continued ...

Also by M. L. Brennan

Generation V
Iron Night

TAINTED BLOOD

A Generation V Novel

M. L. BRENNAN

A ROC BOOK

ROC
Published by the Penguin Group
Penguin Group (USA) LLC, 375 Hudson Street,
New York, New York 10014

USA | Canada | UK | Ireland | Australia | New Zealand | India | South Africa | China
penguin.com
A Penguin Random House Company

First published by Roc, an imprint of New American Library,
a division of Penguin Group (USA) LLC

First Printing, November 2014

 REGISTERED TRADEMARK—MARCA REGISTRADA

ISBN 978-0-451-41842-5

Printed in the United States of America
10 9 8 7 6 5 4 3 2 1

For my mother and my father.

ACKNOWLEDGMENTS

I remain extremely fortunate and grateful to be working with the amazing people at Roc. Anne Sowards provides editorial brilliance and knows when to rein in my inclination for the gross-out, Rebecca Brewer always has answers to my questions, and Nita Basu is a publicity rock star. There are also endless unmentioned people who put this together—cover artists, typesetters, the copy editor, proofreaders, and many many others. Thank you all! Thanks also go to Colleen Mohyde—without whose efforts this series would likely never have made it off my desk.

Sarah Riley and Karen Peláez are going to eventually get sick of seeing their names in print, but they once again answered the call and read the roughest possible version of this book. Where would I be without your keen eyes and encouragement? Thanks are also due to Joe G., John G., and Steve J. for the googly-eyes prank. The tiny eyes on the dishwashing detergent remain one of my favorite mental pictures. Django Wexler patiently answered frantic questions about Japanese—and then I promptly ignored half of his advice, so any errors on that one rest with me.

My family remains delightful and supportive of my work. Particular thanks to my brother, Devon, for his motivational haikus and daily phone calls during the last push on the manuscript. My husband continues to be an utter champ—particularly when I am in the midst of authorial despair. The cats were no help at all and will receive no thanks.

How to thank all of the amazing people who have shown support for the Fort Scott books on the Internet, at conventions, and at bookstores? You know who you are, and you are wonderful, fabulous, and your lovely words and actions humble me.

In planning this book I made significant use of information that I found in *Bear* by Robert E. Bieder and *Dark Banquet: Blood and the Curious Lives of Blood-Feeding Creatures* by Bill Schutt. Schutt's book deserves particular emphasis, as it not only provided invaluable information about obligate sanguivores, but made me laugh many times. Like the best of research materials, it not only answered questions that I had, but also gave me information that I hadn't even realized was out there. Many scenes owe their existence to Schutt's excellent book.

Chapter 1

The sun was low and weak as I walked with my brother and sister through the Common Burying Ground. It was late afternoon in November, and the gray clouds in the sky seemed uncertain about whether they would wholly commit to a full rainstorm or just continue looking atmospheric. The three of us were dressed completely in black, and we would've looked at home in most cemeteries, except that the Common Burying Ground had been declared at capacity before the Nazis invaded Poland. It had been the place of choice for Newport's dead since the sixteen hundreds, and even after its official closure it continued to attract a small but steady stream of history enthusiasts, armed with cameras and guidebooks. Lacking these signature items, our mournful little trio must've looked more than a little creepy.

Since we were vampires, it might've been assumed that a cemetery was a natural place for us to visit. In fact, the opposite was true—we visited here only when there was no other option. Today was one of those days. Bhumika, my brother Chivalry's wife, had died two weeks ago, finally losing her long battle with the illness that had been slowly killing her since the day she and my brother married. I'd spent long, emotionally exhausting days with him, slowly clearing her belongings out of the suite of rooms that they had shared—deciding what would go to her friends, what would go to charity, and which few items Chivalry couldn't bear parting with. Those pieces (a half-empty bottle of her shampoo, the embroidered gold sari that she'd worn for their wedding, a forgotten to-do list written in her looping handwriting, and more) had been carefully tucked into an elaborately carved and cedar-lined chest that had been taken into the attic for safekeeping.

We'd held Bhumika's memorial service yesterday in the grand ballroom of my mother's mansion—beautifully catered, tastefully decorated, well lubricated with wine, and attended by everyone who had known Bhumika, along with several hundred people who hadn't. Chivalry had taken his yacht out alone this morning to spread Bhumika's ashes over Narragansett Bay, and now we were attending to the last sad detail—heading out to view Bhumika's memento mori.

Chivalry was moving slowly, his expression racked with grief. His usually impeccably groomed dark-brown hair looked like he'd run a hand through it this morning and decided that was good enough, and the shirttail on his frighteningly expensive bespoken suit was untucked. The air was cold enough that I was keeping my hands shoved deeply into my pockets, but Chivalry had left his coat behind in the car and seemed unaware of the temperature.

No one looking at him would believe that Bhumika was the nineteenth wife that he'd buried.

Or that his need for Bhumika's blood had been what had wrecked her body and finally sent all of her major organs into a cascade of failure that even the best doctors at the finest hospital in our territory couldn't stop. Both my brother's complete adoration of his wife and the painful grief he'd experienced since her death were apparent to anyone who looked at him. Bhumika was the fourth wife that I'd watched him bury, but even I couldn't claim that his feelings weren't real, though how he was capable of loving his wives so deeply and totally even while he drank their blood and killed them one drop at a time was utterly beyond my powers of comprehension.

To my left was the other person who couldn't understand Chivalry, though she came at it from the opposite direction. Prudence was our sister, a full century older than Chivalry. She had gone on record as recently as dinner last night that she was "getting sick of all this fuss over another dead woman." It had been classic Prudence, and I had expected her to skip out on today's ritual, yet I'd been the only one surprised when she had appeared at the arranged time, decked out in a black Versace dress and a jet necklace. Even her crutches were made of black fiberglass with matching velvet armrests, which she must've had to special-order for the occasion.

With Chivalry moving like a sleepwalker, Prudence was having no trouble keeping up with us, even with her injury. A month ago, she had tried to kill my last remaining host parent, Henry, and push my transition into its conclusion. It would've made me a full vampire, with physical repercussions that I was still not completely clear on, but which I'd spent my entire adulthood fighting against. In her murder attempt, she'd broken one of our mother's direct orders, and the two of them had physically clashed. During the fight, Prudence's left leg had been horribly broken at the thigh. Vampires are very long in reaching our physical maturity—my sister was more than two centuries old, looked like a healthy professional woman in her early forties, and was only just approaching vampire adulthood. Our abilities mature as we do—if I'd suffered an injury like Prudence's, my cast would've come off a few weeks earlier than a normal human's. At Prudence's age, a few days of bed rest, a week of wearing a leg brace and taking it easy, and she would've been back to normal. But my mother had felt that punishment had been in order for Prudence's disobedience, and she had been rebreaking my sister's leg in the same spot every three days for the last month.

Now my sister was hopping along beside us on the uneven ground of the Common Burying Ground, her gleaming black crutches looking almost like an extension of her long black wool coat with its luxurious sable-lined collar and cuffs. A dainty black hat concealed her bright red hair—Prudence was a product of an era that would never have dreamed of entering a graveyard without the correct haberdashery. There was a small bit of veiling, but not enough to conceal the ice in her blue eyes every time I looked over and started to ask if she wanted a little help. On multiple attempts, her expression of barely leashed violence had made my throat dry up halfway through each offer.

The dissolution of our brief partnership had left her feeling angry and betrayed, but despite her terrifying glares, I had caught her staring at me a few times over the last several weeks with an expression that I found much more concerning—curiosity. And a terrible sense of patience. She also hadn't stopped talking to me, which, given recent events, seemed a bit ominous.

It was actually a relief when we reached the mausoleum.

Tucked away in one of the many quiet corners of the Common Burying Ground's thirty-one acres, it rose up unexpectedly from the surrounding sea of weathered and broken slate gravestones. It was built out of granite blocks, with a tiered roof that had been topped off with a large urn sculpted from bronze that had long since gone green from oxidation. The door to the mausoleum was the same heavy black iron as the incredible front entryway to my mother's mansion, worked over with the image of an angel kneeling under a willow tree, and our family name of Scott was carved above the doorway. Unlike everything else in the Common Burying Ground, the mausoleum showed the clear signs of constant care and maintenance, and when Chivalry slid the large iron key into the door's lock, it opened soundlessly.

We filed inside. There was a single carved marble bench decorated with the repeated pattern of the urn, the willow, and the angel. The floor was an alternating pattern of black and white marble, and the three non-door walls were white marble, with bands of black at the floor and ceiling. Thin, concealed skylights in the roof let bands of the dusk light in, enough to see by without having to resort to flashlights. Workers had been here recently, making everything ready for our visit—the air wasn't stale, though I did catch a few whiffs of Febreze.

On the walls was what we'd come to see. Nineteen names were carved into the marble—a woman's first name, then beneath that, the years of her marriage to my brother, then a small border engraving. Chivalry went straight to the newest addition and traced the letters of Bhumika's name with just the tips of his fingers while Prudence and I hung back. Now that we were no longer moving, I noticed my sister's subtle movements as she slid her BlackBerry out of her pocket to discreetly check her messages.

I couldn't help letting my eyes drift around the walls, noting all of the names. There were the women I'd met— Linda, Carmela, and Odette (though my memories of her were very hazy). Then there were all the others, and eventually I traced them back to the first: Mabel, 1886–1890, with a border of ivy and musical notes. The sight of that long-dead woman's name made me shudder. As the first, had she been unaware of what her fate would be? Had Chivalry? Even with nineteen names, there was a huge amount of white space. How many names had these walls been built to accommodate?

Despite the cold air, I could feel myself starting to sweat. The knowledge that a mausoleum like this might be in my own future made me shudder. Those walls suddenly seemed tighter than they'd been a moment ago, and I knew that I had to get out. But just as the thought crossed my mind, Prudence's hand was suddenly wrapped around my left arm and squeezing like a vise. I met her eyes, surprised, and watched as she very slowly and deliberately shook her head. Then she darted her eyes over to the marble bench and lifted her eyebrows.

The message was clear—there was no bailing. Prudence and I settled ourselves awkwardly onto the bench and sat. Chivalry's attention never shifted from Bhumika's name, even as the light from the skylights slowly got weaker and weaker, tinged now with the oranges and purples of what must've been a very good sunset. An hour passed. Eventually Prudence gave up and pulled her BlackBerry completely out of her pocket. The tapping of the keys as she texted was the only sound in the mausoleum.

Marble is not known for its ergonomic qualities, and November in New England is not conducive to sitting outdoors in one place for a long time. My face was completely numb from the cold, though not quite as numb as my ass, when Chivalry finally turned away from Bhumika's marker.

Apparently that had been some kind of signal, because Prudence slid the BlackBerry smoothly back into her coat pocket and said, almost concealing her boredom, "The mason did a lovely job, brother."

Chivalry nodded, an almost spastic jerk of agreement.

My sister's elbow dug hard into my side, and I jumped slightly. This was my cue. "Everything looks so clean," I noted.

Again, Chivalry nodded, but just slightly more smoothly. Prudence and I took our places bracketing Chivalry, and we began the slow walk back to the car, the two of us filling the air with banal comments. The sun had completely set, and any starlight was hidden behind the cloud cover. Before my transition began, just a half year ago, I would've been unable to navigate my way through the cemetery without tripping over at least one of the smaller head-stones that sometimes hid under patches of longer grass, but my eyesight was much sharper now, and we all made our way smoothly back to the car. Had it not been for Prudence's crutches, we might even have been described as stately—since I was usually the one who spoiled the family's more photogenic moments, I couldn't help but feel a small twinge of vindictive satisfaction in Prudence's temporary lack of grace.

Halfway to the car, Chivalry began responding to our comments, his voice hoarse and raspy. He and Prudence struck up a conversation about a headstone that we passed—apparently its owner had been known for par-ticularly wild parties back during the Gilded Age, and I knew that Chivalry's time mourning Bhumika had come to an end. From this point on, he would be searching for a new wife, and before a month was over, we'd be cele-brating a wedding.

In all prior instances, I'd had the luxury of distancing myself from the process, physically and emotionally, and in feeling appalled at Chivalry's callousness. But I'd taken on my brother's job of policing my mother's terri-tory during the last month, when everyone knew that Bhumika wouldn't last much longer, and I'd agreed to continue with those duties for another few months while Chivalry was (to use my mother's term) "occupied." There was no way to separate myself from what was happening in my brother's life, or for me to assure myself that I had no part in his selection of a new bridal victim.

But as we walked (and Prudence hopped), I also no-ticed something different about Chivalry that had been concealed by his overt grief. Even as he sounded more and more like his old self, there was something about him that was making me edgy. His movements were too quick, his eyes in the darkness too bright, and something in his voice was making the hair on the back of my neck stand up. I'd never forgotten what my brother was, but he'd always been the most gentle and approachable one in the family, and this was disturbing on a very deep level.

As we neared the car, Chivalry stepped forward to take charge, and I caught Prudence's sleeve under the pretext of helping her with her crutches. My brother was so thoroughly creeping me out that I was willing to talk to Prudence. It was one of those moments that left me alert for unidentified aerial porcine objects.

"Something's wrong with Chivalry," I whispered to her.

She made a low, interested noise in her throat, and suddenly my chin was snagged in her gloved fingers and wrenched low enough that the two of us were eye to eye. "Ah, the wonders of transition," she murmured, her face filled with an avaricious excitement that made me regret my newly sharpened vision. Her voice dropped further, becoming more intense. "You are seeing more, Fortitude, sensing more." Her fingers dug in tighter, her nails pricking me through the silk of her gloves. I was starting to regret my question. "Chivalry has not fed since Bhumika's death, and will not feed until he selects his new bride." She pulled us even closer, until her wide, disturbing eyes were all I saw, and I felt the heat of her breath on my face. "Watch his actions closely, little brother. Perhaps you will learn to avoid his foolish and sentimental example." Then her eyes narrowed, and I found myself released so abruptly that I almost staggered. My hand shot up to touch my chin, and I was surprised not to find blood. My sister never broke our eye contact, and gave a low snort. "Or not. Knowing you, you will simply find a way to expand upon our brother's ridiculousness."

Chivalry saved me from the awkwardness of lacking a sufficiently withering response by rolling down the window of the car and asking in annoyance why we were still standing out in the cold. The moment was broken, and Prudence returned to her usual state of grumpiness as I helped her maneuver her immobilized leg and crutches into the backseat.

We were loaded into my mother's Rolls-Royce, along with her driver, and there was no conversation as the car backed cautiously out of the Common Burying Ground, onto the aptly named Farewell Street, and turned toward my mother's mansion on Ocean Drive. In my lifetime, she'd never come to any of these visits to Chivalry's mausoleum. It wasn't from (or, rather, not *entirely* from) lack of interest—while I walked under the sun at any time of day, Chivalry required a Panama hat, dark glasses, and preferably some kind of awning during the hours around high noon. Prudence was finding sunlight steadily more problematic, coming outside only when the sun was at its weakest or on cloudy days. But our mother dated back to medieval times, and she lived her days in a suite of rooms that had been built without windows. It had probably been a century or more since she had been capable of even a short stroll on an overcast winter day.

In the summer, downtown Newport is stuffed with cars and meandering tourists. Just getting from the Claiborne Pell Bridge to my mother's doorstep can take thirty minutes of bumper-to-bumper traffic. But as the daylight shortens, the temperatures drop, and the winter storms that roll through the Atlantic brush up against Newport and allow its inhabitants to experience the delight of near-sideways rainstorms, the summer visitors flee and the population plummets. The boutiques either switch to their winter hours or close their doors completely until May, the parking meters are covered over, lines shorten, and service gets better. Best of all, the drive to my mother's mansion becomes less than ten minutes.

After shedding our coats in the main foyer, we filed into the dining room, where my mother was already seated, dressed in a neat black pants suit, its inherent frumpiness adding to her little-old-lady veneer—an illusion usually only broken when my mother smiled and revealed a pair of gleaming incisors that would not look out of place on a tiger. As we each took our seats, my mother extended one thin, deceptively fragile hand to Chivalry.

"My poor boy," she said. "I know how very fond you were of Bhumika."

Madeline's tone would've been perfectly appropriate— if Bhumika had been a hamster.

Chivalry thanked Madeline in a low voice, and with a satisfied nod, she reached down and rang the small silver bell that sat next to her wineglass. A moment later the room was filled with people as Madeline's scrupulously trained staff descended on us with dinner. I glanced down at my plate and stifled a sigh. Maple-glazed ham, smelling delicious. I aimed my fork toward the potatoes and hoped that between that and my side of asparagus I would be able to fill up. My family's approach to my vegetarianism had been to assume that if offered enough succulent temptations, I would eventually buckle under.

Across from me, Prudence ate one careful spoonful of the delicate soup in front of her, then put her cutlery down decisively.

"Mother," she started, but her eyes were fixed on Chivalry, who was stirring his spoon through his own bowl of stew and eyeing my portion of gleaming ham steak with a very uncharacteristic interest that was making me feel uncomfortable. "I was thinking it might cheer us all up if I invited a few people from work down for dinner tomorrow."

I managed to tear my eyes away from my brother long enough to look over at Madeline, but she was also watching Chivalry closely, even as she answered Prudence. "Oh, what a lovely idea, darling. I do so enjoy meeting bright young things."

I choked on a sip of water, but not from my mother's comment, though that was weird enough. My mother had very regular visitors and dinner parties, but her interests were entirely political, while my sister's guests, if they were indeed only her coworkers, would just be a group of stockbrokers and money managers. What shocked me was the sight of my brother's fork snaking toward the ham on my plate. I glanced over—Chivalry's eyes were fixed and gleaming. Awkwardly, I nudged my plate closer to him, but my movement seemed to bring him out of his reverie with a jolt. He cleared his throat loudly, took a large spoonful of his stew, and then said with complete aplomb, "If you want to, Prudence, go right ahead. Though I'm not sure how fifteen conversations about how the Brazilian real is stacking up against the dollar will particularly perk things up."

That at least sounded like my brother, and though I watched him closely, his behavior remained normal for the rest of the meal. I wondered if ham steak–coveting was a normal stage of his grieving process—when Linda, his spouse before Bhumika, had died, I was in college and had left immediately after the memorial service.

Chivalry excused himself immediately after dinner, but he leaned down and gave my shoulder a fraternal squeeze on his way out—his way, I knew, of apologizing for whatever the attempted ham snatching had been about. When he left the room, I looked across the table at Madeline, hoping for an explanation, but she simply fussed with her wineglass. I slanted an inquiring look at Prudence, who was patting her mouth with a napkin.

"What was that about?" I asked.

Prudence arched her eyebrows. "I can't have people over?"

"You know what I mean," I said, irritated. "The ham."

She sniffed, radiating disapproval. "Yes, irritating, isn't it? I told you that Chivalry won't feed until he finds a new wife." She waved her napkin at me, a weird white counterpoint to her black ensemble. "Now you're starting to see why that behavior is so utterly ridiculous."

"Not feeding makes you want ham?"

I was treated to a very evocative eye roll. "Sometimes there's just no talking with you, Fort. But on that note, when was the last time *you* fed?"

I glanced over at my mother, still swirling the last of her wine in its glass. Until my transition was completed, my blood needs were met by my mother. For years I'd fed every few months, as far apart as I could push it, but I'd given in to the requirements of my changing physiology, and now I usually fed every other week. And while I wasn't a big fan of taking my sister's advice, Chivalry's weird dinner behavior had unsettled me. "Mother?" I asked. "I actually am a bit, you know . . . due."

Madeline looked up from her glass, and I was struck by how very tired she looked. She'd always looked ancient (even for a vampire, six hundred plus years don't rest lightly), but tonight the skin of her face seemed to hang from her bones. The blue eyes that were the model for Prudence's were bloodshot. For a moment she looked confused, and I could see her eyes narrow as she mentally counted back the days to when she had last fed me. The answer she found clearly surprised her, and her feathery white eyebrows shot up. "Oh, my darling, how careless of me," she said. Then she paused, and asked, almost tentatively, "I'm a bit under the weather tonight, precious. Would it be very difficult for you to wait a day or two?"

My jaw didn't quite drop, but it definitely wanted to. In my life, my mother had nagged and enticed me to feed, and often despaired over my avoidance of it, but she had never once asked me to wait. "Uh, sure. Sure, it's no problem." My mouth moved through the social protocol, but I couldn't help darting a look toward my sister, but Prudence wouldn't look at me. She was staring at our mother, and despite the studied blankness of her expression, there was a look in her eyes that on anyone less sociopathic I would've called . . . *worried.*

My mother blinked owlishly behind the oversize

glasses that she didn't need for her eyesight but liked to wear for effect. "Unless you're very hungry, darling?"

"No, no I'm fine," I assured her, feeling slightly better. "I'm not even noticing it." Which was the truth—I'd gotten into the habit of feeding every second week, but I didn't feel that uncomfortable sense of hunger that I remembered from the times when I'd avoided feeding for months longer than I should've. Madeline looked relieved, but when I glanced back to Prudence, she was now fiddling with her bracelet and maintaining a look of polite social boredom.

"I was just going to check in with the secretary and then head out," I told my mother, pushing my chair back.

Madeline smiled then, widely enough to display her long fangs, and her eyes brightened. "Ah, what a good little worker. Your brother is lucky indeed that he has you to carry the dull minutiae of business while he is indisposed." She eyed my sister and added pointedly, "Someone who can be trusted to follow directions."

Ah, doublespeak, hidden messages, and awkwardness—Mother was clearly a little tired, but otherwise in fine form. Before Prudence could respond, I babbled my good-byes and fled the dining room.

Chapter 2

Vampires were an Old World import to the Americas. My mother was the first to make the trip, crossing from England in 1662 and establishing a wide territory that included all of New England, most of New York state, a slice of New Jersey, and a healthy helping of eastern Canada. She'd been a vampire in her prime back then and had carved out her lands with almost traditional colonial zeal—anyone or anything that objected to her preeminent status had been very messily slaughtered. After almost a century of these activities, she had exterminated, driven out, or made treaties with all the occupants, and settled down to start a family.

The supernatural species hid among the human populations—humans outnumbered us by a thousand to one, and technology plus an unbeatable superiority of numbers was not a fight that any sane individual wanted to get into. There were plenty of the less sane among us, but even they were strong-armed to toe the party line on this one. There were species that had tried to withdraw completely beyond human communities; that was not only difficult, but it also meant withdrawing from some of the basic necessities of life—like high-speed Internet access. Most of us could pass for human, and plenty of species had developed symbiotic or outright parasitic relationships with humans.

Despite the passage of centuries and the establishment

of an American constitution, my mother's method of rule remained entirely feudal. Nonhumans who wanted to either visit or live in my mother's territory had to petition for entry and then negotiate the terms that they would live by. Madeline was a very big fan of tithing—almost all of the groups in our territory paid a percentage of their earnings to my mother. They also had to avoid conflicts with other nonhuman species in the area and cover any of their supernatural tracks that might otherwise bring unwelcome attention.

As she'd gotten older, Madeline had passed the business of keeping her territory running smoothly to her children. My sister was a natural-born enforcer, striking terror into the hearts of generations of my mother's subjects, but the tasks that involved more subtlety than "kill and terrorize" fell to Chivalry. And as with all thoughtful men of business, that meant that he delegated as much of the mountain of paperwork as possible to his staff.

My brother's office was on the first floor, but tucked toward the back of the house, far away from the glamorous public areas. It was large, and decorated in an almost stereotypically turn-of-the-century gentleman's style. Cluttered bookshelves marched to the ceiling, paintings of yachts, dogs, and horses decorated all available open space on the wood-paneled walls, massive brocade curtains festooned the windows, and a massive oiled mahogany desk dominated the room. But for all the show, it was a functional office—those books were the old bound tithing records. The filing cabinets might have been wood-veneered, but any accounting actuary opening the drawer would see the rows of regimented files and feel right at home. My brother's desk was old and big enough to merit its own zip code, but the computer on it was upgraded every other year. The next room (apparently the old music room) had been carved up several years ago to make a support office that had the desks, phones, and equipment for his secretary and two accountants—all human.

The accountants spent their days balancing the books, sending the tithing bills, and making sure that not a single penny that the Scotts could claim slid through the cracks. It was slightly shady work, but nothing that any good mobster accountant wouldn't be used to. The secretary, on the other hand, had a very different job.

Loren Noka was working at my brother's desk when I walked into the room. A statuesque woman in her late forties whose Native American heritage was clearly advertised in her high cheekbones and dark hair, she greeted me with a sober nod. Loren had taken the job of Chivalry's secretary when her father, Irving, retired after almost fifty years of service. Now she spent her day answering calls and organizing e-mails that came in from the inhabitants of my mother's territory, as well as scanning newspapers and local blogs for any hints of misbehavior or possible supernatural exposure.

"Hello, Ms. Noka. You're working very late tonight." Chivalry referred to her as "Loren," but since he'd known her since she was in diapers, I suppose he had the right. To me, Ms. Noka had always had a very kind of Alfred from *Batman* demeanor. She knew a lot of secrets, would never tell a single one, was capable of a look of single icy superiority that would make a transgressor feel like an ant, and I was fairly certain that if I asked her, she would be able to construct a fully functional Batmobile.

"Just making one last check of the news sites before I call it an evening," she said with a polite smile. With Chivalry in mourning, her workload had doubled overnight, but she somehow never indicated that she was stressed. The only thing about her that looked even slightly stressed was her royal purple pants suit as she stood up, but the fabric that was fighting to contain her curved and zaftig figure was probably held together by Loren Noka's sheer strength of will—or she'd found some sort of experimental military superfabric with enhanced tensile strength.

"Is that for me?" I asked, nodding at the single file still sitting in the in-box on Chivalry's desk, a stark contrast to the orderly but impressive pile organized in the adjoining out-box.

"Yes." She reached over and handed it to me. "I would've called, but Mrs. Scott told me that you were coming back for dinner."

The file's weight was substantial, and I didn't try to conceal my surprise. "Feels problematic."

"No, nothing like that. I just got a message that the rusalka needs a meeting, and since I don't think you'd ever met her before, I pulled the entire file for you to look over."

After twenty-six years of ignoring anything supernatural (including myself), I'd been playing a desperate game of catch-up, particularly in the past month, where I'd suddenly found myself my mother's official delegate and Ms. Noka's boss. There had been quite a lot to learn, and I flipped open the file to its first page in the hope of refreshing my memory on this one—then immediately slapped it shut again. "Chivalry mentioned her once. How exactly does that one place a phone call to you?"

"One of her neighbors placed it at her request. Will you go up soon?"

"Might as well go tomorrow," I said, unable to muster much enthusiasm. Sometimes a picture is worth a thousand words. "It's only up in Massachusetts."

Ms. Noka gave me her Mona Lisa smile. "Remember to pick up the bait. There's a note in there, but Mr. Scott always found duck gizzard the most effective. Especially in this weather, when you don't have to wait a while."

"I *do* read the whole file," I noted, slightly defensively. At least, I did now. On my first fully commissioned task for the family, my friend and designated partner, Suzume, and I had driven up to Maine to deal with a group of selkies who were purportedly running a local protection scheme and sinking the boats of fishermen who

wouldn't pay in. It had actually been a bit more complicated than that, and I'd made the classic rookie mistake
of not reading all of Ms. Noka's carefully collected background information before we'd headed up. While it had
turned out well in the end, there had been an uncomfortable incident where I'd been pushed off a dock by a toddler and Suze had punched a seal in the face. A teenager
had filmed the whole thing on his phone, and there had
been an awkward period where we'd thought that the
video would not only go viral, but that Suze would be
formally charged with endangering the local wildlife.

With the file tucked under my arm for later examination, we exchanged good-byes. I left the house without
seeing any of my family again, but the knowledge that
always pulsed in the back of my brain put them all on the
second floor, probably in their individual rooms.

My battered Ford Fiesta sat beside my family's row of
gleaming cars like a squat mushroom invading a cultured
garden. It took two tries for the engine to turn over, and
I rubbed my hands briskly together to encourage the cir-
culation as I waited for the sluggish heating system to
warm up. I could see my breath in the air as I pulled out
my phone and punched Suzume's phone number in from
memory and listened to it ring. We'd been in a strange
holding pattern for the last month since I'd confessed my
feelings to her. On the one hand, our friendship had continued unabated, and she was my regular partner on all
my official trips and investigations around the territory.
But at the same time, the question of what her answer
was going to be was hanging between us.

Suze didn't pick up, and I left a message outlining the
basics of tomorrow's task. When I'd agreed to work officially for my family, Chivalry and I had negotiated a basic salary. It had been a hotly contested discussion, with
Chivalry arguing high and me arguing very low. I'd supported myself on minimum-wage jobs since I had grad-
uated college, and while I was not a particular fan of the

lifestyle that it had necessitated, I was also very wary about the possibility of my family buying my loyalties. We'd finally settled on an hourly wage for all tasks that was just a bit higher than what I would normally be earning in the open market of crappy jobs. Suzume had had no such ethical quibbles, and for her involvement with me, she was charging a very comfortable retaining fee.

I finished the message and ended the call, wondering what she was up to. With Suzume, there was always a long list of possibilities—anything from beating up problem clients for her family's escort service to scampering around the woods in her natural fox form, with any number of activities in between. Since our visit to the selkies, most of our tasks had been relatively simple—investigations of why some tithes were low (the economic downturn was equally hard on supernatural-run businesses, as it turned out), a few territory disputes, some snooping into suspicious deaths that had uniformly turned out to have entirely human causes. Yet even though our job didn't always have much interest to it, she'd remained committed.

Of course, she was still a kitsune, and was entirely capable of creating her own fun. I'd flipped down the sun visor on my drive down this morning and had discovered that some unnamed prankster (definitely Suze) had glued two small craft-baskety googly eyes to it, so now it appeared that the visor had eyes and was watching me.

It was lucky that there wasn't any traffic on the road back to my apartment in Providence, since the Fiesta's heater never managed to dispel any air that I would've characterized as warmer than "somewhat cool." Since the Fiesta had spent the entire summer with inoperable air-conditioning, I couldn't help but feel moderately annoyed that it was apparently capable of disgorging cool air, but only in the completely wrong season. By the time I got home, I hustled quickly to get into the apartment, sighing in relief when I got into the stairway with its comparatively warmer temperatures. I'd bought my funeral suit and formal jacket new for the occasion—since my transition had begun, I'd put on enough muscle to go up four suit sizes, which had necessitated a shopping trip. After much hunting, I'd managed to find clothing that wouldn't shatter my budget or sear my brother's eyeballs on such a sad day. My suit had started its life in a very exclusive store window, until the store owners apparently realized that not many men were willing to strut their stuff in lime green. It had made its way down to the discount warehouse, where I'd bought it, and then I spent a rather interesting afternoon with Suzume figuring out how to dye it black in my apartment's bathtub. The suit actually had a decent lining to it, but at a certain point in Rhode Island, typically around Halloween, it becomes preferable to just never leave the house if you aren't wearing a heavy-knit sweater and the downiest of down parkas.

I climbed the three flights of stairs that led from the ground-floor boutique lingerie store, past Mrs. Bandyopadyay's, and ended at the two-bedroom apartment that I shared at the top with my latest roommate, Dan Tabak. We'd only lived together for a month, though so far he'd managed to pay his half of the rent on time and not make any particular messes. But with any shared living situation, there would always be compromises—as I scrabbled in my pocket for the keys, I could hear the melodious (and now far-too-familiar) tones of Benedict Cumberbatch's voice.

Inside was a typical Sunday tableau—Dan was sitting on the sofa, a wide assortment of thick law textbooks spread out on the battered coffee table in front of him, along with half a dozen completely stuffed notebooks, and his dreaded flash-card-making supplies. Dan was a second-year law student at Johnson and Wales University, and if I'd ever had even the slightest shred of interest in getting a law degree, seeing Dan in action would've crushed it. In the rare moments when Dan wasn't in class, or in a study group, or studying on his own, he was making flash cards as a study aid. It seemed like a horrible and endless process to me, but then again, I'd called higher education a success after getting a bachelor's degree in film theory—an accomplishment that had involved not a single flash card, and a number of actually good films.

I collapsed into our armchair and looked over at the TV screen. A hellacious storm was whipping through the palm trees on a tropical island while Benedict Cumberbatch gave a stately narration. Dan liked to run epic BBC nature documentaries as background when he was making flash cards or organizing the day's class notes. He claimed that documentaries like *Wild Pacific* had narrators whose voices were very soothing. I'd seen his DVDs of *Sherlock*, though, and had suspicions that Dan simply had a crush on Benedict Cumberbatch, but it seemed a little hypocritical to throw stones. After all, I'd seen a lot of shitty movies simply because Amy Adams was starring in them.

"Hey," Dan greeted me, not looking up from his text. I glanced at the title, *Corporations*, and shuddered. "How'd it all go?"

"How do these things ever go? Mostly it just went, and at least now it's over." I reached down and pulled off my shoes, sighing in relief. Dress shoes were not made with all-day comfort in mind.

"Is it true that you guys go through this every five years?" Dan looked up from his book and raised his dark eyebrows inquisitively.

I shrugged awkwardly. We were really just still in the figuring-each-other-out phase of rooming. But unlike all of my previous roommates, Dan wasn't human. I was still getting used to living with someone who not only knew about vampires and the supernatural, but who actually heard regular gossip about my family. "Usually a little longer than that, but sometimes less," I replied, trying to be polite but really not wanting to keep talking about the subject.

Dan let it drop. "Did you eat? I made too much, so there are still some leftovers in the pot."

I eyed him suspiciously. "Was it one of *those* meals?" Dan was a ghoul, which meant that a certain amount of his intake had to be human organs in order for him to maintain his health. The ghouls in my mother's territory had all originated in Turkey and had acclimated well to America, most of them finding an easy source for their dietary needs by opening funeral homes or working in hospital sanitation. It had made me extremely cautious around Dan's cooking, though, and we'd had to have a few pretty serious conversations about dish cleanup, prompt post-preparation trash disposal, and the labeling of leftovers.

"Just the shepherd's pie. The sweet potatoes are safe." Dan snorted. "I can't believe that you're so squeamish about these things. It's not like I interrogate you about every beverage you store in the fridge."

"Really? What the hell was that soda discussion last week about, then?"

"You know my feelings about high-fructose corn syrup." Dan narrowed his eyes, and a very stubborn and lawyery look crossed his handsome face.

I shook my head, unwilling to reengage on this particular issue, even if it meant that I had to abide by Dan's new list of sodas that were banned in the apartment. I was also not entirely full after my partial dinner at my mother's, so I got up to investigate the sweet potatoes. There was still a full serving in the pot, looking extremely inviting, so I spooned it into a small dish. I carefully avoided looking at the partially empty casserole dish. Since Dan had moved in, I'd learned to my horror about how many sins dishes like shepherd's pie and meat loaf could conceal. I put the now-empty pot in the sink and turned on the faucet, automatically stepping back to avoid the incipient spreading puddle that had been this sink's hallmark for many months. To my surprise, everything remained dry, and the faucet even managed to avoid its usual cantankerous sputter. For a moment, I wondered whether my landlord had finally, for the first time in all the years I'd lived there, responded to a repair request. But that seemed like the kind of out-of-character behavior usually only present in body snatching and encroaching brain tumors, and the last time I'd seen Mr. Jennings, he'd seemed completely normal.

"Dan," I called over my shoulder, "did Jaison fix the sink?" Despite my extreme dislike of Dan's meat products and my unwelcome exposure to so many viewings of nature documentaries, he had come with one very big mark in his favor—his boyfriend, Jaison, who was a general contractor. Since Dan had moved in, Jaison had fixed the broken window in his room, adjusted the iffy thermostat on the living room radiator, and even figured out why the pipes in the bathroom made such a racket whenever anyone showered. (He hadn't been able to fix that pipe problem, since it would've involved completely opening up the walls, but it was nice to have a diagnosis.)

"He swung by with the parts early this afternoon. Said that it was driving him nuts," Dan said, not looking up.

I was distinctly impressed. "He came by on a Sunday and fixed our sink, without you even asking? You can never break up with this man." And clearly, short of Dan setting fire to the curtains, I could never ditch him as a roommate.

"Yeah, I'll pass that one along," Dan replied dryly. "I've got your half of the materials costs written down on a Post-it somewhere." Then he tilted his head backward over the back of the couch to look at me. "Hey, can you put the last of the shepherd's pie in the microwave for me? I think I'll finish it off."

"I'm not touching that thing, even with a spatula." I put my bowl of sweet potatoes in the microwave and nuked it as Dan laughed incredulously at my statement and turned his attention back to the screen, where Benedict Cumberbatch was now discussing the coconut thief crab. My phone gave its incoming-text buzz, and I pulled it out. Suze was up for the trip to Massachusetts tomorrow. I smiled, texted back an acknowledgment, and then polished off the sweet potatoes in short order. A comfortable silence fell between me and Dan, though I found myself glancing over at him several times, wanting to ask a question that I had a strong feeling would be crossing a boundary. I wished I could ask him how he could date Jaison, who was a human with no knowledge of the supernatural world at all, and feel comfortable not only keeping such an enormous secret from him, but also eat three dinners a week that were made from humans. I wanted to know whether it was as easy as he made it look, or whether it was actually much, much harder, and he was just really good at keeping up a facade. I wondered what Dan thought of my brother's relationships with his wives. Did he think Chivalry's approach was sensible, or was he actually as appalled by it as I was by his shepherd's pie?

I opened my mouth to ask the last one, then shut it quickly. I shouldn't ask questions when I might not be ready for the answers, I reminded myself. And even though my half of the rent was paid up for another four months, and between the family work and some part-time floater work I'd picked up, I was more financially solvent than I'd been in the last five years, it was a good idea to maintain roommate harmony by not poking at sleeping dogs. I'd spent far too many months too recently with a sum net worth of less than fifty dollars to not be pleasantly enjoying being able to buy a new DVD or replace a worn-out piece of clothing without worrying about paying my bills. I was even managing to accrue a tidy sum that I hoped would help overhaul some of the Fiesta's more-pressing issues—it would be nice, for instance, to experience a winter that didn't require mittens while driving.

Leaving Dan to his Sisyphean flash-card construction, I headed to bed.

I found two very tiny googly eyes glued to the back of my toothbrush, and one single googly eye affixed to the cap of my toothpaste. I laughed at the sight, but then felt a low feeling of unease as I considered where Suze might be going with this one. I checked my room carefully for any more eyes before finally pulling up my heavy winter comforter and slowly falling asleep, the precise murmur of Benedict Cumberbatch's narration still drifting through my bedroom wall.

Armed with a bag of assorted Munchkins from Dunkin' Donuts and a coffee for each of us, I picked Suzume up from her house at ten the next morning. She was scampering out of her front door the moment I pulled into her driveway. The grin covering her face was nearly as brilliant as her neon green North Face parka. Suzume was very familiar with the Fiesta's winter performance at this point, so she was wearing a heavy pair of blue corduroy pants, and her silky black hair was arranged in two jaunty pigtails that just showed under the bobble-topped fleece hat that matched her parka.

"*Fuck* is it cold in here!" she noted as she pitched her duffel bag into the backseat with a heavy metallic clunk that indicated that she was prepared for whatever we might encounter. "Fort, I'm not telling you that you should buy a new car—"

"I'm sure you aren't, but somehow I think that is going to be the takeaway on this comment," I noted.

She continued blithely over me. "No, I'd never question your automotive decisions. I'm just going to note how glad I am at this particular juncture that my reproductive organs naturally reside inside my body and don't have to try to make the inward crawl that yours probably are attempting at this moment."

I snorted, handing her coffee over as she pulled on a

pair of gloves that she had apparently set aside just for the car ride. "Do you have all of that out of your system now, or am I going to hear variations on this theme for the whole drive?"

"I can make no promises," Suze said, her beautiful almond-shaped eyes crinkling in humor.

Getting from Providence to the small town just outside Lowell, Massachusetts, where the rusalka lived required a cautious snaking around the edge of Boston. Even at ten o'clock on a Monday morning, the roads leading into Boston were stuffed with commuters, and we made our way carefully around and then up, neither of us having any intention of turning an hour-and-a-half drive into a three-hour Masshole-infested nightmare of bad driving and Red Sox bumper stickers.

Resting just below the border into New Hampshire, Lowell is one of the classic New England cities. Farming roots made way to an industrial boom, followed by the slow and painful collapse of the mill and textile industries. Despite a growing student population thanks to the Lowell branch of the University of Massachusetts, and a slow but helpful influx of several high-tech and biomedical companies, driving through downtown Lowell was still a stark and sad presentation of the bones of the town's mighty past. Though some of the old factories had been turned into museums or apartment buildings, many still sat vacant.

We drove through Lowell, across the river, and then we were in the small adjoining town of Dracut. After a circuitous path through a labyrinth of tiny interconnecting roads, we finally pulled up to our destination—the small public boat launch to Long Pond. Possibly one of the least inventively named lakes in New England, it was sizable, its upper third quadrant crossing the line into New Hampshire. It was ringed on all sides by tiny capes and slouched houses that probably all dated back to the 1940s or earlier, all cheek by jowl on minuscule lots, the primary appeal of which was a tiny strip of sand and a wooden boat dock that someone's grandfather had probably built over a few weekends back in the days when building permits were optional and a six-pack of beer was required. A few places stuck out—new construction where someone had bought up one of the old properties, razed it to the ground, and proceeded to shoehorn in a hideous McMansion that overwhelmed the tiny property and completely missed the point of lakeside living.

I parked the car and then grabbed the small deli bag that I'd picked up this morning. The parking area, which in the summer was probably stuffed to the point where cars parked on the grass, was completely vacant now, and the moment Suze and I got out of the car, an icy breeze whipping across the water gave us a clear reminder of why that was. Suze managed to restrain herself to a very speaking glance, and hauled a small blanket out of her duffel bag. It was wool, with a bright argyle pattern, the kind of thing that the elderly tuck around their knees during end-of-season games at Fenway Park.

The dock that we walked down was bleached from years in the sun, but we both sat down cautiously on the spread blanket, well aware that generations of splinters probably remained to attack the unwary. While Suze wrangled the deli container, I pulled a long coil of fishing line out of my pocket, then took up the surprisingly difficult task of tying one end firmly to a raw duck gizzard. Neither the smell nor the temperature was helping, and I was well aware that the easiest route, a hook, would be a very bad idea. I finally succeeded, despite Suzume's ongoing color commentary of the ordeal, and dropped the gizzard down into the lake. The water was clear enough that we could peer down and see our bait hanging there a few inches below the surface, suspended by my line and already the subject of intense scrutiny by some minnows and one fat sunfish.

We stared in complete silence for five minutes, watching the fish, until Suze finally pronounced grimly, "This is going to take all damn day." She sent a dark-eyed glare my way, as if somehow this were my fault. "She needs to get a freaking cell phone like everyone else."

"Pretty sure that phones don't work that well underwater," I noted.

"She could stash it in a beaver lodge when she wasn't using it."

"Beaver lodges now come with electrical plugs for charging purposes?"

Suze reached down and tugged the line, making the duck gizzard wobble in the water. "How exactly is this supposed to work?"

I'd read the entire file last night, but I was a little hazy on this myself. "I think she somehow smells it?" Suze looked unconvinced, and I defended the theory. "Hey, sharks can smell stuff underwater."

Looking down critically to the gizzard, currently being nibbled at by fish, Suze said, "It's a really big lake. Does she usually hang around this dock?"

"Um, I don't think she has a preferred area." I passed the deli container over to her. There were a half-dozen other pinkish-grayish blobs of meat still in it, with a matching (and extremely odorous) liquid collecting at the bottom. "Here, pour the gizzard juice out into the water. Maybe that will help."

The day dragged on while we sat and waited, replacing the gizzard each time the little circling fish managed to completely nibble the bait off the line. For a short time the sun came out and we were warm enough to pull off our hats and gloves, but then the gray clouds rolled back in and the temperature dropped again. We talked while we waited, but they were intermittent conversations at best, since we were both actively scanning the water around us, looking for signs that the rusalka was approaching.

Two and a half hours into our vigil, a ripple in the

water a hundred yards out caught my attention, and I nudged Suze with my elbow. We both eyed it carefully — between the lake's beaver population and one slightly out-of-season loon, we'd had a lot of false alarms. But then the ripple appeared again, closer this time, and my heart began beating faster as I realized that there was a large mass moving under the water.

She broke the surface of the lake about ten feet from us, and her natural camouflage was good enough that if I hadn't been specifically looking for her, I doubted that I would've spotted her. The rusalka was cautious, and the only thing visible was her face from forehead to cheekbone. Her skin was a dull and mottled collection of grays and dark blues that matched the surface of the water almost exactly, and her one visible eye was a hazy white. Then there was a blink, and I realized that what I'd seen was an outer eyelid. The eye now visible was a brilliant blue-green, like a freshly polished aquamarine, but it was a solid color, without a visible pupil or any white.

"You can come closer," I called softly. "I'm Chivalry Scott's brother, Fortitude, and I came to talk with you. I've brought my friend Suzume, a kitsune, so she can keep anyone from noticing you."

I glanced quickly at Suze, who gave a small shrug. "Shouldn't be hard," she muttered. "It's not like anyone would be expecting to see her." All of the kitsune have a kind of magic that they refer to as fox tricks — they can hide things that are happening, or make people see only what they would expect to see, rather than what is actually there. I'd seen Suzume once hide a corpse in a way that would fool policemen, cameras, and even morticians — but that had been very difficult. She always told me that working within people's expectations was the easiest to do.

The eye disappeared beneath the water with barely a ripple, but then a breath later, the rusalka fully surfaced right beside the dock, and it was all I could do to avoid a full jump-reaction. The file that Loren Noka had prepared for me had included a few drawings, but that was a very different thing from seeing the rusalka in all her glory.

From her waist upward, the rusalka looked superficially like a woman. Her skin was that chameleon-like gray and blue all over, but from a distance it did look like human flesh—though now that she was closer, I could see a slight overlapping pattern to it, like the hide on a shark. What at first looked like a long, coiling head of hair that stretched below her waist and was a mix of black, gray, and blue was actually something thicker, and it moved against the wind, constantly coiling and relaxing, like the strands on a sea anemone. Her eyes were that brilliant aquamarine blue, but set on the sides of her face like a fish's. She had no nose, and her long mouth opened and shut as she seemed to adjust to the air. The rusalka was no mammal, so her torso was flat, with no unnecessary breast tissue, even in imitation. And down at the waist was what made my throat suddenly go dry. The lake surface began to slowly churn as the rusalka propelled herself higher out of the water, revealing the tangle of dozens of long, powerful tentacles that made up her lower body. She pushed upward until she could rest her arms on the edge of the dock, an oddly relaxed-looking pose that allowed her to fix one of those eyes on each of us.

There was also, it must be said, a distinctly fishy odor emanating from her.

She was a stunning example of the weird directions that nature and evolution can take. Farther off in the lake, two men in kayaks paddled leisurely into view, apparently confident enough in their craft that they didn't expect to overturn into the icy waters. Suze's fox trick did its work, though, and one gave us a small wave of recognition, not even registering the sight of an honest-to-god sea monster resting against the dock.

Very typically, Suze recovered first from the reveal,

and, for all the world like a good hostess at a boring cocktail party, extended the deli container forward, with a drawled, "Canapé?"

The rusalka took a deep breath, drawing in the odor of the remaining duck gizzards. Then her mouth fell open into a wide semblance of a smile that revealed a set of teeth that reminded me of a porpoise's, and with a brisk and oddly throaty, "Don't mind if I do," she accepted the container in one webbed hand and tipped the whole thing back like an oyster shooter. I somehow restrained a shudder—the smell of those duck gizzards, even on a cool November afternoon, had not been improved by a lack of refrigeration.

Looking about as pleased as possible with her noseless face and fish eyes (she bore, I couldn't help but notice, a small but distinct resemblance to the film version of Lord Voldemort), she made a smacking sound with her mouth that I assumed was some kind of compliment to the cook, and set the now-empty container back on the dock.

"So," I said, drawing on every iota of experience I'd gained during my time in the service industry to just roll with this and preferably get out as soon as possible. "What seems to be on your mind?" From the notes in the file, the rusalka wasn't much into small talk, and honestly, what kind of social pleasantries were there with a sea monster? Ask how the algae level had been this summer?

"Jet Skiers," she said, practically hissing the word, and the water became more agitated as her tentacles thrashed in temper.

"Um, I'm sorry?" Whatever issues I'd considered as being the cause of my visit today, that had definitely not been on the list.

But the rusalka was clearly eager to elaborate. "Those awful Jet Skiers. From the moment the lake unfreezes in the spring, through the entire summer, and practically right into winter, not a day goes by that I don't have to hear them buzzing those horrid machines up and down the lake. This summer was the worst—it was constant. They drip gasoline, they swamp the canoeists so that I've nearly had people dumped right on top of me, and the blades on them are horrendous. Just look at that!" One long tentacle lifted out of the water for our perusal. I noticed that it was the same color as her skin on the top side, but on the bottom, suction-cuppy side, it was a bright, almost electric blue. It also had two long, barely healed slices in it.

Apparently it wasn't just manatees that were in danger from Jet Skis. "That does seem problematic," I said, feeling sympathetic. "And you would like my mother to . . . ?"

The rusalka dropped that hazy white lid down over her eyes in a way that in the female of a lot of other species I would've called coy. "Well, I can't kill any of them without your mother's permission," she said slowly. "But perhaps if just a few unfortunate accidents started occurring . . . ? I'm sure it wouldn't take too long before the town authorities stepped in to regulate things."

Sympathy over injured tentacles only went so far. "We aren't going to green-light the slaughter of Jet Skiers," I told her flatly.

Suzume piped up, that familiar foxy glint in her eyes. "I don't know, Fort," she said, mock-thoughtfully. "They can be awfully assholish. And if she agrees to take out only the problematic ones—"

The look I gave her told her how very, very unamused I was.

"What?" Suze responded, the hurt tone of her voice completely at odds with the grin that she was fighting to suppress. "I'm sure it would make life a lot more pleasant."

As if on cue, the loud buzzing of a Jet Ski filled the air, and from the north end of the lake a particularly douchey specimen roared into view, cutting across the path of the kayakers so that the wake of his machine nearly swamped them. He then turned and went skyrocketing back in the direction he'd come from, leaving the two men frantically trying to right their kayaks and ride out the rest of the waves. The darker-haired of the two, stabilizing himself faster, expressed his outrage in gestures more usually seen on the I-93 interchange into Boston than in the beauty of nature.

I could sort of see what Suzume meant, and it was always difficult to argue against the killing of humans when the ones in question insisted on acting like complete dicks, but still . . . "I'm sorry," I said, making sure that my tone was firm, "but you are *not* going to be allowed to kill the Jet Skiers. No matter how much they might have it coming."

There was no doubt about this one—the rusalka was pouting. "I was worried you'd say that." She sighed heavily, and her tentacles slapped the surface of the water in a desultory fashion that I supposed was meant to convey disappointment. "Things are changing so much. I remember a time when Chivalry didn't mind if I took a few bites out of drowning victims, as long as I hadn't been the cause of it. Now I have to stay away from the bodies, even when they're stuck somewhere for days and I don't see how anyone would notice one little nibble gone."

The nostalgia of the predatory species in the territory was always a little creepy to listen to. "I *am* sorry," I repeated, "but you have to stick to the fish. Birds if you can take them at night when no one will see you hunt. We just can't risk anyone figuring out that there's a large predator in the lake, much less that it's you."

"It's terribly crowded now, though. There used to be quiet areas of the lake, even in the summer." The rusalka's lower lip gave a small tremble, and she fixed that incredible eye on me again. "Are you very sure that you won't let me kill just a few of the Jet Skiers?"

Clearly this had been on her mind for a while. If I

hadn't checked all of the clippings and printouts that Loren Noka had provided in the file and known for a fact that there hadn't been any unexplained deaths or suspicious drownings in this lake for the last three years, I would've been getting worried. "Very sure."

The rusalka's tentacles slapped the water a few more times; then she sighed. "Then I think I'd like to ask your family to find me a new lake. Somewhere very quiet, with healthy fish. Maybe in the migratory path of some ducks."

Despite my instinctual sympathy for any duck populations she found herself around, this was a plan that I could get on board with. Apart from the undeniably problematic Jet Skiers, it looked like the population density of this area was on the rise, which was not a good match with the rusalka. I wasn't very worried about her ability to keep herself hidden—the background in the file I'd read made it clear that she spent most of her time in deep water, and since there hadn't been any local rumors about a lake monster, she wasn't a concern in that area. But there did tend to be higher suicide rates around the lakes where rusalka lived—whether it was a chemical or pheromone they dispersed naturally into the water or something else, it was a fact of their presence. Depression rates would be higher around a rusalka, and suicide clusters common. It made sense, really. The rusalka was native to Russia.

"That seems like a reasonable request," I said. "Do you have any preferred destination?"

"North." That eerie hair of hers curled tightly, wrapping around her head and shoulders. "The water temperature is getting just a bit too high in the summer. I noticed it the last few years."

Somewhere, I thought, some Republican senator had sensed a disturbance in the Force and screamed out that global warming was a myth. "I'll bring it up with my family and see what we can work out," I assured her. North certainly wouldn't be a problem—if we were looking for a relatively remote lake, we needed to get her farther away from the cities anyway.

She dipped lower into the water, her tentacles now completely hidden. "But no Jet Skiers," the rusalka said darkly.

"You might have to compromise a little, but I promise that I'll see what lakes have restrictions." There had to be some privately owned lakes or lakes in protected areas where the authorities shared the rusalka's distaste. "Is that sufficient?" I asked as she slid down even farther, until only her shoulders and head were visible. The rusalki were solitary creatures, not known for being great socializers, and I had a feeling that with our business concluded, she was ready to be on her way.

"Yes. My thanks," she said. There was a sudden flurry in the water, a swatting of tentacles, and a moment later two fat sunfish were flopping on the argyle blanket between me and Suze, and the rusalka was gone.

We both stared at the flopping, gasping fish for a second. "Maybe that's her version of a fruit basket?" I ventured.

"So tossing them back in is out of the question," Suze agreed, and made a face. "Your Fiesta doesn't smell good at the best of times, but this might be a tipping point."

Almost three hours of sitting on a windy dock had left me with a desire to get somewhere with heating that was stronger than my inclination to defend the honor of my car, so we stuffed the fish into the deli container and headed back to the Fiesta. We dumped the now very dead fish four streets away, where we hoped they would make some stray cat extremely happy. By mutual decision, we then broke out the smartphones and made a beeline for the nearest pizza place. While the duck gizzards and the rusalka had not been very pleasant, we'd missed lunch and it was now almost four o'clock.

I couldn't vouch for Suzume, but I hit up the Purell dispenser in the bathroom with more than usual vigor.

Once I'd decontaminated myself as much as possible, I settled back into the booth where Suze was already flipping through the menu. She'd taken off her parka for the first time that day and now looked much happier.

"If we ever have to do that again, I'm doing it on four paws. My winter coat is all grown in now, and I would've been much more comfortable."

"Plus you could've eaten those fish she tossed us," I noted. "Would've saved you the cost of dinner."

She looked up from the menu, clearly affronted. "What, I sit on a dock all day with you to visit something that is probably going to give me tentacle-hentai nightmares, and you can't even spring for half a pizza?"

When we'd first met, that would've had me lunging for my wallet. But I knew Suzume well enough to know how much of her indignation was just an act. "If this is a date, I'll pay. But if it isn't, we really should make sure to ask for a split check. You know, so everything's clear." I gave her my most agreeable smile, watching her eyes narrow.

"So your argument here is that I should date you to get some free food?"

"I'm just saying that there are some perks." She made a grumbling sound, and I grinned. "In fact, as a show of good faith, I'll even get you a beer."

It was an old joke between us, and she couldn't hold back her laugh. "Well, that's the kind of big gesture that can get a woman's attention," she teased, deliberately flipping her pigtails.

"Pizza and beer, Suze," I deadpanned. "I have it on excellent authority that they go together."

Suze pushed her menu away as the waitress came up. "Large pizza, half vegetarian, half meat lover's," she rattled off our standard order as the poor woman, who had only expected to take the drinks, scrambled for her order pad. Suze paused for a moment and looked back at me, tilting her head in that very vulpine way of hers. Not looking away from me, she said, "Split the checks. But," she amended emphatically, "the beer goes on *his*." When the waitress left, she gave me a chiding look. "Don't try to bribe me, Fort."

"It's not a bribe," I said mildly. "Just an incentive."

She snorted, but then changed the subject. I let her—we'd had these small snippets of conversation many times over the last month. If she'd ever told me flat out at any point that she didn't want to be in a relationship with me, then I would've dropped it forever. But she hadn't—and at times I could feel her dark eyes watching me when I wasn't looking, considering and assessing, the same way I'd once seen her in her fox form, staring up at a bakery tin that I'd put on top of one of the high cabinets to keep away from her. She'd been weighing how much she'd really wanted it, and whether it was worth the effort.

As it had turned out, a fox is very capable of jumping straight to the top of a refrigerator, then hopping on top of the hanging cabinets, scampering over to the bakery tin, and gobbling a third of the contents before you can stop her. Since then I'd just had to accept that no food item in my apartment was safe from Suzume.

When I pulled out my wallet at the end of the meal, I discovered that it was now sporting a pair of glued-on googly eyes. I looked over at Suze, who was watching me with a look of sublime glee across her face. I shook my head and pulled out some cash, ignoring her delighted snickering.

We drove back to my apartment, where Suze plopped straight onto the couch and started channel surfing. I called the results of the trip in to my mother, who seemed pleased by the results.

"Talk this one over with your sister," Madeline told me. "I'm sure the two of you can come up with a good plan of action."

"Mother, I'm not sure that Prudence and I work that well together," I said. "The last time didn't work out too well." In fact it had ended in my holding a gun to her head, and then her attempting to kill my host father, Henry. Not a particularly great track record.

"Nonsense, darling. You sorted out that wretched elf problem, and just had a few hiccups at the end." I choked a little at her phrasing. "Besides," she said, her tone sharpening, "you have many more years of sharing each other's company. There's no time like the present to figure out how to get along. Now, when will you be coming down again? She's decided to continue visiting in her old room for another week or so, so you can see her whenever you want." What a very genteel way my mother had with phrasing. Much better than mentioning that Prudence had had to temporarily move back into the mansion when Madeline began enacting her punishment plan. Apparently it was very hard to go to the bathroom with a broken thigh unless there was a helpful twenty-four-hour presence of staff willing to help out.

"In a few days," I told her. "The rusalka won't need to be moved until the springtime anyway, so there's no rush." We exchanged good-byes, and then I hung up.

Collaborating with Prudence again was right up there with a root canal as far as things I'd like to avoid. I put in a call to Loren Noka to check on whether any new messages or jobs had come in while I was out, pulling out and prepping a bag of microwavable popcorn as I went. Suze had given up on channel surfing and was now digging around at the DVD pile. Noka assured me that with the rusalka conversation out of the way, there was nothing that needed my attention.

With the knowledge that I wouldn't be running errands for the family business, I called up my floater job. A few weeks ago, I'd seen a flyer on the side of a bus stop shelter, and after following up on it, I had begun my exciting employment as the substitute dog walker for a local entrepreneur who had managed to corner the market in the College Hill area. Hank was a semi-retired semi-professional marathon runner in his fifties, and years ago he'd hit on the realization that he could get his necessary daily miles clocked up while at the same time hauling along some pampered canines and get paid for it. Since then he'd become something of a dog walker kingpin, with hordes of underlings, a permanently affixed Bluetooth, and a daily e-mail blast of schedules and locations. Working with my family had left my schedule too erratic even for working as a waiter, and so far this had been an almost unqualified success. After all, there isn't that much of a difference between cleaning up after people's dinners and scooping dog poop into plastic bags.

Fortunately enough, one of Hank's regulars was going to be out the next day, so he simply gave me her full schedule. It included a round of basic morning and afternoon poops, which were never more than a quick walk around the block, and also a long set of full exercise runs for a few people who preferred the dog exhausted and their furniture intact.

Suze made a loud noise of disgust when I hung up, but said nothing. She was not a fan of the dog walking—she claimed that all the dogs marking me was really annoying. She'd thrown a fit the few times I'd met up with her after walking the dogs without going through a full shower. I assumed it was some kind of weird canine thing, since the dogs certainly noticed whenever I'd been around Suze—even a dog that might've been practically crossing its legs to avoid an accident had to slow down and give me a complete sniffing before we could make our way to the nearest patch of grass.

The familiar opening instrumental strains of *Wild Pacific* floated through the apartment. "Don't even think about it," I snapped at Suze, who, having made her disapproval clear, gave a superior sniff and flopped back onto the sofa. I poured the popcorn into a container and handed it to her as a peace offering, then popped the DVD out and flipped the TV over to the classic movies channel. Luck was with me as the opening scene of *Shadow of a Doubt* filled the screen. Suze and I had very different tastes when it came to most films and shows, but Hitchcock was always a reliable compromise.

The murderous Uncle Charlie had just been triumphantly squished by a train when keys rattled in the door and Dan and his boyfriend, Jaison, came in, carrying takeout food bags. As a couple, they were a study in contrasts. Dan was five foot five, dressed in an elegant dark gray peacoat, slacks, and a wine-colored scarf that was tied around his neck with a casually perfect knot that I knew would've taken me hours to achieve. Jaison was well over six feet tall, his medium-length natural Afro mashed under a battered Red Sox ball cap and an unzipped parka thrown on over a tan sweatshirt, with the carpenter's pants that he'd probably worn to work that day, judging by a blob of dried mortar still attaching the pants to the top of his steel-toed work boots. And, of course, the small fact that Jaison was entirely human, while Dan was very much not.

A round of polite hellos was exchanged. Both Suze and Jaison were in and out of the apartment regularly enough that everyone knew each other socially at this point.

"Hey, Jaison. Over for dinner?" Suzume asked. I shot a suspicious look at her. Despite how innocuous the question had been, I knew that tone in her voice too well.

"Dan and I grabbed Thai food," Jaison responded.

Suzume made a tsking sound. "Really, Jaison, why doesn't Dan ever make dinner for you? I hear he's a *very* daring chef."

I blanched, and from his position behind Jaison, Dan looked ready to strangle Suze, whose smile had just a bit too much trickster in it to be mistaken for friendly. I knew that my roommate was always extremely careful to cook only on nights when Jaison wouldn't be staying over, and up until now I'd participated in the cover story that Dan wasn't much of a cook.

I hurried into the conversation, "Suze, plenty of people like eating out when they can. And I'm sure that Dan's glad to get a break from washing out the pots." I aimed a small kick at her ankle, but Suze was no stranger to the social-norm protection kick, and she smoothly lifted up her legs and tucked them onto the sofa, never breaking that wide smile.

Jaison remained blessedly unaware of the undercurrents in the conversation, and his white teeth flashed against his dark skin in a wide, though slightly baffled smile. "I don't mind doing a round of dishes in exchange for dinner," he said, before turning one slightly confused look at his boyfriend. "But I thought you didn't really know how to cook?"

Dan very deliberately ignored the question and shoved the line of discussion into a completely new direction with a surprising lack of subtlety for a man currently studying the legal system. "What I'd really like is if we could convince the landlord to put in a dishwasher."

I did my best to help out, saying, "It would take a miracle, Dan. You wouldn't believe the fuss Mrs. Bandyopadyay had to make when her stove had a gas leak." Leaning in close, I whispered, "Be nice," in Suze's ear.

While Jaison began transferring the take-out food from Styrofoam containers to plates, Dan came over to the couch under the pretext of checking out our pile of DVDs. I was treated to an extremely icy glare.

"Turn that look ninety degrees to the right, Dan," I warned. "I didn't start this."

"She's your girlfriend, so she's your responsibility," Dan said in a muttering pitch that nonetheless fully expressed his irritation. "Get her to knock it off."

"Sitting right here," Suzume complained, "and resenting every implication and statement you just made."

"Dan, even if she was my girlfriend, which, for the record, she isn't, I would still do what I'm doing now, which is to take this chance in advance to fully disavow whatever action she eventually takes to get back at you for those comments."

The expression on Suze's face was definitely promising full retribution, and Dan was smart enough to look a bit concerned. Quitting while he was behind, he grabbed a disc at random and got up, grumbling, "I didn't know living with you came with a fox involved. The kitsune are a menace."

Suzume watched Dan retreat, the gleam in her dark eyes hinting at future destruction of property or the ruination of reputations. I scooted closer to her and said softly, "He's just sensitive about Jaison, Suze. That really wasn't nice to tease him about."

She gave a very superior sniff. "If he wants to date dinner, then he should get used to it." Then she fixed me with a sidelong look. "You're *both* too sensitive about this."

"And your poking at Dan has nothing to do with Keiko?" Suzume and her twin sister had been arguing for months over Keiko's relationship with a very nice, and wholly human, doctor.

The glitter in Suze's eyes warned me to back off from that topic. "I don't know if you stuck up for me very well just now. That's didn't seem like very boyfriend-ish behavior."

I took the hint and dropped the family topic, but I couldn't hold back a laugh at her mock-affronted demeanor. "Suze, the last thing you would ever convince me that you want is blind validation."

A very calculating expression filled her face, and Suzume made a surprisingly smooth slinking movement across the sofa that took the distance between us from comfortable and friendly to completely nonexistent, pressing us together from shoulder to hip in a way that made my breath catch. My body went on full alert, and I was uncomfortably reminded of just how long it had been since I'd had sex. Suze was clearly absolutely aware of every iota of her effect on me, and her voice became low and husky as she murmured in my ear. "If you know me so well, what do *you* have that I want?"

Completely ignorant of just how loaded a question had just been asked, Jaison cut through the banal sounds of take-out food being dished out, saying in gleeful surprise, "*The Sarah Connor Chronicles*? Dan, I thought you hated the *Terminator* series!"

Suze and I didn't move. Behind us, I could almost hear Dan gritting his teeth as he very quickly reaped the reward of snagging a DVD at random from my pile. "Well, you and Fort both like it so much," Dan covered. "Maybe I should give it another chance."

Without breaking eye contact with me, Suzume called, "That means giving it a full chance this time, Dan. Letting the series build its momentum. No calling it quits three episodes in." Even as the sexual tension meter remained set on high, I fought a smile—Suze was never one to let a good chance for immediate payback pass her by.

"Fort, are you up for watching the pilot tonight?" Jaison asked as he walked over to prep the evening's entertainment. As he did, Suze leaned away from me, letting a natural-looking position adjustment break our physical contact.

"Robots, time travel, Summer Glau, and violence?" I asked. If my body was destined to remain woefully unsexed, maybe my brain could at least get the condolence prize of sci-fi-induced dopamine. "Do you even need to ask?"

Jaison grinned and offered me a fist bump of geek solidarity, which I was happy to accept. Then he looked over at Suze. "Even Dan's giving it a chance," he coaxed. "You might like it."

"Violence, sure. Summer Glau, maybe. Robots and time travel? Never. I'll call a cab." She gave my knee a friendly pat as she stood up. "Have fun scooping poop tomorrow."

"It's just the career I dreamed about for four years at Brown," I noted.

Chapter 3

I was not a big fan of being awake at six in the morning, especially during the winter months when the sun wasn't even up yet, but it was the unfortunate downside in a temporary career option that revolved around the bladder control of canines. At least today the coffeepot was already going. Still dressed in my usual winter pajamas of a set of old sweatpants and a long-sleeved shirt, I propelled my zombielike self into the main room, where an already-dressed but still-rumpled-looking Jaison was pouring out the first coffee of the day. We exchanged the traditional pre-caffeine greeting of manly grumbles and commenced slurping.

Dan was parked on the sofa, feverishly flipping through a set of his flash cards, muttering things under his breath about alter ego liability and undercapitalization. Jaison and I shared a look of perfect understanding—no salary was worth that. The stressed-out ghoul broke off his prepping for a minute. "Fort, the dish-soap bottle has eyes. Is your girlfriend behind that?"

I shuffled over and checked beneath the sink. Sure enough, the Dawn container now had a jaunty pair of googly eyes. "She's still not my girlfriend, Dan."

"Whatever the hell she is, she'd better remember that whatever kind of grand finale she's working up to had better not involve defiling common property."

Silently, Jaison turned the handle of the coffeepot so that I could properly admire the eyes that were now affixed to it. By wordless agreement, neither of us mentioned it to Dan. I also decided that the addition I'd noticed on the ice cube trays the previous night could wait for a more opportune time.

The early morning passed in a quick series of doggy pee breaks. There weren't that many of them—most dog owners, no matter how busy their work schedules, were able to run their dogs out for a fast poop before they had to head out for the day. But there were a few people who worked third shift and wouldn't be home until almost noon, and one or two families had clearly gotten the dog as some sort of prop for their kid's childhood and now attempted to farm out every inconvenient facet of the dog's existence. Hank's dog-walking kingdom was based on the very marketable importance of reliability—his clients might not always know *who* was going to be walking their dog, but they knew that *someone* would be showing up, and in a timely enough fashion that they wouldn't be coming home to find a puddle of urine in the middle of their carpet. To make that possible, Hank required all of his clients to hang a combination-based keyholder on their doors, the same way that real estate agencies did. Hank changed all of the combinations himself every month, to cut down on theft concerns. Each walker was e-mailed their walking schedule, addresses, and the combination keys the night before their route started, and in all the houses where I'd shown up to collect a dog for Hank, I'd never been given the wrong combination code.

Once the morning sanitary checks were completed without a problem (though Venus, the elderly French bulldog, managed to take twenty minutes to locate her ideal spot before solemnly defecating on the front steps of a synagogue, while the very unamused rabbi watched to make certain that I collected every single particle of poop), I moved on to the exercise runs. For most of the dogs, a half-hour jog at a good pace was enough to ensure that they were left panting and happily mellowed out. Others, like Hercule, the Great Pyrenees, or Mogsy, the Rhodesian Ridgeback, ended up with a full hour. At two o'clock, my schedule temporarily shifted back to poop maintenance, giving several desperately grateful dogs a well-needed bathroom break to tide them over until their owners got home in the evening, but everything ran mostly on track, with the only hiccup being when Pip, the long-haired dachshund, attempted to attack, for no discernible reason, a mailbox. He ended up settling for peeing on it, but looked balefully over his shoulder several times as we departed. Whatever issues lay between Pip and the mailbox, they were clearly far from over.

Despite the ignominy of scooping up dog feces and having my crotch ritualistically sniffed by fifteen different snouts, I enjoyed the work. Jogging around the College Hill area of Providence, even during November, was far less soul-crushing than any retail job I'd ever held, and the dogs were always happy to see me, which made them a cut above most of my former coworkers. Plus, spending the majority of the day jogging was good enough exercise that I didn't have to maintain a gym membership. While there were the occasional moments of watching a dog urinate and pondering the usefulness of my Ivy League degree and periodic spots of weirdness like the day Ella (apparently an inveterate trash eater) pooped out two elastic bands, some chicken bones, and a condom, I'd so far been very happy at how the job was working out.

I was on my last assignment of the day, jogging a matched set of brick red Pharaoh Hounds named Fawkes and Codex, when my phone rang. I checked the caller ID, then slowed down to answer when I saw that it was Loren Noka. The dogs whined pitifully, hauling against the leashes and looking back at me with wide eyes that begged me to *ruuuuuun*, but I ignored them and listened to Ms. Noka's clipped delivery.

"I just got a call on the emergency line. The *karhu* of the *metsän kunigas* has been murdered. His niece discovered the body in his house, and they have requested an investigation."

I was turning the dogs around before Loren Noka was halfway through. "Text me the details, please," I said quickly, then disconnected as soon as we had exchanged good-byes. I tapped Suze's number in and was relieved when she picked up on the second ring.

Halfway through whatever clever joke she was saying as a greeting, I broke in with, "The head bear was just found murdered. Chivalry's still on bereavement, so this is all on me."

One of the things that a lot of people didn't realize about Suzume (probably because they had already fled in the other direction) was that when things got serious, she didn't play around. Without a pause, she immediately dropped all the fun joking and said, "I'm working downtown today. Pick me up." Then she rattled off the address and hung up. I shoved my phone back in my jacket pocket and pulled on the dogs' leashes—Fawkes and Codex, sensing that their precious run was going to be cut short, were doing their best to tug me in the direction that lay *away* from home—and once I had snouts facing correctly, I broke into a full sprint.

While I dodged around pedestrians and avoided being run over at cross streets, my brain scrambled to get a handle on the hot mess that I'd just been deputized to deal with. Reported murders were very rare in the territory—in the months that I'd been officially a part of my family's policing structure, I'd dealt with a few complaints and some minor disputes. Most things had been like my visit to the rusalka—fairly easy to look into and resolve. The most serious call to the emergency line that I'd been aware of was when I was still doing ride-alongs with

Chivalry over the summer, and a member of the territory had tipped us off that some kobolds had gone from eating stray animals to snatching people's pets.

Murder was much different, and this one was serious. I'd done my best to learn about all the major species that my mother ruled over, but I still hadn't met a lot of them. Unfortunately that included the *metsän kunigas*, and I tried to go over what I knew about them in my head as I returned two very disappointed dogs to their home and headed directly to my car.

The *metsän kunigas* were bears. Or, rather, they were humans who could turn into bears. Unlike the kitsune or the Ad-hene, which had specific and very localized points of species origin (Japan and Ireland, respectively), werebears, like both of their natural cousins, had developed in a lot of different places. The two communities (the larger in Providence, and a smaller one in Maine) that were in my mother's territory were Finnish immigrants who had come over in the early eighteen hundreds, but apparently there was also a variety of werebear that was indigenous to the United States, and lived in a few areas out West. They used different terminology, but the logistics were essentially the same. The Providence group typically didn't cause trouble for the vampires, operating within the rules that had been negotiated when they settled, and they delivered very healthy tithes, since the ruling family operated a thriving local insurance company that employed many members of the group. Their leader was called the *karhu*, and basically served as the group's monarch for life. The current *karhu* had been, until a few minutes ago, Matias Kivela. That, unfortunately, capped off most of what I knew about them.

One thing that Chivalry had been very clear on was that they universally hated the term *werebear*. Naturally, that was the first word out of Suzume's mouth as she hopped into my car.

"You smell worse than the werebears, Fort. Did you really have to let every single dog mark you?"

I'd pulled the car away from the curb the moment she pulled her door shut, and was already merging into the brewing excitement of Providence traffic at four thirty on a Tuesday. We were both dressed in work clothes—my apparently dog-funked jeans, a long-sleeved black shirt now decorated with a few sweaty spots thanks to my active day, and a zip-up gray hoodie with bleach stains. In contrast, Suzume was poured into a knee-length black pencil skirt, a dark green silk blouse, heels, and a black wool coat. We were definitely about to present an aesthetically mixed picture, but I was hoping that punctuality would be valued over presentation.

"I'm pretty sure that *metsän kunigas* is the preferred term, Suze. How would you feel if people called you a fox?"

"I would praise them on their accurate assessment of my place on the hotness-slash-awesomeness scale."

"And if they called you a werefox?"

"I would make them eat their own kidneys."

"Consider my point made." I turned onto Route 123 and glanced at Suze, who was glaring at me, the gears in her brain clearly working.

"You don't understand," she complained at last. "*I'm* a fox that turns into a human, which is awesome. *They* are humans who turn into bears, which is lame. It's completely different."

"I'm sure that the nuances of that are really important," I said soothingly, then did my best to shift the conversation.

The town of Lincoln, where most of the *metsän kunigas* lived, had a number of nice things going for it. It was a mere twelve miles from the heart of Providence, *Money* magazine had named it the sixty-third Best Place to Live, and it contained the Lincoln Woods State Park, which covered 627 acres of protected forest. Route 123 curved right along the edge of the state park, which was where a number of the *metsän kunigas*, including their dead leader, had bought property and built their homes.

The house was a tidy little beige 1920s bungalow with a tall wooden privacy fence that hid all views of the backyard from anyone driving down the street. There were at least five cars wedged into the driveway, and more parked on the lawn. I pulled the Fiesta up to the curb, and we both got out.

"Someone's watching us," I said quietly as we started up the front walkway. I could see the blinds in the front windows twitching.

"A whole lot of people are watching us," Suze corrected.

The door opened the moment my foot hit the steps. The man in his late thirties who opened it filled the doorway—he had one of those solid, square builds that can hide a lot of potpie dinners, but his was solid muscle, with no trace of fat. His dark hair was cut short, and the rich natural brown of his face suggested that one of the immigrant Finns had found love south of the border. He was scowling, and the expression brought to my mind so many bad grumpy bear jokes that my hand shot out without conscious thought to give Suze's wrist a cautionary squeeze. Her quiet little "Hrmph" confirmed my instinct.

"So Chivalry Scott actually sent baby brother rather than stirring himself." Even though he was half a head shorter than I was, the man at the door was capable of a very impressive rumbling bass.

"You asked for vampire help, and that's what just arrived," I said, feeling my temper spike. It's not that I wasn't used to being referred to as the baby of the family, but most people at least tried to phrase it more politely. And after a month of my handling my brother's workload, fewer of the territory inhabitants were surprised to see me. "If you want the Scotts involved, then that means that you're dealing with me."

The man was suddenly and effectively hip-checked to the side by a woman whose age and facial features matched his too well to be anything other than a close sibling. Her chin-length haircut might've suggested Busy Professional Mother, but her expression clearly read Irritated Big Sister.

"Calm down, Gil." Her dark eyes were carefully shuttered and her face scrubbed clean of expression when she looked at me. As she nudged her brother out of the doorway, she gestured for both of us to come in. "I'm sorry, we're just a little surprised. We knew that Chivalry probably wouldn't be able to come, so we were expecting Prudence," she explained as we stepped inside and she closed the door behind us. Inside, the bungalow's old floors gleamed with wood polish, and the decorating scheme seemed to revolve around the repeated theme of beige and beige—from what I could see of it. People packed the front hallway and spilled over into the adjoining dining room, all of them completely quiet and staring unabashedly at us.

Our apparent hostess offered me a handshake as professional as the navy blue pants suit she was wearing. "We haven't met before. I'm Dahlia, and this is my brother, Gil. The *karhu* was our uncle."

I returned the handshake. "I'm Fortitude Scott."

Suze caught her hand next. "Suzume Hollis."

Surprise flickered across Dahlia's face, the first emotion I'd seen from her. "Oh, I already called the kitsune."

"I'm not part of the cleanup crew," Suze said, giving a quick smile that flashed all her white teeth and didn't suggest anything friendly. "I'm with the vampire."

"Why don't you fill us in with what you know," I suggested.

"Of course," Dahlia agreed immediately, her expression quickly shuttering again. "Please, follow me."

We were led into the living room, where the beige decor had received a splash of color, literally. The *karhu* had been a tall man in his sixties, still trim and fit, but whose blond hair was streaked with gray. Unlike his niece and nephew, he would've looked perfectly at home on the Finnish ski team—except for his ravaged chest and the large pool of dried blood that he was lying in.

I looked down, feeling very much out of my depth. I'd seen bodies before, and I'd hunted for murderers, but most of it had been on my own time, with my family looking at my actions practically as teenage rebellion. Now I was standing next to a corpse with at least twenty of the *metsän kunigas* watching to see what I would do. Worse, they were right to, since I was very suddenly in charge.

"How about I check the body while you get the background," Suzume suggested beside me. I realized that she'd picked up on my discomfort and stepped in to cover for me. Gratitude filled me, and steadied me at the same time, allowing me to summon an inner Joe Friday as I looked at Dahlia and, in my best "Just the facts, ma'am" voice, ask, "What can you tell me?"

Her brother still a scowling mass beside her, Dahlia began, "He was alive last night when Carmen left the house—"

"Carmen?" I asked.

"His daughter," Gil said roughly, his tone and face clearly stating that this was something I should've known already.

"Carmen is twenty-one," said Dahlia, her cool voice cutting in. "She's in the kitchen, but she's having a hard time with this. If we can leave her alone for a few minutes, that might be best."

"Her father was just murdered," I conceded. "I can talk with her after you and I finish."

Dahlia nodded. "She says that she left around nine last night to go to a party. She spent the night with a boy she met there, so she never came home. When she woke up, she had to go straight to work, so Uncle Matias would've been alone all night." There was just the slightest waver in Dahlia's eyes as she glanced away from me for the first time in the discussion. Her eyes went over at where her uncle's body lay in a pool of blood and, from the smell that even open windows in November couldn't completely disperse, waste. I wondered what this very contained woman was thinking, but then she controlled even that tiny deviation and looked back to me. "Uncle Matias didn't come to work this morning."

"The family owns an insurance business," Gil said. "Most of us work at it."

"I did know that, but thank you," I said as politely as possible.

"Oh, I should've guessed," Gil replied. "The business generates tithes, so that would be important to know. Not like whether or not my uncle had a daughter."

I reminded myself that Gil's uncle was lying dead five feet from us at the foot of his La-Z-Boy, and that misplaced anger and its corollary, misplaced dickishness, were a noted part of the grieving process. I therefore ignored Gil's comment completely and continued looking at Dahlia, who elbowed her brother in the stomach with enough force to make him grunt slightly and take the cue to shut up.

"I assumed at first that Uncle Matias might not be feeling well," Dahlia continued, "but he didn't call, and when I tried getting through to him, there was no answer on either the house phone or his cell."

"Was that unusual?" I wished that I had a pad of paper to take notes. It would've given me something official-looking to do. Beside the body, Suze had finished looking over the wounds on the front, and she now rolled it over with a soft thump that all of us pretended not to have heard.

"For him not to pick up the cell, not really. None of us carry cell phones when we're roaming in our other forms. But it was strange for him not to let me know that he wouldn't be coming into work. He'd had appointments and calls scheduled, which I had to cover. So when I left the office to go home, I swung by the house. I have a key, and I let myself in. That was when I found him, and I called everyone in."

"It was just you?" I asked. Suzume was now giving the dead *karhu* a thorough sniffing—and since she was remaining in human form, that meant getting pretty close to the body. Fortunately no one seemed to be bothered by that—a benefit of dealing with people who spent a good amount of their time in natural fur coats.

"Yes," Dahlia confirmed. "Gil was in the field all day, looking into a flooded-basement claim. My mother was watching my daughters, and I knew they were planning on spending the day in the woods, so I didn't even try calling them."

Suze rejoined us, her sniffing apparently concluded. Her clothing was now looking much worse for wear after crawling around the body—but since she didn't seem to even notice the bloodstains now decorating the bottom of her skirt and her panty hose, I assumed that she had a plan for dealing with it. Since she was giving her hands a brisk wiping on her skirt, I wondered if that plan was dry cleaning or a Dumpster. "Too bad you didn't stay on your own. I don't smell anything on the body but bear, but since you've had half the *metsän kunigas* in the state kicking their heels in here, that's not surprising. When the cleanup crew you hired gets here, we'll give it a more thorough going-over, but did you notice anything when it was just you?"

Dahlia shook her head, her brown eyes giving nothing away. "Whoever did it was long gone. I couldn't smell anyone who shouldn't have been here. I just started making calls."

Gil cut in again—and unlike Dahlia's poker face, it was clear that Gil was angry at even the implication that his sister should've handled the body discovery differently. "Uncle Matias was in his sixties, but he was strong. What killed him could've killed Dahlia, so she was right to call the rest of us." He pointed at the small but visible blood droplets that led from the body to the sliding glass door that led to the backyard. "When I got here, the two of us followed the blood trail. It goes to the deck, but ends in the outdoor shower. There are some containers out there with spare clothes—sweatpants, big T-shirts, just enough to cover anyone who wanted to walk over wearing their fur. Carmen looked through it, and she doesn't think that anything is missing."

"The killer would've needed a shower," Suze agreed. "The *karhu* has a lot of stab wounds in his chest, and judging by what I'm looking at, it wasn't much of a fight. The main blood pool is all in that one spot, with no drag marks. Everything beyond that is either spatter or what dripped off the killer on its way out the back door. Have you called in the ghouls?"

"I did. They'll send the hearse after the kitsune shroud the scene and the police are dealt with." Compared with her brother's impression of a simmering pot, Dahlia was an icicle.

"They'll do an autopsy for us, then, and see what they can pick up." Suze's tone was bland, but I could see her eyeing Gil, and specifically the vein currently throbbing in his forehead, as she waited for the outburst.

She didn't have long to wait. "Well, we all know what caused this!" Gil bellowed, making my ears ring. "Something that could've caught my uncle by surprise and killed him before he could shift forms? Something that could hide their scent even from a kitsune? Something that would *want* to kill Matias? This is obviously the Adhene!"

A low murmur went through the general crowd, and I got the impression that Gil's suspicion was a popular one, and that only my mother's rules were preventing this group from heading over to the Underhill entrance with some torches and farm implements. I'd seen enough of the elves at work recently not to find that a very concerning prospect, but so far, nothing about this looked like the bodies I'd seen them leave behind before. "Why would the Ad-hene want your uncle dead?" I asked.

"Maybe they're tired of their usual prey. We share the Lincoln Woods with them, and my sister and I have both seen what they do to the deer that they hunt. They're dangerous, and now that they aren't allowed to slaughter their own children anymore, who knows what they'll be up to next? Maybe they thought Matias would be interesting prey. Or worse, what if the next Ad-hene population pipe dream involves *metsän kunigas* blood? How long before the Scotts bother to look into it, since according to our treaty, we can't even ask them ourselves?"

Gil was definitely not a member of the Scott family fan club, that was for sure. I pushed him. "My mother just punished the Ad-hene for breaking our rules. Do you think they'd defy her again in less than a month?"

"There's no reasoning with madmen," Gil countered. "And they didn't start breaking those rules overnight. From what I heard, the murders were happening for close to a year before the Scotts bothered to look into them—and only after a corpse got dumped on your doorstep! We use those woods—my nieces *play* in those woods. Our *karhu* is dead, and to me the most obvious culprit is sitting right in Underhill."

Through her brother's passionate tirade, Dahlia had been noticeably silent, and I shifted my attention to her. "You're very quiet. What do you think about this theory?"

Her eyes narrowed, flicked to her brother, and I could see her weighing the possibilities before cautiously nodding. "The Ad-hene like to kill, and they've broken the rules before." She asked Suzume, "Could an Ad-hene hide his scent from you with a glamour?"

Suze's expression was reluctant and very unhappy, so I knew her answer before she even spoke. Nothing irritated her more than having to admit that her kitsune abilities had limitations. "I'm not sure. If we were talking just about the Neighbors, I'd say no—the nose is harder to fool than the eye, and most of them can barely hold a visual glamour. But I can't say for sure about the Ad-hene, and I don't think anyone in my family has had enough contact with them to know either."

A blond girl with a kind of Swiss Miss prettiness who looked just out of her teens walked up to us, the first of any of the bears to break away from the observing throng. Her face was red and blotchy from very recent crying. "Dahlia, the kitsune just arrived," she said, her voice low.

"Good." Dahlia looked at me. "Mr. Scott, this is Car-men, my cousin."

So this was the dead bear's daughter. I felt horribly awkward being introduced to her with such icy polite-ness when her father's body was still sprawled in the middle of the room. "I'm sorry for your loss," I managed, getting a small nod in return. Then the moment was bro-ken by the entrance of the kitsune.

There were three of them, a terrifying thought in itself, and they walked in a small phalanx to us, forcing several of the bears to stumble out of their way or be trampled. In the front was the smallest, an older woman whose dark hair was heavily streaked with gray but who bore a strong resemblance to Suzume. Flanking her were two kitsune in their early twenties who bore the clear signs of more lo-calized parentage. All three were dressed in formal busi-ness wear, but it ranged from the older woman's sedate gray slacks-and-sweater combo to the youngest woman's brilliant canary yellow skirt paired with a black silk blouse.

"Suzu-chan, I should've known I'd find you here," the older woman said, with that touch of exasperation that seemed to affect most people Suzume knew.

My partner gave a broad grin. "Right where I'd be most useful, right, Oba-chan?" As the woman gave a very definitive snort that expressed her feelings on the subject, Suze nudged me with a friendly elbow. "Fort, meet my Aunt Chiyo."

Horrors, more introductions. "It's a pleasure," I said politely.

There was clear interest in the way Chiyo looked at me, but also a subtle wariness. "Hmm. The young almost-vampire my mother seemed so interested in. You're taller than the White Fox described." Her mouth pursed. "These are two of my daughters. Midori is my oldest." Midori towered over the other kitsune by several inches. Her features and eyes were as Asian as her mother's, but her skin was a very dark brown that had clearly come from her father, along with gorgeous curly hair that was not quite the true, deep black that Suze and her aunt had. She shook hands with me, her cinnamon-colored eyes solemn.

"And one of my younger daughters, Takara," Chiyo continued. The yang to her sister's yin, Takara had Irish-pale skin, and each of her cheekbones was covered in a series of freckles. I could only speculate what her natural hair color was since it was barely two inches long and dyed a bright blue that matched her eyes. Clearly Suzume's aunt had not had a set "type" when she'd dated as a young woman.

Compared to her mother and older sister's very dignified bearing, Takara was practically vibrating with energy as she looked me up and down with a keenness that made me feel just slightly objectified. Even worse was the very visible disappointment on her face as she said to Suzume, "I thought he'd be better looking, *anego*."

Suzume was clearly amused by both my discomfort and her cousin's pout. "Next time I'll provide visual supplements, Taka. That way you won't be let down."

Now Midori joined in. "I don't know; given how Keiko talks about him, he could be worse. At least the vampire smell isn't too obvious. Of course, it could be covered up by all those dogs that apparently humped him."

Chiyo cut the conversation short with a sudden barrage

of Japanese that I somehow knew (just *knew*) had not been particularly complimentary to my personal aroma. "We can all chat later," she concluded in English, then nodded to Dahlia. "After all, the *metsän kunigas* have hired us to perform a job."

"We appreciate your time, Ms. Hollis," Dahlia said formally. All three of the bears were watching the kitsune very carefully.

"Oh, I imagine that you do." And then Chiyo gave a very foxy and predatory grin that was definitely not nice at all, and that I had seen several times before on Suzume's face. "Forgive my lack of delicacy, but you are familiar with the price tag on what we're about to do, yes?"

Gil was gritting his teeth. "We don't have many options, do we?"

"That's the beauty of holding a monopoly," Suzume said serenely. She glanced at her aunt and flashed her own smile. "Thirty?"

Chiyo returned her niece's expression in spades. "Yes. Thirty thousand. Cash only, if you don't mind."

Dahlia and Gil exchanged a significant glance. I noted with interest that Carmen was left to stand awkwardly on the side, not involved in her cousins' exchange. A quick flicker of irritation managed to pass through the grief on her face—a flicker that I definitely recognized. It was tough when your relatives insisted on relegating you to the kiddie table during decision making. Of course, I'd certainly learned lately that being the one calling the shots wasn't all it was cracked up to be either. Dahlia was the one to speak. "That might take us a few days."

"More." Gil was reining in his temper, but his tone was grim. I didn't like him very much, but I could sympathize a little. My own sphincter had made an instinctive clench at the number being tossed around. "I don't care how good you are. We're going to have to be careful freeing up that much in cash right after my uncle's death."

"Of course we understand, darlings. You're in your grief, after all." Chiyo's white teeth gleamed. "Three weeks, not a day longer. Don't look for an invoice. We know where to find you."

There was another silent exchange between the siblings; then Dahlia nodded. "All right. But it has to look like a natural death. Something that won't be questioned or spur any kind of investigation."

"Why else would you have called us in?" The older kitsune's eyes narrowed in annoyance, looking moderately affronted. With another imperious sniff, Chiyo very deliberately looked away from Dahlia and shifted the subject. "Suzume, have you gotten a good enough look at the scene?"

"Mostly, Oba-chan. But if the murder weapon is here, I haven't found it."

"Easy to address." Chiyo turned to her younger daughter. "Taka-chan?"

The blue-haired girl nodded, and began unbuttoning her blouse with a very businesslike air. Lacking an ingrained social response for how to react when the younger cousin of a woman I was doing my best to date started disrobing in the middle of a crowded room that happened to include a dead body, my higher thinking ceded completely to my lizard brain response. Almost simultaneously I flushed beet red, dropped my eyes to my shoes, and made a strangled noise in my throat that sounded like a turkey lure. I could feel the puzzled gazes of every shape-shifter in the room lock on me.

Had I not been fully dressed, I would've suspected that this was a nightmare.

"Oh, he *is* adorable," Takara said delightedly as the unzipping of her skirt zipper filled my ears. A pair of now-bare feet deliberately peeped into my line of vision as I stared at my shoes, replaced a moment later by a small red fox with black legs and a white-tipped tail, whose jaw dropped in a vulpine version of laughter before her nose dropped to the ground and she devoted herself to her task.

Her sister seemed less impressed. "If you like the type. Honestly, though, Suzu, what have you *not* been doing with him that he can't even take a little flashed skin?"

Whatever retort Suzume was about to make (and I'd known in my bones that I was not going to like it) was cut off by another explosion of Japanese scolding from her aunt, toward whom I was now starting to feel much warmer feelings. I looked up to see Midori's full lips press hard together in response to whatever had been said, while Chiyo turned her attention to the bears, who had been standing by during all of this. "My dears, it might be useful if we didn't have quite as huge a crowd."

"Do you need them completely gone, or just out of the way?" Gil asked.

"On the back porch is fine."

Even Dahlia's stone facade broke enough to look somewhat relieved to be given an excuse to get away from the kitsune antics, and the two siblings immediately began herding the bystanders. Takara scampered through the legs of the moving people, somehow always avoiding getting her tail stepped on. Midori and Chiyo began circling the body. That left me and Suzume with Carmen.

I gave Suze a small nudge with my shoulder, then nodded at the girl. Suze arched an eyebrow, but stepped away to join her aunt and cousin at the body. That left me with the last person who had seen the *karhu* alive.

It was awkward as hell.

I did my best. "I'm really sorry that I have to ask you this now, with your dad right there, but—"

Carmen interrupted me. "No, it's okay." She rubbed her face hard with the sleeve of her sweater, gave a wet sniffle, and focused completely on me. She had none of Dahlia's icy control, or Gil's anger. What she did have when she focused those pale blue eyes on me was a clear, unhidden disappointment that made me feel about three inches tall. "So it's definitely you who is going to be hunting for the killer? Not your sister?"

I couldn't help but feel sorry for her. Her father had just been murdered, and in her eyes, the person assigned to the job was the C-Team. But at the same time I had no intention of asking my sister for help—not after the fiasco of last time. "I know that Prudence seems like she would be the better person to look into this," I said, keeping my voice firm, but also trying hard not to sound like a complete dick. "But my brother and my mother both put me in charge instead of her for a lot of reasons. I promise I'll do my best." Carmen's huge blue eyes filled up with tears, and her lower lip started trembling. I managed to hold out for one long minute, until the tears broke and started streaking her face, and I knew that I was beaten. With a sigh, I capitulated, promising, "If I don't make any progress, I'll ask for her help."

Carmen brightened immediately, like a rain-soaked daisy. "Thanks," she said sincerely. Then she looked embarrassed. "I didn't want to hurt your feelings, but it's just—"

"I understand. It's your dad." She nodded gratefully. "Okay—well, did you notice anything at all that was unusual when you left home last night?"

Carmen shook her head. "No. I'm sorry, I've thought about it as much as I could, and it was just a normal night. Dad was reading when I left, and he usually would've gone to bed around eleven."

"Would he have waited up for you?"

For a second she looked annoyed, and I wondered whether that had been something that had been a point of contention between the two of them. "I'm living at home to save on rent, but I'm twenty-one. Dad knew I'd be back when I was back." Then her whole face crumpled again, and the tears let loose. "It was a stupid party. I should've stayed home. If there had been two of us, Dad would've been okay."

I gave her shoulder an awkward patting as she sobbed, looking around desperately for assistance. Dahlia was just walking back in from the porch, and caught my expression. She immediately hustled over and collected Carmen, wrapping an arm around her. Gil followed at her heels, and the three ducked away into the kitchen.

That thankfully over with, I looked over at the foxes, and realized that the situation over there was not much better. Takara was back in human form, though still completely naked, and was now muscling the body of Matias up into a sitting position on the La-Z-Boy. Midori and Chiyo were helping, and I was very glad that all the bears were temporarily out of the room. The three kitsune were fighting against the effects of rigor mortis to sit the corpse into a natural-looking pose, and it was incredibly grisly to see Takara throw all of her weight onto the legs while the others shoved against the shoulders as hard as they could, while the body let out horrible cracking and gas-releasing sounds. It was also an extremely messy endeavor, and I could understand why Takara hadn't bothered to put her clothes back on.

While the other three kitsune continued fussing over the body (now there seemed to be some disagreement about how his arms looked), Suze made her way back to me. She leaned, subtly moving me so that I didn't have to look at what was being done with the body, and started talking quietly. "Taka found a nice big decorative geode the size of my fist under the sofa with a good blood smear on it. We think that's what bashed in the back of his head, and it smells like it came from inside the house, so the killer probably just grabbed it. She couldn't find the knife, but I checked the kitchen, and the butcher's block is missing one of the big carving knives, and it wasn't in the dishwasher either."

"So the killer took the knife?" Another loud cracking sound filled the room as the kitsune apparently solved the problem of arm placement. I winced.

"Looks that way," Suze agreed.

The noise had drawn Dahlia, Gil, and Carmen back in from the kitchen. They stared at the spectacle before them—Matias's body was now positioned in his chair, his hands draped over the padded arms and his head pressing back against the cushions. The gory mess of his chest managed to look even more horrific in this positioning than it had when he was lying on the floor.

Gil headed straight for Suze, his eyes wild. "My sister just called the police to report that we discovered my uncle dead from a likely heart attack, just like that aunt of yours told us to." A sound of complete and wordless outrage emerged as he pointed his finger at the scene before us. "That does *not* look like a heart attack!"

Suze gave a slightly superior smile, apparently completely unconcerned at the outraged *metsän kunigas* in front of us. "Are you sure? Why not take a second look?"

We all turned our heads, and at the same moment I felt my whole body cramp up with a pins-and-needles sensation, as if everything was a leg that was just falling asleep. A second later it was gone, leaving only the slightest soreness behind, but I knew that feeling, and I wasn't surprised when I focused my eyes and saw a man lying quietly in the beige La-Z-Boy, his face gray and drawn, but with no blood or wounds anywhere visible. Smoothly inserted into my brain was the thought, *Gosh, the poor guy must've had a heart attack. Not surprising, at his age. I wonder if there was a history of it in the family.*

That was the power of the fox magic. Even knowing that it was an illusion, I couldn't see through it. I knew that if I reached out and touched the exact spots where the knife wounds were on the *karhu*'s chest, my hand would tell my brain that there was unbroken skin. I'd seen Suzume do this once on her own when she needed to hide the body of a vampire's host—it had exhausted her to the point where I'd had to carry her back to where we'd parked the Fiesta. Her aunt and cousins weren't falling over, but they all suddenly looked like the opening scene of a five-hour energy commercial.

"All done," Chiyo announced, and walked slowly over to us. Dahlia and Carmen had joined us—the former clearly fighting to hide her surprise, and the latter just staring with her jaw flapping open. The kitsune reached into her handbag and removed some blank pill bottles, the orange kind that usually had pharmacy labels attached. She held them for a moment as she glanced between the three bears, settling finally on Dahlia. "Everyone seems to be looking to you, Dahlia. So are you the new *karhu* that we'll all be dealing with?"

Another of those lightning-fast and completely undecipherable looks was exchanged, and it was Gil who answered, in as controlled a voice as I'd heard from him yet this afternoon. "My uncle had indicated several times that Dahlia would be his choice, but the formal ceremony won't be until after the mourning period is over."

As if they had never stopped in the first place, Carmen's tears began again. "Another month at least," she choked out.

Chiyo nodded. "Of course. Well, then." She handed Dahlia the pill bottles. "Put these in the medicine cabinet and on the kitchen counter. When the police see them, they'll see exactly the medications they would expect to see in cases of heart trouble." The sound of a siren began blaring in the distance, and she gave a small, satisfied smile. "Ah, that should be them right now. Since I'm sure you can handle them while they come to the obvious conclusions, we'll adjourn to the kitchen." A hard look tightened her tired face, and she glared at all three of the *metsän kunigas*. "The paramedics will rush in and make all sorts of fuss. Let them. They'll see everything they expect in a fatal heart attack, and they'll never see the blood even when they put their hands right in it. *No one* will see it. It won't show up in any photos either. When they shower after their shifts, it'll be washed down the drain and no one will be the wiser. Just look sad, shaken, but not very surprised, and when they ask you, say that your uncle had had some health issues for the last few years, but didn't like to talk about it much. Once they realize that there's no use bringing him to the hospital, and the police agree that it's clearly just a natural event, let *them* ask if you have a funeral home to use. *Then* bring up the ghouls, and either of you can trot off and call them over."

"Will the ghouls be able to see through what you've done?" Gil asked. "We were told that they would be able to do an autopsy."

"My daughters and I will follow them over to Celik Funeral Home and break the illusion for them." Her dark eyes dropped to the rug, which the fox magic had rendered seemingly beige and unmarked again. "Remember that once we do that, everything will break. You'll need a carpet steamer, and definitely get a new cover for that ghastly chair."

Dahlia nodded, her mouth pressed into a thin line. "We can manage, thank you." The sirens were nearly at the house. "If you'll excuse us—"

"Of course." Chiyo motioned her daughters into the kitchen as the bears went out to meet the owners of the siren. Suze caught my wrist and towed me along.

The kitchen was, unsurprisingly, beige, with a few touches of dark wood trim that matched the cabinets. The three kitsune collapsed into the chairs that ringed the small breakfast table. I couldn't help but notice that Takara was still completely naked.

She looked mentally fried, and I wondered whether she needed a reminder about her state of nature. "Um, Takara . . . the police are here, you know."

Suzume snorted and leaned against the counter. "Don't hassle her, Fort. A naked girl in the kitchen is the last thing the police or the paramedics will expect to see. I could pull this trick in my sleep—all they'll see is yet another group of grieving relatives."

"That's very helpful of you, Suzu-chan," Chiyo said in a tone that suggested that Suzume was often much less than helpful. "Speaking of helpful, I wish you'd do something about Keiko. It's silly of her to extend her pregnancy like this. I can't imagine why she would go nine months on two legs instead of seven and a half weeks on four legs."

Suze darted me a quick look, and I suddenly realized that Keiko's aunt apparently knew less about what she was actually up to than I did. "It's hard to say, Auntie. Maybe she saw Yuzumi recently." Suze's voice was completely serene.

And apparently effective at muddying the conversational waters. Chiyo's eyebrows knit together in irritation. "Suzume, *really*, how can you even—"

Takara's head was cushioned in her arms, but she jumped in. "I don't blame her. The triplets are about as destructive as the German Luftwaffe. Saving seven months can't be worth eighteen years of that."

"I was talking with Hoshi last week," Midori added. "She thinks that Keiko has the right idea—she's considering staying two-legged for her pregnancy. Thinks it'll be easier in the long run, even with the cost of maternity clothes. Or maybe spending just two days a week on four feet—cut the pregnancy down a month or two, maybe just end up with a set of twins, max."

"Hell, yeah," her sister agreed. "Have you seen those stupid booster seats Yuzumi has to use? They wouldn't all fit in my car when I was watching the girls, so I had to drive them in fox. Riko peed in a cup holder."

Their mother now looked defensive. "Staying fox doesn't always mean triplets."

"Except for Yuzumi. And you. And twice for Kanon-

obasan." From Midori's expression, these were some rather significant exceptions.

"Do you see what your sister has started?" Chiyo demanded of Suzume, apparently tired and aggravated enough to miss the slight gleam of satisfaction in her niece's eyes at how well she'd distracted her aunt from the original topic. "I expect this kind of thing from you, not Keiko."

"What kind of thing? Kits? Is that what you expect from me?" Suze sounded amused.

Her aunt shuddered dramatically. "Don't even say such a thing, Suzu-chan. I don't want to imagine the kind of demon-spawn you would produce." She focused on me, and said, "My poor sister had to call the fire department three times before Suzume was six."

I had no difficulty at all imagining that. The conversation lagged after that—Chiyo and Midori were both tired after hiding the body, and after a few minutes they were clearly struggling to keep up with a basic conversation about whether we could expect any snow this year before Thanksgiving. Takara was apparently given more slack as the youngest, because she simply shifted back to her fox form and took a snooze on the floor.

After forty-five minutes, Gil appeared in the doorway, his wide face bearing an expression of semi-appeasement. "You were right—they're convinced," he said bluntly. "One of the officers is staying around until the body is taken away, but it just looks like a courtesy thing. I called the ghouls, and they said they'll be here in a few minutes."

"Excellent," Chiyo said, collecting her purse. "My daughters and I will meet them at the funeral home. No reason to continue cluttering up your kitchen." Midori reached down and scooped her four-footed sister off the floor. Takara didn't even wake up, but simply made a small whuffle in her sleep.

Gil focused on me. "And you?" There was a distinct

challenge in the way he was looking at me, and I could feel my temper rising. For just a moment I pictured myself grabbing the other man by the throat and tossing him against the wall a few times, but even as my fist clenched in anticipation, I realized that this wasn't normal. I bit the inside of my cheek hard enough to hurt, and my temper receded. Gil's uncle was dead, I reminded myself, and I was the person he had to trust to find out who had done it. I probably wouldn't be happy in his shoes either.

I should've fed from my mother yesterday, I realized grimly. Transition was bringing my heritage closer to the surface.

I pulled myself back together. "I have everything I need here for now. I'll consult with my family this evening, and then I'll begin investigating." I also planned to feed while I was home.

Clearly reluctant, but having no other options, Gil nodded. "You will keep us informed, though, right?" Temper made his face flush darkly. "If it were up to us, we'd be finding the killer ourselves—"

"Gil." Dahlia's voice cracked from the doorway, interrupting her brother. He clenched his jaw, shot me one last searing look, and walked stiffly out of the room. Dahlia watched him leave, then turned her head just slightly to meet my eyes. "Please pass our thanks along to your mother, Fort. We appreciate your time." Then she also turned and left.

"My, how deliciously awkward," Chiyo said. Gleeful amusement fought with exhaustion on her face, and momentarily won out. "No wonder Matias passed over the brother. That one has no love for the vampires, and he's not bothering to hide it."

"It's a difficult day for deference, Oka-san," Midori said, with a bit more compassion. "If someone killed you, I would be pretty angry if I was robbed of the chance to rip that person's belly open with my own teeth."

Her mother gave a flashing smile. "Another reason to be grateful that we are kitsune, then, and not some half-rate were." That brought a round of smug agreement from the other foxes. I hoped desperately that the bears had all been occupied and not bothering to listen—apparently Suze came by her attitude of superiority honestly.

We all slipped out of the beige house together, past the grim-faced *metsän kunigas* who once again filled the living room.

Outside, I took a deep breath, grateful for the cold air after the stifling emotions roiling inside. The sun had set while we were inside, but the *karhu* had been a fan of those nice little outdoor solar lights, and the curb and driveway were lined with soft blue glows. Suze gave my sleeve a tug, demanding my attention. Looking down, I could see from her expression that my brief struggle for control in the kitchen had not gone unnoticed. After a considering moment, she let it drop, and instead said, "If you're going down to see your mother, Fort, I'll go with them over to the ghouls." She nodded to her family members, who were walking very slowly in our wake. "I'm probably a better driver right now."

Chiyo and Midori expressed their happiness with the plan. Takara was still a bundle of sleeping fox, and had no opinion. Suze walked with me to where the Fiesta was pulled to the curb, and made a show of leaning against the car while I reached inside to fish out her duffel.

"So, what are you thinking?"

"Gil seems pretty set on the Ad-hene theory," I noted. "What do you think?"

"The last time they got the attention of the Scotts, Prudence eliminated twenty percent of the remaining full-blood population. If I were them, I'd think twice about doing something that might bring the one-woman extinction event knocking on my door." Suzume's eyes gleamed. We'd both had a front-row seat when Prudence ripped the head off Shoney, a creature who'd been old during the Bronze Age.

"No one has ever accused the Ad-hene of being reasonable. I'll get in touch with Lilah and see if she's noticed anything." After our encounter with the Ad-hene had ended with bodies on the ground, I'd made a battlefield appointment of the half-elf as the official liaison between the Neighbors and my family. I considered what we'd learned so far about the murder. "All you smelled was bear?"

"Nothing but." Speculation was clear in her face. "Thinking that it might've been one of his loving subjects? The daughter looked broken up, the nephew was pissed off, but that niece was cold as ice."

"Definitely something to keep in mind. There wasn't even an attempt to cover this up, and the Ad-hene might be crazy, but they aren't stupid."

Suzume snorted. "Life is always easier when your opponents are idiots."

We exchanged good-byes and parted. I turned on the Fiesta and headed south for Newport.

Chapter 4

I arrived at my mother's mansion just before nine, and a bit of a surprise greeted me. All of the outdoor lights were on, and the parking area was absolutely cluttered with cars. I stared for a moment, the Fiesta idling loudly, and wondered what exactly was going on.

A sharp rap on the window startled me, and I saw the comfortably weathered face of James, one of my mother's staff.

"Quite a to-do tonight, Mr. Scott," he said with a broad wink. He'd known me since I was in diapers, and every time he looked at me, I had the impression that he was remembering wiping my nose or confiscating my crayons. "A few of the boys and I are valeting the cars, so we'll tuck yours away where it won't be a bother."

"A bother or an eyesore?" I asked, shifting the car into neutral and getting out.

James smiled widely, showing teeth browned by a lifetime of black coffee and lack of fluoride treatments. "Now, now. I have a snug little spot where it'll be nice and safe. You have to be careful with a car like this — one tap and the bumper will probably come right off."

He wasn't wrong. Last year I'd spent a month and a half with the Fiesta's bumper attached by wire ties following a low-speed bumper collision. I'd been short on money at the time, and it had taken a while to save enough to get my mechanic to spot-weld the bumper back where it belonged. I'd left the wire ties on, figuring that it could use the help.

Inside, the house was bustling with women in a mixture of sleek evening wear and professional business dress. Madeline's staff cruised among them in black-tie tuxedos, male and female, holding trays full of wineglasses or hors d'oeuvres.

Prudence appeared at my elbow, looking smug. Her crutches were gone, replaced by a rather dapper ivory cane that she leaned on heavily. Her matching dress was long, and the fabric was stiff enough that I couldn't be sure of what kind of bandaging was currently on her leg. "Why, hello, Fortitude. I see you've come to admire my ladies' networking party."

"Is that what you're calling it?"

"Yes, it seems to be quite popular." She linked her free arm with mine and tugged me toward a quieter part of the room. As we crossed, I noticed Chivalry standing in a knot of women, listening politely as one of them was saying something about how the artwork on the stairway reminded her of some fancy house she'd seen in France. The interest in her eyes as she flirted at my brother was clear, and at a casual glance, Chivalry seemed to be responding. But his eyes were just a little too bright under the light from the chandelier, and there was a keen, assessing look on Chivalry's face that flicked from the woman speaking to the others surrounding him. The situation should've been annoyingly reminiscent of a sultan checking out new applicants for the harem, but instead it reminded me very uncomfortably of Discovery Channel footage of a wolf inspecting a deer herd.

Prudence followed my gaze and gave a very satisfied smile. "This has been quite a successful evening. I'm thinking of throwing a few more of these this week—of course it's so short notice, but I've gotten compliments from the ladies all night, saying what a lovely idea it is to bring together so many clever and successful women to network." To my relief, she slipped her arm out of mine, snagged a wineglass from a passing tray, and took a sip. Then she shot me a calculating look. "Do you remember any lady professors from Brown who would be suitable? Very few women in this day and age seem capable of turning down a couriered invitation."

"Um, one, we just call them professors now. Two, I'm not getting involved, and neither should you."

Prudence rolled her eyes, though whether it was over my correction of *lady professors* or my very deep discomfort over the thought of having any part in Chivalry's dating process was unclear. "Don't be such a child. Whoever Chivalry selects and weds will be in our lives and home for years, and I *refuse* to suffer through the fiasco of Sybil again."

"Sybil?"

My sister took a longer drink of her wine and her face darkened. Apparently this memory still had the ability to nettle her. "1909. She was an anarchist, a follower of Emma Goldman. Constant rallies and arrests. We couldn't get through a single meal without being lectured about the ravages of capitalism. I thought the woman would never die." Prudence shuddered. "She actually lasted for fourteen years, wretched thing. Constitution of a rhinoceros." Her expression lightened as she reflected on the past woman's death, then finished her wine again and surveyed the room, looking more pleased. "The trick of the thing is to make sure that Chivalry is given enough of a selection. For years I kept trying to surround him with debutantes, but that was a mistake. No, he needs a variety of women — professions, ages, backgrounds, interests, all of that. But it's just important to screen out the ones who would be a bother to sit across a dinner table from."

That my brother was busy reenacting his personal Bluebeard routine was bad enough, but the idea of trying to steer certain women toward him for the sake of pleasant dinner conversation while they slowly expired was fairly awful. "I'm not getting involved," I repeated bluntly. "Now listen, Matias Kivela was just murdered, and I'd frankly really prefer talking about that for a while."

That was finally enough to break Prudence's focus on her creepy party, and very effectively. With a few muttered excuses and a promise that he'd be back shortly, she extricated Chivalry from the situation that frankly made me suspicious about her previously professed disgust with dating-themed reality shows (or perhaps she was actually disgusted, but at the same time took notes), and the three of us quickly relocated to my mother's sitting room.

Madeline was ensconced in her favorite padded sofa, and from her elaborately brocaded robe to her Turkish slippers (complete with little curls at the toes), it was clear that she had planned a very quiet night away from the fuss downstairs. Upon seeing the three of us, she immediately turned off the TV (some CNN exploration into the latest scandal of a senator who liked his power to come with a side order of illicit sex) and motioned us to sit. Prudence and I settled on opposite settees, the heavy silk of my sister's dress rustling against the upholstery, but Chivalry began to pace around us. It was a strange inversion—usually Prudence was the one who acted like a large cat on a leash—but I found myself unable to look away from him even as I brought everyone up to speed with the *metsän kunigas* situation. His clothing was loose, even though I knew that every item he ever purchased went straight to his personal tailor, and there was a prominence to my brother's cheekbones that hadn't been present a week ago, suggesting that he'd dropped weight.

My mother's brilliant blue eyes narrowed in irritation when I finished my summary. "Inconvenient, this. Matias was steady, and could've easily ruled another ten, perhaps even twenty years."

"Disruptive," Prudence noted. "We're still mopping up after the elves had their little rebellion, and now a murder like this?"

Madeline gave a small wave to indicate that Prudence was deviating from the topic at hand, but that she didn't disagree with my sister's underlying point. "It needs to be handled, and quickly." She turned to me, and the iron in her voice brooked no disagreement. "Fortitude, you will look into this, and you will find the culprit."

I couldn't help but feel a little nervous, here. After all, to this point I had, with Suzume's help, managed to solve a grand total of *one* murder. "I'll work on it, but—"

"No, not *work* on it, *find* it." Madeline's annoyance was clear. "This won't be like those times you've gone Nosy Parkering with that fox and fallen rump over tea-kettle into a palaver. You're my agent in this, Fortitude, working in my stead. You have *resources*, for heaven's sake, and a responsibility." There was a very icy practicality and ruthlessness in her voice, one that she usually hid behind her silly little-old-lady act. But there was no mistaking how seriously she was taking this situation. "You will find a perpetrator promptly, my son. And if you do not, you will find an acceptable scapegoat."

My mother in these moods scared the crap out of me, but my head was shaking immediately. "I'm not going to railroad anyone," I said.

Prudence couldn't contain her reaction to my statement. "Oh, for the love of—"

I interrupted Prudence, but I was still focused on my mother. "Suze and I have leads, and we *will* find the killer." I sounded a lot more confident than I felt at the moment, but if it meant the avoidance of creating a setup and a fall guy, I was willing to use Fake It Till You Make It as my personal motto. "The *metsän kunigas* suspect the elves, so I'll call up Lilah Dwyer and start looking into it."

My sister gave a loud and wholly unladylike snort.

"Well, brother, if the bears have focused on the Ad-hene, I doubt even you could shed a tear if we have to execute one as an example."

I deliberately ignored her. "We'll find the killer," I assured my mother. And Prudence wasn't wrong—I didn't know much about the bears, but I knew much more than I wanted to about the elves, and if the evidence led to Underhill's doorstep, I wouldn't be bothered in the least.

Madeline had calmed down, and now she even looked amused. "How confident you suddenly sound, my pet. Such music to my ears. Now, do you have everything you need? Clues, information, murder weapon, all of those things they yammer about on procedurals? Such a dull genre. Though I do regret that I have no laboratory of gadgets or brilliant scientists to offer you. They always seem so useful on those shows."

I relaxed a little as my mother slipped back into her usual patter. That was always a good sign. "The ghouls are performing an autopsy, so we should at least find out a little. Suzume thinks that a knife was used, and there's one missing from the *karhu*'s kitchen, so if we find that, it might be useful."

Chivalry was still pacing the room, but now he spoke quietly, his voice sounding like he was straining for normalcy. "You should talk with our retainer witch—she's fairly reliable. Loren Noka can give you her information."

"What a waste of time," Prudence snapped, disgusted. "How many times over the last decade has the witch been able to offer you the slightest help?"

Chivalry's voice stayed measured, but I noticed that his pacing picked up some speed. "Rosamund isn't often able to contribute, it's true, but when she does, it is useful. And anything that involves a body is worth asking a witch about."

"Seems odd to say the word *worth* in a conversation

about witches," said Prudence. "Useless little headlin-
ers."

My sister looked ready to start a monologue on the
subject, but she was cut off by Madeline's smooth inter-
jection. "Yes, precious, you've made your opinion clear
many times. Now Fortitude will find either *the* murderer
or *a* murderer"—she smiled at me, flashing her very long,
fixed fangs—"to mollify the bears. Once this happens,
who will the new *karhu* be?" She looked expectantly at
my brother, but Chivalry was circling restlessly and
didn't seem to notice his cue.

There was a short, awkward silence, which I broke.
"Chiyo Hollis asked them. Apparently Matias had mentioned his niece, Dahlia, but I'm not sure how certain
that is."

Madeline was still watching Chivalry, and despite my
effort, now looked annoyed. "Chivalry? You know the
heirs." Her voice was stern.

That got Chivalry's attention, and his forehead creased
as he considered. "Somewhat." He sounded distracted.
"The nephew would rock the boat and be disruptive, and
Matias felt that his daughter was too young to be considered when we discussed it a month ago. Dahlia seems to
be the best choice."

Distracted was not a good response for our mother. I
spoke up again, hoping to distract her from Chivalry.
"Gil is definitely not a fan of our rules. I don't know
about Dahlia—she plays everything really tight to the
chest. Carmen is twenty-one, though, so not incredibly
young. She's maybe ten years and change younger than
the other two."

To my surprise, Prudence responded by agreeing with
me. "Twenty-one is not too young." She kept talking to
me, but I noticed that she was watching Chivalry out of
the corner of her eye. "Keep an eye on them, Fortitude.
And remember that whoever becomes *karhu* is the one

we have to deal with for the next three or four decades. Best to avoid anyone extremely annoying." She raised her voice and pitched to Chivalry again. "Wasn't that why we didn't want Ilona?"

Another awkward pause, and I did my best to set the question up again. "Ilona?" I asked. It wasn't just to try to help cover for Chivalry—I had no idea who we were talking about, and my confusion was clear.

That finally brought Chivalry back into the conversation, even though he now sounded very annoyed with me, which he normally saved for when it was the two of us on our own. Usually in a group setting he spent most of his time covering for me in front of Prudence. The disruption of our normal family dynamic was almost enough to make me dizzy. "Matias's older sister," Chivalry explained curtly. "Dahlia and Gil's mother. Their father wanted her to inherit, but I thought she would be too difficult. She always questioned everything, never just followed an order. Matias claimed that she'd mellowed with age, but it figures that her son would be a problem as well." He gave a small shrug. "You can get to know Carmen better if you want, but Matias said that Dahlia had the right temperament."

Having watched all of this interplay closely, Madeline now gave a very heavy sigh. "It's just like dogs. You finally get one trained just the way you like, and it dies. Then you have to housebreak a puppy all over again." She gave a grumpy wave of her hand to dismiss us. "Well, enough of this. Prudence, you can't abandon your guests much longer."

Prudence used her cane to pull herself awkwardly to her feet. "Come on, Chivalry. I know they'll be missing you." The implication in her voice was so clear that I was sure that the women downstairs must've somehow felt the reverberations.

Chivalry didn't respond, but simply offered Prudence his arm with the gentlemanly antebellum manners that had been drilled into him over almost a century and a half ago. There was a fixed and intent look on his face as they left, and Prudence glanced over to meet my eyes, lifting her eyebrows in some expression that I couldn't quite interpret.

I stayed behind with my mother and watched as she fussed with the sleeve of her robe. I normally didn't go out of my way to spend more time with Madeline, but unfortunately this afternoon had shown that I couldn't put the feeding off any longer. After a moment it became clear that I wasn't leaving, and my mother made a small noise in her throat and looked up at me. "Don't judge your brother harshly, Fortitude. At least, not for his manners. It's a bit like when our Patricia decided to go on a cleanse. She was in an utterly wretched temper all week, and when she finally gave in, she nearly devoured an entire roast."

That was not a very visually reassuring metaphor, but it did at least offer a segue into my own issue. It seemed odd to have to find a way to bring the topic up—usually it was my mother who offered to feed me (and offered, and offered), and I would either accept or put it off. Asking for it seemed weird. "I suppose that's the thing, Mother. I'm feeling a bit . . . edgy."

She understood my meaning immediately, but there was a slight hesitation before she nodded. "Ah. My apologies, then, my dove." Then she was rolling back her left sleeve with her usual businesslike manner, and I felt reassured. I moved from my current seat to next to her on the sofa, and tried to tamp down the eagerness that rose up inside me as my mother's bony, age-speckled wrist was exposed. "Go ahead," Madeline said, and drew her right thumbnail firmly across her wrist, slicing her skin.

The blood that rose to the surface of my mother's wrist was much darker than a human's, and thicker. I leaned down and latched my mouth over the cut, and as the first drop touched my tongue with a sizzle that sent a shiver down my whole body, I acknowledged at last the relief that I felt at feeding. My reaction to Gil in Matias Kivela's kitchen this afternoon had disturbed me, and if feeding from my mother would stave off a repeat of that, I would embrace it wholeheartedly.

For most humans (barring those results of the creepy attachment parenting trend), the act of being fed directly from their mother's body is one that is usually last performed before long-term memories begin to form. That I still relied on my mother in such a primal way, for sustenance, was always extremely disturbing to me when I thought about it in stray moments, but during the act itself the world seemed to close in around me until all I thought of and experienced was the taste of my mother's blood, the pressure my mouth had to exert to get the thick fluid down my throat, and the deep, yawning hunger inside of me that I was finally able to assuage.

The blood from my mother's cut was even thicker and slower in flowing than usual, and it felt like trying to drink a milk shake through a busted straw. I'd just taken my third full swallow when Madeline suddenly slid a finger from her free hand against my mouth, breaking my suction. Surprise rolled through me—never in my life had my mother ever stopped my feeding before I was ready. I sat up quickly and was appalled at what I saw— my mother's naturally fair skin was so pale that I could actually see the tracings of blue and violet veins up her neck and jaw. She was slumping back into the sofa, not for comfort but from a lack of strength.

I was off the sofa so quickly that I stumbled and smacked my knee hard against the table, setting off a loud clatter of china suddenly shifting, but I didn't even slow down and was already halfway to the door to call for help, when Madeline's voice, weak but with that unmistakable steely command, pulled me back.

"Fort, don't go."

"I'll get Chivalry, or Prudence, and—"

"Stop." She couldn't lift her lids all the way, but even that much was enough for her blue eyes to freeze me in place. "There's nothing to be done, my darling."

"No," I snapped automatically, my brain rejecting the idea that my mother was somehow less than permanent.

"Yes," she replied, her voice inescapable. She stretched her hand out weakly to me, and I saw that the cut she'd made for me was no longer bleeding, but it was still open and red when usually it would've sealed itself by now. "Leave your siblings be. Now, I'm very weary—help me to my bedroom. I think it's best that I have a lie-down."

I put my arm gingerly under her arms and around her back, nervous about how very tiny and breakable she seemed at the moment. It was a strange thing to feel that my mother was vulnerable when only a month ago she had beaten Prudence into a pulp on the floor. And even though it amused Madeline to play at being a harmless little old lady, there had always been that palpable sense of danger to her. But as I half helped, half carried her out of the sitting room and into the bedroom, I couldn't help but remember what my sister had told me recently—that even for our mother, there was only one path that age would lead to. And Madeline was so very, very ancient.

Madeline's sitting room was pink and frilled, with spindly antique furniture. It wasn't my taste, but it did look like the kind of thing that a certain type of grand-motherly woman with a lot of money would create. Her bedroom, however, was full-on Versailles, with brocaded pink silk on the walls and the dominating force of a bed that could've easily slept four. It was massive, carved out of ash wood and completely lacquered and inlaid with mother-of-pearl to give it its own luminescence. All dressers, end tables, and even my mother's baroque la-dy's desk had been built to match. The bed's high posters and frame were hung with old-fashioned gathered bed curtains made of pink silk and embroidered all over with silver thread, with a matching comforter, bed skirt, and at least a dozen extra-fluffy pillows. Overall, it was one of those rooms that seemed to go beyond a question of good or bad taste and just leave the viewer feeling completely overwhelmed.

I helped my mother onto the bed, where she leaned back against the pillows with a deep grunt of relief. For a moment she just breathed heavily; then she turned her head to the side and stared. Curious, I followed her gaze, and I noticed a new addition to her room. A very large portrait of four people in period clothing was resting on an easel.

"Oh, new painting?" My mother wasn't a serious collector of art, preferring just to find pieces that worked for particular rooms, so new items usually appeared only to replace something that had broken or worn out, or as a harbinger of a complete redecoration on the horizon.

Madeline chuckled, but it was a thin, weak sound. "A very old painting, actually. One that I haven't seen in quite some time. Look closer."

I walked around the bed to get a better look. It was a group portrait of four people—three women, one old, one in the beginnings of middle age, and one young, with one man in about his early thirties. The gowns and sleeves were incredibly full and elaborate, with those antique necklines that fell low on the shoulder, dipped very low in front across breasts gathered together and up like a set of dumplings and made me feel nervous about a nipple-slip just looking at it, and then fell downwards in great sweeping drapes of fabric that must've been nightmarish to wear. The older woman sat in the middle of the painting, flanked by the middle-aged woman and the man, who both stood. Just off to the middle-aged woman's side was the youngest woman, who was sitting on some kind of lower footstool, with a small spaniel dog resting almost bonelessly on her lap. There was a similarity in the noses and features of the sitters that suggested that they were family members, and while the old woman had iron-gray hair and the man's hair was a darkish blond, the other two women both had waves of elaborately arranged chestnut curls. My eye was caught by the middle-aged woman — even in that kind of Vulcan-like stare that all people in older portraits always seemed to have, there was something very familiar and uncomfortable about the expression in her blue eyes.

As soon as I realized it, I felt like an idiot for not recognizing it immediately.

"Is this you?"

She smiled. "Yes, we commissioned it in 1650 from Sir Peter Lely. He was the portrait artist to Charles the First, and so much the rage that even after the king's execution, he continued to get scads of work. One of those Dutch imports, but really quite good. Normally he would've just done our heads and left the rest to his workshop pupils, but he did our whole figures and the clothes, and just brought an apprentice in for the background." Her smile widened, and a little bit of color returned to her face as she stared raptly at the painting, lost in memories from over three centuries ago. "Constance insisted on getting her favorite dog into the picture. Silly, really, since she had already had two portraits of him done, along with every other dog she owned. We practically had a whole wing of them, to say nothing of Edmund's horse portraits. How Mother did complain, but I agreed in the end. Such a fuss over a pet whose name no one remembers now."

"I've never seen this before. Was it in storage?" Until now I'd only ever seen one image of my oldest sister, who had died long before even Prudence was born. Madeline had a hand-size miniature of her that hung in her dressing room, beside matching ones of the rest of us. I knew that Prudence loathed her miniature, which had been painted at a time when her hair was stick brown and rolled into the most incredible sausage curls. Mine had been done when I was twenty-one and my acne finally under control, but Madeline had apparently instructed the artist to aspire to accuracy rather than flattery, and I was glad that I didn't have to see it regularly.

"No, it was in England. It's the only portrait of all four of us together. Constance died just eleven years later, and I came to America. Mother died soon after that, and it was just Edmund rattling around in that old and drafty castle. He began traveling then, and he wanted to send me most of the collection, but I didn't like the idea of putting them onto ships—one good leak and the whole thing would've been at the bottom of the ocean. And then in 1830, the whole place was burned to the ground during the Swing Riots."

"Your family's castle?" Mother didn't talk much about life before she'd come to America. Chivalry had told me once that he thought it was because of Constance's premature death, and, looking at her now, I thought that he was probably right.

"Well, it was possibly a bit of a blessing—the whole thing was eleventh century and a misery to live in, but Edmund couldn't just admit that it was far past time to pull the whole thing down and build something comfortable. It was a tragedy about the furnishings and the paintings, though. Edmund was in Russia when it happened—in those days it took almost two months for him to be notified. Fortunately this painting was on loan for a Lely retrospective, and there was one tapestry of my mother and me that was done in 1388 and that Edmund had had sent out for cleaning. It's only representative, of course, not a true likeness, but it was a relief that it survived. After that I absolutely forbade Edmund to risk the painting to travel, and he put it on loan in a nice little museum where it would be safe."

"But it's here now." I watched her closely.

"Yes." There was a very unguarded look on her face— one of pure pleasure and delight. "It arrived late last week. Private plane, four lovely young curators fussing over it. So thoughtful of Edmund. It's been so long since

I saw my mother's face, and Lely did a wonderful job on Constance. Really captured something of her around the eyes. Edmund sent a letter—he was thinking of coming as well, but he's quite tied up in Brussels."

I'd never met my uncle, and I'd never expected to, so the sound of a proposed visit surprised me. And after my last experience with European vampires, I honestly couldn't fake any enthusiasm about the possibility. "Your brother does a lot of traveling. I thought vampires usually stayed inside their territories?"

"Yes, but Edmund is a bit of an activist. He'll just go from one territory to the next, getting nest-mate privileges and then trying to change everyone's mind for a decade or so before moving on." Her happiness dimmed, replaced with an expression of annoyance. But not, I was surprised to realize, directed at me. For once.

"An activist? A vampire activist?" That was a word combination that I had honestly never expected to experience.

"It's just like Al Gore and his silly little slide show. The topic is dull, the damage is already done, and all his work and effort isn't helping a jot."

"Mother, global warming is actually—"

"It's a metaphor, darling," she said wearily.

I let it go, and returned to the weird concept of a vampire activist. "What is his topic?"

My mother gave a heavy sigh. "I'm sorry, Fortitude, but I'm utterly wrung out. Please ring the bell. Patricia will bring me a cup of tea and perhaps read to me for a bit." Over the course of our conversation, she had seemed to perk up a little, but now she was once again looking exhausted. I apologized and did as she asked. When the house had first been built, it had a full set of the old-fashioned bell-cords that snaked down to the servants' areas of the house and alerted them that their masters had some whims to be fulfilled. Madeline had renovated the house many times, however, and those were all gone, replaced by newer technology. In my mother's room was a small toggle on her bedside table that she could hit and summon one of her staff—it was a bit like the button on a plane that you could push to call over a flight attendant.

I slipped out of my mother's rooms when Patricia bustled in, all solid solicitude. I wondered briefly if Patricia would offer my mother more than just a cup of tea—at one time or another I'd seen many of my mother's staff members with small patches of gauze on their wrists or butterfly bandages discreetly placed on their necks. It certainly wasn't often—I knew that most of my mother's sustenance came from the political hopefuls and powerhouses that she so carefully nurtured—but it had slowly become a more common occurrence over the last year. I'd wondered if my mother was becoming slightly lazier, but now I realized that it had been an indication of her flagging strength.

The party was still in full swing in the main hall, so I took a back staircase rather than the grand main one that swept downward in carved and gilded glory. Down a hallway where I passed staff members making their way back to the kitchen with trays of empty wineglasses and half-nibbled plates of food, I headed to the small butler's pantry that concealed the entrance to one of the house's nastier secrets.

A staff member was always stationed in the pantry, endlessly scrubbing and polishing the silver, and the one on duty tonight gave me a solemn nod as she unlocked the door partially hidden behind the woodwork pattern, revealing the basement staircase that, in sharp contrast to everything else in the house, was purely functional and industrial.

Until the murderous scene that my sister instigated a month ago when she tried to kill my host father and push me into full transition, the rooms at the bottom of the stairs and behind a steel door with a keypad lock had belonged to Mr. Albert. He'd been my host parents' guardian and keeper since I'd been a small child, and I took a short moment before keying in the code that would allow me entrance to gather myself together.

The door released, and I pulled it open, entering completely transformed rooms. The main room, with its full-length one-way mirror used to observe Henry at all times, had previously been decorated like an old, comfortable sitting room. But Mr. Albert's scuffed shelves and ancient armchairs were gone, replaced by a set of Spartan, functional furniture, with the showpiece being a long metal desk, looking like it was straining under the massive computer setup on top of it, with three screens, two towers, and a total of three battery backups daisy-chained together. I had privately dubbed this collection "Skynet."

Sitting with his back to me, and looking steadily out the glass and into Henry's holding area was the new keeper, Conrad Miller. Mr. Alfred had been a former wrestler and a big man, but Conrad had the kind of build and muscle mass that should've been illegal under the Geneva Conventions. I was a tall guy, but next to Conrad's six-foot-five frame and easily two-hundred fifty pounds (none of it fat), I felt like a wet kitten looking at a Saint Bernard. His dark hair was trimmed into a jarhead's buzz, and I knew that the even brown of his skin was natural, since he hadn't left these rooms once since my mother had employed him a month ago.

"Hey, Conrad," I said. "Are you AFK?"

Conrad didn't even glance over at me, but as I walked closer, I could see him smile. The computer screens were covered in the saturated colors of *World of Warcraft*, and his character was on the center screen, as much at rest as a night elf with purple skin and greenish blue hair could get. I wasn't sure how exactly my mother found her employees, but Chivalry had shown me Conrad's background information, and he was pretty much a perfect fit for the job. After almost eight years in the Marines and three combat tours, Conrad had been honorably discharged. With his experience, he would've been great in the private security business—except for the post-traumatic stress disorder that was the remaining legacy of his service in war zones. Because of his PTSD, he couldn't stand being in any location that he didn't feel was secure. That included just about anywhere he would travel in private security, plus his local grocery store and most of the rooms of his own house. Madeline's fortified bunker of a basement, with its restricted access and top-of-the-line installations, had suited him very well. A few pieces of exercise equipment and a reliable Internet connection to support his *WoW* habit, and he'd settled right in.

We were still in the getting-to-know-you phase, but he seemed nice enough, and despite how I sometimes teased him about multitasking with *WoW*, he was serious about the job.

"Do you mind waiting until Maire is out?" he asked, his eyes never wavering from the glass. "It's safer to cover only one person at a time."

"It's okay. I just came down for a look, not a visit."

I hadn't talked to Henry since he'd killed Mr. Albert. I'd been told my entire life that my host parents were dangerous, and I'd accepted it on an intellectual level, but the sight of Henry tearing at Mr. Albert with his hands and teeth had finally forced me to realize exactly what he was capable of. That would've been easier if he was always the wild, vicious, ravening thing that he'd been when he attacked Mr. Albert, but the problem was that he wasn't. The process that had made him capable of becoming a part of the vampire life cycle had twisted and warped his mind, but it hadn't broken it. And in some horrible way, I knew that Henry loved me, which somehow made Mr. Albert's death even worse.

But the events that had led to Mr. Albert's death hadn't left Henry unmarked. I looked through the window and watched the other new addition to Madeline's staff, Maire O'Riley. Small in stature and with curling strawberry blond hair that even her no-nonsense short cut couldn't stop from looking angelic, Maire had been a combat medic until her left leg was blown off in an IED explosion. I'd seen her use a prosthetic that mimicked what her old leg had probably looked like a few times, but whenever she was inside Henry's enclosure, she wore a carbon fiber blade attachment designed solely for function and quick motion rather than any aesthetic sensibilities. Both she and Conrad had, as part of the interview process, been shown photographs of all of Henry's victims, including Mr. Albert.

Seeing Maire inside the enclosure made me nervous. "Why don't you go in when she does, Conrad?"

Conrad's smile widened. "She says I hover and get in her way." He didn't break his alert observation, but he tilted his head slightly toward me. "Don't worry about Maire. She's tough, and she knows what she's doing."

Henry didn't look dangerous anymore. Inside his clear plastic cube prison (the outsides now heavily reinforced with steel following Prudence's attack on the original), Maire was changing Henry's feeding tube—never a pleasant sight. In her attempt to kill him, Prudence had done severe damage, which had never healed or even closed. In the process that made him a vampire host, my mother had replaced his entire blood supply with hers, a process that was extremely difficult for a vampire and nearly universally fatal for the prospective host. Henry had survived, and my mother's blood had fundamentally changed him down to the DNA level; among other things, it had made him far tougher and stronger than a human. Yet at the same time, it made him vulnerable, because his body was unable to make new blood or heal itself without my mother's assistance and donation of more of her own supply. All of Henry's wounds from his fight were neatly sutured closed, but they continually seeped fluid and required constant attention. Some of the damage to his upper body had necessitated the feeding tube, as well as a catheter, which required constant maintenance and attention from Maire. They also required Henry to remain still, which he'd been unwilling (or unable) to do, so now he spent his days and nights completely immobilized, strapped to a hospital bed. This enforced inactivity had caused the formation of bedsores, which also needed regular tending.

Until now, I'd thought that Madeline had made a deliberate decision not to make the blood transfers needed for Henry to heal. I'd assumed that she had been punishing him, much like her breaking and rebreaking of Prudence's leg. Looking at his pitiful condition, however, and thinking about how my mother had interrupted my feeding, I came to the reluctant conclusion that it was highly possible that Madeline was currently *unable* to spare the blood that Henry would need to return to full, or even partial, health.

Inside the cube, Maire completed her work, gathered her tools, and left the cell, locking the newly reinforced door behind her. Conrad's hand never wavered from his stun gun until she had entered the room where we were sitting. Then he returned the instrument to his belt and started up his game again.

I greeted Maire, who looked completely unsurprised at my presence.

"He knows you're here. Do you want to talk to him?"

"No," I said, too quickly. I paused and took a deeper breath. "No, just tell him . . . Tell him that I'm not ready yet."

Maire gave a one-shoulder shrug and began unpacking her supply bag and pockets onto a small table. I'd seen this before—every time she left Henry's cube, she always went through everything and checked it against a list to make sure that she'd brought back everything that she'd intended to, and that Henry hadn't somehow been able to steal an item from her. Considering that my host mother, Grace, had died after stabbing herself a dozen times in the chest with a toothbrush that she'd managed to pocket and then sharpen to a knife's edge, Maire's habit was one that was likely to help keep both her and Conrad safe.

"You know," Maire said conversationally, "my grandma used to work at the Franklin Park Zoo in Boston."

"I actually didn't know that," I replied, feeling a little confused at the non sequitur.

"She worked with the big cats. One day one of the feeding cage locks got stuck, and a leopard jumped on her and scratched her up pretty badly. She got out alive, but she had some really bad scarring on her neck and arm. When I was really little, I asked her one day if she'd been mad at the leopard that did it. She said no, that the leopard was just doing what its nature made it do, and that was no reason to be mad at an animal." She glanced up when she was finished, fixing me with her Irish green eyes to make sure that I had figured out the meaning of this conversation.

"Thank you, Maire," I said, giving her a quick glare.

It was about as effective as glaring at a moose. "Just saying," she said, completely undaunted.

"I'll see you both later. Have a good night."

As I pulled the coded door shut behind me, I could hear Conrad say, "Sleeping dogs, Maire. Why can't you ever let them lie?"

Having no desire to talk to either of my siblings again, I slipped around the party by going out the kitchen. That put me in the direct path of Madeline's cook, who cornered me to ask if I'd had dinner yet. I had to admit that I hadn't. I knew that she would've preferred to park me in the dining room and serve a three-course meal, but after I insisted that I had a lot to do tomorrow and needed to head back to Providence, she grumbled but settled for making me a sandwich for the road and forcing me to accept a piece of cake from the party food. I finally made my escape, but got all the way to the parking lines of cars before I remembered that James had my keys, which meant turning around and going back into the house.

"When you're just rushing around, you'll waste more minutes than if you'd just taken your time in the first place," James scolded me when I finally located him. It seemed my night for unsolicited advice, so I just nodded and waited for my car to be brought around from whatever hole they'd stashed it in.

I ate my sandwich on the drive home, my head full of everything that had happened today. There was plenty to brood over, and my mood was pretty low by the time I finally got into Providence. The apartment was dark when I entered, except for the weak light by the front door that Dan and I would leave on if the other person was out late, so I knew that my roommate had already gone to bed. I ate the piece of cake straight from the plastic container that it had been packed in, but I was still feeling fairly in the dumps by the time I had scraped the last forkful of frosting into my mouth. It was well after midnight, and while I had plenty of people to follow up with on Matias Kivela's murder, they would all have to wait until a more reasonable hour.

I took a quick shower to finally get rid of the combination of dog rub and jogging sweat that I'd been carrying around since that afternoon, then brushed my teeth and took a quick stop at the toilet. I was pulling off a few sheets of toilet paper when I suddenly felt a weird bump in the roll, and I paused. A dark suspicion filled me, and I unrolled more paper quickly. There they were—two small googly eyes, glued to the toilet paper roll, staring at me.

It took me almost a full second to process what I was seeing, and then I laughed hard enough that I actually had to wipe my eyes when I was done. What was really impressive was not only that Suzume had decided to do that, but that the eyes were at least halfway down into the toilet roll, meaning that she must've unrolled the paper, glued on the eyes, and then rerolled everything neatly enough that she hadn't tipped off any of the people who regularly used the apartment's toilet. I was also impressed that she'd put all that effort into a prank that might not have even gotten to me — after all, Dan, Jaison, and even Suzume herself regularly made stopovers here.

Still snickering, I pulled the roll down and tossed it into the trash, then dug a fresh toilet roll out from under the sink and set it up. I tugged the first sheet free from its little glue adhesive, then unrolled enough to complete my business.

I paused for a second, then eyed the roll.

I had to check.

I started pulling the toilet paper again, this time not yanking off a few squares, but unrolling the whole thing.

Halfway into it, there were the googly eyes staring up at me.

Chapter 5

Despite the late night, I was up and dressed early the next morning, and as soon as the clock ticked over to eight a.m. and it was socially acceptable, I started making phone calls. The first was to Chivalry's witch, Rosamund. No one picked up, and I was shuttled to her voice mail. It was the standard "Leave a message" blah-blah, but then it was repeated in Spanish, and then in a third language that I couldn't even identify beyond its being definitely of Asian origin. I left a brief variation on "I'm Chivalry Scott's brother. Call me."

The next call I placed was to Lilah, and it yielded better results. She picked up on the fifth ring with a sleepy, "Fort?"

"I'm sorry, Lilah. Did I wake you?" She had that tone of a person whose brain was still coming online.

"Little bit," she admitted. "What's up?"

"There's a bit of a situation, and I need to talk with you."

"If you're free tonight, we can grab dinner."

That sounded very nice, and friendly-casual, but unfortunately the situation was anything but that. "I'm sorry, but it's pretty important. Family business." God, I felt like a mobster as I said that, and I corrected myself. "What I mean is that it's about the Ad-hene. Can you do any earlier?"

"Oh." Her voice flattened, and became almost resigned. "Well, I guess it was a matter of time."

Alone in my kitchen, I raised my eyebrows and wondered what that implied. Maybe the Ad-hene really *had* found a way to hide their scent from kitsune noses. Well, I couldn't pretend to feel sorry about the possibility of Prudence killing another of them. Frankly, they had it coming. Meanwhile, Lilah continued talking. "Yeah, just give me an hour or so to shower and swing over to my apartment. You remember where it is, right?"

I'd spent a few hours hiding in her closet and seen my sister break a woman's neck in Lilah's bedroom. Her address was well and truly seared into my brain, and I assured her that I'd be fine getting there. We exchanged good-byes; then I dialed Suzume to fill her in on the morning's planned activities.

"No, you should head over alone," she said to my surprise. "I can be magnanimous in victory."

I wished she were in front of me. Glaring at a phone was very unsatisfying. "If you're the victor, then I'm the spoils. Any plans to, you know, *despoil* me?" I knew that I sounded grumpy, but the day was still very young and now I was going to be heading into a potentially awkward situation with a very nice woman whose pass at me I'd had to turn down because of my feelings for Suze, and at this point, though it was rather churlish to note it, it had been a *really* long time since I'd had sex.

"You're being awfully backtalky for spoils," Suzume said, but there was an underlying sassiness in her voice that clearly said that she was enjoying this situation far more than she should've. "Go find out what Keebler knows, and call me when you've gotten the info we need to go kick some elfish ass." Typical Suze, she sounded positively peppy at the thought of impending violence.

"Hey."

"Hrm?"

"If you think that seeing Lilah again is going to change my mind, you're wrong," I said seriously.

There was a pause on her end, and if we'd been playing *Battleship*, she would've had to acknowledge a direct hit.

"Maybe I'm not sure if I want a boyfriend who would call me on my shit," she said.

I snorted. If Suze had wanted a toady for a boyfriend, she could've had a dozen of them. Simultaneously. I'd seen guys get so distracted by her as she walked down the street that they'd bumped into walls. "Nice try. I'll call you later, and I'll still be single." I hung up before she could respond.

Dressing was trickier than usual. On the one hand, Lilah had kissed me once, and there was an element of masculine pride in not wanting to show up looking like a hobo and making her regret her past attraction. On the other hand, if I put too much effort into this, I might accidentally give her the wrong impression, and that would be a jerk move. However, I was going over there in a fairly official capacity, which suggested that jeans were not the order of the day. But then again, Lilah and I were kind of friends, and I didn't want to seem like I was showing off. Looking at it a different way, though, it was entirely possible that Lilah wasn't the only person I'd be talking to about this today, which pushed me back into the direction of dressing carefully. But if at some point the day erupted into violence, I really didn't want a pair of business dress slacks destroyed.

There were too many branches on this particular decision tree, so I gave up and went with a clean pair of khakis and a striped button-down shirt. True, once dressed, I looked like I was ready to go volunteer at a Christian ministry program, but it wasn't necessarily a bad look. I pulled on a hat and parka and headed out, knowing that in the cold morning air it would take at least four tries for the Fiesta's engine to catch.

Lilah lived in a ground-floor unit of a squat brick apartment building. There were four side-by-side units, with one shared slanted roof, and it was one of those places that real estate moguls had pooped out by the dozens in the 1950s during the clamor for cheap housing. When it was first built, there had probably been open green space behind each of the small units, maybe a garden for each, since there was one window in Lilah's living room that was weirdly placed, as if its spot had once held a back door, but that area had long ago been paved over and turned into an almost identical building that faced the opposite road, with only a small strip of pavement just barely wide enough for the Dumpsters in between. In front, there was a narrow band of grass between the building and carefully marked resident parking. At least the uniform bushes along the front were pruned back, though their bare branches certainly weren't winning any beauty contests.

The temperature had dropped from yesterday, and I could see my breath in the air as I picked my way up the walkway, listening to the quiet crunch of the frost-covered cement under my shoes. Lilah pulled the door open before I could even lift my hand to ring the bell. She was simply dressed in jeans and a sweater, and her bright coppery gold hair was still damp from the shower. As she ushered me inside, I noticed that she hadn't put on her glamour yet, and the delicately curved and furred tip of her left ear was poking through the wet strands of her hair.

"Thanks for seeing me," I said.

"It's no problem. I still haven't found another job yet, so it's not like I have to head to work." When I'd met her, Lilah had been the store manager at a New Age store. Unfortunately it had turned out that her boss was a murdering fanatic, and after he'd been killed, the store, which had never turned much of a profit to begin with, had closed.

"I'm really sorry." I never knew quite what to say after those kinds of disclosures. I'd spent plenty of time
myself in that between-jobs twilight, and knew from experience that there wasn't really anything you wanted to
hear except news of a job opening.

She gave a loose shrug. "Yeah, everyone is telling me
that retail is tough right now if you want a manager's
spot. But I've got five more months of unemployment
before I have to give up and take a cashiering position,
and I've done a little under-the-table housecleaning to
make ends meet." Lilah looked at me, and I saw that
there was more gold than brown in her eyes, a clear sign
that she wasn't quite as calm as she'd like me to believe.
"But a few things have come up lately, and having a free
schedule has actually come in handy."

I was about to ask her what she meant, but then the
door to her bedroom opened, and Iris, her younger sister, walked out. The last time I'd seen the nineteen-
year-old, she'd been drugged, naked, and sitting in an
inflatable kiddie pool with a very grim immediate future ahead of her.

Unlike Lilah, who was half human, three-quarters of
Iris's heritage was Ad-hene. Apparently morning in the
Dwyer household was a break from the glamours that
they would have to make and maintain for the rest of the
day, because Iris was also walking in her natural state,
and unlike Lilah, there was no way that she could've just
covered up her ears and gone without.

Iris's straight hair gleamed like polished copper pip-
ing, a shade that no human had been born with and no
dye could've achieved, and the face that her shoulder-
length bob framed had more in common with a Komodo
dragon than with any primate. I'd seen a three-quarter
elf hybrid before, but never one without a glamour, and
it was a sight that forced me to repress the urge to look
away. The Ad-hene themselves had even more severe

features, but they'd also had an eerie and dangerous beauty to them that this scion lacked—she looked like one of those weird crossbred Chihuahuas and Chinese Crested that always seemed to win the annual World's Ugliest Dog Competition—which I was sad to say I watched religiously every year.

There was a blankness to that bizarre face as Iris looked at me, everything that might be going on in her head tucked in so well that nothing showed on the surface. She was probably amazing at poker. "So, what are the vampires interested in talking to my sister about?" she asked with an undercurrent of hostility. I felt a tug of relief—not from her words, which put me in an awkward spot, but because I could at least pick up a bit of emotion from her voice.

Lilah answered her sister before I could think of anything to say. "Iris, this is Fortitude Scott, the one who helped us."

There was something flat about her eyes when Iris looked at me. "Oh." The hostility was gone now, leaving her voice expressionless, almost like a computer reader. I missed the hostility—it had felt more human. She moved a little closer to me and stepped in the sunbeam coming in from the window. As the light hit her face, those flat eyes adjusted, and I realized that the pupil wasn't formed like a human's. Instead of being round, it was vertical, like a lizard's. The colored area around it was also disturbing—it lacked the softening brown that Lilah's eyes had, leaving just a bright, buttery gold. "Didn't see much that night," Iris said. She took one more slow, precise step closer to me, then tilted her head carefully. "Heard you shot Nokke in the knee."

I nodded, wondering where this was leading. Nokke, after all, was Lilah and Iris's grandfather. And also Iris's father, but that wasn't something that was generally discussed. Incest wasn't exactly the most genteel of conversation topics, and the Ad-hene had engaged in it regularly, resulting in some very weird biological relationships among the Neighbors. "Yes, I did."

Iris's mouth twisted in some private amusement, the first emotion to cross that blank face. "Too bad you didn't shoot higher."

Lilah saved me from that particular conversational anvil. "Iris, you should put your glamour on and head to school. You don't want to miss class."

That glimmer of emotion vanished like smoke, and Iris gave a small one-shouldered shrug. "Failing half of them."

Lilah's voice was firm. "Then there are still half of them that you can pass."

That impressive display of big-sistering broke through even Iris's near-lobotomized lack of involvement, and she snorted. Then she paused, and for a brief second I almost thought she looked concerned as those eerie yellow eyes flicked from her sister, to me, and back again. "You'll be okay?" she asked Lilah.

Lilah walked over to Iris and put her hands on the younger girl's shoulders. "I'll be fine," she said, and leaned in to kiss Iris's cheek. "Now get going."

Iris blinked slowly, which did not help alleviate her resemblance to an iguana; then as I watched, her face changed, the glamour filling things out and making her look like one of those crazy-cheekboned high-fashion models that look more creepy than attractive—which was still a definite improvement. The metallic gleam of her hair dulled slightly, enough that while it still drew the eye, it no longer looked unnatural, the furred tips of her ears disappeared, and her pupils softened and rounded. It wasn't like the kitsune's fox tricks, because unlike with the foxes, my knowledge of the truth made her glamour weaker. When I looked at it, there was a haziness to her false face, and if I stared hard, I could get glimpses of the reality that lay beneath it.

Lilah handed Iris her backpack and ushered her out the door, giving her emotionless sister one last kiss on the cheek before she left. She gave a cheery wave, probably as her sister drove off, then dropped her hand and closed the door slowly. When she turned to face me again, I could see a weariness in her that she'd hidden from her little sister.

There was a brief silence, and then I asked, "So how long has she been staying with you?"

"Since that night. My parents gave her those drugs and handed her over to Tomas and the others. They say that they didn't know what they had planned for her, but that was because they never even thought to ask." Lilah rubbed her hands hard on her arm, and I could see that the last month hadn't made a dent in her anger toward her parents. "Iris can't go back to them, not now. There'd be bodies on the ground if she did." The look on Lilah's face suggested that she was trying hard to convince herself that that would be a bad thing. Then she visibly shook off the thoughts of her parents and shifted the topic. "So someone tipped you off about what's been going on. I guess I should be glad I'm talking to you and not Prudence." She sat down on her sofa and looked at me bleakly. "What are you going to do?"

I felt a sharp sting of betrayal—not because the elves were the killers, but because Lilah had known, and she hadn't called me. She at least wasn't trying to hide it now that I knew, but it was hard for me to push down my irritation at her and force my tone to be strictly professional. "Tell me which of the Ad-hene killed the *karhu*, and if anyone helped him. Then we can decide—"

"Wait, what?" Lilah cut me off, confused. "The *karhu*? Someone killed a bear? You think an Ad-hene killed a bear?"

Lilah's poker face had never been great, and we stared at each other for a second, both of us realizing that we'd been talking about completely different subjects. I clarified. "Sometime either Monday night or early on Tuesday, Matias Kivela was stabbed to death. Are you saying you didn't know that?" It was a relief that she hadn't been sitting on a murderer, but on the other hand, I had a very bad feeling that this situation had suddenly gotten a lot more complicated.

"Why would I know that, Fort?" she asked testily. "The *metsän kunigas* have a right to use the Lincoln Woods, but we don't do much socializing. If either group has a problem, our treaties say that we have to take it straight to the Scotts. I'm not sure I've even seen any of the bears in their human forms, much less talked to one. I definitely don't get e-mail blasts about dead *karhus*."

"Okay, you didn't know," I conceded, though that didn't mean the elves were off the hook. "Do you know whether any of the Ad-hene killed him?"

Lilah was shaking her head immediately. "Fort, the Ad-hene haven't left Underhill since your sister killed Shoney. As for stabbing . . ." She paused, and suddenly looked uncomfortable. "Fort, don't you know the punishment your mother levied on Themselves?"

"Just that there was one." Frankly, for the first week Suzume and I had been chasing selkies in Maine, and once home, I'd still had my hands full figuring out Chivalry's job. "Why, what happened?"

Lilah cleared her throat awkwardly, then muttered, "Chivalry cut off the hands of each of the remaining Ad-hene."

"What?" My brother was not the enforcer for the territory. That job lay with—and abruptly I realized why it had been my brother. Prudence had been suffering her own punishment.

Lilah began speaking quickly, apparently deciding now that she'd rather just get the revelations over with. "That was for being involved in the murders. Nokke and Amadon fought against you and your sister, though, so Chivalry cut off their tongues and . . . well, you know."

I dropped onto the sofa next to her. "Whoa." I'd known that my brother was willing to get his hands dirty for our mother, but apparently I hadn't realized *how* dirty. And while a part of me felt a very nasty sense of justice done with the Ad-hene having to experience some of the suffering that they'd forced onto my friend Gage and several other young men, I recoiled at the thought of my brother inflicting it.

"It'll all grow back, of course. I mean, it'll take a while. They can heal a lot of wounds pretty fast, but amputations are apparently more complicated." For a moment I thought that Lilah was trying to cover her discomfort with babble, but a moment later I realized that I'd underestimated her, and that unlike me, she'd kept her mind on the topic at hand when she said, "But believe me, none of them could've held a knife."

That definitely shot a hole in Gil's suspicions. Hands were definitely needed to stab someone to death. Of course, the last time the elves had been involved in murders, other hands had held the weapons. "What about their fanatics? It was the Neighbors who did most of their dirty work during the sacrifices."

Lilah had seemed to calm down, but now her eyes got rabbity again, and there was a long pause. I narrowed my eyes and looked at her. "Do you want a drink?" she asked suddenly. "I need a drink right now."

I followed her into the kitchen and watched as she opened the fridge and removed a half-empty bottle of vodka and a pitcher of orange juice. "It's nine thirty, Lilah," I reminded her.

"I'm unemployed, Fort," she snapped. "You can drink in the morning when you're unemployed." She pulled a mug out of a cabinet and mixed a quick screwdriver, then took a swig. She blinked her too-bright eyes, then took another sip, and I noticed that the color began fading back to her usual, human-looking golden brown. She cleared her throat, removed a second mug from the cabinet, and filled it with straight orange juice. Then she slid the mug toward me wordlessly.

I took it, watching her carefully, and took a drink. High pulp. I waited another moment, then asked, "Lilah? What don't you want to tell me?"

She toyed with her mug, which, like mine, had a comic from the Oatmeal printed incongruously on its side. "When you said that you needed to come over, I thought that meant you'd found out somehow." She took a deep breath, and, not meeting my eyes, said, "Whoever killed your bear, Fort, it wasn't the Ad-hene's pet fanatics. It couldn't have been, since they're all dead."

The words hung there between us for a long moment while I tried to wrap my head around them. "What?"

"Really dead," Lilah clarified, and took another drink of her screwdriver. "All of them."

I stared at Lilah, putting the pieces of what I was seeing together. The Ad-hene were what one could term murder-enthusiasts, and I'd seen them kill one of their most loyal followers with less concern than I showed when throwing out fruit that had gone squishy. If frustrated and maimed, or even if they were having a cranky day, I could certainly see the elves going on a killing spree of their followers. But I had a bad feeling that that wasn't going to be the explanation here. "Lilah," I said slowly, "if the Ad-hene were the ones who killed them, you wouldn't be drinking right now. Tell me what happened."

She still didn't look at me, but she did nod, once. "People were killed, Fort." Her voice was very soft. "If we hadn't arrived when we did, Felix would've been killed. Four women were raped—it doesn't matter if they were given drugs that made them willing, or that made them forget afterward. It was rape. More was planned." She looked up at me, and her expression was grim. "You put me in charge, Fort, and I made sure that every single person in the community heard the truth of what hap-

pened. I had to do it, to make sure that we couldn't gloss
it over or look the other way—that we had to face the
hard truth of what the Ad-hene were willing to do, and
what those of our own were willing to do in their names."

My voice was just as soft as hers. "What happened?"

She laughed suddenly, but with no humor whatsoever.
With quick movements she tossed the remainder of her
screwdriver into the sink, and turned on the tap to send
it all down the drain. "Well, for one thing, they got pretty
pissed." She looked pensively at the water. "It wasn't my
parents' generation—they were shocked, yeah, but they
wouldn't have done anything. But Dr. Leamaro and the
others did their work well—the largest numbers of the
Neighbors are my age and younger." She shrugged and
turned the tap off. "So we acted."

"This was your idea?" I couldn't keep the surprise out
of my voice.

"We lack the equipment for any kind of long-term
imprisonment," she said defensively, but then she looked
over and met my eyes, and seemed to calm down. "I argued that we could try some sort of house-arrest situation, and there were a lot who agreed with me. But there
were those who wanted blood—and they started group-
ing around Cole, one of the older three-quarters." She
grabbed a sponge and started wiping down her counter
as she spoke, and I remembered that she was a stress-
cleaner. "It would've happened with or without my permission. By agreeing to it, I was at least able to get Cole
to agree that all the names had to be voted on before
anyone was executed. It's a very Star Chamber–style of
justice, but at least it's better than a vengeful mob." Lilah
found a spot on her counter and scrubbed it with more
vigor than necessary. "We killed the last of them more
than a week ago, so I'm sorry to say that whoever murdered the bear wasn't one of them."

This lead was drying up before my eyes, and I had an
uncomfortable flashback to my mother's directive to ei-

ther find the murderer or locate a scapegoat. "So the
Ad-hene couldn't. There are none of their flunkies left
who would've—Lilah, do you know any of the Neighbors at all who might've wanted to hurt one of the
metsän kunigas?"

"I'm sorry, Fort, but I can't think of a single one." Her
scrubbing slowed, and she looked over at me uncertainly.
"What do you have that's leading you to the Neighbors?
Was there a glamour on something? Did Suzume smell
a Neighbor?"

"Neither," I admitted. "But the *karhu*'s family thinks
that the Ad-hene were involved."

Now she snorted, and some of her anxiety momentarily receded, replaced by the protectiveness that I'd seen
her display toward many of the Neighbors her own age
and younger. "Well, I'm sorry, Fort, but I think they're
looking for honey in the wrong tree. Believe me when I
say that we have more than enough internal issues keeping everyone busy."

I paused, considered, but I had to ask it. "How were
the fanatics killed?"

"We let the women do it, the ones who were their
victims." Now she looked me straight in the eyes, almost
daring me to question her. "They wanted to, and it was
pretty hard to argue that they didn't have a right."

"Did Iris participate?"

She nodded silently, her face pale enough that her
scattering of freckles showed against her face in sharp
relief, but she didn't back down.

There was another long pause while I tried to weigh
what to say next. "Lilah, murders are supposed to be reported to the Scotts. Why haven't we been told about
these?"

Lilah shook her head with enough force that small
drops of water flicked off her damp hair. "We don't have
to report murders, Fort. We just have to report a death if

we want it investigated." Her mouth twisted. "I was in charge, and I didn't need anything investigated. All of those who died were Neighbors, so we weren't poaching any of Madeline Scott's humans. We destroyed the bodies in Dr. Leamaro's old incinerator and no one is going to call the police, so there's nothing that the Scotts would worry about."

"You were glad it was me instead of Prudence, Lilah." I pointed out. "You knew that my family wouldn't be thrilled to hear about this."

"Madeline Scott wants stable communities, Fort. Solid vassals who pay their tithes and don't cause trouble." She laughed a little, with a harsh cynicism that she hadn't shown when I'd met her a month ago, before she had known what some of the Neighbors were capable of. "We're keeping the tithes flowing, but we are really far from stable right now." Lilah was pensive as she looked at me. "It *was* a good thing it was you, Fort," she agreed.

"Are you going to be okay, Lilah?" I'd made her the Scott liaison to the Ad-hene to keep her safe from their retribution, and I'd encouraged her to try to reorganize the power structure because I'd known that she had a desire to protect Neighbors who had been abused under the old status quo, but I had the very stark realization that she was in a potentially very dangerous position now—largely thanks to me.

Lilah didn't bother to pretend not to understand what I meant, but she shook her head. "Don't worry about me, Fort. I'm riding the tiger right now, but they know that they need me." At my questioning look, she smiled just a little, an expression that reminded me that she might've looked more human than her sister, but half her DNA belonged to a species that had driven itself right to the edge of extinction because its members had thought killing one another was fun. "They all know that I helped you when you were trying to find out who killed Gage, and you were the one who made me the Scott liaison to the Ad-hene. So no one is going to do anything to me, since they'll want me to be the one to contact you later on."

"Later on?"

"There's been talk. The treaty with Madeline was negotiated by the Ad-hene, with their interests in mind. There are a lot of people who want to negotiate a new treaty, one that's with the Neighbors instead." The nervousness and guilt were completely wiped from her face, and now she leaned forward, looking every bit the political operative that usually graced my mother's dinner parties.

"I'm not sure that my mother—"

"Not with Madeline, Fort. With *you*."

And looking into her eyes, I realized that the Neighbors knew that my mother was dying.

Her voice dropped, and I recognized my friend again. "Those who were truly loyal and devoted are dead, and the Ad-hene themselves are safely in Underhill. Nothing will happen until your mother is . . . gone, and there's a new opportunity for change, and for the things we want. We're all waiting, Fort, and I can't think of a single Neighbor who would jeopardize the situation by killing one of the bears."

"Tell me what the Neighbors want," I said.

"You're my friend, Fort. I'm trusting you not to tell this to your family. You know what would happen if they learned what was going on." There was a stubbornness on her face, but I tried one last time.

"The *metsän kunigas* are what my mother told me to look into, and that's all I'm looking into for her. But tell me what the rest of the Neighbors want."

She shook her head firmly. "No, Fort. I told you what you needed to know—that you have to look somewhere else for your killer—and I trusted you with a lot. But we're still in discussions about the other thing, and I won't talk to you about it until we're decided."

I watched her closely. I knew that she meant everything she said, and I knew that she'd told me a few things that would've had my sister arguing for her death. But I also knew that Lilah had never had a poker face. "This thing," I said quietly. "You agree with it, don't you."

It hadn't really been a question, but her face gave me my answer anyway. She picked up a small dish towel and wiped her hands, then folded it precisely and set it back down. "Tell Suze that I said hello," she said, and I knew the conversation was over.

Back in my car, I checked my phone, which I'd turned off when I'd gone to talk with Lilah. There were two missed calls, both from numbers that I didn't recognize. I returned the first, and found myself speaking to the extremely polite Catherine Celik, at the Celik Funeral Home, and being told what the ghouls had found when they had examined the body closely.

"The blow to the back of the head was the first strike," Catherine informed me. "It had enough force behind it to fracture the skull, and without quick medical attention, the bleeding into his brain would probably have been fatal on its own. It also knocked him unconscious."

"There were a lot of stab wounds in his chest," I noted. "It looked like there must've been a fight."

"No defensive wounds on his hands or arms to suggest that," Catherine said. "The state medical examiner is one of ours, and she was kind enough to come in last night after her shift was over and perform a full examination, so this is the same level of information that the police would be given."

It was clear that she'd felt insulted, and I hurried to smooth it over. "I didn't mean to imply that you didn't know what you were looking at," I said, even though I suppose I had been, a bit. "I guess I was just confused about why so many wounds."

"Seventeen," she said, her voice sounding slightly less

frosty as she apparently accepted the apology. "All in the chest. Even disregarding the head trauma, he would've been long dead halfway through."

"This is sounding a bit personal," I noted. "Was the examiner able to find anything new about the attacker?"

There was the rustling of papers. "Ah—well, from the angle of the wounds, the attacker was probably straddling the body when the stabbing began, so no ideas about the height. She was able to determine that the weapon was steel, straight edged and ground along both sides, and eight inches long."

I rubbed my face. "So, probably the missing kitchen knife?"

"It does sound a bit like my best vegetable chopping knife," she conceded. She might've said vegetables, but given what I'd observed of Dan's dietary requirements, I was betting that her chopping knife was used on a lot of meat as well. I shuddered a little. I'd made the mistake only once of talking to Dan while he was cooking—and there had been no disguising the organ meat he used.

Catherine Celik's calm and precise voice, clearly honed from years of being a funeral director, cut into my thoughts. "Mr. Scott, will you have any further need of the body? The Kivela family would like to know if they can schedule the funeral."

I hesitated, then asked, "When will the funeral be held?"

"Not for at least two days, possibly more. I know they'll need to schedule a long wake to accommodate the out-of-town *metsän kunigas* who need to travel."

"Okay, tell them they can schedule it. But, please, Ms. Celik, could you put off doing anything to the body for as long as possible? Just in case I need something else from it." I was fumbling in the dark here, and I wished heartily that someone was with me who could help out. Unwillingly, my thoughts turned to Matt McMahon, former cop, private eye, and the man who had been my surrogate uncle and the last remaining link to my foster parents until a month ago when he'd received a very sudden initiation into the world that most humans lived their entire lives blissfully unaware of. We hadn't spoken since, and I pushed the thought of him away.

"Of course, sir. I will inform the family that the body will not be ready until the day of the funeral, and that we will instead set up a closed and empty casket for use during the wake."

"That might not make them too happy," I observed, imagining Gil Kivela's reaction, "but I appreciate it, Ms. Celik."

"It is a pleasure to assist the Scotts in this delicate matter, sir," she said smoothly, and we exchanged good-byes.

The second call was a bit stranger. It was from the witch's assistant, explaining that Rosamund was on vacation and out of the country. Apparently Rosamund had designated a substitute for any calls from the Scott family, but at that point in the conversation the assistant started sounding weasely.

"Rosamund said to pass you along to Esmé Adams, who lives in Vermont, but . . . well, I heard that you were investigating this yourself. . . ."

The subtextual hinting was pretty heavy. "Yes . . . ?" I prompted cautiously.

"Well, I have another number. . . . Valentine Sassoon lives in-state, and . . ." If the witch on the phone had been in front of me, I would've had to suppress the urge to strangle her during all of these charged pauses. "He's really interested in meeting you," the assistant finally concluded.

Given the way that my morning with Lilah had started, I really didn't want to deal with any more undercurrents in conversations, but I sighed and gave in, saying, "Why don't you give me both numbers, then?"

The assistant was almost overcome with her eagerness

to read Valentine Sassoon's number out to me, but then she started verbally backtracking, apparently finally realizing that she hadn't exactly been subtle. I agreed three times not to mention the private recommendation to Rosamund, assuming I ever met her, and finally got off the phone.

I pondered the situation for a moment, then called Suze. I gave her an edited version of my conversation with Lilah—I wasn't sure exactly how much of the inner workings of the Neighbors' problems she would be okay with me telling Suze (and, by extension, telling the kitsune in general), so I kept that part as bare bones as possible, saying only that the Ad-hene weren't exactly equipped to carry knives right now, and mostly focusing on filling her in on what the ghouls' autopsy had shown and my sudden surfeit of witch phone numbers.

"Call the one the assistant recommended," she said immediately.

"Why, do you know him?" I asked.

"Never even heard of him, but I'm curious. Usually assistants who change a boss's recommendation have a good reason."

"Fine, I'll call."

"Come pick me up," she insisted. "I'm missing all the fun."

"And whose fault is that?" I asked. She made a very rude noise and hung up, which I took as an acknowledgment of my point.

I turned the Fiesta on and headed over to Suze's, dialing as I went. Fortunately Rhode Island didn't require hands-free sets yet, and since I was over the magical age of eighteen, the state assumed that I could multitask maturely. I slowed down anyway. There might not be laws against it, but the police took fairly dim views toward people driving while talking on their phones, and they had been known to hand out speeding tickets to people going thirty in a twenty-five miles per hour zone just to make their feelings about phone use known.

Another assistant answered the call, and I was immediately assured that *Dr.* Sassoon had left clear instructions, and that I was to come over at any time I wanted. I pulled a pen out of the glove compartment and, probably pushing multitasking just a bit too far, held the phone with my shoulder while I wrote the address the assistant rattled off to me down on my hand. Once I had it, I ended the call, stuck the pen back in its holder, tossed my phone into the passenger seat, and shifted gears. In New England, the speed limit is for when you're doing something you shouldn't be or when it's snowing. At all other times the flow of traffic demands at least fifteen mph faster than the posted signs.

"Sorry, I really don't have any plans to accept Jesus as my personal savior." Suzume stood in her doorway and gave me an extremely amused look.

"Ha, ha," I deadpanned as I hung up my jacket. Normally I would've just had her run out to the car and hit the road, but the cereal I'd eaten for breakfast this morning was already long gone, and I needed a pit stop.

While I made a beeline for Suzume's fridge and the Hot Pockets that I knew she kept stashed, her focus never left my attire. "Am I expected to dress to match, Fort?" she asked. "I'm not sure my wardrobe is equipped for that level of blah."

I pulled open her freezer. Jackpot—four-cheese pizza in microwavable sandwich form. She had two packages, and I pulled them both out for myself, then snagged one of the Philly steak ones for her.

"It's barely eleven, Fort," Suze noted.

"Then if you get hungry in the middle of interviewing this witch, don't blame me."

She considered that, then conceded the point. "Fine,

cook them up. Better throw in a few more, though."
There was the distinctive clicking sound of claws against
tile, and I looked over to see two small, inquisitive fox kit
faces peeping out of the cracked bathroom door—one
gray and one red. Apparently Yui and Riko were visiting.
Suze didn't look at the fox kits, but she did raise her
voice very pointedly. "But if anyone violates their time-
out, they're going to see me feed their lunch to the
crows." There was a flurry of scampering noises and the
kits disappeared back into the bathroom.

"They're not coming with us to Sassoon's office, Suze,"
I said flatly. My mind filled with images of how much
destruction kits could wreck in a doctor's office. Frankly,
just bringing Suze along was risking menace to property.

"Since you have not kit-proofed the Fiesta, I would
say not." She gave a snort that clearly outlined her feelings about that.

"Suze, I've got to go talk with this witch. If you're
babysitting, I've got to go on my own."

"What, without me?" Suzume sounded hurt, and she
gave me a full dose of big sad eyes. I wished that I were less
vulnerable to big sad eyes. "I'm just watching the kits for
half an hour. Tomomi woke up with an earache, and Yuzumi had to take her to the pediatrician. It's not going to
take long, and then she'll be back for the others and we
can head out."

I pulled open a Hot Pocket package with unnecessary force, feeling irritated. Somehow it felt less than
professional to have the murder investigation sidelined
by babysitting. "Doesn't your grandmother usually watch
them?"

"Wednesdays she's got her senior swim group down
at the Y." She raised her eyebrows at my expression.
"What? It's important for the elderly to stay active. Besides, Sassoon's receptionist told you that you could
come over whenever. Let's test that theory a little."

"Fine," I groused, though I knew that I'd been beaten

even before I'd shown up, "but this had better not take long." I put the first plate of Hot Pockets into the microwave and hit the reheat button. "By the way, I'm still single, not that you asked." The smell of melted cheese filled the apartment, and I pulled my plate out as soon as the microwave gave its little dinging noise. Plate in hand, I turned, and was suddenly brought up short by Suzume, who had come right up behind me, well inside my personal space, and had waited patiently for me. I froze automatically as she placed her hands very deliberately on my shoulders, leaned in close, and took a deep sniff of my face and chest.

She quirked an eyebrow at me, her expression unreadable. "Not even a hug from Lilah? Interesting." Then she stepped back and busied herself by pulling out more freezer food for the kits.

If I hadn't had anything else on my schedule, watching the kits wouldn't have been a half-bad way to spend time. Once Suze released them from their time-out in the bathroom, they were energetic little bundles of fur and teeth. My willingness to continually throw a small, spit-soaked rubber ball down the hallway for them apparently endeared me greatly to their foxy hearts, and then I was given the very important job of distributing tummy rubs, and finally the kits collapsed on the end of the sofa for their naps.

My clothing was a bit worse for wear (Riko really liked nibbling at my shirttail), and I was wiping kit saliva off my shoes with a paper towel when Suze asked, in completely conversational tones, "So, what did Lilah tell you that you aren't telling me?"

"What?"

"Seriously, Fort. I might not have caught a scent of anything but bear at the scene, but one conversation with Lilah and you're basically crossing the elves off the suspect list. Spill the beans."

I paused and considered her. I thought back over my conversation with Lilah, and how much she'd empha-

sized that a lot of the information she'd told me was potentially dangerous to her if it got back to my mother.
"How much of what you see when we're working do you
report to your grandmother?" I asked. Atsuko Hollis,
after all, was Madeline's closest ally.

Suze's dark eyes narrowed, and she didn't say anything.

I nodded, my point confirmed. "Exactly, Suze."

"Madeline might've given the Ad-hene a slap on the
wrist—"

I gave a snort so loud that it made the kits twitch
across the room. "Oh, you did *not* just make that pun."

Suze ignored me and kept going. "But I've heard rumors that there are Ad-hene down in Underhill that no
one has ever seen. Did your buddy mention those?"

I weighed her point. "Lilah told me about them when
we were trying to find the skinwalker. She said that there
are Ad-hene who are basically imprisoned in Underhill
so that the ones that we see have someone to torture
every day." The elves were such a delightful species. Really, it was hard to imagine what could have inspired
some of the Irish to try to trap all of them in Underhill
for good.

"And whatever she told you that you're not telling
me, did that alibi out these mystery elves?"

"No," I acknowledged, "but I'm not sure that I'd be in
a hurry to go run errands and kill bears for the sociopath
who would normally be torturing me if they hadn't gotten their hands chopped off."

"Me neither, but let's just keep them in mind before
we write the elves completely off."

The conversation concluded just as Riko stirred from
her nap, kit batteries apparently fully recharged, and
then it was back to throwing the ball. Unfortunately I
really did have other things that I should've been doing
(namely, interviewing a witch), and as the promised "half
an hour" morphed into "three and a half hours," my pa-

tience started running short. The only reason I didn't finally throw in the towel and head out on my own was that Suze was equally annoyed and began sending pissy text messages to the kits' mother.

When Yuzumi finally showed up, she was revealed to be in her mid-twenties, looking exhausted and about as much in need of a shot of whiskey as I'd ever seen a woman. So, basically she was the universal embodiment of all mothers of three-year-old triplets.

"Ear infection," was her grim opening statement, completely foregoing any regular greeting. Riko and Yui capered around her legs, and she petted their heads absently as she continued talking to Suzume, whose expression was clearly indicating that she was not pleased at the inaccuracy of Yuzumi's babysitting estimate. "You would not believe the line at the doctor's, and then the pharmacy took forever to fill one round of amoxicillin."

"Tomomi in the car?" Suze asked, beginning to look a bit more forgiving.

"Yeah, she's completely conked out. Thanks for watching the girls." For the first time she looked over at me. She looked a lot like her sister, Takara, with incongruous blue eyes and freckles contrasting with her dark hair and Asian facial structure. "Is this the vampire?" she asked, a hint of curiosity making its way through her exhaustion.

"Sure is," I said, giving a forcefully cheery wave.

She looked at me as if I were the dog that had just talked, then turned back to her cousin. "Thought he'd be better looking."

"That does seem to be the consensus," I noted wryly. Suzume just looked amused.

"Sorry, I know you probably have places to be," Yuzumi said, and then rattled off some quick Japanese. I had no idea what she'd said, but both kits suddenly made similar hacking coughs, shuddered from the tips of their noses to the last hair on their tails, and then shifted into a pair of redheaded little girls whose only hint of their Japanese heritage was the shape of their eyes. They weren't identical, but they were very naked, which immediately resulted in a crash course in how surprisingly difficult it is to get a pair of three-year-olds dressed for winter temperatures. Suze and Yuzumi turned practiced hands to the basics, but I ended up helping Riko into her shoes and mittens.

By the time Yuzumi and her brood were fully loaded into her station wagon and Suze and I were in the Fiesta and heading to the doctor's address, it was just past three o'clock.

"You realize that if I can't talk to this guy today, we have to call up the one in Vermont? I really don't want to drive up to Vermont today, Suze."

She just gave me her best foxy smile. "Much as I love maple syrup candy and eco-friendly co-ops, Fort, I don't think we're going to be hitting Vermont today."

There was something altogether too smug and knowing in her voice. "*Do* you know anything about this guy?" I demanded.

Suze lifted her hands up with a laugh. "I don't, really and truly. Just observing the situation, that's all."

I peered at her closely as we sat at a traffic light, but I could tell from her expression that she wasn't lying on this one. I shook my head, the light turned green, and I concentrated on shifting the Fiesta smoothly through its gears.

The office of Dr. Valentine Sassoon, doctor of sports medicine and orthopedic surgery (as we were informed by the sign beside his door) was, by doctor standards, lushly opulent. Located in one of the more upper-tax-bracket neighborhoods of Providence, it was a beautifully maintained Victorian house that at some point had been retrofitted to suit the needs of a medical practice rather than a private residence, yet at the same time it retained all the beauty of hardwood floors, original crown molding, and two incredibly elaborate stained-glass windows.

As we walked into the waiting room that in some prior age had probably been a front parlor, the first thing I noticed was that every available inch of wall space was packed with a very interesting style of artwork. While most doctors' offices featured framed prints that were mainly picked with all the daring interior decorating instincts of the average hotel chain, each frame on these walls contained the same set of items—one newspaper clipping detailing an athlete's near-career-ending injury, a second clipping extolling the athlete's incredible comeback, and a picture of the athlete in question with an arm wrapped around the shoulders of one smiling man in a white doctor's coat.

"Typical witch," Suze noted quietly as I eyed one of these little collages in the place of pride above the old fireplace. I was no sports aficionado, but I would've had to be a hermit living under a rock not to be able to recognize Curt Schilling. Just to make sure that no one was missing the implications, this one even included a close-up picture of the famous bloody sock.

"Not a fan of subtlety," I agreed. Not that witches could really afford to be. The first time I'd visited the late Dr. Lavinia Leamaro, who employed a witch, I'd noticed a similar decoration style. Since she'd specialized in women's infertility, she'd covered the walls with pictures of the children that her practice had produced—and Suzume had explained to me at the time that intense emotions fed into a witch's magic and made it stronger. I wasn't exactly clear on how that worked. I knew a bit about what witch magic could do, which was manipulate the body and coax it to do things that it normally wouldn't, like allowing an infertile woman to conceive, or, judging by Dr. Sassoon's wall of triumph, enable a man with a torn tendon sheath on his ankle to pitch a successful Game Six of the ALCS.

That put magic firmly in the category of things like my iPhone; I was completely unclear on *how* it worked, but I could identify its results.

The receptionist immediately recognized my name, and did something I'd never seen before in a doctor's office, which was get out of her chair herself to lead us out of the waiting room and down a hallway. She knocked on a closed door softly, and when she heard "Come in," she ushered Suzume and me into a completely occupied examination room.

There was a young woman in her late teens sitting on the examination table with her left pants leg rolled up to her thigh, revealing a long, muscled leg. Her knee was sporting a number of long pink surgical scars and a line of black sutures that looked disturbingly fresh. Sitting beside her on one of those stools with rolling wheels was the man who'd been sporting a doctor's coat in all of the collages in the waiting room. It was always hard to judge height when someone was sitting, but it was easy to judge clothing, and his shirt and slacks would've earned a nod of approval from Chivalry and probably paid for half my month's rent. He was African American, with his hair trimmed very closely to his head, and he had the type of features that made him look like a TV actor playing a doctor—namely, he looked like the kind of guy who could've been strutting catwalks rather than sweating through medical school. I couldn't help but resent him a little on sight—he was all too reminiscent of the football quarterback in my high school who had *also* been at the top of all the AP classes. Seeing someone attractive, popular, *and* intelligent had always made me feel like they'd just gotten a few too many of life's gifts.

Fortunately my resentment was offset by the incredible awkwardness of walking in on someone else's medical appointment. "I'm sorry, we're interrupting. We can wait—"

"Not at all," Dr. Sassoon said in a rich baritone that

made me immediately think, *Of course.* Was it too much to wish that this Nubian god would end up sounding like Gilbert Gottfried? "I left instructions that you be brought in. Please, do sit down." He gestured to the wall, which had two chairs, one of them occupied by an older man with a luxuriant white mustache and a slight similarity to a walrus. Valentine's eyes noted Suze, and I was interested to see that he suddenly looked more cautious. The expression quickly vanished when he realized that I was watching him. "I'm sorry, I hadn't expected you to bring company. Bill?" The walrus man looked up, and Dr. Sassoon smiled politely. "You won't mind waiting in the front, will you?" It was phrased like a question, but there was no doubt in anyone's mind that it was clearly a command. The walrus cleared his throat and stood up.

Now I definitely felt like we were crossing a line, and I held up a hand to Bill and spoke to the girl on the table. "No, no, we aren't going to kick out your dad."

The girl never glanced away from her knee, and responded flatly, "He's my coach."

"Well, then we don't mind kicking him out at all," Suze said, and gave the man a dismissive nod. "Bill." He cleared his throat and slipped around us with a muttered apology, closing the door behind him without even a glance at the young woman he was leaving behind. Suze and I exchanged glances, then sat down in the vacated chairs.

Dr. Sassoon gave us another of those polite smiles, but his eyes were clearly sizing us up. "If you'll just give me a moment." He turned his swivel chair around and returned to his examination of the girl's knee.

I looked over at Suze, who gave a small shrug and then turned her full attention to the doctor. We watched as he probed the girl's damaged knee, carefully running his hands over it, and at one point he straightened the leg entirely. The girl didn't make a sound, but her face whitened and sweat showed at her forehead while her hands gripped the side of the table hard. But despite her obvious pain, she didn't protest or even flinch back from what Dr. Sassoon was doing. I was amazed at her control, since in her position I would've at least been bitching up a storm, if not shrieking in pain.

After a long minute, the doctor carefully let the leg return to its original position. "Thank you very much," he told the girl, then looked back over his shoulder and addressed his next words to us. "I'm not sure if you recognize her, but Crystal here is the fourth-best gymnast in the United States, according to the last round of Nationals." He glanced back at the girl inquisitively. "And you probably would've placed higher if it hadn't been for the knee troubles, correct?"

Crystal nodded, and I was struck by the intensity on her face as she continued to stare down at the sutures covering her knee.

"Well, Bill is out of the room, so we have a chance for a bit of an honest chat," Dr. Sassoon said to her. "According to what your trainer told me when he scheduled this appointment, you've been a gymnast since you were five, and training seven days a week since you were eight. You missed the age requirement for the last Olympics by one month last time, and now if you want to compete, you have to stay at the top of the sport for another two years. How am I doing so far?"

"You're right," Crystal replied.

"Now, you suffered a stress fracture in the knee a year ago and had surgery to repair it. You continued training and competing on it, and the knee got worse. Another round of surgery, more training, and competition. You got out of surgery three days ago, and the surgeon informed your coach that your career is over."

The young woman was absolutely stone-faced during this recital of facts. "Yes," she responded bluntly.

"Well," Dr. Sassoon said, giving her an odd smile, "do you want your career to be over?"

She blinked, and looked completely thrown. "What?"

"Let's put a pin in that question," he said, that smile still firmly fixed on his face. "Why don't you explain to me what your plan is for the next two years—assuming I could make that knee last for you?"

Crystal started talking, and it was a terse, focused monologue of training plans and competition schedules. She would graduate from high school next year, then take a gap year before college in order to train full-time in order to qualify for the U.S. Olympic team, then head out with the team and win gold. Everything was detailed and thought out—this had clearly been the plan she'd gone over in her head for years, and she had a focus and intensity that honestly made me a little uncomfortable. At one point I glanced away from her, and I noticed something that I hadn't before. In the corner of the examination room was a large ceramic pot that housed a jasmine plant. I'd caught the scent upon entering, but the thought of growing plants in an examination room was so far outside my own experience that I had subconsciously attributed the scent to an overenthusiasm with an air freshener. As Crystal continued to detail exactly how she intended to bring home an Olympic gold medal, I realized that the delicate white flowers were shifting and taking on a strange tinge—while a moment ago they'd been milky white, now they gleamed a sickly and disturbing green, tinged with a putrescent yellow and a bruising red. Then I blinked, and the colors were gone. But I thought that there were more blooms on the plant than there had been a moment ago, blooms that struck me as growing with an almost eerie vigor. I glanced over at Suzume, but her eyes had never wavered from Dr. Sassoon, and from where her chair was located, I wasn't sure she could see the pot of flowers.

Crystal's chronology of intended glory had wrapped up, and now Dr. Sassoon was speaking again. "Sounds like quite a plan. Now, I can fix your leg." Her poker face shattered, and Crystal flushed with excitement. But just as her mouth started opening, Sassoon held up one cautionary finger. "Ah. Let me clarify what I mean, because you have a choice in what I do. In one treatment, I will help the surgery that you just underwent. It will turn out to be much more successful than the surgeon originally thought, and your knee will heal. You'll have some stiffness to it, and some loss of flexibility, but it will function well enough that you will be able to get through a perfectly normal life for the next sixty years. But your gymnastic career will indeed be over."

Crystal's face fell. Clearly that was not the kind of *fixing* that she'd thought he meant. "And the other treatment?" she muttered.

"You will have full function back." He put one hand on her knee, and while there wasn't anything remotely sexual about the gesture, there was something about it that made me uncomfortable watching it. It was the way that he looked at her knee, as if his eyes could see through the skin, down to the tendons and the bone, and he was pondering all the things there that he could reshape. "Full flexibility, strength, all those things that you haven't had for the last year, and honestly probably a bit longer before that, given the state of your tendons. This knee will make it to the Olympics, and you will compete on it with no fears that it will crumple and betray you."

Crystal was beaming. "Y—"

Sassoon cut her off again, firmly. "Not yet, Crystal. This path has a cost." He lifted his hand and raised her knee one precise inch. It clearly didn't hurt her, but it focused her attention on the joint in question almost as if it were separate from the rest of her body. His voice shifted, and this time when he spoke again, there was almost a brutality to it. "Your knee will be ruined. The cartilage will wear too quickly, your bones will grind, tendons will snap like old rubber bands, and the knee will fracture like poorly fired china. Before you're a year past the Olympics, you'll be walking like an old woman, and you will need total-knee-replacement surgery by the time you are twenty-five." He was completely focused on her, and his incredible voice was deadly serious. "This is not an estimate, Crystal. This is a promise."

"But . . ." I knew just from the look on her face which path she had already picked, and my heart sank in my chest. "But I'll get to the Olympics, right?" Valentine nodded, and then there was nothing on her face except raw drive and ambition. "Then that's what I want. Fix the knee, make it work. I need to be back in the gym as soon as possible."

There was a complete lack of surprise on Sassoon's face when he heard this, and he wheeled the small padded stool he was sitting on over to the pot of jasmine flowers. Reaching one hand down, he selected one bloom, and broke it off. With a smooth motion, he lifted it to his mouth and ate it, chewing with a slow deliberation as he then moved to the storage area set beside the pot. He opened a low drawer and removed a plain earthenware jar, about the size of one of my old girlfriend's makeup containers, and then wheeled himself back to his former spot in front of Crystal. He swallowed the flower in his mouth, then opened the jar and took Crystal's knee firmly in his left hand, dipping the first two fingers of his right hand into the jar and emerging with a dollop of cream. The cream at first glance looked no different from a blob of sunscreen, but as his hand moved, I noticed a weird opalescent shimmer to the cream that encompassed a rainbow of colors.

He began rubbing the cream firmly into the knee, and the moment the substance touched her skin, Crystal gave a full-body flinch that was so extreme, she might've tumbled right off the table if Sassoon's grip on her knee hadn't been so tight. Sweat was steaming down her forehead, and her hands locked onto the table in a death grip. She wasn't trying to get her knee away from Sassoon, but small, strangled noises of pain began emerging from her throat.

"It burns, it burns, it *burns*!" Her voice was suddenly very high and very young.

I tensed at the sound, but Dr. Sassoon looked completely unperturbed. "It will do that, Crystal. Now," he rubbed one last dollop of the stuff into her line of stitches, which resulted in a full-throated scream that left me flinching. He remained unaffected, and simply gave a small nod as he removed his hands from her leg. "You're going to stay still for the next hour and give that a chance to soak in. Then I'll be back, and I'll put another layer on." I'd thought Crystal was pale before, but now she went stark white at the knowledge that she was going to have to sit through a second round of that, but Sassoon wasn't even done yet. "You'll be back in here every morning for the next two weeks for another two layers. Keep the knee lightly wrapped between treatments, stay out of the gym, and, Crystal, this one is very important, *don't shower*. Don't even wash your hands. Do all of this, and when two weeks are over, you can go straight back into a full training and competition schedule, and the knee will do everything you need it to."

Crystal blinked at him owlishly, the combination of the pain in her leg and the strange barrage of directions apparently overwhelming her. Sassoon put the top back on the jar, slipped the jar into his shirt pocket, and stood up, turning his attention to me and Suze just long enough to indicate that we were all heading out together. He gave Crystal one last, thin smile. "I'll send Bill back in, and you can bring him up to speed on the plan."

We followed behind Sassoon as he led us up the stairs to the second floor of the restored house, and into an office that had probably begun life as one of the bedrooms. The decoration style was more of the same from his waiting room, though I noticed one of the collages sitting unhung, propped on the wall behind his desk. This one featured Lance Armstrong, and, given recent events, I had a strong feeling that it used to hang in a point of pride downstairs.

"So what was all of that, Sassoon?" I snapped as we all settled into chairs. These, I couldn't help but note despite my irritation, were much comfier than the ones in the examination room.

"Please, Fortitude, call me Valentine." He steepled his fingers, and I again felt the full weight of his attention fix on me. "You don't like the choice I offered Crystal." He didn't bother to phrase it as a question, just as a statement.

"No, I don't," I replied flatly. "I don't think a seventeen-year-old has the perspective to make the decision to trade a lifetime's use of her joint in exchange for a short-term goal."

"Interesting," the doctor said, and meant it. He leaned forward, his brown eyes intent. "And who should've made that decision instead? Her coach has a very strong financial incentive for getting that young woman on an Olympic podium, and very little concern about whether she'll be capable of walking without a cane at thirty. Her parents stood back and watched while she ignored every doctor's order and competed on a severely compromised joint. Maybe they'll wring their hands later, but if they'd had worries about her future health, they would've pulled her from her current trainer months ago."

"*You* could've made the decision," I said, my voice icy. "Told her that gymnastics were over and sent her on to the rest of her life with a functioning left leg."

"And assumed that I knew better than Crystal herself about what she needed to be happy in life. Seems a bit paternalistic, I think." For the first time since we entered the room, Sassoon looked over at Suzume, who'd been watching this exchange with interest. "I wasn't expecting you to bring company, but given what I've heard about your activities, Fortitude Scott, I should have. I presume that you are one of the White Fox's granddaughters?"

"That's right," Suzume said coolly. "I notice that you don't seem interested in my thoughts about the gymnast."

"I'm not, actually, though of course it's somewhat rude of me to admit," Sassoon was definitely going for bluntness here. "Do you agree with your companion, however?"

Suze gave a sharp smile that showed off her teeth. "It was her body to ruin. Why fuss?" She leaned forward, and all joking was gone as she focused on the doctor. "The gymnast isn't important, of course. You knew very well what she was going to choose before you even brought the subject up. What you were interested in was how Fort was going to react. Why don't you tell us why that is?"

Sassoon registered Suze's demand, but when he answered, he spoke directly to me again. "I believe you are acquainted with one of my colleagues, Ambrose?"

"The witch who used to work for Lavinia Leamaro? Yes, we met a few times." I didn't try to pretend to be anything other than grim when I spoke about him. At the behest of his fanatical employer, Ambrose had cooked up the roofie potions that had been fed to the Neighbor girls who had found themselves unwillingly involved in the Ad-hene's murderous plan to breed themselves back to power. Ambrose hadn't known what his potions had been used to do—but he also hadn't asked why his boss wanted a potion that would render its drinker compliant and without memories of certain events. I'd prevented my sister from killing him, but I hadn't been sorry when she left him with several long gouges in his stomach.

"I spoke with him recently, and he told me that you had stopped your sister from gutting him like a fish. I find that extremely interesting."

A few pieces were beginning to come together for me. "Interesting enough that you convinced Rosamund's assistant to give me your contact information," I noted.

Sassoon nodded. "Yes. I wanted very much to meet

you." He spread his hands gracefully, and a thoroughly charming smile spread across his face. Clearly salesmanship was among his many talents, and some used-car lot had missed out big when Valentine Sassoon had applied to medical school. "And, whatever you were contacting Rosamund about, I'm confident enough to say that I can do just as well. A bit better, possibly. Certainly better than poor old Esmé would've."

I eyed him carefully. That too-charming smile did nothing but inspire suspicion in me, and my feelings about the doctor at the moment were pretty far from signing up for his fan club, but there was clearly something that Sassoon wanted from me. I weighed my options, then decided to go ahead. "All right. Here's the situation."

Sassoon was attentive while I explained, taking notes and occasionally stopping me to ask a clarifying question, but otherwise quiet. I finally finished, and looked at him expectantly, curious to hear his response.

Suzume had been unusually silent during this exchange, watching Sassoon with all the close attention of a cat that has spotted a mouse. Now she gave a slow, taunting smile, and said, "Go ahead, Valentine. Here's that chance you've wanted so badly to impress the youngest of the Scotts."

Sassoon allowed only the briefest flicker of a look toward Suze, but it was a revealing one, and I realized during that moment that she'd hit on something important, and something very true. Then the witch's expression smoothed again, resetting to pleasantly professional, and he focused on me when he spoke. "When I was very young, my grandmother told me that she had once been able to make a corpse's body bleed fresh in the presence of its killer. But that magic would work only when the body still carried an imprint of the killer, and that would've been gone by the time rigor mortis set in."

"That's very helpful of you, telling us what you can't do." There was a lot of sarcasm from Suzume's corner, but this time Sassoon must've been ready for her, and he didn't acknowledge her comment except for just the slightest twitching around his left eye.

I'd already lost a lot of time today, and while a full list of what witches could do with a murder victim's body was academically interesting, I needed something a bit more focused now. "Why don't you just tell me what *can* be done?"

Sassoon smiled thinly at me. "You are tracking down a killer, so I understand a certain amount of disinterest in background. Very well. You tell me that the murder weapon is missing, and I'm sure that to find it would be helpful. Well, then. Blood calls to blood, Fortitude. If your killer was clever and tossed the weapon in a bucket of bleach, there will be nothing that any witch could do for you. But if even a trace of that blood remains on the blade, I can help you find it. Stabbings are very intimate—a lot of blood, and a lot of direct emotion. It's not an easy thing to do, and I'll need to call some of my colleagues to assist me, but I can give you an object, a compass of sorts, that will lead you straight to that knife as long as even a speck of blood remains on it."

That was definitely something useful, no doubt about it. I readied myself for the weight of the other shoe dropping. "And what will this assistance cost me?" Not that my mother was hurting for money, but that would probably determine the price tag. I'd worked briefly in landscaping, and I'd seen my boss throw more than a few rich-bastard tax line-items on a job estimate.

Sassoon smiled, his perfect teeth gleaming. "On the house. I am, of course, quite happy to assist the Scott family."

"Shenanigans," I said bluntly. "Either you come clean now, or I hit the road for Vermont and see if Rosamund's substitute can do this."

His mouth pursed, and a flash of annoyance crossed his face. "She wouldn't, that I can tell you."

I didn't bother to respond, just watched him. He stared back at me for a long minute, but then he broke and glanced over to Suzume. Answering his unspoken question, she said, "Your song and dance in the exam room was to find out if Ambrose was telling the truth about Fort. You got your answer, but in case you're still wondering, I'll confirm. Yes, Fort will absolutely go out to the car and leave you in his dust for a principle." Sassoon looked at me, just a bit nervously this time, and I did my best to stay calm and cool as I stared at him. I wasn't sure whether Suze was completely right on her last statement—I'd made plenty of compromises in the past when other people had been in danger—but I trusted that Suze was figuring out a way to get the witch to spill about his ulterior motive in getting involved.

It worked. Sassoon dropped the act and sat back heavily in his chair, annoyance now showing clearly on his expression. "Plain dealings seem odd when speaking to a vampire, but very well." Something about him relaxed just slightly, the overt and almost annoying effort to charm being dialed back. "How much do you know about the witches, Fortitude? About our history in your mother's territory?"

"You want to tell me something about that history, so why don't you go ahead and do it?" I suggested.

Sassoon's smile seemed more natural now. "You don't like me very much. But you didn't like Ambrose, or what he'd done, but you wouldn't let your sister kill him. Let me talk about witches, then." He dropped his hands onto the arms of his chair and leaned backward, clearly settling in for a long session. "Most witches earn a livelihood in medicine. Some of us went to medical school, but others find ways to work around that. Magic works with the body—some of us will lay our hands on our patients and change their bodies, but most of us choose to use the intermediary of potions and salves. The results are the same, but it is easier for our patients to assume that the cure came from a concoction rather than magic. Safer as well, of course. Witches, after all, have always had trouble hiding from the eye of humanity."

"I believe Salem has a tourist trade based solely on that fact," Suze noted.

"Salem gets all the attention, but Connecticut was the first colony to execute a suspected witch," Sassoon said. "And there are a few countries today that still maintain official legislation against sorcery, though only in Saudi Arabia will the state still perform an execution. But to be what we are isn't a choice—unless a witch regularly uses their power, siphoning it out and into humans, we sicken. And when we begin to sicken, the power will force its way out, oozing out and seeking humans. Without control and direction, our power will twist human bodies. Cancer rates will skyrocket, and there will be sudden increases in birth defects or miscarriages. Today that will result in a visit from the CDC and investigation of local chemical plants, but in past years that led to a witch hunt."

"That's interesting," I said, and I meant it, since that was a fact that I had been previously unaware of, "but what does this have to do with me?"

"Witches don't live in close communities beyond the immediate family structure. Large numbers meant a greater risk of detection, and for a very long time, doctors and healers whose patients showed a high instance of surviving as a result of attention were more suspect than those whose patients died by the cartload. So when witches came to your mother's territory, we didn't do so as one group, like the *metsän kunigas* or the ghouls, and we didn't have a strong position to bargain with. And your mother had a strong desire to keep us from getting attention. We aren't allowed to live close to one another outside the immediate nuclear family, or work together, and we're strongly discouraged from any large gatherings. Children have to leave the family home at eighteen and settle elsewhere, regardless of whether or not they have the means to support themselves." The smooth charm from before was completely gone now, and Sassoon's voice was getting charged and excited. There was an expression of barely leashed outrage on his face, and for the first time I recognized who Valentine Sassoon really was—he was a believer and an activist, just like those people I'd known at Brown who had gone into the Peace Corps or taken gap years to work for Habitat for Humanity. It was a strange thing, this recognition, because suddenly he seemed much more like a person to me, and I very unwillingly found myself associating him with a dozen old friends who I'd listened to late into the night in bars, and I liked him better for it. And because he was being truly honest with us, he didn't even notice and capitalize on that change of heart I was experiencing, instead rolling forward, his voice getting louder and more worked up as he went. "And things have tightened. It's been fifty years since any new witch was given permission to settle inside Madeline Scott's borders. Your sister Prudence was open about the fact that she was behind that. She also began harassing witch couples who had large families. Twenty years ago she murdered two witches and their six children, giving the justification that the family was too large and would've drawn attention— not *was* drawing attention, but *would have*. Since then, any couple who has more than three children lives in fear that Prudence Scott will show up at the door, because once she does, that family has twenty-four hours to be out of Scott territory, or Prudence comes hunting."

He paused for a second, breathing deeply and clearly trying to pull himself back on track. I watched but didn't say anything—my sister's dislike of witches was something that she certainly had never hidden from me, but I hadn't known the extent of what she'd done. I didn't doubt what Sassoon was telling me—I knew Prudence, and I'd seen her murder my foster parents in front of me in the name of how they *could have* been a risk to our secrecy. It wasn't hard to picture her killing a family of eight, and then using that to terrorize and control something as fundamental as family size.

Sassoon picked up his narrative again, and as much as he tried to control it, I could hear the thrumming excitement in his voice. After all, I remembered it from a dozen phone calls from Brown alumni telling me about how they'd quit their jobs to join Occupy Wall Street and be part of the movement that changed America. "But things are changing. Science has caught up with a lot of what magic does. The illness that our magic cures is often the same one that would be cleared up with antibiotics. We can make a tumor smaller, and over time even eliminate it. Chemotherapy can do the same thing. We can allow an infertile woman to carry a child to term—just like countless clinics. And better yet, when I do something with magic that goes beyond the boundaries of medicine, my patients simply regard it as a scientific marvel. Even if a scientist saw under a microscope that something I had done would not be possible, she would bend over backward and simply credit it as being beyond current scientific knowledge rather than even suggesting for a moment that magic could possibly exist." Yeah, I definitely recognized that look on his face as he described what could be. "There are places that are still dangerous for us to live, but the cities in America are bastions for weirdness. Wiccans set up shop in Salem, and I see flyers for spiritual healing and crystal healing and alternative medicine covering public bulletin boards. This part of the world is *safer* for us now, safe enough that many of the old rules aren't necessary anymore."

"And you think I'll be more open to changing these rules than my sister?" I asked.

Sassoon nodded eagerly. "Yes, but not just changing the rules. Allowing us to build a community, and to negotiate with your family as a group rather than as many individuals."

Suze's jaw dropped. "Oh, for fuck's sake—you're trying to *unionize* the witches?"

"Is that accurate?" I asked. "Because that actually sounds a bit accurate."

He nodded. "It is."

The kitsune whistled, long and low, and I saw that she was, despite herself, impressed. "Well, look at this. Sisters doing for themselves." She'd always had an interesting way of showing that she was impressed. Then she became deadly serious. "You know that Prudence will never go for this, and neither will Chivalry."

"But would Fortitude?" And he looked at me, both fiercely determined and painfully vulnerable.

I held up my hands. "Listen, Valentine, you're making some good arguments here—I'm not going to pretend otherwise. But this is something that I'd have to look into a lot more, and I'm certainly not going to just agree with you based on a five-minute spiel."

To my surprise, what I said actually seemed to rev him up more. "But you're not immediately saying no, Fortitude, which is what is important." With a clear effort, he forced the enthusiasm down and got serious again. "A succession is coming. We all know it, and we're all bracing for it. If Prudence rules when Madeline is gone, then things for the witches are definitely going to stay bad and probably get a lot worse. But you stopped your sister from killing a witch, even one who had done some pretty morally gray things. So I want you to see more of us, Fortitude, and be aware of us and what we can do and how we could live. Because you could be a voice for where we could go, and for changes in the way things have been done." That was definitely enough to make me uncomfortable, and I opened my mouth to explain that whatever hopes he was pinning on my ability to convince my sister to do something she didn't want to, he was *so* barking up the wrong tree, but he held up a hand to stop me and my jaw snapped shut again. He just looked so very painfully earnest. "That's all I wanted to say for today. Now, about your murderer problem. Just get me at least a cup of Matias Kivela's blood, and a few hours for everyone I need to drive down. Let's say, my house a bit after eleven tonight?" He wrote down an address on the back of one of his business cards and slid it across the desk to me. I glanced down at it, noticing that unlike most doctors, Sassoon had very legible handwriting.

I considered, then accepted that I really did need this compass thing. And it probably wouldn't hurt to keep an eye on Sassoon. "All right." I paused, then had to ask. "You're not going to tell me not to tell my family about your big plans?"

All of his activist fervor from before was back under control, and Sassoon gave that cool smile that made me remember my earlier vestigial high-school desire to punch him. "You know very well that if you tell them, Prudence will see me dead as soon as possible."

That was certainly unfortunately true, but still. "You're pretty confident about my ability and desire to keep my mouth shut."

"I'm a gambler. Besides, you protected Ambrose, who had done far more than me to deserve death," the witch said dryly, then turned to look at Suzume.

"You aren't so sure about the odds of my keeping this to myself, are you, Sabrina?" Suzume's voice was amused, and she was clearly feeling peppy enough to start assigning nicknames. From the expression on Sassoon's face, he not only caught the reference, but was highly offended by it. Again, Suzume's instincts for antagonization were proving flawless. "Well, don't fret. You're being so nice and useful for us today—it would be a shame if Prudence ripped your arms off."

That seemed like a solid exit line if I'd ever heard one, and so Suze and I showed ourselves out of the office and back to the Fiesta.

"Okay, so that was a bit more complicated than I expected," I said to the world in general. Then I looked over at Suze, who was fiddling with her seat belt. "Think he's worth working with, or should we see if the Vermonter can cook up that compass he was talking about?"

"Fort, your sister has the kind of attitude and outlook that I'm going to very politely refer to as *unionbusting*. Valentine stuck his neck out pretty far to try to recruit you, which to me suggests that he's desperate because not many witches have been willing to sign up for his cause. They might agree with him on every line-item issue, but they're not going to risk death by vampire." She shrugged, not looking overly concerned at this assessment. "He needs you a lot right now, because he thinks that you can save the movement he's trying to put together. If he promised to make you a compass, he's probably going to just about kill himself to make sure that this is the best damn compass that any witch could give you. I don't see the Vermont subwitch having that kind of motivation. Use him as long as he's useful, and if he starts becoming a problem, just report him to your sister and she'll take care of him."

"Yeah, that's nice," I said sarcastically. I wished fervently that I could decide whether I liked Valentine Sassoon or thought he was a jackass, since I was sure that would help sort out my feelings about the likelihood that at some point my sister was going to show up on his doorstep in a killing mood. "Seriously, Suze, is what he's saying about the witches right?"

"Fort, if you'll listen to me for once, you won't even go there." There was a clear warning in Suzume's voice.

"*Suze.*"

"Fine, yes," she snapped, sounding pissed. "The witches have a bit of the short end of the stick."

"If things are so bad here for them, why wouldn't they leave? And why would others actually be trying to get in?" I tried to think through what Sassoon had told me again.

"Madeline Scott isn't exactly benevolent, but she's not bad," Suze noted. "She at least prevents most interspecies warfare or predation, which is pretty different from a lot of other areas, where it's just a question of which gang controls your area, and whether they want to kill you or recruit you. Some places are even worse—Des Moines is basically Thomas Hobbes's state of nature, with each individual looking out for their own skin, and your neighbor can go fuck themselves."

The knowledge that putting one foot outside the boundaries of my mother's territory would require the escort services of Chivalry had been enough to keep me solidly inside New England for my whole life, but I'd always assumed that it was just because I was a young vampire. Now I rethought my view of the wider world, and realized that things were even more complicated than I'd previously known.

"So Valentine is pinning his hopes for a brighter tomorrow on me." That was enough to induce an instant headache, and I rubbed the heels of my hands hard against my eyes. The witches were so, *so* screwed. "Suze, everyone seems really interested in *me* all of a sudden."

"That's natural, Fort," she said soothingly. "After all, your milk shake brings all the boys to the yard."

I gave a deep sigh. "I value these chats we have. But, seriously. First with Lilah, now with Valentine, I've got people thinking that I can somehow protect them or change things after my mother is gone." I blinked my eyes open again and turned to face Suze, staring at her beautiful, opaque black eyes, and I felt a small but insistent flutter of suspicion. "Do the kitsune think that as well?" I asked, feeling like the familiar assumptions of my life had suddenly been replaced by a set of fun house mirrors.

Suze looked amused rather than offended, and the blunt honesty in her voice steadied me. "My grandmother sees the value in having a foot in both camps, Fort, but if you think that's my sole reason for hanging out with you, think again. The kitsune have the closest ties to the vampires. We've seen enough to know that your influence on Prudence is about as substantial as an ant's on a hippopotamus."

Wasn't that the damn truth. I perked up slightly at the other implications in that small speech. "So you're hanging out with me primarily because of my rugged male allure?"

"Maybe because of your scrappy puppy-struggling-out-of-a-cardboard-box appeal."

"I'll take that," I said. That cleared up, I put the key into the ignition and started the Fiesta. It died. I started it again . . . and it died. Third time, and this time it caught. I shot a triumphant look to Suze, who returned it with a withering expression of *Get a new car*. I ignored that. "Now, let's go see a ghoul about a cup of blood."

Chapter 6

Celik Funeral Home was just like every other funeral home I'd ever seen—tastefully decorated in neutral colors and rigorously dusted antiques, with careful plaques on each room (OFFICE, VIEWING ROOM, RESTROOM) and black-suited employees who had all perfected a facial expression that combined *I can't wait to help you with whatever question you have* with *I'm so sorry for your loss*.

Dan had previously been the only ghoul I'd ever met, and I'd assumed that he was on the short side. But in the first minute of stepping inside Celik Funeral Home, I met about four different ghouls, and I discovered that Dan was actually on the tall side for his species. Most of them just barely topped five feet. I wondered if their height made it hard for them to find suits that fit, or if some entrepreneurial ghoul had gone into the tailoring field.

Catherine Celik, a tiny woman in her late sixties, ushered us into her office (the sign on the door listed her as registered embalmer and funeral director, and also listed half a dozen other Celiks who held similar, though junior, positions). We were quickly settled in wingback chairs and asked whether we wanted drinks.

"One of my granddaughters is fetching the item you requested," Catherine said, with no implication whatsoever that someone calling her up and asking her to extract a cup of blood from a two-day-old corpse was out of the ordinary. Maybe it wasn't. While my mind wrestled with that possibility, the ghoul was extracting a thin manila folder from the pile on her desk, which she handed to me. "We also prepared these for you."

I flipped open the file, revealing a grisly collection of Matias Kivela's autopsy photos. I was grateful that lunch had been a few hours ago. "That was very ... thoughtful of you. I'm sure these will be useful." Or, I'm sure they would've been useful if I'd had any idea what I was doing, though I supposed that if I hit a brick wall, I could just stare at the photos and hope that a brilliant deduction would strike me, like I was the star of a police procedural.

Suze peered over my shoulder and made a small, unimpressed noise. Over what, I had no idea, but then she turned to look at Catherine and said, "It must bother you," with a nod to the pictures.

"Oh, well, when you're in the business, you end up seeing just about everything," the older woman said comfortably.

"No, no," Suze said, and I noticed the sly gleam in her eyes and braced myself. "Seeing good meat treated like that," Suze said, completely straight-faced.

All this got her was a very chiding look from Catherine. "Really, Ms. Hollis. The *metsän kunigas* are hardly on our menu. The condition in which Mr. Kivela arrived here had no influence on us save for the state of the bill we will produce."

I couldn't help the unwilling curiosity that comment stirred in my brain. "But ... if he'd been a human ... you would've ... *eaten* him?"

"Of course," Catherine said patiently. "After all, he would hardly be needing his organs where he is going, and waste is so shameful." There was apparently quite an expression on my face, because she made a little *tut tut* sound at me. "Really, Mr. Scott, there's no need for that look. I can assure you that we take the utmost care when harvesting. A kosher supervisor would be hard-pressed to find fault with our methods."

"Oh no, I'm sure . . . ," I responded automatically, then, unable to stop myself, qualified, "Except for the *source* of your meat." The conversation was interrupted at that point when the door opened and a young woman, about my age and looking like a minus-fifty-years version of Catherine, walked in. She was dressed in yet another black pants suit and was carrying a very incongruous ice chest, the thick plastic kind used for small picnics.

"Ah, Karli, thank you," Catherine said as her granddaughter set it on the desk. The older ghoul opened the lid, and the moment the seal popped, my nose practically began twitching as my salivary glands went into overdrive, as if I'd suddenly walked past the open door of a KFC (the greatest ongoing threat to my vegetarianism). Catherine tilted the container so that we could see that it contained a plastic container, the same kind used by my favorite Chinese place for take-out soups, filled with blood. The soup container was packed tightly with several bags of frozen peas, but there was still a little surface movement on the dark liquid from being carried up, and the inner sides of the container were coated with a thin layer of the red fluid from the slosh. I found myself weirdly curious at the patterns it made, and for a second I pictured myself running a finger around the inside of the brim, gathering the fluid up just like leftover batter after making a cake. That was finally enough to set off my internal alarms, and I forced myself to look away from the container and back up to Catherine, who was still blithely talking. "You said over the phone that you only needed a cup, but I had my nephew gather a full pint, just in case."

"I appreciate that, Ms. Celik. Ah . . ." I forced myself to peek down once more, but fortunately the strange urge was gone, and I was able to consider the rest of the ice chest's contents. "Now, about the peas . . ."

She smiled, revealing what were almost certainly not the teeth she'd been born with. I wondered if it was racist to find a ghoul with dentures weird. "Yes. I find that they work just as well as ice packs. It should keep everything cool for a few hours. If you need it to last longer, simply throw in a bag of ice cubes. Just be careful not to freeze the blood—I doubt you really want to have to thaw it. When you're all done, give the chest to Dan and he'll drop it off the next time he comes by."

I reached over and closed the top of the ice chest firmly. My reaction to the blood was still creeping me out, and I felt a part of me relax as the seal was locked back into place. I grabbed onto Catherine's last comment like a life preserver back to safe conversational territory. "Oh, you know Dan?"

Now she looked distinctly amused. "I've known Daniel Tabak since he was in diapers. Do pass the peas along to him—I know his father always frets that Dan doesn't eat enough vegetables." That expression must've been back on my face, because the old woman now looked *extremely* amused, and gave me a little needling. "If you're going right home, I'd be happy to have Karli go and fetch Dan's portions for the week. He usually picks them up from the butcher shop, but I'm happy to save him a trip."

It was the look in her eyes more than the context of her statement that tipped me off about what she meant by the term *portions*, and I nearly fell over myself to try to avoid that scenario. "Oh, no, no, we're making a few stops tonight . . . and I'm sure Dan doesn't mind the trip." There was a small giggle behind me, half smothered, and I had a feeling that Karli was enjoying the sight of a squeamish vampire just as much as her grandmother was. Frankly I was impressed that Suze wasn't joining in for once. "Well, this has been so helpful. You've really thought of everything, but I'm afraid that we really do have to go." I grabbed the handle on the ice chest with one hand and Suzume's elbow with the other, and continued spewing social niceties as I backed out. Catherine and Karli's matching smiles were the last thing I saw before the front door finally closed behind us. Back outside, the temperature dropping, I gave Suze a very unfriendly look as she finally let out the snicker at my expense that she'd been suppressing out of some vestigial sense of solidarity.

"Lots of help back there, Suze. Thanks for that."

"Anytime, Fort," she said, ignoring my sarcasm. From her point of view, of course, she probably thought that she *had* been helping. There was a short pause as we began walking to the car, but then I had the distinct feeling of being closely observed. I glanced over, and saw that Suze was eyeing me with an unusual intensity—an intensity that she usually reserved for bacon products. "Do you have any plans for dinner tonight?" she asked abruptly.

Even after the previous conversation, and my very creepy reaction to the blood container, I was definitely more than ready to eat, but her question surprised me. We'd eaten dinner together plenty of times, but there was something just a bit formal in Suze's phrasing, and it made me cautious. "Not as yet. Why?"

"We've got a few hours to kill before we have to get the blood over to Valentine Sassoon's." Her eyelids became heavy, and the smile she gave me was slow and had a lot of undertones, all of which I was more than willing to explore. "Have dinner with me."

I was certainly not going to turn down an invitation like that, and I rushed to tuck the ice chest safely into the trunk. Suze got into the passenger seat and immediately began issuing directions.

An hour and several stops later, Suze directed me to pull up in front of a wholly unfamiliar brick town house on the South Side. The sun had set, and the lights were on in the town house, with shapes moving behind the window shades.

I gave a heavy sigh. "So clearly we aren't heading back to your house." I would've picked up on that earlier (since we were in a completely different neighborhood), but I'd been following her directions through three separate stops for dinner, wine, and dessert. I wasn't sure what I'd been expecting, but clearly my hopes for the evening were about to be completely dashed.

"Just grab the stuff," she said as she snagged the wine and the gourmet brownies.

I grabbed the other bags—one roasted chicken, one vegetarian quiche, and an assortment of sides—all at Whole Foods prices. I made a firm mental note to clarify all dinner plans with Suze before I willingly shelled out the big bucks ever again. I wasn't saying that I expected sex in exchange for buying dinner, just that I would've suggested a different venue—like Pizza Hut.

Suze hushed me as we walked up to the door, so I must've been muttering something along those lines under my breath. I shut my mouth tightly while she rang the bell, though I could've saved myself the trouble, since it just dropped again when I saw who opened the door.

Suzume's twin sister, Keiko, looked very unhappily surprised to see us, but Suze shoved the container of brownies into her hands and trilled loudly, "Keiko! Thanks so much for inviting us!"

Keiko's boyfriend, Farid, walked up behind her, wearing bright blue scrubs and looking befuddled. "Honey, we had dinner plans?" he asked.

With her back to him, Keiko's expression was murderous, but Suze gave a patently false, "Oh no. Did you say *next* Wednesday, Keiko?" She shot me an apologetic look. "I'm so sorry, Fort. And here I made you spend all afternoon making your famous quiche!"

I felt that was pushing things a bit far, especially given the clearly marked Whole Foods bags, but Farid jumped in anyway with a loud, "No, no, tonight is fine! I'm on night shift, but we have time for dinner!"

"Oh, I wouldn't want to intrude . . . ," Suze started.

"Well, actually—" Her sister tried to capitalize on that statement, but this was clearly not Suzume's first rodeo. She pressed immediately forward. "But we did get a chicken, and all the sides. But don't let us intrude, Keiko."

"Of *course* you're not intruding!" Farid lied, early training in good manners springing into action. "Everything smells amazing. Please come in—right, hon?"

Keiko was clearly pissed beyond rational speech, but she had no choice but to paste a patently bright smile across her face and step back to let us through the door.

I was already a permanent fixture on Keiko's shit list, but I muttered a desperate, "I knew nothing," in her ear anyway during our hello hug. The prickle of her nails in my back told me that I would be held accountable regardless.

Farid put himself to work cleaning up what was clearly the beginnings of their planned dinner, and I tried to be useful by pulling out all the food that we'd brought and setting it up on the table to eat family style. The town house was one of those built tall rather than wide, with the floor we were on consisting only of an eat-in kitchen and a small TV area that barely accommodated a love seat and a matching armchair. An open closet next to the sofa revealed a stackable washer and dryer.

"Your place looks great," I said to Farid. The sisters were currently in a staring match that was clearly speaking volumes to each of them, but it did manage to make things a little awkward for the rest of us. If they had been in fox form, I was sure their tails would've been lashing in agitation.

"Thanks," Farid said, setting out dishes and utensils.

"It's a little tight, but I'm only five minutes from the hospital, so it makes my commute pretty easy."

Suze broke away from her twin's death glare and gave Farid a wide smile. I hoped for his sake that he didn't realize that it was not one of her nice smiles. "That's very convenient," she said. Then, with an innocence that immediately pinged my radar, "How many bedrooms do you have?"

"Two," Keiko said through gritted teeth, and when Farid turned his back to put the old dinner fixings in the fridge, she gave us both a slashing look. "So we use the extra one as an office."

"That all sounds great," I said quickly. Apparently Suze's sudden interest in real estate was crossing into areas that Keiko was definitely marking as off-limits, so I forced brightness into my voice and tried to shift the conversation. Keiko was far from my favorite person, but I felt bad for Farid, who seemed like a normal nice guy who thought that he was dating a normal human woman. "Do we have everything we need?"

"Got the glasses right here, so it looks like we're all set." Farid settled the wineglasses at the hastily reset table, and we all settled in. It was one of those little circular tables that worked well for two, and barely accommodated four, so we were all elbow to elbow.

Suzume popped the cork on the wine, and immediately snagged her sister's glass. "Keiko, I know you like Australian wines, so Fort and I picked up a Yellow Tail." She was pouring before the other kitsune could answer, and her dark eyes looked particularly foxlike as she watched Keiko alertly. "I sure hope you like it." Since Suzume knew full well that Keiko's loose peach sweater was concealing her five-month pregnancy, I could feel my eyebrows arching up my forehead. Whatever Suze's plan was for this dinner party of the damned, this was clearly what she'd been maneuvering toward.

Keiko's expression would've been appropriate for a French aristocrat standing next to the guillotine. "That was so thoughtful of you, Sis," she said grimly, and I could see her trying to work out a way to avoid accepting the glass that Suze was holding out to her.

Before she could, however, Farid broke in, reaching over himself to take the full wineglass. "Oh, actually, Keiko is sticking to water these days."

The last time I'd seen a facial expression like Suze's had been during the 2012 presidential debates, when Barack Obama had uttered the fateful phrase, "Proceed, Governor." "Really?" She leaned toward Farid. "Anything I should know about?" And I could almost hear Suze's trap snap closed. Unable to do anything, I sank down into my chair, as if by less visibility I could separate myself from what was unfolding.

Keiko was cornered and she knew it, but she was still struggling for a way out. "Well, it's just—"

And then Farid started talking, and it was all over. He looked at Keiko, and I cringed at the expression on his face. He was head over heels in love with her, and had no idea that he was unwittingly helping her sister put the knife in her back. "Sweetie, really, we're way past the first trimester. I really think we can at least tell family." The barely suppressed excitement in his voice was the worst part, and I wished that I could cover my eyes.

"Trimesters? That sure sounds specific," Suze said brightly. Enough was enough, and I kicked her hard under the table. She winced but never looked away from her sister.

Trapped, and with no escape, Keiko gave in. "You're right, Farid," she said, then looked over at Suze with a very unsisterly expression in her eyes. "You'll be an aunt in another few months." Of course Suze had probably known before poor Farid, but Keiko did her best to sell it. "Yays," she gritted through her teeth.

The whole table devolved into a flurry of hugs and

congratulations. The ones from Suze were distinctly insincere, and I did my best to divert Farid with a manful handshake to distract him from the fact that the future mother of his child's hug for her sister looked a little bit like an attempted choking. After a minute we were all seated again.

Either Farid was as dense as a brick usually, or what had been apparently the first public announcement of his impending fatherhood had rendered him insensible with joy, or one of the kitsune in the room was doing some subtle smoothing of his perception, or maybe a combination of all three, but he directed a smile at Keiko that was so blissful that it was painful to see. "See, honey?" Then he looked over at me and let the floodgates open. "I've been dying to tell everyone, but Keiko kept saying that we didn't want to get ahead of ourselves." He laughed suddenly, gleefully. "But it's just killing me — I can't wait to get the nursery all set up, and tell my parents—"

Alarm bells went off inside my head. "Your parents?" I asked weakly.

"Yeah. I'm not going to lie. They emigrated from Tehran thirty years ago, so they can still be a bit traditional, and I don't think they're going to be too thrilled about us not being married." He looked right over at Suze and became extremely earnest. "But I'm just going to tell them that it's our decision, and I definitely am not going to let them start trying to put pressure on Keiko."

"You'll be just like all those Hollywood starlets," Suze said with a smile. "So glamorous."

I felt a sudden rush of air under the table, and the wince on my friend's face indicated that Keiko had had enough. "You always know how to phrase things, Suze," she said. Apparently her kick had been a lot harder than mine, because I noticed Suze suppressing a grimace and reaching down to subtly rub her shin.

This conversation had more sharp edges and loaded statements than a Katharine Hepburn movie, and I for one wanted out. I was also really hungry, and I didn't think it was wrong of me to want a slice of the vegetarian quiche before it was stone cold. "So with that great news, let's get eating!" I said forcefully.

Farid immediately joined me in reaching for the serving dishes. "Yeah, I hate to say it, but I really do have to leave for work soon." As he began carving a wing off the chicken, he leaned in and kissed Keiko on the cheek.

Dinner stabilized slightly after that. It was clear that Suze's goal had been to push the acknowledgment of Keiko's pregnancy out into the open, and now that she'd achieved that, she and her sister were just biding their time until Farid left. What Suze's motivation had been, I had no idea. After all, Suze had known for months. Normally I would've resolved to ask her about it later, but from the way she and her sister were exchanging glares, the truth was likely to come out as soon as Farid was out of hearing distance. I envied him. Being at a minimum safe distance once the sisters threw down would've been a blessing.

Awkward atmosphere or not, I was hungry, and I concentrated primarily on eating as much as possible and keeping my eyes off the roasted chicken, which did smell incredible. When Farid pulled on his coat, grabbed a brownie for the road, and waved a jaunty good-bye, I did have to strongly suppress the urge to yell, *Take me with you!* just to escape the sisterly fight that I knew was coming.

Sure enough, it started the moment the door closed behind Farid.

Suzume dropped her bright facade immediately, and even I was taken aback by the level of anger on her face when she rounded on her sister. "You fucking told him," she said dangerously.

"I think I'll clear the dishes," I said quickly, hopping to my feet and grabbing what remained of the sides.

"Yes, I told him," Keiko snapped back, getting right into her twin's face. "You didn't need your brilliant plan of interrogation either, Suze. You could've just asked me."

"Oh yeah, ever since you swore that you'd dumped him, I've completely trusted your honesty. No, not only have you *moved in with* the human, which I have already been completely covering up for you, but now you decided it would be *fun* to break one of Grandmother's biggest rules? If this is your version of teen rebellion, Keiko, it sucks a big one!"

The kitchen was small, and I honestly wasn't sure that there was anywhere in the tiny town house where I could escape from this fight. "I think I'll wait in the car," I suggested.

"She'll just tell you anyway." Keiko said to me, looking annoyed. "Besides, *you* of all people should be on my side. I hear that you practice catch and release on problem humans—I'm not doing anything like *that*."

Apparently the story of my saving Matt McMahon from my sister had been making the rounds. I definitely did not appreciate Keiko's particular choice of phrasing, but I looked at Suze, whose eyes had a lot more in common with a fox's than a human's right now, and realized that I couldn't just run back to the car and let her rip her sister apart. I hadn't ever seen the twins together at a time when they weren't fighting, but I did know that Suze loved her older sister, and while she wasn't one to express a lot of regret about her actions, I had a feeling that if I left the house, this conversation would go even further downhill.

I really wished that I could go hide in the car.

Instead, I forced myself to walk slowly back to the table and sit down in my chair. I snagged the bottle of wine, refilled Suze's glass right to the top, and nudged it toward her. Maybe that would help the situation, or at least distract her for a moment. Then I turned my attention to Keiko. Forcing my voice low, and in as reasonable a tone as I could muster, I said, "All right, Keiko. So you've told Farid that he's going to be a father. You're not insane." I cut Suze off before she could even open her mouth. "No, Suze, don't even start. Keiko, you're not crazy, so you have to have some kind of plan here."

Whether it was my words or my voice, Keiko calmed down a little. "Thank you," she acknowledged, then reached over and snagged the bottle herself.

Instincts garnered from a lifetime of American films and TV kicked in. "Wait. You're—"

Keiko cut me off, rolling her eyes. "Half a glass with dinner, Fort. This is not going to result in fetal alcohol poisoning." She poured about two inches into Farid's empty glass, then took a slow sip. "Oh, this *is* good."

"See? You and Australian wines," Suze muttered.

Another sip, and then Keiko started talking to me again, sounding a lot calmer, but carefully ignoring her sister. "Grandmother's rule is that we can't have long-term relationships with humans, and when we choose one to be the father of a litter, we have to make sure we never see him again after we become pregnant. These are the rules for secrecy, and they are the same rules that Grandmother's family observed back in Japan."

"Rules that have worked very well for us, Keiko."

Keiko didn't even react to Suze's voice, continuing to speak only to me. "But our grandmother broke those rules. To get to America, she seduced an American GI and convinced him to marry her. He brought her back to Rhode Island, and they had four daughters, each a year apart."

"Oh, Keiko." All the anger was drained from Suze's voice, replaced by a mixture of exhaustion and deep, deep sadness. "Yes, that happened. But think about how it ended—" She looked over at me as well, and filled me in. "Grandfather Hollis returned home early from a business trip. Grandmother was doing the laundry in the back of the house with her older daughters, and she didn't hear him come in. He went upstairs to the nursery, and found a fox kit in the bassinet. That was our aunt, Kanon. She was just a baby. She recognized her father, and without Grandmother there to guide her behavior, she just shifted to human form to greet him."

"What did your grandmother do?" I asked. Atsuko Hollis had only four daughters, so I had a bad feeling that I knew what she'd done.

"She heard him shouting, and she ran upstairs." The corner of Suze's mouth twitched. "We can set illusions, we can fool the eye, but we can't change a memory. And Grandfather Hollis was stone cold sober, and he knew what he'd seen." A pause, a long sip of wine, and then Suze said, flatly, "So Grandmother killed him, and faked an accident."

Keiko rushed back into the conversation. "Yes, and she always tells that story to convince us that the old way is better, but her way worked for *four years*, and would've kept working if she'd known that his travel plans had changed." She started sounding excited. "I've got Farid completely trained—he texts me to tell me if he goes to a different sandwich shop for lunch, even if he thinks I'm in a completely different state!"

I stared at her for a second as it slowly dawned on me what she was heading toward. "So you're—oh, oh man." Suzume didn't say a word, instead just staring at her sister in mute horror.

Keiko was rolling now, speaking so quickly that her words almost ran together as she outlined her plan. "No, you're not really thinking about it, but I have, and I know that I can make this work. Farid is an ER resident. He works eighty hours a week. I barely see the poor guy as it is. And I haven't gone fox *once* since I started trying to get pregnant—not *once*. That's how my grandmother handled it when she was married, and she had single births each time. I can handle keeping one kit a secret from him."

I tried to cut in. "Keiko, this isn't the fifties anymore. Farid is going to expect to spend some time actually, you know, *holding* the baby."

"Of course he will—when he's away from work, he can hold her all he wants. But I'll be there. And when kitsune kits are little, they always mimic their mother. When I'm human, she'll be human."

"And what about when you're not around?" I reasoned. "Farid strikes me as the kind of guy to pop the baby in a sling and walk around the corner for coffee every now and then for a little daddy-baby bonding time."

"Attachment parenting," Keiko said triumphantly. "I can keep my daughter with me all the time, and it won't even be seen as weird." She paused, considering. "Well, not too weird."

I couldn't help it; I was starting to think that she'd actually thought through a potentially workable plan. I scrabbled for another argument, and then asked, "What if it's a boy?"

This prompted a very loud and derisive snort. "So Suze has been telling you bedtime stories? Fort, my grandmother spent just about every minute of her pregnancies human, and all she had were girls. Kitsune breed true, and that means daughters. All those stories about kitsune having human sons are nothing more than another way to scare us away from forming long-term relationships. There is no biological impact of my love for Farid on our daughter."

Suze had buried her head in her hands, but now she looked up and said, quietly and pointedly, "Keiko, I notice that you have not filled Grandmother in on your marvelous little plan."

"I'd rather ask forgiveness than permission. And once she sees that everything is working out, there will be no reason for her to intervene." There was a stubborn line in Keiko's jaw that I was very familiar with.

"Don't mistake a wish for a truth," Suze warned.

"Grandmother is going to be pretty unspeakably pissed about this."

"But you're not going to tell her." Keiko's voice was wobbling somewhere between an order and a plea.

Looking at Suze's face as she listened to her twin, I wasn't sure what she would say next. I had a feeling that Suze didn't know either, but I broke in reluctantly. "Suze, I hate taking Keiko's side, but I don't see how telling your grandmother right now would help anything. Farid already knows, so it's already really complicated. If your grandmother somehow was able to make Keiko dump Farid right now, the first thing he'd do is get a lawyer and start a custody battle, which is good for exactly no one. Right now Keiko at least has things under control. I'm not sure destabilizing things is a great idea at the moment."

There was a silence that stretched a long minute; then Suzume gave a sharp nod. "Fine, I won't say anything." Then she leaned in very close to her sister, and her voice made it clear that this was a deal breaker. "But I don't give a shit where you are when you go into labor. You ditch Farid and get back to my place."

"I was going to have to do that anyway," Keiko admitted, somewhat reluctantly. "I can't risk a hospital delivery." There was another long pause, and I could feel the tension easing from the room. If they'd been in fox form, this would probably be the point where they each began focusing on grooming their tails and ignoring the other.

I frowned a little. "Farid's a doctor. How are you going to explain that to him? The guy spent ten minutes discussing his ideal birth plan with me, no matter how many hints I dropped about not giving a shit about dimmed lighting and banking cord blood. He's definitely planning to be in the delivery room."

Keiko sighed heavily. "How else, Fort? I'm going to lie my ass off. I'll figure out a decent cover story when we get closer, or if I can't, I'll just ask for forgiveness."

"We'll say it's cultural," Suze interjected. "Everyone always backs off if you claim that it's cultural."

"I don't know. That might not work on Farid." Keiko slanted a glance at me. "Now if it were Wonder Bread over here, no problem."

"I'm not even going to respond to that," I said icily. Mostly it was annoying that it was true.

"Don't be snippy, Fort." Suze cut in, her voice chiding. "We can't all have white male privilege, so stop being resentful about the occasional consolation prize."

While I choked on that one, Keiko shifted her attention to a more pressing matter and said, "Now pass that plate of brownies this way. I'm going to eat the crap out of them."

Suze snorted. "I was wondering how you were controlling yourself." Reaching over, she grabbed the item in question and plopped it right in front of her sister, noting to me wryly, "Never get between a pregnant woman and chocolate." She gave Keiko a quick, assessing look, and shook her head. "You might as well let Farid start making announcements. Loose shirts and padded bras are not going to cover that baby bump much longer."

The speed at which the sisters had gone from at each other's throats to completely mellow had left my head spinning. "Padded bras?" I asked, confused.

Keiko rolled her eyes at my apparent ignorance, but her mouth was already full of brownie, so Suze leaned forward and enlightened me. "Secret to concealing, Fort. She just keeps getting more and more padded bras to make her chest stick out as much as her belly. Pop on a loose shirt, and it just looks like she's getting fat."

I sighed. "Yeah, that answers the question I never needed answered ever." I'd eaten a more than generous dinner, but I was surprised to realize that there was still a little room left, and I reached over and snagged one of the brownies before Keiko could inhale them all. Apparently stress made me hungry.

The sisters maintained their reluctant détente, and we managed to get through the remainder of the evening. When Suze and I were finally heading out, Keiko stopped me at the door with a soft touch on my arm.

I looked down at her face. She and Suze were fraternal twins rather than identical, and without the expression of severe irritation that I was used to seeing her with, I had to note that the features of Keiko's face were more refined and classically beautiful than her sister's, though she lacked the sheer force of personality that Suzume exuded. Keiko looked extremely reluctant, but forced out, "Thanks for being willing to listen tonight, Fort. It really helped."

"No problem," I said awkwardly. I'd been much more comfortable just disliking her.

Removing her hand from my arm, Keiko pulled back out a bit of her usual superior attitude, and said, "So here's just a bit of advice in return—your sister is going to be in charge of the territory soon. If I were you, I'd start mending some fences."

I wasn't grateful for her advice, but I could tell that for once she hadn't actually been trying to insult me, so I restrained myself to a short nod.

Outside, the temperature had plunged further, and I shoved my hands as deeply into my pockets as they could go and wished that I'd brought along my nice woolly scarf. As I unlocked the car, I looked over at Suze, who was huddled in her bright green parka. "A lot of people are paying attention to my mother's health, aren't they?" I asked.

Suze nodded, setting the bobble on her hat jiggling in a weirdly festive counterpoint to the seriousness of her voice. "The succession affects the lives of everyone who lives in eight states and a chunk of Canada, Fort. Saying that this has been the subject of some conversation is a bit of an understatement. Now let's see if this witch can deliver on his promises."

Getting to Valentine Sassoon's house involved driving almost completely across the city to Blackstone. Blackstone was one of the newest neighborhoods in Providence, and one of the most affluent. The houses suddenly got substantially bigger and newer as we drove around the streets. Sassoon's house was in a nice enough neighborhood that a guy out for a late-night jog gave the Fiesta a second look, and glancing in the rearview mirror, I could see him scribbling down my license plate number.

"Great, now I'm a person of interest to the neighborhood watch," I muttered.

"It's like we're seeing the progression of a medical career," Suze noted. "Sassoon probably started in a place like where Farid and Keiko are living."

"See, you're warming up to him." I saw her expression, then corrected myself. "Or not."

"He seems very nice. I'll definitely keep that in mind when he figures out what Keiko is and she calls me up to help dump his body somewhere."

"Or it all works out really well and you become the first person in your family to have a brother-in-law. Plus, free medical advice!"

"I think you've made this situation worse," Suze accused me, her dark eyes narrowed.

"Don't say that," I implored her. I wanted absolutely no ownership in the impending fiasco of Keiko trying to pass a kitsune kit off as a human baby to her boyfriend. I realized that her plan had seemed much more doable when she was describing it to me than now, when I just thought about it. "Look, we're here."

Sassoon definitely knew how to live in style. The house was in the Tudor style, with all of the neat angles and sloping roofs, and from the look of the chimney, at least one truly boss fireplace. There was a single-car garage that had been designed to look like a carriage house, and a decently long driveway that was cluttered with four different cars. Two had Massachusetts license plates, one was from Connecticut, and the last one bore the distinctive "live free or die" of New Hampshire, that eternal stronghold of Ron Paul supporters.

"Looks like those people he called in have all arrived," Suze noted.

I pulled up to the curb, and we got out. The sidewalks in this neighborhood were all freshly paved and free from encroaching grass. I was impressed—even in the nicer parts of College Hill, very few of the sidewalks looked this good. We went to the front and knocked. There was a little bit of movement at the window curtains while someone checked us out; then Valentine Sassoon was opening the door and ushering us into the living room. The fireplace was, I was pleased to note, exactly as amazing as I'd expected.

There were five people sitting on Sassoon's sectional sofa, one man and four women. I recognized the man as Ambrose, and he looked his usual badger-like self, but the women ranged from looking one step in the grave down to a woman who looked like she was just ready for her high school prom. All were dressed for some kind of cocktail party, and I had a brief instinctual wish that Suze and I had snagged a second bottle of wine. Instead I handed over possibly the worst guest offering ever—a plastic ice chest filled with frozen peas and a take-out container full of blood.

"Did you get the full cup?" Valentine asked.

"It's a pint, just to be sure."

"Excellent. Always good to have some wiggle room." His smile made me make a mental note to send some kind of thank-you note to Catherine Celik. I wondered if Hallmark had something appropriate for this situation. "Now, if you and Ms. Hollis can just wait here . . . this might take a while." As if that were a signal, all of the witches in the living room stood up and picked up a potted plant. They'd been tucked discreetly to one side of the sofa, out of sight of the entryway, and I had the impression that each witch had brought their own. Thanks to my very brief career as part of a landscaper's grunt crew, I recognized a few of the plants—daisies and nasturtiums in small pots that could be tucked onto a kitchen counter, one larger pot of jasmine that reminded me of what I'd seen in Sassoon's examining room, and (for Ambrose) one huge outdoor planter of lilac that he lifted with a loud grunt. Without a word of acknowledgment to either Suze or me, they all headed into the kitchen. Sassoon gave us another encouraging gesture at the couch as they left, and then handed me the TV remote.

At my expression, he explained, "Really, I'm not kidding. This is going to take a bit. I've got cable, though, so you can watch whatever you want."

With that, he followed the others, closing the heavy wooden door to the kitchen firmly behind them.

I looked at Suze, and she looked back at me. Given that we'd been told to arrive after eleven at night, being told that this would take a while was not something I'd been hoping for. After a second, she leaned over and snagged the remote.

"Dibs."

Two hours passed. And despite the presence of cable, it was a long and very boring two hours. Television is not exactly at its best past a certain time, and the few things that I was willing to watch, Suze was vehemently opposed to, and vice versa. We ended up settling on a Hedy Lamarr movie on AMC, but while it did have the benefit of one of the queens of the silver screen, it unfortunately also had a really shitty script and plot. We'd also tuned in about halfway in, so there was a lot of confusion about what exactly was going on.

From the kitchen, there was the low murmur of conversation, several extremely weird smells, and once a cloud of sluggish gray smoke oozed under the door. It smelled remarkably like one lecture room at Brown where my film theory class had been scheduled immediately after a senior seminar for chemists. Chemists, as I had learned that semester, apparently did not make much use of deodorant, and the room would develop enough of a funk that it became common practice for whoever arrived first into the film theory class to immediately open all of the windows in the room, even on days when it was snowing.

It was shortly after one thirty in the morning, and the AMC host had just announced the title of the next movie to be shown (which I was personally bracing for, since when AMC hosts referred to a movie as "not one of the better regarded films" of a star's oeuvre, they were never kidding, and it was turd city ahead), when Sassoon emerged from the kitchen. He'd removed his tie, loosened his top buttons, and the sleeves of his shirt were rolled up to his elbows. He looked like a man who'd just spent four hours at the gym, and the muscles of his arms were actually twitching as I watched.

He gave me an exhausted but very proud smile. "All set," he said, and handed me a jelly jar.

I looked at it, feeling slightly underwhelmed. It was a normal-size Welch's Concord Grape Jelly jar (and I could tell, since that was what it said on the lid), halfway filled with a weird liquid that would look like blood for a minute, but then slowly start shifting color until it was the same color as the gray water that had been leaking out of the bottom of my kitchen sink until Jaison had fixed it. Once it looked like sludge for a second, the color started shifting back to red. On the surface of the liquid floated one of those fancy toothpicks, the kind that came with one end wrapped with a piece of colored cellophane and were meant to be used for party hors d'oeuvres. The green cellophane on this one was spinning lazily in a circle.

There was a long pause as we all stared at it. Suze broke that silence. "We waited two hours for this shit?" she said. I couldn't help but silently agree with her assessment.

Valentine looked distinctly annoyed. "Yes, two hours and six witches, and I made exactly what you need." He pointed at the jar. "Follow where the green end points you, and it will lead you to your murder weapon."

I peered at it again. Sassoon had clearly put a lot of effort into this, but I had to point out my observation. "Um, Valentine . . . it's spinning. That's . . . not quite helpful."

"Oh, that," Sassoon said. "Well, this is kind of on the edge of what we can actually do since it's almost getting too far from the physical body. So, this won't work until the sun is up." His tone implied that that should've been obvious.

I thought about it for a second, and still found it rather less than obvious. I'd also had a really long day that had not been improved by two hours in a strange living room, listening to Suze's running commentary about a movie that neither of us had enjoyed. "Why is the sun important?"

Sassoon gave me a look that let me know that he hadn't exactly had an easy day either. "Do you really want that answer, or are you just being annoying?" he asked.

"Fair enough," I conceded. I gave the jar another leery look as Valentine handed the empty ice chest to Suze. "Well, I appreciate you making the . . . thing. And I'll give you a call to let you know how it works out. You probably want to lie down or something, so, you know, Suze and I can just show ourselves out."

Somehow Suzume managed to restrain her summary comment until we were back on the sidewalk and heading for the car. "I'm starting to empathize with your sister's position on the witches."

"Maybe it's solar powered," I suggested, trying to pull the collar of my jacket high enough to warm up my nose. Suze glared at me. "Some things are! I had a calculator that had a solar-cell battery." It had actually been a pretty good calculator too. The battery had never died, and it had ended up being swiped by one of my series of asshole roommates.

Suzume did not look appeased. "It's one thirty. The sun rises . . ."

"Six thirtyish." Thanks to my dog-walking duties, I was unfortunately very familiar with sunrise times in November.

She rubbed her face as I unlocked the car. "I'm not getting up that early," she stated.

I yawned and began the process of starting up the Fiesta. I could see a thin layer of frost on the hood, and I knew that this was probably going to take at least four attempts. Cold weather was not a friend to an ancient engine. "We're hunting a killer, Suze," I pointed out.

"With a compass that only works if they haven't cleaned the murder weapon yet. Our killer either cleaned it already and we're going to be shit out of luck, or they haven't cleaned it yet, in which case they probably aren't planning to do it. So I'm getting up when I'm getting up."

I conceded to her logic. In my current brain-fogged state, it seemed like more than enough justification for a few extra hours of sleep. "Sounds like good reasoning to me." I glanced at the dashboard clock as the engine caught and perked up. "Hey, Wendy's has late drive-through hours. Let's get some fries on the way back."

By the time I'd driven Suze completely across town to her place in Silver Lake, then back to my apartment in College Hill, it was a quarter past two. Deciding that dental hygiene could wait a few hours, and enjoying the feeling of French-fry fullness in my belly, I toed off my shoes, chucked my pants and button-up shirt, and was asleep as soon as my head hit the pillow.

When I woke up, the sun was shining through my windows, and I had that weird knowledge that someone was watching me. Sure enough, it was Suzume. Dressed in an eye-searingly bright red turtleneck and blue jeans, she was straddling my hips in a somewhat concerning manner and staring down at me.

"Um, hi," I said cautiously. My tongue felt completely furred, and with regret I remembered last night's decision to forego toothbrushing.

"Hey." Her black eyes were unblinking. There was a short pause. "I brought over a carton of eggs."

I blinked, my sleep-muddled brain attempting to process both the non sequitur and her presence in my bedroom. "You drove yourself over . . . with eggs?" I rubbed my eyes and tried to gather more facts to clear this up. "What time is it?"

"Almost nine. C'mon." She poked my belly. "Time for eggs."

I dropped my hand and stared up at her again, comprehension sinking in. "You want me to make these eggs, don't you?" I wondered if this was some kind of bizarre relationship signal, or if Suze had woken up in her own bed and decided that the easiest way to obtain her breakfast was actually to drive over to my apartment and demand that I cook it for her.

"Well, I mean, I'm certainly not going to instruct you on the proper rules of hosting, but it *is* usually considered good manners to provide food for your guests." She smiled at me helpfully.

I sat up, scooting my hips back toward the headboard and out from under her, grateful that my winter bedding included a thick comforter and an old quilt. Suzume's presence had sent all of my partially remembered dreams completely out of my head, but it had definitely been enough to confuse the lower half of my body. I shifted myself carefully. "Last night you were all about a late start," I noted.

"Technically that was this morning."

She'd dodged the question. I eyed her suspiciously. "Normally a late start means I call you at around tenish."

Suze gave a lazy shrug. "So today it didn't." I noticed

the way her eyes darted around the room, scanning everything.

Looking for something. Abruptly I recognized the expression on her face and realized what was going on. Curiosity wasn't just the killer of cats—it also applied to foxes. "Under the bed, in the shoe box."

She immediately combat-rolled off the mattress and, after a moment of rustling, emerged with the magical jelly jar. We both stared at it. The liquid this morning was now an even swirl of red and gray, and the toothpick was no longer spinning, instead pointing in the direction of my framed poster of the original *Dune* movie. Suze moved the jar around a little, first in one direction, then the other, and each time the toothpick adjusted itself to continue indicating the same spot. "Huh." She raised her eyebrows. "Guess Sassoon wasn't useless after all." She set the jar down carefully on my bedside table, then looked back at me. "Now. Eggs?"

I kicked Suze out of my room long enough to pull on clothing for the day—I wasn't sure where the magical blood compass was going to lead us, but I decided that I probably couldn't go wrong with jeans and a sweater. My own stomach was indicating that eggs actually *were* a fantastic idea, so I headed straight to the stove, where Suze had helpfully positioned the open container. Suze was occupying herself by reading the newspaper (actually, I had strong suspicions that she was reading *Mrs. Bandyopadyay's* newspaper, and I made a quick mental note to drop it off in front of her door on our way out) and I gave her clothing a quick scan for any visible googly-eye attachment paraphernalia, but there were just too many places for her to stash them, and I gave up.

I tossed a few pats of butter in the pan and cracked six eggs into the mixing bowl. I paused for a second, considered, then tossed in another two. I had no idea how long it would take to track down a murder weapon with a blood compass, and I definitely wanted a full belly. While

I whisked the eggs, I remembered my days-old promise to my mother, winced, and called my sister. At least if I was cooking, I'd have a built-in excuse to escape the conversation quickly.

Prudence listened with surprising mildness to my update about the rusalka situation.

"That sounds fairly straightforward," she noted when I was done. "I'll ask Loren to look into whether any lakes in the territory have restrictions on Jet Skis. If that doesn't work, I'm sure there are some lonely places in Canada where we can stash her." There was a pause. Then she said, knowingly, "You could've done that yourself. Mother wanted you to call me, didn't she?"

"Um, yeah." I poured the mixed eggs into the pan, then started poking them with a spatula to scramble them.

"That's fairly typical of her." Prudence sounded mellower than usual today, though. I wondered if she was still distracted by Chivalry's dating life. "How are things going with the Kivela murder? Have you located an appropriate suspect yet?"

I winced at Prudence's clear acknowledgment that all she wanted was a scapegoat rather than the actual killer. "Some good progress on that, actually," I said. And with my conversation with Sassoon from yesterday about Prudence's attitude toward the witches still fresh in my mind, I noted, "I actually got a nice bit of assistance from a witch," and then filled her in about the blood compass.

"Really?" Prudence sounded impressed. "I didn't think old Rosamund had it in her."

"Oh, actually she was on vacation. This was the recommended substitute." And that was all technically true, I congratulated myself. Valentine Sassoon *had* been recommended . . . just not by Rosamund.

"Well, even vermin can be useful sometimes, I suppose. Broken clocks and all that nonsense." Prudence's interest was clearly exhausted.

I winced at her phrasing. Apparently warming Prudence up on the witches was going to take a longer campaign. The eggs were ready, and I said a hasty good-bye to my sister.

Suze shook her head at me as I brought the plates to the table. "Fort, this is like watching someone fall in love with a twenty-year-old cat that limps. Follow my advice and stay out of this. Your sister has had more than two centuries to build up this dislike of the witches—you aren't going to be able to do anything about it. Save yourself the trouble and don't even try."

"I was only telling her the truth, which was that Sassoon *was* useful." She gave me a patently disbelieving look, and I shoveled a huge forkful of eggs into my mouth in response.

Eight scrambled eggs disappeared from our plates with surprising speed, with Suze making a playful show of defending her share from me. I was still a little hungry even after we'd eaten all of them, and I regarded the last four eggs in the carton speculatively. Suzume followed my line of sight and snorted. "Jeez, Fort, you're a bottomless pit lately. I told you that the vegetarianism would do this—I bet your poor body is protein deficient."

"It's not that," I said, irritated. "My activity level is just a little up with all the dog walking." I checked my watch. "Come on, I'll grab a bagel for the road, and we'll see if we can figure out how to use a magical jelly jar blood compass."

Bundled up for the weather, and with my Colt .45 and Ithaca .37 stashed in a handy duffel bag, just in case the compass led us to the murderer along with the weapon, we settled ourselves into the Fiesta and pondered the compass.

"Hey," Suze suggested. "I'm figuring that unless the compass starts doing something wacky, we should just drive over to Matias Kivela's house and follow it from there. After all, the killer left out of the back sliding door—there's a shot that they just dumped the knife somewhere in the woods behind the house."

I nodded. "Sounds like a good plan," I agreed, and backed the Fiesta out of its spot.

"Oh, *now* you're listening to my plans?" Beneath her fleecy bobble hat, her expression of irritation should've looked comedic. It didn't, probably because I knew that she had at least one knife on her, and that since I couldn't see them, she was using fox tricks to hide them from me.

"Suze, I was not going to tell Mrs. Bandyopadyay that I saw local hooligans steal her newspaper, pursued them, fought with them, and liberated it." I merged into traffic.

"No, you told her the truth, and now I'm going to get geriatric stink-eye every time I walk by her door."

"If it makes you feel any better, Suze, I'm not sure she liked you that much even before she knew you'd snatched her newspaper."

"*To check the weather*, Fort," she protested loudly. "And with almost every intention of returning it."

"It's a dying industry. Just pay seventy-five cents and get your own damn copy. Look at it like throwing a few quarters in the Salvation Army bucket."

It was a weekday, but late enough into the morning that the majority of commuters were already at work, and the drive over to Lincoln went smoothly. We were, quite quickly, cruising in front of the beige craftsman that used to house the late *karhu*, and I reflected that this kind of commute was probably why the bears had settled in this area. I pulled the car up to the curb and peered out the window.

"The house looks empty."

"Should be," Suze said. "I made a quick call to the Celik ghouls this morning—the Kivelas have a two-day wake planned, and it started this morning. They're expecting just about every bear for the duration—they rented the biggest room the Celiks had, plus two side rooms for spillover. No one is going to be at this house."

We both looked at the compass. The green cellophane of the toothpick was now pointing down the street and a little to the side.

"Think we should park and hit the woods?" I asked.

"Cruise forward a little. If it swings all the way over toward the woods, then we'll get out. But the state park is a big place—I'd rather not do any extra walking if I can help it."

I could definitely get behind that reason. "Hey," I said. "Pull off your hat and sit up a little higher."

"What?"

"I'm going like ten miles per hour through a residential zone. I want to make sure that people see that there's also a woman in the car."

"Why?"

"So they don't panic and think I'm a pedophile," I grumbled.

Suze snickered and did as I asked, keeping her eyes on the compass. We inched down the street, past more little houses, and the occasional big one. I shook my head a little. My foster mother, Jill, had always found it incredibly annoying when new developers overbuilt on tiny lots, and I supposed that I had fully inherited that particular prejudice.

"Hey, the compass is swinging."

I pulled the Fiesta over to the curb and looked over. Sure enough, the cellophane was now pointing fully away from the street, and toward another of the houses that was on the state-park side of the road. It was one of those long one-level ranch styles, with light yellow siding and a brick foundation.

"We're only about ten houses down from Matias's house," I noted. "Think the knife is in the woods behind the ranch?"

"Or in that house," she said. "Maybe a neighbor war got out of hand?"

"Neighbors like the elves or like a Robert Frost poem gone wrong?" I drove down a few more houses before finding a parking spot for the Fiesta. If the killer lived in that house, I had no desire to park right the hell in front of it.

"Either could work." Suze patted her leg, and for just a second her fox trick lifted and I saw her long twelve-inch knife (fondly referred to as "Arlene") strapped to her calf, where the hem of her parka wouldn't interfere with her ability to draw it. I reached into the backseat and felt around in my duffel for my Colt, which I tucked securely in the shoulder holster that I'd put on before we'd left the apartment. Winter wasn't my favorite season (mostly due to the Fiesta's lack of a functional heating system), but I had to admit that it made carrying concealed weapons quite a bit easier than in the summer.

There were no cars parked in the driveway of the ranch house, but I took a quick peek in the window of its one-car garage as we walked up to the property. Empty. A long privacy fence surrounded the property, just like at Matias Kivela's. I raised my eyebrows at Suze, who was sniffing furiously.

"*Metsän kunigas,*" she said. "Either living here or visiting often enough that the scent is thick on the property."

The fence was not a little one—six feet high. We poked around cautiously, but there wasn't a gate, so the only way through was the house—or a hop. Suze crouched down on the ground, enough to give me a quick foothold to boost myself up with. As I scrabbled over the fence, I had the awful vision of a busybody neighbor looking out their window and then rushing to call the cops about a break-in. "You're masking us, right?" I muttered to Suzume.

"Don't worry, Fort. No one is seeing you huff and puff your way over that except me."

I grumbled a few choice phrases at her, but finally made it over. The yard was that dull brown that just about everything in New England turns in late October, with a bright yellow children's swing set and a few of those big plastic toys that people with little kids seem contractually obligated to litter around their property. At the edge of the yard were the tall trees of Lincoln Woods State Park.

From the other side of the fence, Suze tossed me the magical jelly jar, which I caught. Then I heard some scuffing sounds as she backed up, took a running leap, and got enough of her upper body over the fence to hook a leg and pop over.

"Nice," I complimented her as she brushed off her jacket.

"Eh. On four feet I could've just hopped it. How's the compass?"

I looked down. It had sloshed a bit during the toss, but as I waited, the fluid settled, and the toothpick began turning again. But instead of pointing at the woods, it was aimed directly at the house.

"Interesting," Suze said. We walked up the back patio to a sliding glass door, which she knocked loudly on. I looked at her and lifted my eyebrows—apparently the "stealth" part of our plan was being ditched. She ignored my expression and waited, then knocked again—this time really pounding hard. Another pause, then she smiled at me. "No one home."

"And if someone had been home?" I asked. "With their setup, I bet most people knock on the *front* door."

Suze was already kneeling, and she slid her lockpick kit out of one pocket. As she started picking through her small tools, she answered, "So we would've said that we'd gotten lost in the woods, and could we please use their phone." A few twists of her slender picks, and there was a small click. She smiled. "Everyone always cheaps out on the sliding-door lock."

"Probably because if someone really wants to get in, it's not exactly hard to just break the glass," I noted, following the kitsune as she slid the door open and walked in. We found ourselves in a combination kitchen and dining room. There were at least a day's worth of dishes piled haphazardly into the sink, and a woman's business jacket was slung over the back of a chair. Children's drawings papered the front of the refrigerator, and I had to step carefully to avoid the toys scattered around the floor.

Suze nudged a pile of bright purple DVDs decorated with animated characters with her foot. "Dora sign," she noted. "The kid in this house is little. Two to five, probably."

I checked the compass again. The toothpick was moving, now pointing us to the left. We walked to the side of the room, where there was an outside door. I flipped the locks and opened it. There was a pair of steps, which led down into a small laundry room, with a cement floor and a screen door on the opposite side that clearly led into the garage. This spot had probably started its life in the house as a possum-trot or a screened-in porch, and had been converted into a full laundry room.

The washer and dryer were shoved against the woodsside wall, and a folding table was across from it. Three overflowing laundry baskets were on the floor, with one filled with nothing but a very rancid collection of weird white fabric.

"Oh crap," Suze said as we eased into the room, slapping a hand across her nose. "Fucking cloth diapers." She made a low sound of disgust. "And someone's at least three days behind on the laundry." She pulled up the turtleneck of her shirt so that the fabric covered her face up to the eyeballs and gagged.

I lacked a kitsune nose, so my full experience of the

rank odor of baby poop was probably a bit less Technicolor than what Suze was currently suffering through, but there was something else in the room. I sniffed again, harder, and there it was, teasing me below the poop. It reminded me of being in a crowded room and catching the hint of an old girlfriend's favorite perfume. The compass was spinning now, not pointing, and I handed it over to Suze, who was still bitching loudly.

I followed my nose straight to the basket of dirty diapers.

"Fort?" Suze asked behind me, confused.

"Something's here," I said. "And . . . I think . . . no, it's definitely blood."

She appeared at my shoulder, red fabric still stretched over her nose, but now her dark eyebrows arched in surprise. I reached down and started tugging the diapers out of the basket and onto the floor, careful only to pull them by clean edges. I was two-thirds of the way down the basket and pulled away a particularly vile diaper (diarrhea had apparently been an issue that day) to reveal a long kitchen knife, with dried blood covering it from tip to handle. "There you are," I muttered.

Real surprise, and just a hint of concern, covered Suze's face. "You smelled that when I couldn't."

"Apparently my nose is more specialized than yours," I said, feeling uncomfortable. I reached up onto one of the shelves and found a clean, folded washcloth. Grabbing it, I used the washcloth to pick up the knife and extract it from its diapery nest. It was a solid knife, with a good heft to it—just like Caroline Celik had suggested, I could easily imagine using this to chop up an onion. Apparently someone had pictured something very different, though. I paused, and considered the knife and the room around me again. "Why would the killer leave this here? It hasn't even been cleaned."

Beside me, Suze shrugged. "Maybe they had to stash it fast." Then she tilted her head to the side and thought it through more carefully. "This house is messy, but it's not long-term messy. This is probably only a few days of clutter."

"Like the kind that would accumulate if the usual cleaners were distracted? Say, by the death of a close family member, and having to set up a funeral?"

"Or distracted by covering up that family member's murder?" She reached past the diaper basket and slid over a basket filled with dirty clothing. "Let's see who lives here." She picked the first item off the top, a small child's shirt decorated with another appearance of Dora the Explorer. Tugging the neck of her shirt down and away from her nose, Suze buried her face deeply into the shirt, inhaling heavily. After a moment she looked up. "One little girl, *metsän kunigas*." She dropped the shirt and pulled out the next item—a little girl's nightgown, decorated in teddy bears. ("For fuck's sake," Suze muttered. "Can they give the theme a rest?") She sniffed again. "A different girl, also bear, a little older than the first." Next was an adult woman's blouse. "Female bear. Don't know her. Too old to be the parent." She sniffed her way through another few pieces of clothing, some children's, some adult's, then snagged a cream camisole. She sniffed, and this time when she raised her head, she had a wide smile. "Ah. Now this one I've smelled in person. Dahlia."

"The *karhu*'s niece." It took a second for it to sink in, but the dots came together and formed an interesting picture. "The one Matias wanted as his heir."

"Maybe she decided she didn't want to wait around," Suze said.

I thought about it, but there was still a snag there. "Why stash the knife in her own house? She's had two days now to dump it."

Suze dropped down to her hands and knees, brought her face close to the floor, and started sniffing carefully around the room. She was usually in fox form when she did this, and I couldn't help but notice that the view was a little different when she was doing it as a woman. I forced myself to look at the ceiling. Unaware of my internal conflict, Suze began talking as she followed her usual grid pattern around the room. "Maybe Dahlia couldn't get a chance when she was alone? Or maybe she wanted a trophy?" There was a pause. Then I heard her getting to her feet. I looked back down to see her dusting off the knees of her jeans. "Apart from the clothing, the only one I smell in this room is the older woman. So she's the one who is here often enough to lay a scent that could stand up to that reek. I think she probably does the laundry."

I considered that. "You stash a murder weapon where you don't think anyone else would find it, or in a spot where only you go," I said, thinking out loud. I tried to remember what Chivalry had said about Matias Kivela's family when I'd seen him the other night. "Dahlia's mother is the *karhu*'s sister. Chivalry mentioned her— her name is Ilona." A useful snippet reemerged, and I got excited. "Apparently her grandfather wanted her to inherit, but Chivalry wanted her brother, because he thought Matias would be less trouble."

Suze nodded, immediately following where I was going with this. "So Ilona got passed over for the top job. Maybe she bided some time, and then took her chance to get her daughter in the captain's chair."

"Maybe they're working together on this," I suggested.

"Maybe," she echoed, and looked around, her forehead creased thoughtfully. "Or one did the murder, and the other learned about it after the fact. Or just one did it, and is keeping it secret from the other." Having worked through that big list of possibilities, Suze looked over at me and raised her eyebrows. "Sounds like something a nice joint interrogation would clear up."

I considered, then shook my head. "I'm not sure. Right now this is just circumstantial. They could go back to the old Ad-hene theory—say that an elf planted the knife where it could do the most damage." I paused, remembering Suze's earlier comment about the other Ad-hene, and my brain suddenly started running through that possibility. "Maybe that happened."

"I don't think so, Fort. Seems a little roundabout for the elves or the Neighbors, and I'm not sure what causing a ruckus with the *metsän kunigas* actually buys them, especially since the bears were quick to finger them. I think it's Occam's razor on this one. The knife is here because the killer lives in the house and decided to stash it rather than dump it."

There was definitely some reasonableness there, and I conceded with a nod. "Okay." A sudden thought occurred to me. "Suze, your nose is sharper than a bear's, right?"

"Absa-fucking-lutely." Suze was no fan of false, or even real, modesty.

"Would you be able to know that we were here?"

She shook her head immediately, setting the bobble on her hat jiggling. "I can't even tell that Dahlia and the kids were here other than their direct clothing, and they probably go through this room every day. Between the diapers, the dirty clothes, and the puddles of dripped Tide, plus it smells like she uses that utility sink for some regular bleaching, there's just too much going on."

I nodded. "Okay. So we take the knife with us. When the killer comes back for it, they won't know who has it, and who knows their secret. That'll put them on edge. We start by sitting tight and seeing if someone breaks— if we get a call that Dahlia has suddenly made a run out of the territory, we know she's the killer. Person identified, no need to kill a scapegoat, and we can send Prudence after her." I had to admit, that plan was particularly appealing to me because no one innocent got killed, and the killing of the guilty party would be handled by my sister rather than me.

"And if the killer sits tight?"

"The funeral is in two days—whoever stashed the knife will definitely come to check on it or move it before then. If she doesn't panic or identify herself, then you and I go to the funeral and see if either Dahlia or Ilona is looking suspicious and twitchy."

"Okay. But Dahlia's one cool customer, and her mom might be as well. What if they aren't doing us a favor and guilt-sweating?"

I shrugged. "Well, then we haul both of them into a room, put the knife down, and see if we can question it out of them." After all, according to television, that worked all the time with real crimes. And I wouldn't have to worry about anyone lawyering up either.

Suze considered, then grinned. "All right, I can get with that plan." She eyed the knife that I was still holding in the washcloth. "Let's get a plastic bag or something to carry that with."

We went back into the kitchen, both of us gratefully breathing in the scent of air that was free from the reek of baby diapers. Suze checked in a few of the cabinets and located a gallon-size Ziploc bag. She held it open for me so that I could dump the knife and its washcloth wrapping into it.

"Suze, not that I wasn't impressed by you sniffing clothing, but we could've just checked their mail." I pointed to the pile on the counter that I'd just noticed.

I received a very irritated look. "Well, now I've got their scents," she said with a confident and thoroughly superior air.

"Oh, of course." I paused, then indicated the pile. "So, should I . . . ?"

Suze glared. "Fine, check the damn mail." I shuffled through it—it was the usual mix of bills, junk circulars, catalogues, and offers from credit card companies, but it was enough to verify that there was mail addressed to both Dahlia and Ilona at this house.

"So Dahlia's mom lives here," I confirmed.

We did one quick check around the house. There were three bedrooms—one with purple walls, a child's bed, and a crib, which the girls apparently shared. Framed prints of Winnie the Pooh, Corduroy the bear, and Paddington Bear decorated the walls, prompting more irritated comments from Suze.

"Oh, just let it go," I told her. "It's kind of cute. I bet you wouldn't be complaining if there were fox pictures hanging."

"Of course I wouldn't. Foxes are fantastic. Roald Dahl based a whole book on that fact."

"And the problem with bears being . . . ?"

"They're stupid."

I sighed heavily. "Let's set the species-centrism aside and get on with this. Also, don't turn around—I just spotted a picture of Baloo the bear."

Suze was able to sniff and identify the next bedroom as Ilona's—it was another small room, with just enough space for an adult-size twin bed, a bureau, and a nightstand. The bureau was covered with framed photos. Most were of a Nordic-looking woman (clearly Ilona) posed with Dahlia and Gil at various ages. Another picture was more recent, judging by the heavy streaks of gray in her formerly blond hair and the iPhone sitting on a table, posed with two little girls who had inherited Dahlia's dark hair and skin. One large photo that was framed and hung on the wall looked like a wedding photo—I recognized Ilona, Matias, Dahlia, Carmen (looking about thirteen, and definitely in the awkward stage of puberty), plus a guy I didn't recognize with pale skin and light-brown hair—all lined up and flanking Gil, who was standing beside the mystery guy. He and Gil were in matching tuxes, with shiny new wedding rings glinting from their left hands. There were also several photos of Ilona and Matias at various ages, sporting some pretty impressive early

1970s hairstyles and generally looking like a tourism ad for Switzerland. I frowned at the pictures.

"Do you think you'd have so many pictures of a guy you were planning on killing?" I asked Suze, who was following behind me with a bottle of Glade air freshener that she'd found under the kitchen sink. She gave a few squirts into the air in general to cover up our presence.

"Sure, if I wanted to avoid looking like a suspect," she said. "These people are Finns. They can probably hold these kinds of grudges for years without letting on."

"I am not even remotely familiar with that cultural stereotype, Suze, and I think you just made it up."

The last bedroom was Dahlia's. It was a fairly standard master bedroom, though she hadn't bothered to make her queen-size bed this morning, and there were some clothes piled up on a chair in the corner. There was only one picture, this one of Dahlia and her daughters at the beach, framed and set next to the computer on her desk.

"Hey, who's the father of Dahlia's kids?" I asked.

"Beats me. I don't follow bear gossip. She probably just did what the *reasonable* kitsune do and shacked up." Suze sounded approving of that plan. Apparently the conversation with Keiko last night was still rankling.

"There was a wedding photo of Gil, though," I noted. "So the *metsän kunigas* do get married."

"Who knows, Fort. Maybe she and the dad broke up." Suze gave another squirt of the Glade, this one aimed just close enough to my face to give me the hint that Suze apparently thought that we'd gotten about all the information available, and it was time to make an exit. I conceded the point.

We let ourselves out the back slider, with Suze fiddling with her picks to pop the lock back into place. Then it was over the fence again, to the car, and then cruising out of Lincoln and back toward home.

"Okay, well that was a pretty productive morning." I

looked at the Ziploc bag now riding in the foot of the passenger side next to the still-spinning blood compass. "Hey, now that we're away from the diapers, can you sniff anything off that?"

Suze leaned down and opened the bag, being careful to only touch the knife with the washcloth as she pulled it out. She stayed leaning down, keeping the knife well below the line of the windows. Apparently giant knives covered in blood were something to be cautious about flashing when surrounded by cars on Route 146. She gave it a careful sniff, then shook her head. "Blood on the blade, but I'm not smelling anything from the handle."

"Is that normal?"

"On a murder weapon? Well, usually there's at least a little sweating when you knife someone seventeen times, so maybe the killer wore gloves." After that disturbing little insight into her own familiarity with murder weapons, she gave a shrug. "Know anyone who can check it for prints?"

"I was kind of hoping that you could."

She laughed. "Fort, I might be awesome, but even I have limits. And none of the kitsune decided to go into forensics, so you're shit out of luck on that. But I'll let my cousin Rina know that she totally let you down by going to cosmetology school instead."

"Okay, back in the bag," I said, disappointed. I had a strong moment of missing Matt McMahon, and wishing that there was some way that I could show up on his doorstep with a bloody knife and get him to figure out whether there were fingerprints on it, and if there were, what on earth to do with those prints. Of course, the odds of that situation were right up there with me buying the *Star Wars* prequels. I forced myself to stop thinking about Matt and focus on the problem at hand. "Maybe my family has some kind of person on payroll who does that. I can ask Loren Noka." It wouldn't surprise me if Loren Noka answered my query by revealing that fingerprint analysis was her personal hobby. She had that kind of air about her. I considered the idea, reminding myself that this time I was doing a sanctioned investigation, and that I supposedly had resources available to me. "Actually, I should probably talk to my brother about this one. Chivalry knows both Ilona and Dahlia—maybe he'll know which of them is a more likely murderer." I looked over at Suze, who was fiddling with the Fiesta's radio. "Ready for lunch?" My stomach had been letting me know for a while that it was *very* ready for lunch.

"It's eleven oh five in the morning," Suzume said flatly. "Start eating meat."

"My nutrition is fine!" I snapped defensively. I paused and forced myself to take a calming breath. Suze was a fox—a natural carnivore. She'd given me a weird look when I'd bought a side order of salad and another of asparagus for last night's doomed dinner party. She couldn't help her cultural predispositions. I changed the subject. "Do you want to swing down to Newport with me?"

"Doesn't sound like much fun. Just drop me off at my car, and you can call me later and fill me in if you learn anything helpful."

I couldn't quite blame her for skipping a visit to my mother's mansion, since it was almost an hour's drive each way and would probably eat up most of the day in between, though I couldn't help but feel a bit annoyed, given that I'd been forced to sit through *her* family's dysfunction just last night. It seemed like a bit of a double-standard for her to immediately pass on a helping of my familial crap.

I drove back to my apartment, dropped Suze off at her car, and then immediately hit the road for Newport. I stopped just outside of Providence to fill the Fiesta with gas, discovering as I did that at some recent point Suze had glued a pair of googly eyes to the inside of my gas tank flap. I shook my head, then went inside. This was my preferred gas stop on the way to Newport—not only because gas was usually at least a nickel cheaper than in the borders of Providence, but they also had a cooler filled with prepared lunches from a local deli, along with a lineup of meals that managed to have a vegetarian option that was a bit better than the usual gas station go-to of a bag of pretzels. I snagged a macaroni salad, a container of yogurt, and on my way to the register succumbed to temptation and tossed on a Little Debbie apple pie.

Since the inside of the Fiesta would not be markedly improved if a spill happened, I inhaled the macaroni salad and the yogurt while parked, tossing the containers in the outdoor trash and gnawing contentedly on the apple pie as I got back on the road and aimed myself toward Newport. I hit a little bit of congestion as all the drivers on their lunch break filled the road, but my time down remained fairly good. It was as I was crossing the Pell Bridge, my window cracked just enough for me to enjoy the smell of salt air and the sounds of shrieking seagulls without freezing, that I realized that I was hungry again. Not just hungry, but ravenous, as if the food at the gas station had been from last night rather than less than an hour ago.

I cursed as I felt my stomach actually rumble, and wondered whether I could've somehow contracted extra hunger cravings from being next to Keiko last night. I didn't usually come in contact with pregnant women, after all, and my resistance to whatever weird pheromones they emitted might be low. I snickered a little, wondering how quickly she would throat-punch me if I ever mentioned that theory to her, and reluctantly considered whether Suze was actually partially correct on her nutrition theory. I'd become a vegetarian two years ago, when I'd first started dating my now ex-girlfriend Beth and she informed me about her policy of not kissing any mouth that consumed meat (which I still couldn't entirely hold against her—after all, I had no plans to ever date a smoker), and I'd never actually sat down with a vitamin and nutrition chart to check my diet. Firstly, I was a vampire, and I had a strong feeling that feeding on my mother's blood was helping with my iron and protein intake. Secondly, I'd survived several years of college where my primary food groups had consisted of pizza and ramen noodles, and I had managed to avoid developing scurvy. But I'd turned twenty-seven in June, and for the first time I'd had a friend complain to me about acid reflux, so maybe this was some weird by-product of getting older.

Or maybe another weird quirk of my transition into becoming a full vampire meant that my stomach was returning to how it had functioned when I was a teenager—a bottomless pit that required at least five solid feeds a day. I definitely hoped it wasn't that—I had little desire to fund a return to my teenage eating requirements.

But regardless of why I was hungry, the result was impossible to ignore, and I pulled into the Bellevue Gardens Shopping Center and headed straight into my favorite greasy-spoon diner, the Newport Creamery. As another sign that the tourist season was well and truly behind us, I got a cheery wave and a "Be right with you, honey" when I stepped up to the take-out counter, rather than a snapped "All ice cream orders have to go to the outdoor window!" I snagged a menu and flipped to the sandwiches, wondering what exactly I needed to finally appease my belly.

I ate at the Newport Creamery often enough that I could've listed their vegetarian options from memory, but today I found myself fixated by the picture of the turkey sandwich. Vegetarianism had never been a particularly easy lifestyle for me—from an environmental standpoint, I certainly agreed that it made sense for people to reduce their meat consumption, and I was a supporter of people trying to at least have a meat-free day in their weekly menu, but I didn't object on a fundamental level to the consumption of meat itself. I'd gone meat free for Beth, but I had stayed meat free because it had helped me suppress my vampire instincts—at least, until my transition had begun at the beginning of the summer. I still ate eggs and dairy, so while I'd missed a few dishes (namely bacon), I hadn't felt terribly deprived before. There had been a few real moments of temptation, and I was certainly no stranger to the occasional backslide, but I'd never felt quite so fixated as I did at this moment, staring at the picture of the turkey sandwich, feeling my mouth fill with saliva, and picturing just how good that turkey would taste.

"Sir?" The waitress, a woman in her fifties with chemically assisted blond hair, was giving me a look that suggested that she was seriously considering calling over her manager. I blinked, and suddenly realized that my eyes felt weirdly itchy, and my vision was sharper than it should've been. My upper jaw was aching just a little, and there was a bubble of something cold and dark rising up in my chest. A shudder went down my spine as I realized that some instincts had been easing their way to my forefront while I'd been staring at the sandwich.

"Sorry, sorry. I missed breakfast this morning," I lied, forcing as much contrition into my voice as I could, and snapped the menu closed. That explanation seemed to relax the server, who gave me a commiserating smile, and we slipped into a comfortable server-patron patter about the harsh penalties of skipping breakfast.

While they were processing my order, I hurried into the bathroom and stared into the mirror. My pupils were huge, not quite enough to completely obscure the brown of my irises, but enough to make me look seriously drugged-up and creepy. My hands were shaking as I splashed water on my face, running my tongue anxiously over my upper teeth as I checked my canines for any changes. I rubbed my face hard with a handful of paper towels, then checked the mirror again. My pupils weren't normal yet, but they looked better than a minute ago. I panted with relief, balled up the paper towels, and threw them into the trash with a lot more force than necessary.

I definitely needed to talk with my brother. Since transition had begun, my vampire instincts had edged out during a few times of high stress, but unless getting a turkey craving was somehow my new stress threshold, this was neither normal nor okay.

I went back to the take-out counter and picked up my order, tipping the waitress as generously as my wallet would allow to try to make amends for inadvertently being That Creepy Dude. I didn't even wait until I was back in the Fiesta before I fished my veggie quesadilla out of the take-out bag and started to gobble it down. I ate it as fast as I could—not out of any desire to relieve my hunger or even any interest in the quesadilla itself, but just out of desperate hope that it would take the edge off whatever was bringing out my instincts.

My stomach felt uncomfortably tight when I swallowed the last of it, and gurgled slightly in protest at the speed of my consumption. I sat anxiously behind the wheel for a second, then tugged the rearview mirror down to check my eyes. Relief shuddered through me when all I could see was a completely normal-looking guy with melted cheese on his chin and shirt.

I cleaned off my face and dabbed at the shirt stain with a napkin, calming down slowly. That had been weird and freaky, but it was over now. I took a long sip of my chocolate Awful Awful and felt another bit of stress drain away. There was nothing about this situation that a great milk shake couldn't fix, I coaxed myself.

I put the Fiesta in gear and drove slowly down the street to my mother's mansion. My car had been built back when cup holders in cars were considered a luxury item for the rich, and I was holding my chocolate Awful

Awful in one hand while holding the strawberry Awful Awful I'd snagged for Chivalry between my legs. I was finally calm enough to start noticing my surroundings again, and I reflected that driving in November in a car with no heating while having a thirty-two-ounce milk shake concoction resting snuggly against my testicles was not precisely ideal.

Inside the mansion, I paused in the entry hall and reached inside me for my internal sense of my family. As always, my mother was the strongest beacon, and I could tell that she was upstairs in her room. Prudence was somewhere on the ground floor, but I tugged on the mental string that tied me to my brother and followed it up the grand main staircase and down the hall to the suite of rooms that he'd shared with Bhumika.

He'd felt me coming, of course, and my knock on his door was perfunctory as I walked into the main room of his suite. There were several bare spots on the walls where artwork that had been Bhumika's taste rather than his had been removed, and one sofa as well as a few decorative tables had also disappeared, probably to molder in my mother's extensive attics. The biggest change was botanical—Bhumika's passion had been breeding and showing roses, and it had not only resulted in the replanning of my mother's gardens, and in the construction of a conservatory greenhouse on one side of the mansion, but had also spilled over in a very big way into the rooms that Chivalry and Bhumika had shared. At the time of her death, their sitting room had been a near jungle of potted miniature roses, the smaller ones resting on tables while the larger ones sat on the floor and snagged your clothing if you passed too closely to them. Today, however, the room was nearly stripped of the pots, except for a cluster of them gathered in the center of the room, which Chivalry was currently studying.

My brother looked up at me. "Fortitude. This is a bit

of a surprise." His cheekbones were in even sharper relief today, and he was overall starting to make the term
heroin-chic spring unfortunately to mind, and I suddenly
felt uncomfortable about coming to see him.

"Yeah," I said awkwardly, and held the strawberry
Awful Awful out to him. Chivalry stared at it, and then a
ghost of a smile crossed his face, and for a second he
looked like my affectionate, amused, and indulgent older
brother again. I relaxed as he took the milk shake from
me and sipped it. "Well, I had a few questions about the
bears . . . and some other stuff." I wasn't quite sure how
to phrase a fear of my appetite without instigating another discussion of my dietary habits, and I decided to
get his thoughts about Dahlia and Ilona first.

"Ah, yes, the *metsän kunigas* murder," he said, but his
mind looked occupied by something very different from
the bears as he set the Awful Awful down on the table.
He stared at the collection of roses, each carefully housed
in an elaborately decorated glass mosaic pot, commissioned especially to give Bhumika's collection of roses a
bit of decorative continuity. "I'm sorry that I have not been
of more assistance." He was pacing around the roses now,
a weird, stalking motion that made my earlier discomfort
creep back up my spine.

"Chivalry, are you okay?" It seemed like a stupid
question to ask someone whose wife hadn't even been
dead for a month, but I also really didn't like the way he
was eyeing Bhumika's roses. "Is there anything I can do
to help?"

"I'm trying to figure out which of Bhumika's miniature
roses to keep." Now he finally sounded engaged with the
conversational topic, but it was too far to the extreme, and
he was almost manic. As he circled the plants, he reminded
me weirdly of a monologue scene from *Richard III* that I'd
seen in college. "She left a list of other rose fanciers who
she wanted plants to go to, but a lot of them chose to take

a full-size bush from the garden instead, and now I have two dozen."

From the hiss in his voice, apparently this was somehow an unpardonable sin. "It's a big house, Chiv," I said soothingly. "I'm sure we could find spots for them."

I don't think he even heard me. Instead Chivalry just paced faster, and his fists were clenching and unclenching in a way that would've made me very worried for the object of his fixation had these not been roses, which are notoriously difficult to throttle. "It was Bhumika's hobby. The outdoor gardeners already have their hands full with the new rose garden, and now they'll have to be permanently taking over the plants in the conservatory as well. Mother won't say anything, of course, but I don't feel it's fair that she suddenly finds herself with a pair of rosebushes in each room disrupting her decor. And they require constant maintenance, which is not something that I want to ask the indoor staff to have to take on just because I don't want to throw a plant away."

He kept talking, but as he became more worked up and angry, I realized that it was spilling down that thread that had connected us for my whole life, rolling over me as if I were at the beach and had suddenly been caught by a wave that I hadn't seen coming. It was much stronger than I was, pulling me down and holding me in a place that was somewhere cold and powerful. I could still see Chivalry's mouth moving, and see him walking, but everything was moving very slowly. Meanwhile I was suddenly aware of everything around me—the heartbeats of all of the staff as they moved through the house, the smell of every place in this room where a human had been in the last hour, and the minute sweat from their skin on everything they had touched.

I wasn't okay, not by any stretch of the imagination. I tried to tell my brother, but as I struggled to push the words past my suddenly bone-dry throat, everything inside of me fixated on the door, and the knowledge that one of those vulnerable, taunting heartbeats had come closer and was now just behind that flimsy piece of wood.

My body turned without my brain's permission, and the seconds stretched as the handle of the door turned and the mechanism released.

"Mr. Scott, I was just speaking with Patricia, and she says that her aunt actually—" James's voice filled the room.

But my mind was gone, all rational thought crushed by the throbbing of instinct. The man in the doorway was shorter than me, the thinning gray hair and the stoop in his body indicating age and weakness, but the flush in his cheeks advertised how hot and sweet his blood would be.

I jumped him, knocking him over with pathetic ease, using my weight and body to pin him to the floor. I wrapped one hand in what was left of his hair and yanked his head to one side, exposing all of that pale, pale skin and those veins that jumped and pulsed with blood. The man's breath was shallow and fast, whistling high and nasal, but he stayed completely limp.

Someone said something, a word, and a dim voice in the back of my brain told me that this was my name. I kept my prey immobilized. It wasn't fighting, and I had it—it couldn't get away, and I looked toward who had spoken.

That was my brother, I realized through the fog. That was my brother, crouched down, with both hands wrapped around the edge of that table as if it were a life raft and he were adrift in an ocean. His eyes were black, and his fangs were fully extended.

"Fortitude," he repeated, his voice hoarse. Sweat was dripping down his forehead. I stared at him—he was trying to tell me not to do something, I remembered, but I didn't know what. The fog in my mind started thinning.

Then Chivalry made a noise, a high, hungry noise, and for a moment leaned forward like a dog scenting dinner. He caught himself almost immediately, pulling himself back, but that moment was enough, and the fog came rolling back in and I was gone again. Everything was gone, except the thought that he was bigger and stronger than me, and he might take my prey away—but it was mine, *mine, mine*, and I would take as much as I could before he stole it.

There was resistance under my teeth, but I gnawed through it, and then there was a coppery taste in my mouth. It was familiar and yet strange, thinner than what I was used to, and as I got my first good swallow, it tasted *wrong*, and sour. I paused, unsure. There was a high, frightened panting in my ear—my prey. But it wasn't moving or fighting back, and I hesitated, running my tongue cautiously over the wet puddles, not understanding why it was so sour when I knew that it should've tasted different, better. I wasn't sure whether to take another bite—maybe I'd done something wrong, or maybe this prey was the problem and I needed to find another—

Then there was a hand wrapped around my throat, and I was pulled back and off my prey. I grabbed for it, but the hand squeezed my neck in an iron grip, and I had to let go. I thrashed my hands angrily at my assailant, but I already knew—that binding thread in my mind told me—that it was my sister.

"James, run downstairs immediately and get yourself bandaged up," Prudence snapped. My prey moved, *escaping*, and I automatically lunged to stop it, but I couldn't break away from Prudence. Her left arm was wrapped tightly around my waist, and her right hand moved from my throat to my forehead, pinning me against her. "No, little brother," she crooned, and the sound of her voice began cutting through the fog, driving it out of my mind.

Reason rushed back, twinned with horror. I turned my head, terrified, and I saw my brother still pressed against the table, but his upper body was turned away from the door, and he'd slapped a hand across his eyes. I understood suddenly why he'd done that—so that he wouldn't be able to see James escape, and wouldn't have had to fight the urge to snatch at running prey.

"I attacked James, Prudence. Oh my God, I attacked," I started babbling, but then stopped as fire streaked through my body, cramping my stomach so painfully that my legs buckled under me. "Something's wrong," I managed to whisper.

My sister was already moving, hauling me bodily as I hung in her arms, unable to move or help her, unable to do anything except try to pull my body tighter together in some animal urge to huddle around the screaming agony in my belly. Prudence half pulled, half carried me into the bedroom of Chivalry's suite, and she slammed the closed door to the bathroom with her shoulder hard enough that the lock splintered and the door flung open, but it was too late, and I was already vomiting. I vomited on the floor, and on myself, and on the tile as Prudence continued to yank me, and then finally in the toilet as she pulled the lid up for me. I was vomiting and I wasn't stopping. It was continuous, a deep, awful retching as if a hand were trying to shove my guts up and out of my mouth. My eyes were closed from the force of it, and my nose was running. Every part of me was soaked in sweat, and still I threw up, and threw up.

Prudence's one hand was on my forehead, holding me in place, and I could feel her other hand stroking my back as each retch ripped through me. "I know, Fort; I know," she whispered in my ear, and there was real sympathy in her voice. "It hurts; I know it hurts. Don't fight it."

Then I could hear Chivalry's anguished voice from the doorway. "I'm sorry, Fort; I couldn't stop you."

"Sniveling won't help," Prudence snapped. "If you want to do something useful, go get Mother."

I puked again—there was no more food now, just bright yellow bile that felt like it was ripped out of me, and I managed to gasp, "What, what," and then I was vomiting again.

Prudence's hand tightened on my forehead. "You're too young for human blood, Fortitude. Your body can't handle it yet."

And then I puked again, and everything went black.

I was in my old bedroom when I woke up. I felt empty and wrung out inside, and as if I'd just gotten over a two-week bout of the flu. Even opening my eyelids felt like lifting weights. My bedside light was on, but a glance out my window showed that it was fully dark—I'd slept for hours. I tried to lift my head, but dropped it back onto the pillow when the movement made my skull feel ready to split open like an old melon.

I closed my eyes again, trying to gather my strength. As minutes passed, I became aware of the susurrus sound of pages being turned. Gritting my teeth, I turned my head to the left and forced my lids open again. Prudence was reading the *Wall Street Journal* while ensconced in her favorite Louis XVI armchair—the one that normally resided in the family sitting room. I blinked for a moment—the idea of my sister sitting by my bedside was discomforting. The fact that she'd required her favorite chair to be carried up a flight of stairs and down a hallway was oddly reassuring—at least I knew that this was still Prudence.

My throat was dry and very painful, but I managed to rasp out, "Is James okay?"

Prudence closed and folded the newspaper with precise movements before meeting my eyes and giving a measured nod. "James has worked on the estate since he was a young man," she said. "Fortunately he kept his head when you attacked him, and stayed passive."

"That was a good strategy?" I croaked.

"Very much so. He needed stitches, but he'll be fine." I couldn't suppress a shudder at the visceral memory of his flesh under my teeth, and Prudence's bright blue eyes sharpened. "I know what you're thinking, Fortitude.

Don't beat yourself up over this one. Your body is changing, and these things happen."

"These things happen?" I echoed, disgust and venom filling me. I tried to push myself into a sitting position, ignoring the jagged claws of pain that shot through my skull, though it made my vision go spotty. I felt Prudence beside me, tucking a few extra pillows behind me for support. When the pain passed, I looked down at myself curiously. I was in a T-shirt and sweatpants, but they were too loose on my frame to be anything that I owned. I realized that I was wearing Chivalry's clothing.

Prudence settled back in her chair, and waited. I could feel her intense stare, and though I tried to resist, eventually the charged silence in the room got to me and I turned to meet her eyes. Once I did, she gave a small nod. "I attacked two women during my transition. One was a friend of mine. I was fifteen, and we were looking at dress patterns when it happened. She was dead before Mother could reach me." I had to look away from the stark honesty on Prudence's face, but she continued relentlessly. "Chivalry attacked five—four of them when he was nineteen, and two of those died. I'm amazed this hasn't happened before with you, given the way that Mother has put off your transition."

"What's happening to me, Prudence? No one will tell me what is happening."

"You are becoming what you were meant to be, little brother," she said. "There is no more mystery than that."

This was worse than the way everyone had held out on the truth of sex for so long, until when I finally got the whole story in eighth grade, I'd been certain that the entire adult world was still holding out on me. "If it's so self-evident, then why can't you just tell me?"

"That lies with Mother." She paused, and a thread of irony entered her voice. "And I have no plans to defy Mother again on this issue."

I glanced down automatically at her leg. Tonight she

was wearing a pair of light camel-colored trousers, and I noticed that the heavy brace was gone, replaced with just a few Velcro straps. "It's looking better," I said cautiously.

She nodded. "I am forgiven." She touched her leg lightly, on the spot that had been broken so many times over the last month, then looked up at me. There was something in her expression that was too complicated for me to understand. She leaned closer to me and touched my left arm very carefully with one finger. "It can be hard to control your instincts during the change, Fortitude. That is surely apparent after today."

I tried to explain. "I was so hungry . . . but it wasn't really bad until I drove over the Pell and was in Newport. And even then I was holding on . . . until I saw Chivalry."

She understood. "Close contact with me and Chivalry helped you before, but not now. Chivalry has no control to give right now, not when he has pushed himself so close to starvation." Her voice became extremely serious. "I spoke with him earlier. He has agreed to avoid you until he finds a new woman."

"Why won't he feed until he finds a new wife?"

She lifted her finger from my arm and pressed it lightly against my mouth. Her face was close to mine, and the look in her blue eyes was a snake's, and I froze like a tiny bird. "Because he is foolish, unreasonable, and a romantic. But he seems to be finally focusing in on someone, so hopefully this overblown sentimentality will be over soon." She relaxed, that dangerous expression sliding away, and she pressed the back of her hand against my forehead in that universal gesture that all women seemed to possess that was capable of making any person instantly feel like a toddler. "How are you feeling?"

"Like the Hulk used me as a lawn chair."

She shook her head over my reference. " 'Not well,' would've sufficed. Let's bring you to Mother."

There was a collapsed wheelchair in the corner that I recognized as Bhumika's. Prudence brought it to my bedside and set it up. I was discomforted to discover that not only was it necessary, but that Prudence had to practically lift me into the chair, with me offering little more than token assistance. I was panting and every nerve ending was on fire by the time I was settled, and then Prudence pushed me out of my room, down the empty hallway, and into Madeline's suite.

Prudence rolled me through Madeline's empty sitting room and into her bedroom, where my mother sat propped up in that massive bed, the covers tugged up to her waist, a beautifully embroidered bed coat on, and a Kindle in her hands. But there was no disguising the way the skin on her face seemed to hang from her bones, and the exhaustion and delicacy that emanated from her.

She looked up as we entered. "My poor little sparrow," she said, and I could hear the regret in her voice. "I am so sorry that you had such an unfortunate experience, darling. It's my fault—your body needs more help right now, and I stopped you the other day before you were done."

There were things that I wished I could ask her, but just sitting in the wheelchair had honestly exhausted me enough that all I really wanted was to lie back down and sleep for at least a week. Prudence rolled my chair right next to the bed, and my mother didn't hesitate before slicing her wrist and presenting it to me. With the events of the day clearly seared into my brain, I wasn't going to object—I wrapped my hands around her limb and clamped my mouth around the cut, drinking as quickly as I could.

The moment her blood touched my tongue, part of me relaxed. This was the consistency, the taste, and overall, the *power* that I'd missed before; this was what had made even my raw instincts pause in confusion during my attack on James. I shivered in relief, knowing that this would not hurt me as the other had, and that it would also protect others from me. It was the memory of James's terror as I jumped at him, and the painful memory of my own animalistic glee at the sight, that had me gripping my mother's arm hard as I drank as much as I could.

Every mouthful of my mother's blood soothed the ache in my throat, and as it slid down, I could feel the still-painful clench of my gut relax. The headache making my eyeballs throb eased a bit more with each swallow, and the feeling that my whole body was one shin that had slammed into a dresser dulled into a distant throb.

It was my mother's own body that stopped me this time. After several minutes, each mouthful became smaller, until I felt what I had never felt before—the flow of blood ceasing, and the flesh of my mother's wrist knitting itself together while I still fed.

I paused, then pulled away. Madeline's face was gray, and she was visibly shaking from the effort.

"Mother?" I asked, unable to hide my fear.

She didn't try to normalize the situation or comfort me, simply lying backward into her throne of pillows and closing her eyes.

"Go to bed, my little sparrow," she said thinly. "I've asked Prudence to give you a small demonstration tomorrow. It's clearly time."

Prudence was wheeling my chair out of the room before I had a chance to protest. I craned my neck back at her and stared into my sister's best poker face.

"Is she going to be okay?"

She sighed, then looked down at me, those blue eyes serious. "For now, Fort."

We left it at that. Back in my room, I found that even with my mother's blood coursing through me, I needed my sister's help to get back into bed. Once I was settled, Prudence tucked the wheelchair back in its corner and leaned over to turn off the bedside light. The warm yellow glow was replaced by the icy moonlight from my window, and the darkness finally gave me the strength to ask my sister what I'd been wondering since I woke up.

"Prudence, why are you being so nice to me?"

"You are my brother," she said simply. "Whether I hate or love you, that fact will never change, and what ties us together can be broken only by death." Her voice softened, not in emotion, but just in volume. "Now go to sleep."

And I did.

Sunlight was streaming in through my window when a rap on my door woke me. The door cracked widely enough that I could see Loren Noka's face. It took a long second to remember that I was in my old room at the mansion, rather than my apartment.

"Loren?" I blinked, trying to get my muzzy thoughts in order. Then everything came back, and I sat bolt upright in the bed and scooted back until my spine smacked against my headboard, letting me know that there was no way to put even more space between the two of us. The image of James's fearful expression as I'd tackled him to the ground filled my mind, and I stuttered, "Listen, I'm not sure you should be—"

"It's all right, Mr. Scott," she said, and pushed the door the rest of the way open. "I brought your breakfast." In her hands was a wooden bed tray, with a silver cover, like hotel room service.

That was definitely not what I'd expected, and I was derailed for a second. "Breakfast?" I parroted, feeling like an idiot. That was definitely not in Loren Noka's job description. Also, given that I normally felt distinctly overwhelmed and outclassed when I was around Loren Noka, the situation was definitely not helped by having her standing in my childhood bedroom in a business pants suit (navy blue today), holding my breakfast, while I sat in bed in pajamas that weren't mine.

For a second I wondered whether this was actually just the start to a stress nightmare.

While I was pondering that, Loren Noka had busied herself by settling the tray down over my lap. "Now, I was informed by the kitchen staff that this is your favorite thing to eat when you're sick." She drew back the silver lid with a bit of a flourish, and laid out in front of me was the go-to comfort breakfast from my teen years — oatmeal, a small container of honey, toast, and a cup of tea.

"Oh, that was really nice of them. It really does look good. . . ." If there was any one thing that was tempting about moving back into my mother's mansion, it wasn't the money or the comfort; it was the cooked and prepared meals. There was a residual soreness throughout my body, and my stomach still had a hint of uneasiness, but the smell of the fresh oatmeal wafting up to me, and the honey already slightly warmed and ready to be poured over it, made me feel cautiously optimistic. This didn't solve the problem of Loren Noka standing over me, and I said, "But you have so many important things to do, and I'm sure carrying my breakfast up isn't one of them. I mean, really, Ms. Noka—"

"Loren," she interrupted.

"Um, what?" I peered up at her, which was a very long, intimidating view, up a very formidable bosom.

"You called me Loren, Mr. Scott," she repeated patiently. "We work together. It's okay if you call me by my first name."

"I don't know. It feels like being asked to call the queen of England 'Lizzie.'" A small crinkle of amusement played across her face, and I relented. "Okay, I can try to get used to it. If you can start calling me Fortitude."

She frowned. "Really, I'm not sure that's appropriate at all."

"Then I guess I can start using Ms. Noka again?" The frost in her expression probably made my oatmeal drop a few degrees. "Really, every time you say 'Mr. Scott,' I feel like Chivalry is standing behind me."

Loren still didn't look particularly happy, but she seemed to acknowledge the point. "Fine, I suppose." Then she reached up and removed a bag from her shoulder, which I hadn't even noticed thanks to my fixation on breakfast. It was one of those expensive store bags, made of stiff paper and with fabric cords for straps. "Speaking of, your brother sent along some clothing for you to wear today."

"What happened to what I was wearing?" She gave me a significant look. "Ah, right. Puke." I looked at the bag now resting on my legs. Even the font of the store logo looked expensive. Chivalry's attempt to reform my clothing habits was ongoing, but I had to at least try to weasel out of it, and I appealed to Loren. "He does know that I can just run those through the wash, right? Even the sneakers? I mean, knowing the staff around here, I bet that probably already happened."

Loren just arched one terrible eyebrow. Clearly there was no help from that quarter. Though given her commitment to business dress, she might actually be in my brother's corner on this one. I sighed and tugged the bag closer. "He picked these out himself?" It was a rhetorical question—of course my brother would never trust someone else to pick out my clothing. One of the weird things about Chivalry's age was that he came from a time when gentlemen apparently spent a serious amount of time primping. The modern-day metrosexual would be completely unprepared for one of my brother's discussions about picking the right colors for your skin tone. That was why I was surprised by the contents of the bag—a long-sleeved gray shirt, jeans, and shoes. It was a high-cost recreation of what I normally would've worn. That was a clear message. "These are clothes that I'd actually wear, rather than what he'd like me to wear. He's feeling guilty, isn't he?"

"I certainly wouldn't presume to say." Loren pursed her lips.

I gave an even heavier sigh. The tags had already been clipped out of the clothes, so I didn't even have the option of trying to return them at a later date. At least I wouldn't have to face the visual proof that my brother had probably paid an average family's weekly grocery bill for a long-sleeved T-shirt. I remembered the sound of my brother's voice last night, when he'd been apologizing for being unable to stop me from attacking James, and a shiver ran through me. If it made Chivalry feel better to replace my clothing, then it really didn't make much sense to keep fussing about it. "Fine." Though having Loren standing there was still feeling awkward, and I looked back up at her. "Of course, now I feel even worse. Shouldn't you be orchestrating the entire Scott empire, rather than delivering me clothing?"

"If it makes you feel better, I can multitask," she said dryly. "Gil Kivela has left a rather impressive number of highly irritated messages. He apparently feels strongly that he should be given an update on how the investigation is going."

"Interesting," I said, meaning it. If I ignored the part where I was in my pajamas with my breakfast balanced on my lap, this could almost be a normal work conversation with Loren. "Anything from his sister, Dahlia?"

"Nothing."

"*Very* interesting. Well, please tell Gil that I'll see him tomorrow at the funeral, and I'll give him an update on things then."

"Excellent." She gave a small nod. "I'll leave you to your breakfast."

"Thank you, Loren," I said. Ugh, it still felt like an offense against nature to call her by her first name.

She smiled. "You're very welcome, Fortitude."

As she turned to leave, a thought occurred to me. "Oh, one last thing."

"Yes?"

"You wouldn't happen to know how to take finger-prints off a knife, would you?"

Her mouth quirked slightly. "I can see if there are in-structions online. But you do realize that even if I some-how was able to manage it, we don't have any of the equipment necessary to use those to narrow down an identity?"

I sighed. "Maybe we can ask my mother about turning the billiards room into a CSI lab."

"I'll draft a memo," she said dryly.

Loren left, and I poured the honey over my oatmeal, drizzling it the way I had in high school—into the em-blem of the *Star Trek* Federation. I took a bite, and felt it slide down my throat and into my belly, practically ema-nating nostalgic goodness. I waited one more minute, then said, "You can come in, Prudence. I know you're standing out there." I'd felt the pulse of her presence as soon as my brain had managed to organize itself.

My sister walked calmly into the room, as if she hadn't been hanging out in the hallway waiting to see if I was about to attack someone again. "You're looking much better this morning, little brother."

I ignored the comment. The truth was, even that small leftover achiness was fading somewhat, and I felt almost back to normal. Aside, of course, from the horrifying memory of attacking James and having to be pulled off him like in one of those videos of circus animals gone amuck. "You were waiting to see if I was going to attack Loren?" My temper started to fray, and I dropped my spoon back into my oatmeal, ruining the honey drizzle.

"It was very unlikely, Fortitude, but it seemed best to make certain that you were in command of yourself again."

"Did you let her know that she was your canary in the mineshaft?" Prudence just smiled. I shook my head—of course Loren must've known. Not because my sister told her, of course, but how could she not have known? I wondered what kind of discussion in the staff room had resulted in Loren volunteering (knowing her, it would've been volunteering, not being deputized) to bring in my breakfast and find out whether last night had been the start of a pattern. "So what exactly is this demonstration that you're supposed to give to me today?"

Her smile widened, and she nodded down to my breakfast. "Best eat while it's still hot, Fort." Her blue eyes flicked over to the clothing bag, and a small look of approval passed across her face. Her preference was to complain about my clothes rather than overtly try to redress me, but Prudence also had high sartorial standards that I consistently managed to underperform against. "And don't dawdle. We have an appointment."

She left. As I hurried through my breakfast, eating as fast as my stomach indicated it was comfortable with, I reflected that it was typical of Prudence to tell me that we had an appointment, but not *when* that appointment was.

We drove to Prudence's tidy town house in South Portsmouth, the next town over from Newport. I was feeling well enough to drive, so I followed my sister's Lexus, and took a small amount of pleasure in tucking the Fiesta next to that gleaming red automotive masterpiece on my sister's pristine asphalt driveway. The Fiesta had been leaking oil lately (okay, for a while), and I had a feeling that my sister would be remembering my visit for some time after the Fiesta marked its territory.

I followed my sister into her house. It was a three-story house, the first floor devoted to her garage and storage, so I followed her up the stairs to her main living area. We passed through her living room, decorated in modern lines in creams and whites, which was probably meant to look clean but went too far and just looked sterile and forbidding. Or maybe that was the look she was actually going for. We ended up in her kitchen, which was more white, broken up this time by the occasional stainless steel appliance. Unfortunately this just increased my impression of being in an alien examination chamber. Prudence didn't even stop to offer me a drink, instead crossing straight over to a tall white-doored pantry.

"Mother has babied you far too long, Fort," she said, picking through extra bowls, an electric mixer, and similar accoutrements of food preparation. "I first saw this done when I was barely six."

"What are we doing?" I had the feeling that she was not about to show me how to bake a cake.

"I'm going to show you how I feed." She emerged from her pantry with a beautiful wooden box. It was rosewood, carefully oiled, with no metal hinges, just wooden joints. She set it on the kitchen island between us and opened it, revealing an interior that had been lined with black velvet, with specially made sections to hold each of the items inside. I stared at those items, which in a kitchen setting really should've looked innocuous, but instead looked, thanks to the presentation and my knowledge of my sister, extremely creepy. There was a large silver bowl, marked on the inside with concentric circles, each numbered, about the size of the Pyrex bowl that I used to hold chips during a party. Beside it, each in its own nestled spot, were a number of wickedly sharp knives—the blades short but slightly curved, their handles silver to match the bowl and decorated with carved flowers. Tossed inside the bowl, casually and in a small plastic Baggie, were a bunch of rubber ties, the kind that doctors used during blood drives.

It was a lot to take in.

"I know we're vampires and all, Prudence, but . . . isn't this going just a little too far?" I pointed at the bowl, wondering if focusing on the aesthetics of the situation would help give me a few minutes to figure out exactly how I was feeling at the moment. On the one hand, my family had been extremely closed-mouthed about giving me any information about my transition, and that ignorance had nearly gotten someone killed last night. So a big part of me felt extremely relieved that some answers were apparently going to be forthcoming at last. However, there was a part of me, the part that had spent so many years pretending to be human, that acutely wished that I were anywhere but here in this moment.

Prudence gave an irritated sigh, looking offended on behalf of her box of horror. "Fort, this is a set of bleeding instruments. I know it's hard to understand now, but for hundreds of years bleeding was as common as telling someone to take an aspirin. This set is very similar to the one that George Washington owned." Her mouth gave a small, ironic twist, and she looked amused at some internal thought. "We'll just try not to follow his example with its use."

I stared at her blankly, not following the reference.

Now Prudence rolled her eyes broadly and looked extremely put upon by my inability to follow her cutting-edge references to one of the founding fathers. "He was drained of eighty ounces of blood in a thirteen-hour period. Not surprisingly, he died. Typical doctors—you were practically safer not calling them in those days." Her voice turned sharply irritated. "Didn't you learn any history at all?"

This was an older, familiar argument. Both Prudence and Chivalry were often decrying my lack of knowledge of tiny minutiae that had been dropped off school curriculums a century ago in favor of fitting in more relevant information. "In fairness, Prudence, they had a pair of world wars to cover, to say nothing of Korea and Vietnam." These were events that my siblings, of course, had lived through. Playing Trivial Pursuit with my family was extremely frustrating.

"I suppose," Prudence grumbled, then returned to instructor mode. She pointed to the big silver bowl. "Now, this is the bleeding bowl. These little darlings are called lancets." Her finger hovered over one of those wickedly sharp implements, and she glanced at me. "I have the rest of the set somewhere, but I really don't think it's necessary to break out the scarificators, the fleams, or the cupping syringe."

"I agree with that assessment." Just the names sounded horrifying enough.

Prudence reached under the kitchen island, where there was a small built-in wine rack, completely filled. She removed a bottle and popped the cork expertly.

"What's *that* for?" I asked suspiciously. Had wine been another required item in bleeding kits? I wondered for a moment if my sister knew about modern-day methods of sterilization, like neatly packaged alcohol swabs.

She gave me a withering look, and I wondered just how much of my thought process had been showing on my face. "*This* is a 2005 Bodegas Roda Cirsion, and it needs to breathe before being served."

"Really, Prudence? It's like nine in the morning. We're in alcoholic territory right now." And unlike Lilah, Prudence definitely didn't have unemployment as an excuse.

The sound of the doorbell interrupted what I'm sure would've been an exceptionally cutting conversational riposte. Instead she gave a little huffy sigh. "Early. Eager little thing."

Following her down the stairs, I watched as she ushered in a man who, I was quickly informed, was Jon Einarsson, one of the young stars of her company's legal department who had come over to discuss a few financial issues with her. Dressed in an immaculate gray suit, Jon was tanned, blond, and almost disgustingly fit and healthy. He had the slightly squarish, blunt good looks of a former frat guy who had done well and was on his way to doing even better. Prudence ushered us all back up to her living room, where we all settled on her white, expensive, and shockingly uncomfortable matching love seats. Jon wasted no time in flipping open his briefcase, removing a set of file folders, and proceeding to explain to my sister a series of financial options that I found completely incomprehensible—though I was able to pick up enough references to off-shore companies and other things that really seemed like they *shouldn't* be legal. Had I not recently slept for almost twenty straight hours, I would've passed out from boredom. This was worse than watching one of those foreign films where all people did was sit at a table, smoke cigarettes, and have a conversation in French, without subtitles. I wondered if Dan was going to start sounding like this in another two years. It was a frightening thought.

After twenty minutes, which I knew because Jon Einarsson was sitting conveniently under Prudence's large art deco wall clock, my sister thankfully interrupted him. "How rude of me not to offer you a drink, Jon," she said. "My brother and I will fetch some refreshments." Jon opened his mouth, but it had clearly been an order rather than a request, and all he could do was snap his jaw closed again and shuffle his papers around a little as my sister and I left the room.

Prudence set three wineglasses on the kitchen island. They were hand-blown, with just a single thread of color curving from the base up the stem. Each glass had a different color—blue, green, and red. Prudence selected the red glass, and placed it in front of her. Then, very matter-of-factly, she selected one of the lancets from her box and made a quick, deep slice across her left palm. She positioned the glass under her hand, and allowed her blood to drip into it, slowly filling up the bottom of the glass.

"I really don't like where this is going," I said, feeling like it was somehow important that I at least make some token protest.

"Hush. And grab me one of those paper towels."

Her blood continued to flow. It wasn't as dark as my

mother's, I noticed, but it was definitely a bit more of a dark raspberryish hue than a human's would've been, and I realized to my horror that I was actually echoing the language used on the back of the wine bottle label. Prudence continued to let her blood flow until the glass was nearly half full, then pressed the paper towel that I'd handed her against the cut, blotting the wound.

"Pour the wine, Fort."

I wasn't happy, but at this point I was pretty much committed to seeing exactly what the hell went on during a vampire feeding. After all, it was somewhere in my not-too-distant future. As I poured, however, I wondered why this couldn't be as comparatively less traumatic than watching that horrific video of childbirth in sophomore year of high school. Prudence rinsed her hand off in the sink as I attended to my assigned task. The wine was a very dark red, almost black, and once each glass was filled, I couldn't visually tell the difference between the regular and the blood-spiked. "Not sure this is a good way to improve a vintage."

Prudence gave another eye roll at my comment. She was patting her hands dry with a soft white cloth, and when I looked, I could see that although the cut on her hand had stopped bleeding, it was still red and open. She folded the cloth and held it in her left hand, like a normal fabric napkin, but positioned so that her cut was concealed, and picked up the red wineglass with her free hand. At her indication, I picked up the blue and green glasses, with their contents of regular wine, and followed her back into the living room, grimly aware of just who that spiked glass was for.

Prudence handed the red glass to Jon along with a wide, perfect-hostess smile. "Here you go."

He looked decidedly taken aback. Clearly the poor guy had pictured something more along the lines of a glass of water. "Oh gosh, it's just a little early for me —"

My sister began talking blithely over him. "Now, some

Rioja traditionalists will say that they're skeptical, but I've found that this is quite a lovely Spanish red. A bit decadent at three hundred per bottle, I suppose, but I thought you'd enjoy it. Such a concentrated, yet ethereal balance, such elegant structure."

Jon had visibly paled when Prudence rattled off the price, and he clearly knew he was beaten. "So thoughtful of you," he managed, accepting the red wineglass that Prudence offered him and taking a polite sip. I barely repressed a shudder at the sight, a reaction that I tried to cover by taking a quick mouthful from my own glass—a disappointing one, since I honestly couldn't tell the difference between what I'd just taken a sip of and the ten-dollar grocery store bottles that I used to periodically spring for back when I dated Beth. And I frankly couldn't imagine that Prudence's blood was helping out that ethereal balance that she'd been harping about. I knew it was kind of hypocritical of me, given that I drank my mother's blood on a regular basis and had a future trajectory that included drinking other people's blood, but I couldn't help it—it was kind of gross to know that poor Jon Einarsson had just gotten a mouthful of Prudence's red stuff.

He gave a polite compliment, and Prudence talked a bit about fragrance and texture and notes of flavor—those almost stereotypical natterings of wine enthusiasts that I'd always secretly suspected to be a complete sham. Jon nodded as she spoke, the look in his eyes suggesting that he agreed with me, but he continued taking small sips. The conversation then shifted back to financial black alchemy, and Jon took the reins. But I noticed that as the minutes passed, his descriptions of various legalistic loopholes became slower, and more lethargic, while every time he took a drink of his wine, it was deeper than the last. Prudence watched him, taking little tastes from her own glass, a tiny smile playing at her lips as she looked at him with horrible patience. Jon began blinking more, looking hazy and just a little owlish, and his pale blue eyes began to dilate. His hands shuffled through his papers awkwardly, but he began openly staring at my sister, apparently unable to help himself. By the time another twenty minutes had passed, his glass was completely empty, and he was just sitting, gazing at my sister like he was Moses and she a burning bush, his lips slightly parted like a Hollywood starlet waiting for a kiss.

Prudence had that small smile fixed on her mouth, and she leaned forward, setting her glass down carefully on a coaster. "Jon, would you be willing to do me a small favor?"

"Of course, Ms. Scott," Jon said, perking up and sounding like this was just the opportunity he'd waited a lifetime for. "Whatever you need."

"I'd like just a pint or so of your blood." Prudence's voice was very calm and friendly. "Would you mind terribly?"

Jon blinked very slowly, and mulled over the request for a second, then said, with a terrifying placidity, "That doesn't sound like a problem." The bright, sharp lawyer who had appeared on Prudence's doorstep not even an hour ago now seemed entirely gone, replaced by Forrest Gump.

"I'm *so* happy to hear that," my sister said. "Fort, let's all relocate to the kitchen."

"Um, why?" I asked.

She shook her head at me. "This sofa is *linen*, Fort. Stains will *never* come out of it."

With Jon following at our heels like a contented little puppy, we returned to the kitchen. My sister's box of historical horror remained displayed in all its glory on the island counter, but Jon seemed completely unfazed, simply looking around and saying, "You're very into modern design, aren't you, Ms. Scott. I feel like I've seen this kitchen in magazines." He continued chattering happily like that, my sister just nodding agreeably to everything he said while she busily settled him on a tall stool, then assisted him out of his suit jacket and rolled up his shirt-sleeves. He responded like a helpful toddler with his mother, watching all of her actions with benign sanguinity.

I was feeling quite a bit less calm, especially when Prudence tied one of those rubber medical bands around his lower bicep with disturbing expertise.

"Prudence, you aren't going to hurt him, right?" I asked as she helped Jon curl his left hand into a tight fist, making the veins in his arm begin to pulse.

Another eye roll, as if somehow that question were utterly ridiculous, even though we had just roofied this guy and were now settling him down within arm's reach of a whole collection of sharp knives. "I have no desire to dispose of a body today. Mr. Einarsson will be leaving here under his own power." She tucked another of those soft white towels under his left arm, then asked, "Now, Jon, you wouldn't mind if I bit you, would you?"

He looked surprised, and a hint of mild concern was seeping through his bovinelike demeanor. "Bit me?"

"It will only hurt a little. Just a tiny prick," she reassured him. Internally, I couldn't help but root for Jon's brain to make a comeback here.

"Oh." He considered, and that flicker of self-preservation melted away like a snowflake caught on a palm. "Well, that doesn't sound too bad."

"You're being so helpful, Jon. I do appreciate that." Her eyes darkened, the pupil expanding to completely encompass the blue of her iris, and her fangs slid out. To my relief, feeding from Madeline appeared to have put my instincts back under control, and I didn't have any overt reaction to this apart from a deep sense of worry and discomfort on behalf of Jon, and a general sense of being horribly conflicted about what I was seeing, like the time I went to a party and walked in on a girl snorting cocaine off a very nice coffee table. My sister leaned down until her mouth was just above the bend in Jon's elbow; then she looked over at me. "Now, Fort, despite what modern culture might've led you to believe, this is only as sexual as you'd like to make it. Just like eating a strawberry, or a hamburger." With that helpful comment, and without further ado, she bit Jon quickly and neatly. He flinched at the contact but remained calm. My sister pulled back quickly, allowing me to see that her fangs had left two perfectly round, deep marks that were already flowing with bright red blood. She retracted her fangs, though her eyes remained dark, and leaned back down to drink, locking her lips tightly against Jon's arm to form a seal. Just as she had promised, there was nothing sexual about what followed—though there were some extremely uncomfortable slurping sounds, and I could see her throat working steadily as she swallowed.

Jon looked over at me with those calm, pale blue eyes. "She's right, you know," he assured me. "It really doesn't hurt so much."

"That's really great, Jon." I said. Holy fuck, was this creepy.

Meanwhile, Jon was settling comfortably into social patter, as if we were at a cocktail party instead of sitting in my sister's kitchen while she drank his blood. "So, what line of work are you in, Fort?"

I winced. "Well, I'm doing a bit of floater work for this small, privately run firm. Very exciting business model. Providing very specialized services to the home."

"Sounds great," Jon enthused, and I had a strong feeling that five years earlier in his life he would've appended that statement with a "brah."

After just a few minutes that nevertheless felt even more torturously long than when Jon had been talking about money management, Prudence pulled up. With one hand she smoothly lifted the side of Jon's towel to press against his wound, while with the other she dabbed delicately at her mouth with her white cloth napkin. It occurred to me that my sister had made some ridiculous choices in her color scheme.

"Jon, could you hold that for me?" she asked, and he obediently reached over with his right hand to press the towel, while she untied the rubber band and dropped it onto the counter. "Excellent, Jon. Just keep steady pressure on that for a moment." She then returned her attention to me and resumed lecturing academically. "You should feed directly from the vein every ten to fifteen days at least, and don't stop drinking until you feel comfortably full. Usually that will be about a pint and a half, sometimes a little more. I didn't take much from Jon today, but that's fine because I fed very recently. I know Mother let you get into bad habits and stop feeding from her before you were completely satisfied, but you'll need to understand that that kind of behavior simply won't work when you feed from humans. Any less than a full feed, and at your age you'll start sickening very quickly. When you're a bit older, you might be able to go longer in between direct feedings in emergency situations, but ten to fifteen days is the rule for full health, even for a vampire our mother's age."

"Ten to fifteen days, gotcha." I'd now seen my sister feed, and all I wanted to do was beat feet for the door.

She gave me a very quelling look. "That's your minimum for a *direct* feeding, Fort, straight from the vein to your mouth. But that won't fulfill your full blood needs."

My heart sank. "It won't?"

"No. One pint every three days will be necessary for that. Now, you can use the vein if you like for that as well, but here you should keep in mind the corrosive nature of our bites. The more each feeding source is used, the shorter the life becomes, eventually ending with full organ failure and death."

"Like Bhumika," I said painfully.

"Not quite. But you bring up a useful point." She reached over to her box and removed the silver bowl and another rubber band, setting both on the counter. Then she flipped up Jon's towel and nodded in satisfaction when she saw that her bite had stopped bleeding and was clotting up at the surface. She adjusted the towel so that it now stretched completely across Jon's lap, then settled the silver bowl on top of it so that it was nestled snugly in the V of Jon's legs, with the towel completely draped beneath it. Then she positioned Jon's right arm so that his forearm was resting across the bowl, underside up, revealing paler and somehow more-fragile skin. All with that very practiced air, Prudence tied the new rubber band around Jon's right bicep, and this time he made a fist without even having to be cued, smiling proudly at his own cleverness. Prudence rewarded him with an answering smile that filled my veins with ice, and I almost flinched when my sister returned her attention to me. She didn't seem to notice, focused as she was on lecturing me. "Now, like our dear brother, I imagine you will probably make a fuss and raise all kinds of objections to the human impact of feeding directly every three days, so I'm going to show you the workaround. Please hand me one of the clean lancets."

Not trusting myself to speak, I reached into the box and removed a lancet, feeling the solidity of its silver handle, and passed it to her. She accepted it with her right hand, while with her left she carefully palpated and poked at the veins now bulging in Jon's arm. Then she checked the silver bowl again, cautioning Jon not to let it fall. He nodded obediently. Finally, she rested the blade of the lancet gently on the skin of Jon's arm. "Direction is important on this," she said to me. "Always cut lengthwise, little brother. Otherwise you can sever the vein." Then she made one deep, smooth slice across Jon's arm. The blood rose up immediately, and she turned his arm carefully so that all the blood began draining into the bowl. All three of us watched silently as the bowl began to fill up, Prudence quickly untying the rubber

tourniquet and wrapping her own hand around Jon's fist
to encourage him to continue squeezing. When the blood
level in the bowl reached the numbered sixteenth ring on
the inside of the bowl, she drew the towel over the wound
and pressed down firmly.

"Fort, if you wouldn't mind setting the bowl on the
counter?" I reached over hurriedly and performed the
transfer, flinching at the way the blood rocked gently
against the sides of the container and the way that I could
feel its warmth through the bowl. "Now, sixteen ounces is
a pint," she continued. As she talked, she opened a side
drawer, revealing a very thorough collection of gauze and
medical supplies. She removed a thick white bandage,
which she taped across Jon's wound. "Be a dear and hold
that, would you, Jon? Thank you." Walking around Jon,
she came over to me so that we were standing beside each
other, looking at the bowl of blood sitting on her kitchen
island. "Now, that slice was no more harmful to the good
Mr. Einarsson than a visit to a blood drive, but it becomes
a rather significant hassle for us." Another cabinet was
flipped open, and her hand emerged with a small metal
hand colander, which she passed to me. "Start agitating
the blood, Fort."

"Um . . . what now?" While I often failed to understand my sister on an emotional level, this time it was
very literal.

"It's a bit like hand-beating eggs," she explained. Prudence took the colander from me, dipped it down slowly
to the bottom of the bowl, then lifted it in a slow scooping motion until the bottom of the colander just barely
broke the surface of the blood. Then she handed it back
to me. "Just like that."

This was definitely a whole new level of weird, even in
my family, but my brain was feeling almost bludgeoned
by the entire exercise, and I just followed her instructions.
While I continued the bizarre action of mixing a bowl of
blood, my sister busied herself by getting her plastic gar-

bage can out from under the sink and changing out the bag for a fresh one. She brought that over and began positioning it fussily just beneath the area I was working. I watched her for a second, trying to figure out what could possibly be coming next, but when I glanced down at the bowl of blood, I nearly jumped out of my skin. There was something forming at the top of the bowl, something filmy and weirdly fibrous. "What is *that*?"

"Oh, wonderful, Fort. I'm glad to see that all that time spent working in food prep has had some use after all." Horribly, I could see from her face that she was actually sincere in this compliment. She leaned over the bowl, smiling. "That, my brother, is a blood clot. Now, scoop it up and drop it in the garbage."

Ew, I thought, but I did as she asked, fishing it out with my little colander, and dropping it into the trash. "Um, why are we doing this?"

"Keep mixing, Fort." I did as she asked, and she nodded, pleased. "Because we are agitating the blood, we are forcing the clots to form. By removing all of the clots, we will be left with a bowl of blood that is minus the clotting factors. In point of fact, we will have a bowl of defibrinated blood, which will remain liquefied and clot free when we put it in the refrigerator."

As I had many, many times before, I wondered what horrible wrong I had committed in some past life that I'd been born a vampire. Surely a benevolent deity would simply have made me into a dung beetle? I scooped out another few clots, and then stared at my sister. "The refrigerator?"

"Just so." She glanced down into the trash, where more clots were piling up, and sighed. "Of course it's so terribly wasteful, to say nothing of the proteins that you lose by removing the clots, but there's no way to store it otherwise."

"Why don't we just use bagged blood, from hospitals? I'm pretty sure that they keep all of this stuff in it." For a

moment I wondered if I was being forced to whisk a
bowl of blood out of some bizarre character-building exercise, like the time in Cub Scouts when they gave us
cups of cream and made us hand-churn butter.

"Ah, a question Chivalry and I asked ourselves a
number of years ago, as it happens. Well, what we discovered is that hospital or research blood has been citrated,
meaning that they have added trisodium citrate to it. It
has no effect on humans, but we both tried it, and it
made us horribly nauseated. Defibrinated blood may
mean extra work, but it's far better than uncontrollable
vomiting. Such a process, of course—all this work, and
you have to deal with more humans. Ah, it looks like
you've gotten all the clots. You can stop mixing now."

I tapped the extra blood off the colander and set it
down in Prudence's sink. My sister was reaching into yet
another cabinet, and this time she emerged with one of
those tall, thick, 1980s Tupperware rectangles with the
removable lid on top and the handy bunghole to pour
with. My foster mother, Jill, had used exactly that type of
Tupperware to make lemonade from concentrate when
I was little, and I watched in a detached kind of horror
as my sister unknowingly defiled a small piece of my
childhood as she carefully poured the blood from her
silver bowl into the Tupperware and pressed the lid securely on.

She looked at her handiwork and gave a little moue.
"Fort, I am sorry to say that the taste of blood is most
definitely *not* improved by sitting in the fridge, and this
will be rendered utterly undrinkable in two days. And
unlike revenge or a fine mint julep, this is not a beverage
that is best served cold—you will want to make certain
that it is body temperature. Microwaves can be a dance
with disaster—I'd suggest sticking to warming it in a
saucepan. But when you do, remember that it's just like
warming up milk—too much heat and it's ruined." She
popped the Tupperware into her fridge.

"Okay, that's pretty much seared into my memory."

"I'm glad to hear it," she said, with zero irony. "Now here are a few more important details—Chivalry drinks one pint of harvested human blood every three days, then roughly a pint and half directly from the vein from his wife every fifteen days. It's my understanding that his wives watch their diets very closely, take vitamin supplements, and will usually receive a blood transfusion later in the day that Chivalry feeds from them."

I looked directly at my sister. "And how do *you* feed?"

She smiled. "I drink directly from the vein every three days."

"Do you . . ." The thought of those numbers shook me deeply, and my mind raced. "Are you feeding from multiple people?"

"Mother does that with her politicians. She must have a stable of at least a hundred, really. That spreads the impact, since she rarely feeds on the same individual more than once or twice in a single year." Prudence's voice became cautionary. "But she's old, Fort, and her blood is very strong. One tiny sip and a human's loyalty is hers—you saw for yourself how much of mine it took for Jon. Chivalry would need an entire glass at least, and I'd suggest that you just go straight for a roofie and knock the human out, or ask one of us for help. No, I have no desire to waste the blood and energy to maintain a stable. I'll feed on our nice Mr. Einarsson every three days as I need, and when his health starts deteriorating, I'll find a new source." Still seated on his stool, Jon smiled at the sound of his name.

I could feel a part of myself curling up inside. How I was continuing to stand here talking with my sister was incredible to me—maybe I was in shock. "How long will he last?" I looked at Jon, trying to wrap my head around the idea that because of what my sister, no, what *we* had done to him, he was going to die.

"For me to feed on? Perhaps five, six months before

he becomes visibly ill. He'll be receiving regular transfusions, of course, the same arrangement that Chivalry makes, so he won't dry up of anemia on me. If I stop feeding when the illness becomes obvious, he might live a year before everything falls apart. But since I have no desire at all for some bright young thing at a hospital to think she's found a new chronic disease, generally it's a good idea to arrange an accident around that point. Muggings gone wrong, brake failures, house fires." She was so calm, so flippant. Listening to my sister talk, I was viscerally reminded of who she was, and who I would have to become—that I would have to choose between Prudence's high body count or Chivalry's slow murder. While I was absorbed by the echoes of my internal trauma, Prudence was turning to Jon with another of those small, cruel smiles. "Now, you wouldn't tell a soul about any of this, would you, Jon?"

He thought it over, then asked, "Would you want me to?"

"No, not ever."

"Oh, okay, then." It was so easy for him, and he smiled sunnily at her.

"Would you like to come over here on Sunday and feed me again?" Prudence asked.

Jon nodded immediately. "Of course."

"Excellent," she praised him.

It was horrible. The whole thing was beyond horrible, a theft of willpower. "He's like your own zombie, Prudence," I said hoarsely.

"They're always like that initially. Given an hour, however, and he'll be back to normal." She reached down and traced her finger in one drop of blood that had dripped down during her transfer of the whisked blood into the Tupperware, one tiny little dot of red against the pristine white marble island top, and smiled. "The only thing that will have changed is how he feels about me." Then she looked at me with those brilliant, and so very, very cold blue eyes. "Have I answered all of your questions, little brother?"

I was already edging toward the door. "Very thoroughly."

Those blue eyes glinted dangerously. "You will come to me, of course, if you have any follow-ups that you think of later. I do so want to make certain that you are prepared when your transition is completed, and you must remove yourself from Mother's skirts and obtain your own dinner."

I muttered something—I had no idea what—but it was enough for Prudence to nod and give me that terrifyingly cheery wave. I pounded down the steps, and was out her door and to the Fiesta as quickly as possible without quite running. My hand was shaking badly enough that it took three tries for me to unlock my door, and how I got myself home without an accident I couldn't even imagine, since I was running basically in a fugue state of shock, my mind replaying over and over that placid, peaceful look on Jon's face as he watched his blood flow steadily into that silver bowl.

The apartment was empty, and I went straight to the bathroom, dropping my clothes onto the floor while I cranked the water on. The ancient pipes started groaning, and I got under the spray without waiting for it to warm up all the way. The water was so cold that it actually hurt, but I ignored it and squeezed a dollop of shampoo into my hand and started scrubbing. I looked down and watched the water circling around our perpetually partially clogged drain. It was all clear, which surprised me. Between my attack on James yesterday and what I had helped Prudence do to Jon in her kitchen today, I felt like the water should've been stained red.

I scrubbed until the water was warm, and then kept scrubbing until the upper layer of my oversaturated skin started peeling off under my washcloth. It wasn't until the water started cooling down on me again that I finally turned the tap off and got out of the shower. I hadn't brought clean clothes in with me, and looking down at the pile of new clothes puddled on the floor, I knew that I didn't want to put those back on. I tied the towel around my waist, then wadded up the clothing and carried it with me into my room, tossing it in the corner, behind an old box of DVDs, where I wouldn't see it.

I didn't want to think about how my brother had bought the clothes for me, because I didn't want to think about Chivalry at all right now. I didn't want to think about the decisions he had made, and what I suddenly understood about them now. I didn't want to imagine Chivalry with a bleeding bowl, finding people to siphon his pints out of. I didn't want to think of my brother bent over Bhumika's arm twice a month, his teeth piercing her dusky skin, feeding even though it meant that he was killing her just a little at a time.

I didn't want to wonder whether at some point, maybe on one of their initial dates, or maybe even earlier, when he was first interested in her, my brother had mixed his blood with a little wine and handed it to Bhumika and watched her drink it down. Bhumika had told me once that Chivalry had told her everything about who he was, *what* he was, and that she had made her decision to be with him with the full knowledge that it would lead to her death. But now I remembered Jon Einarsson's face, how willing and eager he had been to do anything Prudence wanted him to. And I couldn't stop myself from wondering whether Bhumika's decision had been real.

I pulled on sweatpants and a long-sleeved T-shirt, running on autopilot. My mind was running numbers. Chivalry's wives died slowly before him, while Prudence killed fast. My mother fed from more than a hundred, but how much did she shorten the lives of her victims with that bi-yearly bite? Numbers rolled through my head as I sank down onto my bed. I'd been delighted when I'd finished my last required math classes, never feeling like I had any particular aptitude for the subject, but now equations were putting themselves together in my brain with horrifying ease.

If Chivalry fed from his wife twice each month, how many bites were enough to kill healthy women in the prime of their lives? How many times would Prudence feed from Jon in the kitchen before she felt that he was a liability to be disposed of? My brain, suddenly my most unhelpful organ, conjured a picture for me of Bhumika, the last time I'd seen her—tucked into bed, surrounded by IV drips, attended by home hospice nurses. And my brother, looking so pained—had he looked like that when he had leaned down to bite her arm and feed? Had he removed her IV, or just bitten in a different spot to avoid disturbing it? Had she looked at him with that terrifying passivity that Jon had shown, even as each new bite rushed death forward?

Would that be me? A hundred, fifty, thirty, ten years from now? One year from now? Or would I be standing in Prudence's kitchen, where her newest victim, caught for me, would be asked if he minded at all if Prudence's baby brother took a drink?

I could hear Jon's voice so clearly. "Well, that doesn't sound too bad."

There was a ringing sound, my phone. I hit the button to ignore the call. It started ringing again, though, and I hit ignore a second time. The third time, I threw my phone against my wall, and that stopped the ringing.

I heard Dan come home, and he must've seen my car in the lot, because he called a hello. I didn't say anything, and I heard him walk into his own room and close the door. The light from the window dimmed, then finally died altogether, but I didn't bother to turn on my bedside light. I just sat in the dark and thought.

I thought about math, and numbers, and whether I could be brave.

My clock was behind me, so I didn't know what time it was when my bedroom door opened and Suzume walked in. But I wasn't surprised. Her floppy fleece hat and her green parka were tucked under her arm, and as she dropped them onto the floor and shoved the door closed with a lazy swipe of her foot, I realized that I'd been waiting for her.

"You weren't answering my calls," she said. She looked thoughtfully over to the mangled wreckage of my phone, lying in a small pile of abused electronics and drywall chunks. "I guess now I know why."

There was no need to answer that. I looked up at her face, which was clearer to me than it should've been in the darkness of the room. Her dark eyes were cautious, probing, but not afraid. I wished with all my heart that I could've been born a fox.

"Suze," I said as she walked closer. "If your living meant that other people would die . . . how many people would you be willing to kill? For you to keep living?"

She stopped, one of her feet still half lifted. I'd seen her do that as a fox many times—freezing, then holding still with perfect balance as she used her long, sensitive ears, her nose, or those bright eyes to locate the source of whatever had disturbed her perfect understanding of her surroundings. A moment passed; then her head tilted slightly to one side.

"Do you want to die, Fort?" she asked, cutting to the heart of my question. Her voice was soft, and so very carefully neutral.

"I should," I whispered, and my voice broke along with that icy fog that had protected me until now, and everything inside me hurt so badly that it made what had happened to me physically when my body had rejected James's body seem like a picnic. "I should be saying that my life isn't worth someone else's. I mean, if we're sitting in an ethics class, that's what I should be willing to do, right? If I die, all those people down the line over the next five or six hundred years ..." I knew that number, because I'd thought through it for hours, and I'd run the numbers inside my brain for Prudence's method and for Chivalry's, and those numbers felt branded across my soul. "All those people who would die early because of me would live...."

Suzume sank slowly into a crouch, as gracefully as a ballerina into a plié. Her face was right next to mine. "But."

I hated myself. The answer was so clear, so undeniable, and I was craven and foul and rotten, and I said, "But I don't want to die," and I shuddered with the truth of it.

She watched me through mirrored eyes for a long moment, then leaned in, bridging the inches between our faces. Her dark hair fell around our faces in a curtain as she pressed her mouth against mine, not gently or deeply, but a hard press of lips. Nothing offered, nothing being coaxed, this kiss was a demand, and a promise. It went on for a long minute; then she pulled back. Her face was unreadable, but there was nothing unclear or unfeeling in what she said next. "I don't want you to die either, Fort."

I had no words, and just watched, my mouth still feeling the imprint of that stamp of ownership as she sank completely down, kneeling on my ratty secondhand rug. The long line of her side was pressed against my left leg, and she slid one hand up the leg of my sweatpants to rest against the back of my calf. My skin was so cold compared to the furnace of her body, and I could feel that heat spreading into my flesh.

"Now tell me what you learned," she said, and her hand squeezed my leg ever so slightly. Looking in her eyes, I suddenly knew that she would hold me here until I told her, even if the walls of this apartment building fell down around us.

So I did. About attacking James, about helping my sister feed from Jon, about the numbers and the corrosion and death that my bite would bring, and what the unavoidable future in front of me was. During the entire recital, Suze never interrupted me, simply stayed where she was, kneeling at my feet in the dark and listening.

When I was done, silence hung between us. Then she moved her head to the side, just a little, so that her cheek was now resting against my knee as she looked at me.

"Your sister didn't say that feeding from the same human each time was required." No lawyer looking for loopholes could've sounded more focused than she did.

"No, but," and then I paused, seeing what she had pointed out with a brain that had been shaken loose of the terror that had clung to me. "Oh." I looked down at her, and my hands slid onto her shoulders as if it were the most natural thing in the world. "You're right. Prudence and Chivalry use the same source for convenience—Chivalry tries harder to maintain his wives' long-term health by supplementing with stored blood, but he's still biting them over and over. There's nothing physiological to prevent me from biting a different human each time, to spread out and minimize the effects." My mind raced now, thinking about how that could happen. My blood couldn't entrance a human or steal their loyalty like my siblings' blood could, and from Prudence's inference, it would be decades at least before I gained that ability. But coaxing wasn't my only option, and I only had to feed from a human two or three times each month. Providence was a big city—a bi-monthly mugging, perhaps, but one in which I stole the blood I needed rather than money? Something like chloroform, maybe, to disable my victim, prevent them from remembering my bite? Or maybe—

Suze's laughter interrupted my thoughts, and I looked down at her. She was smiling widely up at me. "See?" she asked. "Now you're figuring a way around it."

I leaned closer, and pressed my forehead against hers, pressing my eyes shut to prevent myself from the ignominy of tears. "Thank you, Suze," I said, my heart laid bare in front of her. She'd saved me—not just from the possibility of death, but from the worse one, of making the choice to live no matter what the cost.

We stayed like that for a few heartbeats. Then she slipped backward and bounced to her feet, wiggling with gleeful energy, and snapped on the light. I blinked hard at the sudden light, and she laughed again and spun playfully in a circle, stretching her hands out to brush against my wall. She spun until I was dizzy from watching her, and I caught her hand on one of her rotations, tugging her to a stop. That brilliant smile was still spread across her face.

I knew my own expression was matching it, but the feeling of her hand tucked so comfortably in mine, warm and just slightly sweaty, made my smile fade a little. I looked at her and asked, "Are you going to kiss me every time I get suicidal during my transition?"

Her smile faded, but she didn't pull her hand away from mine. Instead she leaned down, close to me, her hair swinging forward to frame her face. She brought her free hand forward and brushed the tips of her fingers along my jaw, leaving a trail of fire behind. "I am a fox, Fort," she whispered, her words a warm breath against my ear. "And when something is mine, I keep it. If I bury it in a hole to keep it safe, it may stay there for months while I roam and run, but I will never forget where I have put it, and I will always come back for it, because it is mine."

Then she slid away, across the room to perch by my window, where the ancient radiator hissed. With one hip propped in my windowsill, she stretched one leg out casually to rest on my computer chair, as if nothing were different. But there was a flush across her cheeks, and the pounding of my heart in my chest was radiating down to my fingertips. She wasn't touching me anymore, but I could feel the ghost of every place that had felt her skin, and looking at her, and her perfect casualness, I knew that it was the same for her.

"I called your secretary when I was tracking you down," Suze said, looking out the window rather than at me. "According to her, you've got another half dozen messages from Gil, who was sounding more pissed with each one and demanding to know what we're doing about the investigation, and one very polite and measured text from Dahlia, asking if there are any resources she can offer to assist us." She tilted her head, glancing at me over her shoulder. "An interesting dichotomy of reactions—don't you think? One definitely seems more eager than the other to see our investigation move forward."

I stayed where I was sitting and just watched Suzume. Even in jeans and an old corded fisherman's sweater, she was perfect. "The plan still holds. We'll go to the funeral tomorrow, and see whether it's Dahlia or Ilona looking twitchy."

"Tomorrow, then," and her eyes gleamed. "Bright and early."

Dan was in the living room when Suze left, and even though she and I didn't touch or say anything unusual, the air between us was charged enough that when I closed the door behind her, I turned to see the ghoul giving me a wide, inquisitive grin.

"That seemed promising," he said. I just shook my head at him and headed for the fridge, to see what I could put together for dinner. "Just remember," he continued, undeterred. "Once you've slept with her, and she's all mellow from endorphins, remind her about the sanctity of mutual property."

There were googly eyes glued to each of the eggs left in the carton. "I wouldn't hold your breath, Dan," I said.

Chapter 7

Matias Kivela's funeral was well-attended, filling the stone confines of Saint Paul's Evangelical Lutheran Church and packing the pews to the point where a small line of overflow participants began lining the side aisles. Suze and I arrived half an hour before the scheduled start, but we would've been relegated to the cheap seats had it not been for Suze's kitsune chutzpah. She marched us straight up the center aisle to a pew that was just behind the ones set aside for family use. It was full, but she leaned down and said, sounding exactly like the bulky bodyguard in a mob film, "Mr. Scott appreciates you making room for him." I stood back and attempted to look entitled.

Reluctantly, everyone in the pew shifted over, making just enough room for the two of us to wedge ourselves in. Suze upped her glare, and after a little muttering, a few of the younger sitters collected their belongings and left for other, less desirable seating. Those who were left slid farther down, so that when Suze and I sat, now we had room to spread out.

"Not sure that was necessary," I muttered to Suzume as she unwrapped her scarf and pulled off her gloves. After our interlude the night before, I'd expected things to be different—instead, she had arrived on my doorstep in completely appropriate funeral wear and a chipper bounciness that pretty much defied me to make things awkward.

"Of course it was," she scolded me with a grin. "You're Madeline Scott's kid—you don't get squished up against some grandma bear. Also"—she nodded to our left—"tell me that this isn't a good observation post."

I followed her gaze. On the other side of the aisle and just two rows up was the full Kivela family. Dahlia was standing, looking tired but completely composed, and speaking with an ever-shifting circle of people.

"Looks like someone is settling into the leadership spot," I whispered to Suze.

"Check out momma bear," she muttered back.

I craned my head—Ilona Kivela wasn't crying, but she definitely was in a different emotional place than her daughter. She looked like a bomb-blast victim, pressed up against the shoulder of her son and rocking slightly.

"Maybe she realized that we snagged the knife, and she's had a few sleepless nights?"

Suze was frowning, though. "Not sure. That doesn't look nervous. Looks more like she's trying to hold off a full throwing-herself-on-the-casket breakdown. And look at the way Gil's keeping close to her. Did your brother say anything about Ilona having some kind of acting background?"

"I didn't actually get a chance to talk with him," I admitted. Then Gil Kivela swung his head around and met my eyes, making me have to work hard to avoid slinking down into the pew. That was a person who was definitely not happy with me, but in addition to his mother, he was also pinned down by the four-year-old girl sitting on his lap. Beside him was the guy from the wedding picture, who had his hands full wrangling Dahlia's younger daughter.

"Someone just spotted us," Suze said.

"Yeah, Gil looks like he's trying to force-choke me with his brain," I noted.

Suzume's elbow dug into my side. "Not him—the *karhu*'s daughter."

I pulled my eyes away from Gil's glare of death, and realized that Suze was right—Carmen Kivela, looking extremely fragile and breakable in a black dress and matching cardigan that emphasized her pale skin and hair, had gotten out of the family pew and was making her way over to us. As she got closer, I could see the redness of her eyes and nose, but she was managing to keep it together.

"Thank you for coming to honor my father," she said to me when she reached us. Her chin wobbled a little. "It would've meant a lot to him that the Scotts sent a representative."

It was an awkward moment, but I winced and went with that explanation. "Matias Kivela was a valuable ally," I said gravely, "and he will be missed."

"Dahlia seems to be stepping into his shoes very smoothly, though," Suze said, fishing around.

It worked, and I noticed how Carmen's cheeks flushed—the curse of the Finnish complexion, because there was clearly no hiding it. "She hasn't even cried," Carmen said, and there was a hard layer of anger in her voice. The young bear clearly heard it, and immediately moved to cover it, "Of course, she has so much to do, I'm sure she just hasn't had time. It's hard to be the one in charge—my father was always saying that the *karhu* had to be strong for everyone."

I nodded toward the pew. "Your aunt looks pretty distraught. Were she and your father close?"

Carmen nodded, looking puzzled. "Of course. Aunt Ilona and my dad were almost inseparable. For a while they were even talking about Aunt Ilona selling her place and moving in with us. You know, I wasn't going to be living there forever, and that way they could keep each other company."

"And why didn't that plan go through?" Suze asked.

"Because of Dahlia, of course. After Parker was killed, Aunt Ilona moved in with Dahlia to help with Anni and Linnea."

"Wait—who was killed?" I asked.

"You didn't know about Parker?" Carmen sounded utterly gobsmacked, her jaw dropping. "How could you not know?"

"Save the pearl clutching and just tell us," Suze said, annoyed.

Carmen's eyes were still round with shock, but she leaned closer and dropped her voice. "Parker was Dahlia's husband. They got married right out of college, and Dahlia had Anni, then Linnea. Her job with the family business brought in more money, so Parker took care of the kids. I guess he got sick of it, or maybe sick of Dahlia, 'cuz things got pretty rough right after Linnea was born, and last year they separated." She paused, and looked at us, clearly expecting a bigger reaction to that latest bit.

"And . . . the *metsän kunigas* don't believe in divorce?" I asked. Well, we were standing in a Lutheran church, so apparently I was learning a lot about the bear culture today.

Carmen couldn't control a snort, "If both spouses are *metsän kunigas*, we don't give a shit. But Dahlia and Gil both married humans."

I could feel my stomach drop a little, and I carefully avoided looking at Suze. "And the human spouses know? About, you know . . ." I looked for a way to explain.

Carmen spared me the phrasing difficulties. "Of course," she said. "How can anyone keep a secret like that from a spouse? And with kids? You'd have to be crazy to try that." She shook her head. "Well, Parker swore that he'd keep his mouth shut, said that he'd never do anything that would put his own kids in danger, but my dad said that we couldn't risk it. My dad thought that Parker might start trying to use the secret as a way to get leverage during the divorce—custody of the girls, maybe

more alimony from Dahlia, stuff like that. Dahlia promised that he wouldn't, and she even said that she'd try to
reconcile with Parker if it came down to it, but Dad said
that it wasn't her call, and so he killed Parker." From
Carmen's face, she knew she was dropping a bombshell
on us, and there was just a hint of enjoyment in her eyes.

"How did Dahlia react to that?" I asked, looking over
again at Dahlia and her very, very dry eyes.

"She wouldn't even talk to Dad for six months," Carmen said. "And they work at the same company, so that
says something. Aunt Ilona was the one who finally
patched things up, but it was still really tense."

"But Matias still wanted to make her the heir?" Suze
asked.

"He announced it a month ago," the bear explained,
but from the press of her mouth, this was clearly not a
happy memory. "It was just a precaution, you know. I
mean, he was in good health. But he said that it was important to just get a name out there in case something
happened, and he said that I was too young right now."
Carmen's jaw clenched. "But Dad would've lived another twenty years, easy. Dahlia was the heir now, but
that would've changed in another five years."

"Carmen," I asked carefully, "your cousins think that
this was the Ad-hene. But who do *you* think killed your
father?"

She paused, and a series of emotions passed quickly
across her face, too many for me to identify. People were
starting to settle into their seats, and the service was
about to begin. But she leaned forward, quickly, her face
intense, and said, "Maybe it was the Ad-hene. They're
dangerous, and Gil thinks that they probably blame us
for the fact that the Scotts figured out what they were
doing in the Lincoln Woods, and for their punishment.
But it's just—" The minister was walking up to the podium, and I could hear Gil Kivela hissing Carmen's name

urgently. She leaned close to me, and whispered, "It happened *now*, and Dahlia got *everything*." Then she broke off and hurried back to her pew.

I looked over at Suze, who raised her eyebrows very significantly. The first hymn was announced, and as everyone stood, I muttered to her, "Well, that changes things a bit." She nodded grimly, and her dark eyes were narrowed. For the rest of the funeral, she kept that steely focus on the family pew.

When the funeral was finally over, the pallbearers lifted the coffin and headed down the aisle, followed closely by the family. Dahlia's face was completely blank the whole time, but her arms were wrapped around her mother, who had broken down completely into high, anguished wails. Carmen walked on Ilona's other side, tears trickling down her cheeks while she helped support her aunt. Behind them were Gil and his husband, each carrying one of Dahlia's daughters. But Gil's eyes were locked on me, and he leaned over to whisper something to his spouse, and then passed the little girl over so that now the husband was carrying both. With a quick kiss, he left his husband and the funeral party, heading straight to me with all the subtlety of a wrecking ball.

I braced myself as he got right up in my personal space and wrapped one huge hand in the lapel of my suit jacket. "We need to talk," he growled.

"Oh, I very much agree," I said.

We ended up in the corner of the church, by the stone baptismal font, as everyone else continued to stream out the doors. It was a good thing too, because Gil was definitely not able to whisper, and frankly, even his attempts to keep to an inside voice were of middling success.

"What the hell are you playing around with?" he snarled at me, and it was very easy at that moment to picture Gil in his bear form. "None of us have heard a thing from you about the state of this investigation since you left my uncle's house. There's been no activity near Underhill, no indication that you've caught whichever Ad-hene did this. Do you at least have a name?"

I glared right back at Gil, keeping my voice as cool as possible. "Actually," I said, "given the information we've turned up, we are fairly sure at this point that the Ad-hene had nothing to do with your uncle's murder. Right now we feel that it was probably one of the *metsän kunigas.*"

"You're insane," Gil snapped, shoving a hand into his hair and gripping tightly, as if that were all he could do to keep from punching me right in the face. "Or you're completely incompetent."

"Assume I'm competent for a minute here, and why don't you give me some background. Your sister was married to a human—how exactly does that work?"

Gil looked flummoxed at the shift in direction. "Parker? What the hell does Parker have to do with this? He's *dead*. *That's* your suspect? A dead man?"

"Indulge us for a moment, Gil," Suze said, watching him carefully.

The sheer shock of this conversation seemed to have knocked Gil away from the desire to commit violence against me, and he blinked his brown eyes a few times. When he started talking, he sounded almost reasonable, albeit flummoxed. "We're not like the ghouls or the witches, and we can produce viable offspring with humans. We have to be careful about it, since if more than one generation in a row marries a human, then the children start having problems. Partial shifting only, uncontrolled shifting, and eventually it's possible to breed the shifting out completely. There are plenty of Finns who could trace back to a bear ancestor without having any of the traits themselves. So if one generation marries a human, then the next generation has to marry a *metsän kunigas*. That can happen pretty normally, but it's important to keep the gene pool from getting stagnant, so a lot of times there are arranged marriages between different bear communities. Sometimes the marriages work out, and the couple stays together. Sometimes they don't, and they separate once each partner has a daughter to bring back to their communities, with any sons staying with the mother. My mom was one of those—my dad was from Mexico, and as soon as my little sister was born, he took her back with him, and we haven't had any contact since then. But because of that marriage, Dahlia got free choice in her partner—human or *metsän kunigas*. She married her college sweetheart." A little smile tugged at his mouth, the first I'd ever seen from Gil. "So did I, but I hope things turn out a lot better with me and Kevin than what Dahlia had with Parker." Almost immediately, though, the soft look on his face disappeared as the storm clouds of being pissed off with me rolled back in. "Why the hell is this news to you? Why the hell is a Scott who doesn't even know the first thing about us investigating? This is so goddamn typical—the moment we need the Scotts for something other than just taking our money, the only competent one is too busy dating to stop by and help out."

My temper sparked—not from the insult to me, but at the suggestion that somehow Chivalry was off having fun and ignoring his job. The image of my brother as I'd last seen him, wrapped around a table, barely holding himself together, flooded my brain, and I got right in Gil Kivela's face. "So how did Dahlia feel when Matias killed her husband, Gil?"

"How do you think she felt?" he snapped, not backing down by an inch. "Parker was being an asshole, but the last thing Dahlia needed in the middle of the destruction of her marriage was to feel responsible for the murder of the father of her children. She argued like hell—" Then Gil broke off, his face suddenly changing, looking at us in near wonder as he realized the direction that we were actually heading. That didn't last long, and he crossed his arms, stuffing each fist up into his armpit as if that were the only way that he could prevent himself from punching me. It was a good thing that the church was empty, because he was yelling now. "What the hell are you implying about my sister? How dare you even suggest that? Instead of throwing around these kinds of lazy accusations, you need to be following the actual trail—"

I cut him off. "We did follow that trail, Gil. The murder weapon was in your sister's house."

"Then someone planted it there," Gil said immediately, without even blinking. "Probably a Neighbor trying to cover their tracks, and hoping that some asshole vampire will be *stupid* enough—"

He broke off when a young guy in his late teens, wearing an awkward expression and a suit that he'd either borrowed in haste or outgrown recently, hurried up the aisle, waving one arm. "Gil," he called, "Dahlia sent me to get you. The funeral procession can't leave until you get into the main car."

"Fine," Gil snapped. Then he turned back to me, his face set with dislike. The young guy was hovering at his elbow, clearly wanting to tug, but just as clearly unsure that that would go over well. Mostly his hands just fluttered with indecision. But there was no such uncertainty from Gil, who poked one huge finger in my chest, hard. "You go to those goddamn woods. Whatever the Adhene and the Neighbors are doing that they had to kill my uncle, it's in Lincoln. I know it is." With that, they turned and left—Gil a barely contained block of rage, and the young guy practically falling over himself at his heels, a lanky muddle of adolescent physical misery.

"Some interesting dynamics," Suze said, watching them leave. "The more we're hearing about Dahlia, the more I think she had a lot of motive to kill Matias."

I looked over at her, raising my eyebrows. While I'd been Gil's focus, she'd been observing closely. "Gil didn't even blink when we told him about the murder weapon. Think Dahlia confessed to him?"

"I don't know." Suze shook her head, her mouth tight. "That felt knee-jerk to me. I don't think he knew about the knife being in Dahlia's house. He didn't even consider for a second that what you said could be true. It was just one more strike against the Ad-hene for him."

"It's all pointing at Dahlia," I noted. "Her brother might believe in her, but her cousin was right in that Matias's death works out pretty well for her—she gets the top job and revenge at the same time."

"I think we should check the woods," Suzume said unexpectedly. I turned and stared at her, and she shrugged. "The whole family is going to be tied up in funeral shit for the rest of the day. If we hit the Lincoln Woods, I can sniff in the areas around Matias's and Dahlia's houses, see if I can get a whiff of any Ad-hene activity."

"Suze, do you *really* think it's possible?"

"I'm not as quick to take Lilah's word as exoneration as you are," she said. "A full Ad-hene might've been able to hide their scent at Matias's house from my nose. And given the state of that laundry room, I'm not sure I would've been able to scent an Ad-hene if they were only there briefly and were careful about what they touched. We know that there are Ad-hene unaccounted for down in Underhill." She shrugged. "Plus, if we do the sweep and come up with nothing, that's one more nail in Dahlia's coffin."

I considered it, and I had to admit that there were some valid points in her argument. "Are we completely eliminating Ilona from the suspect list?" I asked.

Suze snorted. "Hell no. The woman could be the next Meryl Streep, for all I know. Dahlia has a good motive, but Ilona could've done it. Her brother trusted her? Well, then that would explain how he was cracked over the back of the head with that rock before the knifing started."

"Well, that visual is enough to make me hope that it

ends up being the Ad-hene," I noted. "Into the woods we go."

"We're going to have to make a stopover for a wardrobe change," Suze said. "These heels were not made for spelunking."

After a quick lunch and a clothing swap, Suze and I were heading toward the Lincoln Woods State Park. Thanks to a map check, we'd figured out which parking area was the closest to where the bears lived, so the neatly graveled lot with a helpful wooden sign enumerating all of the important rules of park usage (mainly revolving around our trash, and how we needed to carry it out with us) was different from the one that we'd used during our last, very climactic trip to the Lincoln Woods.

I looked up uneasily at the sky as I turned the Fiesta off. The day had begun overcast, and the weather had not improved over the last few hours. Heavy gray clouds loomed overheard, and I was very grimly aware that my parka was merely water *resistant.*

Beside me, Suze was rustling around in the duffel bag at her feet. She emerged with a brown paper bag, which she passed to me. "Hey, got you a present."

That probably should've set my heart pounding a bit after the events of last night, but I'd hung around with Suze for a while now, and I knew to regard her gifts with significant caution. I reached carefully into the bag and withdrew a long, white aerosol can. I read the label and turned to Suze with a distinctly unamused expression. "Bear spray?" I asked flatly. According to the label, it was Sabre Frontiersman Bear Attack Deterrent, and the container actually felt like a miniature fire extinguisher.

She nodded, looking affronted at my lack of enthusiasm. "Fuck yeah, Fort. There are *actual* black bear sightings in Lincoln, and I don't think all of them are the *metsän kunigas.* Besides, if we happen to bump into an

Ad-hene, I bet that stuff would screw them over pretty well too. That shit is *effective*."

I narrowed my eyes suspiciously. "Suze, when have you been spraying this stuff?"

Her eyes widened innocently. "Me? I would never abuse a product as serious as this." Then she leaned in, and she grinned. "But just between the two of us, I nailed a kobold with this stuff full-on once, and it actually passed out."

I shook my head, but attached the accompanying hip holster to my belt. My bag with the Ithaca and my Colt would be staying in the trunk today. I had zero desire to end up chatting with a member of the state forestry service about firearms that I technically did not have a license for, plus, as Suze had pointed out, the Ad-hene looked very thoroughly inhuman, and so spent their days safely tucked away in Underhill, where no one would catch a look or, worse yet, a picture.

While I stood with my back to the car, Suze slipped out of her clothes and into something a bit fluffier. When I heard a high yap, I turned around to see a black fox eyeing me from the passenger seat of the Fiesta, her tail whipping excitedly from side to side. I opened the door to let her hop out, reflecting as I did just how much Suze's full winter coat made her look like a walking plushie toy. It was one of those bone-cold days, and she actually looked a lot more comfortable than I did. I grabbed the park map, and we headed into the woods.

What followed was a three-hour reminder of why I hated outdoor sports, particularly hiking. November wasn't exactly the ideal time for a walk through the woods to begin with, but Suze's need to hunt for Ad-hene activity took us well off the hiking trails. We went down inclines, back up inclines, picking our way over loose rocks and piles of dead leaves. There were little streams throughout the area, which meant that we also spent a lot of time balancing on moss-covered rocks, and my boots quickly became soaked. I stepped in three separate piles of rabbit poop, which Suze seemed completely incapable of avoiding, and the bare trees around us lent an extremely creepy air to the woods that was not helped by the incessant croaking of crows that found either my presence or Suze's (or both) extremely upsetting.

The whole time we were walking, Suze's nose was stuck close to the ground as she zigged and zagged, hunting for a trail, but she never gave me that classic pointer dog's pose that she usually struck when she found what she was looking for. We passed within sight of the back of Matias's and Dahlia's houses, but we found absolutely nothing except confirmation that the beauty of nature was all a crock of marketing shit.

We'd just finished picking our way around a few fallen trees near the back of Dahlia's house, making me fervently hope that we were truly past tick season, when Suze looked up at me and gave a small huff of disappointment.

"Nothing?" I asked, knowing what the answer was. I rubbed the back of my sleeve over my forehead—it was cold, but we'd been walking enough that I'd managed to build up a sweat.

Which was right when there was a crack of thunder, and the rain started falling.

The rain meant the end of any scent trails that Suze might've been able to pick up, even if any trails had been there in the first place, which I was now very sincerely doubting. Both of us were quickly soaked, Suze looking particularly sad as all of her puffy fur became drenched and stuck to the sides of her little body. Even her whiskers looked wet. My parka did the best it could to resist the rain, but my saturated socks squished with every step I took, and I could feel a line of water leaking down the back of my collar.

The map, now also wet, was stuffed into my pocket, and I was very grateful that Suze had a better sense of direction than I did, since I was sure that I would never have been able to find my way back to the car on my own. The rain eventually started lightening as we walked, settling down to a sullen and periodic drizzle, but the wind picked up, blowing straight into our faces and sending the temperature dropping. Adding to the fun, the sun was now getting lower in the sky, and in the extending twilight I would've been really screwed had my eyesight not been significantly sharper than a human's.

"When we accuse Dahlia of murdering her uncle," I muttered to Suze as the parking area finally came into sight, "she is also going to have to pay for this miserable afternoon." Suze gave a grumbling yip of full agreement, and paused to shake her coat, spraying my pants with water. Had I not already been soaked, I might've been pissed, but it seemed a bit unreasonable to fuss.

We were halfway to the car, the gravel of the lot crunching under my boots, when Suze suddenly froze, her ears pricking fully up and her tail lashing. I was spinning around before my brain even fully registered what was going on, and then it was a good thing that my instincts were running my body, since my brain nearly shut down in shock at the sight of the full-size black bear just stepping out of the woods and onto the gravel. The moment my eyes locked onto it, and it knew that I'd seen it, it gave up all attempts at sneaking and broke into a full run toward me, its mouth open to reveal an extremely terrifying set of teeth.

Bears were typically presented as slow and meandering, but now I suddenly discovered that bears could move really fast when they wanted to, and this one was barreling down on us with clear intent. Adrenaline pounded through me, and I ripped the bear spray off my belt. One hand snapped off the safety cord, one tiny sliver of my brain registered that the wind was at my back, and then I pointed it and hit the button as hard as I could. The bear was only five feet away from me, and the blast took it right in the face—*now* the bear made a sound, a full-throated roar of rage as it stopped in its tracks and started rubbing its face with those dangerously clawed paws.

I didn't wait around to observe further, instead spinning around, yelling, "Car, car, car!" and sprinting to the Fiesta with Suze right at my heels. I was shoving my hand into my wet pants pocket as we went, scrabbling desperately for my keys, and I yanked them out with so much force that I could hear my jeans pocket rip. I most certainly did not give a shit, since behind me I could still hear the bear bellowing, and I shoved the key into the Fiesta, the terror of breaking the key off in the lock the only thing that slowed me down long enough to turn it carefully. The moment it released, I yanked the door fully open, and Suze bounced straight in on four feet, landing in the driver seat and then immediately hopping into the backseat, her shape changing into a human even as she went. The moment she was off the driver seat, I was slamming into it, yanking the door closed as fast as I could.

"Shotgun?" Suze yelled from the back. "Tell me you packed the fucking shotgun."

"It's in the goddamn trunk!" I yelled, never regretting basic gun safety so much as I did at that moment, my hand shaking so hard that it took me three tries to get the key into the ignition. In front of me, the bear was still rubbing at its face with its paws, but I was horribly aware that its movements didn't seem quite as frantic as they had a moment ago. In the back, Suze had hit the release button that allowed her to fold one of the seats down flat, and also opened access to the trunk. She was reaching her arm into it and yanking, clearly trying to catch my gun duffel and get it into the main car.

I turned the ignition, and the Fiesta stalled out. I

screamed an obscenity that I normally pretended that I didn't know. In front of me, the bear had apparently shaken off the effects of the spray, and was now breathing heavily and staring straight at me with pain-squinted eyes. Behind me, Suze was still rifling through the trunk. I turned the key again, and this time the ignition caught. As the engine slowly rumbled to life, the bear growled and started coming toward the car, moving fast.

"Oh fuck, oh fuck," I muttered as I automatically threw the car into reverse and started backing up quickly. The bear was between us and the tiny gap in the trees that was the entrance and exit to the lot from the main road, and I was deeply and horribly aware that the fine craftsmen at the Ford company had built the Fiesta for fuel economy and not with the intention of withstanding a concentrated bear attack. Behind me, Suze was cursing loudly and inventively, and in front of me, the bear had just broken into a run, heading straight toward us. I could see the gleam of its teeth and the heavy muscle under its black fur.

My hands gripped the steering wheel convulsively as I ran out of room to back up. Then it occurred to me — the Fiesta might not have been designed to keep bears out, but it was a one-and-a-half-ton potential weapon. Not allowing myself to think this through any further, I yelled at Suze to brace herself. The bear was charging when I slammed the accelerator straight to the floor, shifting through the gears desperately to keep the Fiesta from stalling out. Gravel flew everywhere as the wheels spun, and the Fiesta kicked forward with everything it had. The bear saw what I was doing, and I could see it try to stop itself, but the gravel slid under its paws as its momentum continued pulling it forward, and I plowed the front of the Fiesta straight into the bear at twenty-five miles per hour.

The impact was incredible, rattling through the car and sending my head smacking into my deployed air bag, which puffed out with enough speed to prevent me from dashing my face against the windshield, since I had not been wearing my seat belt. The bear was completely draped over the crumpled remnants of the Fiesta's front end, which bowed around its body as the bear blinked up at me, stunned. There was a long minute of complete silence as we stared at each other, and it crossed my mind that the bear looked rather freaked-out all of a sudden.

Then the bear started moving, extricating itself slowly and with clear pain from the crumpled metal surrounding it, and I realized that this wasn't over yet. Then there was sudden movement behind me, and Suze shoved my gun duffel into the front seat. My hands started flying, and I pulled the zipper open so fast that it tore, but I kept ripping it, and then I yanked the Ithaca .37 sawed-off shotgun out and broke it across my lap while my other hand snatched out the box of shells. I was moving as fast as I'd ever moved before, popping the box open and spilling the shells out into my hand, but Suze had already stuck her own hand into the bag and hauled out my Colt .45, which I kept loaded in the bag. She'd always professed herself more of a knife fan than a gun person, but today she was clearly willing to make an exception, and she thumbed off the safety, popped open her door, and started firing.

The first shot went wild—she was doing too much, and she was still clearly physically shaken up from being tossed around in the crash. But that was more than enough for the bear, and it turned and started running for the woods. It was limping badly, its chest and face covered in blood, and Suze managed to land a few shots in its furry butt as it went. It flinched upon each impact, but kept going—bears had a thick layer of fat that made it difficult for most bullets to penetrate deeply. I had the Ithaca fully loaded, but when the bear hit the tree line and kept going, I just let the shotgun drop down onto my lap while the events of the last minutes caught up to me and I started hyperventilating. Suze collapsed into the backseat, panting hard as well, and I noticed, in a horribly, horribly inappropriate moment, that she was still completely naked. I pulled my eyes forward with an effort.

"Holy fucking shit, Suze," I gasped out. "What the fuck just happened?"

"That was an ambush," she said, reaching over and dropping the empty Colt onto the bag. "The wind was in our faces when we came into the parking lot, so I couldn't smell it. It waited until we were halfway to the car before it started coming toward us—that's when I heard movement."

"That was a *metsän kunigas*, right?" I asked.

"No doubt about it—a normal bear would've run after you sprayed it. Plus, all those normal bears should be hibernating right now!"

"Why did it wait for us to get close to the car? It let us get by it before it attacked us!" I glanced back at Suze, meeting her eyes, and felt my stomach sink. "It had a plan."

"One that we disrupted by not getting eaten," she said grimly.

"I am stating for the record that *I don't like this*," I gritted as I reached over, stuffed another clip into the Colt, and tucked it into my pants. Suze slid back into her fox form, and we cautiously got out of the car. I held the Ithaca carefully with both sweaty hands—even for a bear, this wasn't a gun to mess around with. Next to me, Suze had her nose pressed to the gravel and was snuffling loudly. The damp fur along her back was standing completely on end, showing that at least she was as terrified right now as I was. I wanted nothing more than to get back in the Fiesta and find out if it could still drive. The ignition was somehow still running, albeit with several extremely concerning rattles, so the impact hadn't completely demolished the engine.

Suze led us back to the spot where we'd exited the

woods, and when her ears pricked up, I knew that she'd caught the scent that she wanted. Then her ears swiveled around like alert little radar dishes, listening for any hint that the bear wasn't completely gone, and she moved very slowly and cautiously, with me right behind, keeping my Ithaca raised and ready the whole time.

The scent led us to a small outcropping of rocks and fallen trees with a clear eyeline to the parking lot and the Fiesta, along with the broken path in and out, but that offered good cover for anything hiding. And waiting there was a small, red plastic bucket, the kind that little kids played with at the beach. There was even a price tag still hanging off the handle. We both stared. Then I reached over and grabbed it. There was something inside—a sealed gallon-size Ziploc bag, with some light blue fabric inside. I opened the bag carefully and withdrew a woman's button-up shirt. I leaned down and let Suze shove her eager black nose into the folds of the shirt. She inhaled deeply, and her tail whipped suddenly in surprise.

Something moved near us, a flash of black, and we both jumped apart, me swinging the gun desperately and her baring her sharp teeth. A crow scolded us loudly from a tree, spreading its black wings and cawing. I shuddered with relief, but that was definitely enough of a reminder. Stuffing everything back into the bucket, I slung it over my arm, and we hightailed it back to the car.

Even in the long and lengthening shadows, the Fiesta was in *bad* shape. The front bumper hung down, barely still attached, while the hood was crumpled back. My left headlight was completely shattered, and the right one drooped drunkenly. The engine continued to groan dangerously, and I could smell burned oil in the air.

However, it didn't even merit discussion, because this was the last place in the world that I was willing to wait for a tow truck. The Fiesta was still running, and I needed to try to limp it home. I reached forward and tapped on my hazard lights (in small mercies, the Fiesta's back end was still completely intact), tucked the deployed air bag as much out of the way as possible, then carefully let off the emergency brake, massaged the clutch, and eased onto the accelerator. The sounds that the engine made were horrible, but the car faithfully responded and rolled forward. "I'm sorry, old girl," I said, patting the dash and feeling guilt ripple through me. "You're a good car, and you don't deserve this. You deserve a ride of honor on a flatbed truck straight to the nearest mechanic."

In the passenger seat, Suze had returned to human form and was busily yanking clothing back on at near-warp speed. It was, after all, still the middle of November. "Stop anthropomorphizing your car, Fort," she grumbled, struggling into her shirt.

"The Fiesta saved us from a bear attack today," I said severely. "You will never bad-mouth this car again."

"Fine." She finally got the hem of her shirt pulled all the way down, and I glanced over. I couldn't help but notice that she had not bothered to put on her underwear, which was still lying on the floor of the passenger seat. After noting that small, yet salient fact, I forced my brain back on target.

"What did you smell on that shirt, Suze?" I asked. "I know that way you flip your tail. It was something important."

Leaning down, she started yanking on her socks as the Fiesta finally made it back to the main road, and I tentatively accelerated to fifteen miles per hour. "That was Dahlia's shirt," she grunted as she started putting her shoes back on. "And thanks to that plastic bag, all it was going to ever smell like was Dahlia. That bucket was new, too new to pick up any defining house smells or anything other than what was probably a CVS and the fifty people who likely handled it there."

"Frame job," I said, the pieces coming together. "Someone is setting Dahlia up to take the fall for killing the *karhu*."

"We were meant to find that knife in Dahlia's house," Suze agreed. "Wasn't Dahlia. Probably wasn't even Ilona. Someone stuck that knife there for us to find." She started wiggling into her sweater. "How much stronger is your sister's nose than yours?"

"What?" I eased the Fiesta onto Route 147, creeping along and watching as other cars passed me, their drivers shooting incredulous looks at us.

"You smelled the blood on that knife when I couldn't pick up anything except the diapers. It was put there for a vampire to find. Now, Chivalry is mourning his dead wife. Usually he's the one who would investigate a murder in this territory. But he can't right now—that leaves you or Prudence."

I followed where she was going, slapping my forehead with one hand. "Someone killed Matias *now* for a reason. If Prudence was investigating, she would've found that knife and just killed Dahlia *and* Ilona on the assumption that one of them was the murderer!"

"Exactly. But Prudence didn't get the job—you did. And you found the knife, but you didn't point to a suspect."

"Which must've completely frazzled the person doing this setup, since they must've assumed that we missed the knife. Until we went to the funeral today and told one of the *metsän kunigas* that we *had* found it."

"That same guy who seemed awfully fixated on us checking out the woods today."

"Gil," I said grimly. I was really looking forward to shooting him. "I thought I saw a pair of balls on that bear."

But Suze shook her head. "That wasn't Gil that attacked us. I've gotten a few good, close whiffs whenever we talked to him, and that wasn't him."

"So we've got more than one—shit!"

The Fiesta's horrible rattles had suddenly gotten much louder, and the heat sensor had just whipped right up to the highest possible marking. It was hard to tell in the dark, with only one barely functioning headlight, but I realized that there was smoke billowing out of what was left of my hood.

I pulled the Fiesta hard into the breakdown lane and tumbled out of the car. The smoke was now dense and black, billowing out of the front as I scrambled out, ran to my trunk, and started hunting for my fire extinguisher. On the other side, Suze was also out, and she set to work immediately, grabbing stuff out of the car (starting first with the duffel bag that contained the Ithaca and the Colt) and tossing it into the grass, well away from the Fiesta. Everything in the trunk was still all tumbled around from the bear-ramming impact, and everything that wasn't the extinguisher I threw out over my shoulder. Finally I laid my hand on that blessed red canister, and ran back to the front of the Fiesta. Flames were licking out from it now, and the heat was incredible. With my hood already pushed back from the crash, I just aimed the nozzle at the engine and deployed.

There was a tiny hiss, and about a teaspoon of foam emerged. I stood there, stunned, for a second. The extinguisher had been in the car when I bought it, and had probably been waiting twenty years for its heroic moment to arrive—and now had completely failed.

Suze grabbed my arm and yanked me backward as the fire spread, until we were standing on the dead grass beside the road, surrounded by the pile of all the stuff that she'd pulled out of the car. She had her phone against her ear and was discussing the situation with the fire department, but I knew that they weren't going to get here in time, and there was nothing to do but watch as my faithful Ford Fiesta died in a pyre.

Hours later, after talking to the fire department, and the police department, and after watching the steaming remains of the Fiesta be hauled away to the dump, then waiting for Dan to drive over and pick us up, I lay prone on the sofa, staring up at the ceiling and mourning my car. The police had definitely taken notice of the crumpled front end. We'd explained by lying, claiming that we'd hit a deer near the state park area, and after the deer had run off into the woods, we'd tried to limp the car home.

My hair was still wet—it had taken two straight shampoos in the shower to get rid of the scent of burning metal, plastic, rubber, and oil. I'd thrown my clothing and Suze's into the wash along with a double dose of detergent, and was hoping that it took care of the odor. I heard the pipes stop rattling—Suzume must've finally finished with her own shower.

There was a scuffing at the door, and I was sitting and aiming the Colt all in one motion. I waited, frozen, as the door opened to reveal Dan. He glanced at the gun I was currently pointing at him, and raised his eyebrows. I tucked it back onto the coffee table, where it sat next to the Ithaca. Both were fully loaded.

"I just checked on your laundry," Dan said. "All done, and the worst of the funk is out. I tossed everything into the dryer, so Suze will at least have something to wear tomorrow when you guys head out."

"Thanks," I said. "Listen, some bears might come and try to murder us in the night, so you might want to go crash at Jaison's."

Dan looked remarkably calm about my statement, and simply crossed over to the fridge to take out the ice cream. He set it on the counter, then removed two bowls and commenced scooping. "Fort," he said, "firstly, I knew that rooming with you was going to entail a certain level of being in the shit."

"You did?"

He paused in the act of scooping ice cream, and gave me a very level stare. "Your last roommate got murdered, Fort. Exactly how dumb do you think I am?"

"Sorry," I apologized meekly. "Continue."

"Like I said, I knew this kind of thing might come up. At least you wash your dishes and clean the bathroom when it's your week, so it's not the end of the world. And as for Jaison, the guy lives with his grandma. That's not a morning-after walk of shame that I want to experience."

I winced, then nodded in understanding, and watched as my roommate re-covered the ice cream and put it away. "I'm sorry your car died," Dan said, and handed me one of the bowls.

"It was a really good car." Ice cream seemed small solace for losing my car, but it was certainly better than nothing. I ate a bite.

Dan paused, and seemed to be considering my statement.

"It was," I defended. "It rammed a fully grown werebear in defense of our lives."

"At least it died in battle, then," Dan noted. "Gloriously, even. And then got a full Viking funeral."

"There is that," I acknowledged.

Suze walked into the room. Her hair was still wet from the shower, and she was wearing my Doctor Who T-shirt, which hit her around midthigh, and apparently nothing else. I looked at her and blinked a few times, feeling my brain shudder to a full stop. It completely tented her in a swath of Dalek-emblazoned fabric, covering her arms down to the elbow, and I knew that logically I'd seen her in outfits that showed more skin (and, technically, that I'd also actually seen her naked multiple times pre- and post-shifting), but somehow this just seemed *naked-er*. And really sexy.

"So, what are we talking about?" she asked.

"How I'm going straight to bed, and you kids have fun catching a killer tomorrow," Dan said, clearly able to read a room. He grabbed his ice cream and retreated.

"Watch out for bear assassins climbing up the fire escape," Suze called after him, and he gave a wave of acknowledgment before closing his door firmly behind him. She looked over at me and gave a small smile. "Subtle of him."

"Screw subtle—he just won best roommate of the year," I said, watching her closely.

At that, she grinned widely, and sauntered over to the couch before tucking in beside me comfortably and reaching over to confiscate my ice cream. I let her have it, enjoying the feeling of her soft body pressed against my side. Until that moment, I'd felt ready to conk out and sleep for a week, but with her here, I decided that plan could wait a bit.

"So, are we all set for tomorrow?" she asked, snuggling close and spooning some ice cream into her mouth.

I watched as she swiped her tongue over her bottom lip. "We catch a few hours of sleep, then wait until Kivela Mutual Insurance is open for the day. We head down there and corner Gil at work, with lots of superior firepower, and beat a confession out of him," I recited, then paused. "Not that I want to move right now, or possibly ever again, but are you sure it's not a good idea to do it tonight?"

She shook her head, her wet hair flicking me with water droplets. "He sent that bear after us, but right now he doesn't know that we know he's trying to frame Dahlia, so he won't be trying to run. We wait, and then we can get him when we're surrounded by other bears, rather than at his house where we won't have backup."

I nodded. "Okay, seems like it would work." I looked down at her, feeling my pulse pound in my ears, then said slowly, feeling the heaviness of the possibilities in the room, "So now we just go to sleep."

Suzume's eyelids dropped down slowly, nearly shutting, and she gave a very slow nod. "That's the plan." Her voice was low and throaty. She stood up smoothly, then handed me back the now-empty bowl. "Guess we should head to bed, then." She turned and strolled into my bedroom. I stared for a long second, then hurried to rinse out the bowl and set it in the drying rack. I ran my hands over my hair, wishing that it wasn't drying in weird little shapes and cowlicks, but definitely not willing to make a pit stop in the bathroom to make a styling attempt. I breathed experimentally into my palm, but all I could smell was chocolate ice cream, which I believed would count rather firmly in my favor. I carefully straightened my T-shirt and adjusted my sweatpants, and followed Suze into my bedroom.

She was lying naked on my bed.

Well, naked except for her fur. The black fox wagged the snow-white tip of her tail in greeting.

I couldn't help but laugh at the foxy look of amusement on her face. I walked over and leaned down to rub the soft fur behind her ears, watching as her fluffy tail twitched with enjoyment.

"Trickster," I whispered affectionately, then turned off the light and slid under the covers. After a moment, I felt her get up, turn around a few times, then settle down again, this time with her furry body pressed against my arm. In the soft glow coming through my window from the streetlights, I could see the prick of her furry ears and the glint of her eyes, and I knew that she would be on guard in case bear assassins actually did break through the door. Feeling safe and comforted, I slipped into a dreamless sleep.

Chapter 8

By seven in the morning, Suze and I were both dressed, fed, and engaged in the serious business of figuring out exactly what the line was between concealing weapons in winter clothing yet also keeping them accessible. Parkas were turning out to be problematic, so I'd had to break out my zip-up hoodie. It had enough bagginess and drape to conceal the Colt when I wore it in a belt holster, but it also was easier to flip up and maneuver than my parka. For the Ithaca, I'd been a bit flummoxed, until Suze told me to just calm down and stuff it in my laptop bag. Well, actually she'd used the term *man purse*, but the outcome was the same.

As for Suze, she'd turned out to have an impressive array of knife sheaths in her car, which she could strap to her forearms, lower legs, and various other spots in addition to the traditional ones at her waist, or the near-scabbard that she strapped to her leg to contain the twelve-inch single-edged terror that was Arlene. Her fox tricks would enable her to walk around without anyone suspecting her of being a one-woman alternative to a Cuisinart, but the sleeves on her corded sweater from yesterday had been a little too tight for the fast access to all of her knives that she apparently preferred, so I'd lent her one of my button-down flannel shirts. When I'd asked whether she'd be cold, since after all it was still

November, and she only had a long-sleeved cotton shirt under the flannel, she just shook her head and looked amused, commenting that any woman who wore evening attire on New Year's Eve got used to being chilly for the sake of fashion, and that if she got really uncomfortable, she could at least stab someone to make herself feel better.

I'd just tucked the last few boxes of extra ammo into my laptop case (which had not been what I'd had in mind when I purchased it, but I was suddenly appreciating its roomy and convenient pockets in a whole new way) when Suze's phone rang. She looked down at the number, raised her eyebrows, and handed it to me.

It was a Newport area code, and I flipped it open. "Hello?"

"Good, Fortitude, I was hoping I'd reach you at this number." Loren Noka's voice echoed in my ear, and she sounded relieved. "You aren't picking up your phone"— the phone I had destroyed the other day, I suddenly remembered—"and the *metsän kunigas* just called in an emergency."

"What's going on?" I asked, my heartbeat picking up significantly. Maybe Gil Kivela had figured out that we were on his trail and had made a break for it.

"An early-morning employee at Kivela Mutual Insurance found the body of a young man in their office. It's one of the bears, and they think it looks like the same type of attack that their *karhu* suffered."

"Give me the address, Loren," I said, grabbing my laptop bag and heading for the door, Suze following in my wake. "We'll be heading over there immediately." I rattled off the address to Suze as we pounded down the stairs—she had an incredible memory for those kinds of things, and ended the call to Loren.

"Why would Gil Kivela kill again?" I asked Suze as we jumped into her Audi Coupe. I missed the Fiesta almost viscerally as I tucked my laptop bag at my feet.

There was little that the Fiesta could boast, but at least it had had four doors and a sense of scruffy comfort. The interior of Suze's car was nothing but immaculate leather, and I was terrified to so much as think of bringing a soda into it.

It was also an automatic. As Suze merged into traffic and began an extremely aggressive style of driving, I couldn't help but think about how much better her gas mileage would've been with a manual transmission.

Meanwhile, Suzume was actually answering my question. "Maybe the kid got close and saw something Gil didn't want him to see. Maybe he was actually involved, and got scared, and Gil had to eliminate him. But after what happened yesterday, I can tell you what I'm sure we'll find." She looked over at me as she merged across two lanes of traffic with a single turn-signal. "Something of Dahlia's."

"You think he'll still be trying to pin this on her?" I asked, one hand automatically wrapping itself around the "oh shit" handle of the car as Suze blew completely through a red light.

"With a second body on the ground? I'd say he's pretty committed." Suze's speedometer was flirting with ninety, and I decided to let her concentrate on driving.

The parking lot of Kivela Mutual Insurance looked neat and orderly—all the spots were full, but no one was roaming around. The illusion of normalcy was gone the moment we walked through the swinging glass doors, where the fairly standard reception area was filled with a crowd of extremely anxious and stunned people, all dressed in various assortments of business casual. From the looks of it, some people had been more dressed than others when the news of the killing went out. One woman in a blouse and slacks was standing next to a man who had apparently just thrown his business jacket on over his pajamas. Whoever that guy was, he was the one who immediately stepped forward and led us through the crowd.

"Rhoda does the cleaning in the morning, before the rest of us come in, so she was the one who found Peter," the pajamas guy said as he led us through a large main room filled with an assortment of cubicles.

"Bear or human?" Suze asked him. There was a glint in her eyes that was clearly assessing cover-up requirements.

He caught on to what she was asking, and immediately shook his head. "No one works here who isn't either *metsän kunigas* or one of our spouses. Rhoda married in forty years ago, so she's no threat. She's in the back." There were three rooms with actual doors at the far end of the main area—one had Matias Kivela's name on it, so I assumed that was the corner office. The other was the bathroom, the break room, or some unholy combination of the two, and the last was what pajamas guy gestured for us to enter before immediately turning and trotting back to the reception area.

From floor to ceiling, the room was edged with tall metal file cabinets. Down the middle of the room was a long table, surrounded with chairs, so this probably served as a conference room when the company needed one. I immediately picked out Dahlia and Gil, standing side by side against one of the cabinets, their faces grim. A smaller, gray-haired woman was huddled in one of the chairs, crying—that was probably Rhoda, who had found much more to clean up than usual. The kitsune had beaten us here—Chiyo, Midori, and Takara all gave me small nods of recognition, and they were clearly waiting for us to finish up before they could make preparations for the police.

And at the far end of the room, between the table and the farthest cabinet, was the body of a young man. I'd thought that Matias Kivela's body had been tough to look at, but this one was worse—his face was a mass of bruises and cuts, his arms were covered in slices, and his chest was simply a mess.

I looked over at Dahlia, and that coldly professional look on her face. I could see the cracks now; there was a haunted expression in her eyes. Looking at Gil, all I could see was barely contained anger.

"What can you tell me about this man?" I asked, directing the question to Dahlia.

"Peter Utrio," she answered, rubbing her face. "He is"—she coughed, suddenly, and corrected herself—"*was* nineteen. He's a college student, and no one can remember seeing him after the funeral last night."

Suze was crouching down next to the body, leaning close and poking around. "There's a lot more damage here than Matias suffered." She glanced over at the bears. "Did anyone examine him closely?"

"I did," Gil said. "When Rhoda found him, she locked the door and called Dahlia. I was already on my way in to get some paperwork done early, so I arrived first. He's got at least half a dozen broken ribs, plus all those defensive wounds on his arms. He was definitely awake when whoever did this started stabbing him." The bear paused as Suze leaned down close and sniffed. She scuffled in his pockets for a second, then tossed me something, which I automatically caught.

It was the boy's wallet, which I flipped open. I stared for a second at his college ID—I'd seen that face before, and recently. I tried picturing it with some more acne, then it hit me—this was the guy who'd been sent to fetch Gil yesterday at the church. I looked up and caught Suze's eye. I nodded down to the wallet, and she gave a subtle tap on the body—we'd both found stuff. She tilted her head quickly at Dahlia, and I got the message.

I looked over at the kitsune, who looked ready to go. "If Suzume has everything she needs, you get started," I said, then paused. "Another heart attack? Won't that be a little weird?"

Midori shook her head. "He's too young to be a clear candidate for a heart attack, so that isn't what the police's minds would naturally accept. There's just been a tragedy in the death of Matias Kivela, someone he knew. We'll have to work off that."

Chiyo reached into her purse and produced a bag of extremely illegal paraphernalia. "We're going heroin overdose on this one," the older woman explained.

"Suze?" I looked over, and she was already getting up. I turned to the bears. "Gil, I'd like you to stay with Rhoda in the cubicle room while Suzume and I have a discussion with Dahlia, privately." He opened his mouth, and I cut him off before he could even voice his inevitable protest. "*She* is the acting *karhu*."

He glowered at me, but there was nothing he could trump that with. Dahlia herself just gave a small nod and a murmured, "Of course," as we all trooped out of the file room. Dahlia led us down to her uncle's office. After seeing the inside of the man's house, I was not surprised at the temple of beige that awaited us.

Suze shut the door and produced a piece of fabric. "This was in his hand." She passed it to me, and I looked. It was the cuff of a shirt, ripped off and spotted with blood. Suze looked over at the bear standing beside us. "It's yours," she said.

Dahlia frowned. "What do you mean? How would Peter have something of mine?"

"Someone has been working very hard to set you up for your uncle's murder," I told her. "The knife that was used to kill Matias was hidden in your laundry room, we found a shirt of yours that was going to be planted at the scene of an attack on us, and now here's another piece of your clothing left with a second body." As I spoke, Dahlia paled and wobbled on her feet, reaching one hand out to steady herself against the wall as she stared at me.

"Given the state of his broken ribs, and the amount of oil, metal, and fuel that I smelled on him, I think I can safely say that Peter was the bear that attacked us last night," Suze said.

"He attacked you?" Dahlia shook her head, and I could see her struggling to follow everything we were throwing at her. "Why would he—no, Peter wouldn't have done that."

"Believe me, it happened," I said. "There were only two people who knew that Suze and I were going to do one last check of the Lincoln Woods for Ad-hene activity near your uncle's house. Peter overheard it, but Gil was the one who told us to go there. Now Peter is dead, and someone is trying to lay evidence that points it toward you. Dahlia, we think that your brother is trying to frame you."

"No!" The color rushed back into Dahlia's cheeks, and for the first time I saw her get mad. "That's insane, and it's not true." At our expressions, she clearly tried to pull things back, but her voice was still shaking with anger when she spoke. "I know he wants to be *karhu*, I know he feels he could be the leader we need right now, but I *know* my brother. He wouldn't do this."

"If not him, then who?" Suze asked. "If you're taken out of the picture, then who benefits and becomes *karhu*? Your brother, your mother? Matias's daughter?"

Dahlia pressed the heels of her hands against her jaw, hard enough that I could see the skin whiten, and she shook her head. Her eyes pressed closed, and I could see her trying to run through what Suze was saying, trying to weigh things. "Mother is too old—the *karhu* is always from the generation in their prime. The new *karhu* would be either Gil or Carmen, but Gil would never do this to me, and Carmen wouldn't kill her own father—her mother is dead, and Uncle Matias was all she had left."

"*Someone* is trying to frame you for murder, Dahlia," I put in. "Try it from the other angle—what do you know about Peter? He was working with whoever is orchestrating this—who was he close to?"

"None of us, not really," she protested. "Peter is, *was*, an only child, from the *metsän kunigas* community up in

Maine. His mother was human, so he was going to have to marry bear, but he was never close with any of his peers in that community. He came down to go to college here because everyone hoped that he would meet one of our bear girls and form a natural attachment, that the matchmaker wouldn't have to be brought in. He was sweet, but so awkward, and I can't even think of a single one of us who he would've so much as talked with outside the general group meetings and business."

"Think, damn it," Suze snapped at the bear. "Who would want you dead?"

Dahlia just shook her head. "This is my family," she insisted. "It has to be an outsider, someone trying to start an internal fight. The Ad-hene—"

Suze was shaking her head and cutting Dahlia off before she could elaborate. "It's not them, Dahlia. It's someone you've been trusting. Now get with the *not* trusting, and give us some goddamn suspects!"

Dahlia's mouth thinned, and she was back to looking pissed. I sighed—Suze's methods of interrogation sometimes ran into difficulty. "Listen," I said, trying to inject some calm. "We're not getting anywhere like this, and Dahlia clearly doesn't have any ideas. So we need to figure out a way to flush our killer out."

Suze huffed, then said, "Give them what they want."

"What?" I stared at Suze. "I don't think killing Dahlia is a good plan!"

"I agree with that," Dahlia said quickly, edging away from us. "That's actually a very bad plan. Very, very bad."

"No, you idiots," Suze said, looking disgusted. "We just let the killer think that the frame job has worked." She paused, then added, "Admittedly, that is going to be tough to do without killing Dahlia."

"Wait a second," I said, holding up a hand. "Am I correct in saying that I've gotten somewhat of a reputation as being a less murder-happy vampire?"

"Do the *metsän kunigas* shit in the woods?" Suze

asked rhetorically. I wondered how long exactly the kit-sune had been sitting on that particular gem. Dahlia's expression suggested that had the situation been any less fraught, those would've been fighting words.

I pushed forward. "Okay, we can use that. We pretend that we believe that Dahlia is guilty, and we put her under house arrest."

"That might be tricky, Fort," Suze said cautiously. "We're not using my house. Dan would definitely not go for this, and Dahlia's house is kind of baby central."

"No, no my house is empty today," Dahlia said. "Gil and I were so sure that it had to be the Ad-hene. . . . We talked at dinner last night, and I agreed to send the girls somewhere safer until the situation was cleared up. Mom and I packed everything they needed, and she hit the road. They arrived in Greenville, Maine, at five thirty this morning."

"That makes things easier." I actually felt a deep sense of relief. Not only was this going to clear up logistics, but I was glad that her daughters were well out of the line of fire. "Is there anyone out there in the reception area who you can say for sure, based only on logical proof, *couldn't* have been involved in either of the murders? We need someone who we can say is your prison guard, so it would help if this was a bear."

Dahlia thought it through, then nodded. Clearly, trusting people was something she was a lot better at than coming up with possible suspects. "Alison could do it. She's been backpacking in Australia for an entire month. Someone texted her, and she caught a plane home. She didn't get in until the morning of the funeral."

"Then she's your guard while you're under house arrest." I looked over at Suze. "Peter wasn't killed until after I hit him with the car and he ran off, so the killer might've just acted quickly to cover some tracks. We'll search Peter's place, just in case he was helpful enough to leave *karhu*-murdering plans in writing. Then we'll swing back to your house, and we'll all sit tight and see what happens."

There was general agreement. Dahlia whipped out her iPhone and looked up Peter's home information for me, while Suze went out and then returned a minute or two later with our recruited prison guard/bodyguard. From the expression on her face, Suze had probably had some fun with that "random" selection criteria. Fortunately Alison didn't look like a strange pick for that job—she was tough, and solidly built, the kind of person who definitely looked like she could backpack solo around the Australian outback for kicks. She also looked like the kind of woman who I would call for help if I needed to move a fridge.

While we filled her in on what her job was going to be, I removed a plastic bag full of industrial wire ties from my laptop case. Our original plan had been to use these as part of subduing Gil, but they now served as a way to help with our ploy. Suze fashioned a set of cuffs. "Too tight?" she asked solicitously.

"Actually, yeah," Dahlia replied.

"Good." I stared at Suze, and she gave a small shrug, explaining, "It'll look more authentic. Oh, and we should punch her in the face to make it look like we roughed her up during questioning."

"I think the cuffs are enough," I said. "Now, is the crowd gathered?"

"Everyone's in the cubicle room right now," Alison said.

"Good. On our marks . . . aaaaand, everyone acting!"

"Ladies, gentlemen, and bears—I am pleased to say that we have apprehended the murderer of Matias Kivela and Peter Utrio." A huge gasp went through the room, and everyone looked stunned and horrified at the sight of Dahlia at my side, her hands bound with wire ties and a blank expression on her face. I continued, pressing my advantage. "Dahlia Kivela will be under house arrest while I discuss her punishment with my mother, but let me assure you, it will be severe." People were already leaning over to talk with their neighbors, and many were pulling out cell phones to call or text the news to everyone else. I noticed how many people were shaking their heads, still looking amazed, while others wore smug I-knew-it-all-along expressions. Even when they could turn into bears, people were still people.

Alison strong-armed Dahlia through the crowd, presumably out to her waiting car, followed by Suze, who, I noticed, snagged her cousin Takara's sleeve and had a whispered conference. I would've been following closely, but halfway to the door, Gil finally shoved his way through the crowd and wrapped one huge hand around my arm, stopping me in my tracks.

"What is *wrong* with you?" he bellowed in my face, attracting the fascinated attention of the entire crowd. "This is outrageous—my sister would never do that! What the hell did you do to her to make her say that she did that? Who did you threaten?" His other hand locked on my free arm, and I had a feeling that I would have a matching set of bruises in the shape of his fingers. I stepped back and broke his grip before he could deliver the teeth-snapping shaking that he clearly wanted to inflict, then grabbed him by the collar and towed him into the reception room and away from the crowd. I was not forgetting for a moment that, for all Dahlia's protests, Gil remained my prime suspect.

In the reception room, with no audience of his hopeful future subjects to play to, I got up in his face. "I didn't need a confession," I said loudly. "The evidence spoke for itself. The murder weapon was in her house, and there was a piece of your sister's clothing on Peter's body today."

Gil shook his head wildly. "That's circumstantial evidence! Anyone could've put that knife in Dahlia's house, and who the hell knows how Peter got a piece of her clothing? How are you even so sure it's Dahlia's clothing? None of this would be enough for a human court!"

I was impressed—Gil was doing a great impression of a frantic and loyal brother, but I shook my head coldly and said, "It's a good thing that the vampires don't need courts, then," and turned away. Suze had just come back into the building, and through the glass doors, I could see Alison loading Dahlia into her car.

"Where are you going?" Gil demanded, grabbing a handful of my jacket.

I looked over my shoulder. "To finish my investigation."

"You're going nowhere without me," he snapped. "I'm not going to let you railroad my sister on shoddy evidence."

I shook him off me again and glanced over at Suze. She gave a small, curious look, then held open the door and gestured for Gil to precede us. He did, shooting us both extremely foul glares. I followed, pausing next to Suze to whisper in her ear. "Exactly what is this plan of yours now?"

She leaned in close. "Methinks the gentleman doth protest too much. Let him come along. We'll see what he does, and if he makes one wrong move, I'll slice him before he can shift to bear."

I glanced down to where I knew Suze's knife was strapped to her leg, even though her fox magic forced my eyes away from it. "Agreed," I said.

We loaded into Suze's Audi. I was driving, with Gil uncomfortably close in the passenger seat. Suze had clambered into the backseat (another reason to loathe two-door cars—even she was unable to make her entrance into the back look graceful), and was now sitting directly behind Gil. While he continued a loud soliloquy on the subject of his sister's innocence, I glanced behind me and noticed the gleam of one of Suze's smaller knives, held carefully in her hand. Apparently she was not taking any chances, because she looked ready to slit the bear's throat at a moment's notice. It seemed like a solid precaution to me, and I started the Audi up.

Peter's apartment turned out to be in the student area near Roger Williams University, in one of those tired but massive apartment buildings that are such a staple of off-campus housing that the owners have realized that they never have to do maintenance ever again, because naïve young students will continue forking over their parents' money regardless of the size of the rat infestation. I remembered such living well—in my first off-campus apartment at Brown, the cockroaches had been so giant and aggressive that I had given up even trying to keep food in my cabinets, and had kept everything in my fridge.

Normally Suze would've picked the lock on Peter's door, but as we stood in the hallway of the building's ninth floor, with the light above us flickering ominously and what looked like fossilized vomit on the carpet, it was clear that her services were unnecessary—the lock was already broken. I pushed the door open and walked in, followed by Gil (who had finally stopped talking after Suze had openly threatened him while we walked up the stairs—naturally, the elevator was broken), then Suze, who was shadowing the bear's every movement.

It was a typical efficiency apartment—bed, bureau, and desk in the main room, doors leading into the tiny kitchen and the tinier bathroom. The single window had a bath towel tacked to it to make up for the lack of curtains. It also looked like a bomb had exploded—every drawer had been yanked out of the dresser and dumped onto the floor, and papers were thrown everywhere. The computer keyboard, mouse, and monitor were resting neatly on his desk, but the plugs had been yanked out and the hard drive removed. There was the usual assortment of college-guy posters on the walls, but there were several noticeable blank spots where something had been removed. On a few spots that remover had been in such a hurry that the corners of the picture still remained, with the rest torn away.

"Someone was already here," I noted, a second later kicking myself for becoming Captain Obvious. There was a weirdly strong smell hanging in the air, and not the usual one I would've expected for a college guy's apartment. "And that someone brought bleach." I looked over at Suze. "Is there any way you can still—"

Never taking her eyes off Gil, who was staring around the room and looking distinctly taken aback, or was just admiring his own handiwork, she shook her head. "I can't get a scent, Fort. Not once bleach gets thrown around."

"Shit." I looked around and nudged a pile of paper. "Whoever did this must've grabbed anything incriminating."

"You don't know that," Gil said sharply, giving me that very familiar glare. He knelt down and started sorting through a pile of papers. "The killer was probably in a hurry, and they could've missed something that will prove to you that my sister is innocent."

As he turned his attention to the papers, I exchanged a glance with Suze. She gave a little shrug and said, "Well, we did drive all the way over here."

"All right." I turned and looked at the demolished room. "Now, if I were a nineteen-year-old guy, and I had something incriminating to hide, where would I put it?"

Of course, I *had* once been a nineteen-year-old guy in crappy student apartments (my current apartment, while still moderately crappy, was still a cut above the cesspools that students lived in), so all I had to do was remember where I had stashed my treasures. I went straight for the closet, and started shaking out all of the shoes, then dug my hands into the pockets of all of his jackets. I found a very nice watch, probably a graduation gift from his parents, but nothing incriminating. I looked around the room again and saw the pile of books against the side of his desk. Gil was still picking away at the papers, with Suze focusing on emulating upper management and not doing anything but watching. I grabbed the top book on the stack and flipped through it. Nothing. Next one, again nothing. I was halfway through the stack when I hit pay dirt in his copy of *An Introduction to Literary Criticism*. It was a photo, and I stared at it for a long second.

"Guys," I said, with enough intensity that Gil and Suze both turned around. I handed the picture silently to Suze. Her eyebrows lifted slowly, and she gave a low whistle as she looked at what I'd seen—there was poor, awkward, acne-ridden Peter lying on his bed. And snuggled up next to him was the beautiful blond Carmen, with a very sly smile on her face.

Gil looked over Suze's shoulder and gaped. "Carmen and Peter weren't dating," he said, staring at the photo as if he couldn't quite process the information it was conveying because it just didn't add up—like two and two suddenly equaling twelve. "She's always chasing some of the older boys—*metsän kunigas* in their twenties. She told me once that Peter had a puppy crush on her."

While Gil was trying to wrap his head around things, I pulled the next book off the stack—*Ivanhoe*. Apparently Peter had been a literature student, because I found another picture. This was quite a bit more explicit—it was just Carmen on the bed, and she was completely naked. "Looks like someone found that crush useful," I said, and passed the photo over. I stared at Gil, realizing that the whole time he'd been defending his sister, he'd been absolutely sincere. Meanwhile, there had been Carmen, just hanging around the edges, so willing to tell me all about how Matias had killed Dahlia's husband, or, *Jesus*, even making me promise to bring Prudence into the investigation if things stalled out.

Suze was clearly thinking the same thing. "Carmen

was working on this from the beginning, and she figured out how to get Peter to help her out. She tried to pin it all on Dahlia, and she waited until she thought that she'd be dealing with Prudence rather than Chivalry."

"She got Peter to attack us, maybe to kill us, or maybe just kill you and maim the hell out of me and plant the evidence, who knows, but that definitely would've brought Prudence up here in a killing mood." I looked at Gil. "But she was just focusing on Dahlia—why is that, Gil? Why didn't she try to frame you for anything?"

Gil was still staring at the photos of his cousin, shaking his head. When I said his name, he jerked a little, and finally looked up at me, horrified. "Uncle Matias tapped Dahlia as his successor at the end of last month. I knew that he didn't agree with my opinions, and that Chivalry Scott just saw me as another version of my mother, so I knew that I wasn't going to be named the heir. But my mom asked why he wasn't considering Carmen at all—she's young, but she's twenty-one now. But Matias said he didn't want to go into it, but that she didn't have the temperament."

"I've heard that phrase a lot in these conversations," I noted. "Now what exactly did he mean by that?"

Gil coughed, uncomfortable. "When she was five and I was eighteen, I caught her pulling the wings off flies. Stuff like that. She was kind of a creepy little kid."

"Great, a budding sociopath," Suze said. "Now what exactly was done about it?"

"I told my aunt, and she said that she'd take care of it."

Suze's eyes narrowed. "Would this be Carmen's dead mother?" Gil nodded, and her voice became suspicious. "And how did she die again?"

"It was an accident," Gil said. "She . . ." I could tell the exact moment he thought it through and connected the accident to what was currently going on, because he suddenly looked like he wanted to vomit. "She fell down the stairs and broke her neck. Carmen was the one who found her. But she was just a little kid—she was only six."

"We need to find Carmen right now," I said, and Gil nodded jerkily, still looking locked in shock. "Where would she be?" I pressed, when the bear didn't automatically answer.

"Work?" he blinked. "She's the assistant manager at a bridal boutique downtown. But why would she go to work the day after she killed Peter?"

"She went to work the day after she murdered her father," Suze noted. "Apparently she believes in saving her sick days for something important."

"Carmen was locking in alibis the whole time," I said as the realization hit me. "She killed Matias, showered, then put on clean clothes and went out to a party. Slept with some guy, spent the night, then went to work and let someone else find the body." I mentally kicked myself. Not that I'd even pushed on her alibi—I'd fallen hook, line, and sinker for her innocent routine.

"But that was planned," Suze said. "Everything that night, from when she killed him, to the party that was probably already scheduled, to how she'd clean up her part of the scene. This, though"—she nudged one of the dumped drawers with her foot—"this was her having to improvise. Having Peter attack us to plant the clothing was also risky—she exposed an accomplice. Then she dumped him in the main building—trying to force us to take action."

"So we have a sociopath who is getting sloppy and desperate," I said. That wasn't a comforting thought. I felt a rush of relief that Gil and Dahlia had shipped the little girls up north. I focused on Gil. "Listen, if you call her at work, maybe have her meet you somewhere by saying that you guys need to talk about Dahlia—"

The sound of Suze's phone cut me off, an explosion of techno dance music. She was a fan of personalized ring-tones, and I had yet to psych myself into asking her exactly what she'd assigned to my calls. "That's Taka," she said, whipping the phone out of her pocket and pressing it to her ear. After an intensive minute, she cursed vehemently. "Go home. Don't go near a bear until I give you the okay."

"What's going on?" I could feel the hair on the back of my neck standing on end.

She hung up and shoved the phone back in her pocket. "I asked Taka to keep an eye on the house. She was in fox form when Carmen showed up and went inside. A minute later she came out with Dahlia. Carmen had a gun, so Taka stayed where she was. Carmen forced Dahlia into the car, made her drive off somewhere. Once they were gone, Taka ran down and into the house. The bodyguard is dead, shot at close range, and Taka just called me from the house phone."

"Oh my God," Gil said, then shook his head. "Alison is *dead*?"

"Focus, Gil," I said. "We need to focus on Dahlia. Why would Carmen take her rather than kill her?"

"She must've smelled a trap when we didn't just kill Dahlia outright." Suze paced. "So now we've got a sociopath who realizes that we know that there was a frame job happening."

"But why take Dahlia?" Gil pressed. "And take her where?"

"Everything Carmen has been doing, she's been doing to angle herself into the job of *karhu*," I said slowly, thinking things through. "Her father must've said something to her that made her realize that he was never going to give her the job, so she killed him in a way that would also knock out the other contender for the spot. Now she knows that we don't suspect Dahlia, so—"

"It's *me*," Gil burst out. "She's going to kill Dahlia and try to pin it on me, leaving her as the only possible heir."

"But you're—," I started to protest.

"But I'm with you guys. Oh my God," and he had his

phone out and dialing even as he talked, his words running over one another as he tried to spit all of them out. "She'll use my husband. He's at home, and if she can somehow make it look like Kevin and I were working together to try to make me *karhu*—"

"Car, right now, car," I said, and we tore out of the room and ran for the stairs.

"Kevin's not picking up his phone," Gil said, terror lining his face as he started taking the stairs three at a time and pulled ahead.

"Maybe he—"

"No," Gil insisted as the two of us started struggling to keep up with him. "Kevin's a web designer. He answers his phone on the toilet, at two in the morning, at the movies—he *never shuts it off.* That means Carmen is *already there*."

"But they could be heading anywhere," Suze protested. I agreed with her, but I was concentrating on breathing as we pounded down nine flights of stairs. "You were with us. She just grabbed Dahlia—she must already have had Kevin stashed somewhere."

"No, it's in our house; it would have to be—she needs to imply that I was involved with the whole thing. She thinks she stripped everything out of Peter's room that tied him to her—*crap*, the way you guys were looking at me this whole time, you thought it was *me*?"

Hopefully there was a gift basket somewhere that managed to capture that *Sorry I suspected you of murder* sentiment. If we got through this one, I'd have to look into it. For now, I saved my breath and focused on keeping up with Gil and Suze.

We emptied into the parking lot and raced to the Audi. I tossed Suze's keys to her, saying, "We need aggressive driving right now, but don't kill us. Gil, directions." I tried to think through Carmen's actions. "You were with us. That meant that if Kevin works from home, he would be alone. Everyone was calling with the news about Dahlia—Carmen hears that and figures out her plan. She goes to Kevin first, disables him, stashes him at your house. Then she goes to Dahlia's, kills Alison, grabs Dahlia." I shuddered. "Gil, for the love of everything holy, just tell me you don't live two doors down from Dahlia."

Fortunately it turned out that Gil didn't. His distrust of the Ad-hene and dislike of sharing woods with them had apparently been enough motivation that he and Kevin had bought property not in Lincoln, where most of his family lived, but over in the town of Johnston, which pressed up against the Snake Den State Park, the second-largest of Rhode Island's state parks. This meant that since we were driving from Providence, we were actually closer to Gil's house than Carmen had been starting from Lincoln. She'd had at least a ten minute head start on us, but between the distance and Suze's incredible ability to drive with reckless disregard for life and property yet never be noticed by the police, I was able to clench my fists and hope. And looking at Gil, whose husband and sister were both in danger, I noticed a strange shifting and mottling in the flesh of his jaw and neck, as if the shape of his mouth were trying to change into something else. I remembered the jaws on Peter the bear when he'd been charging the Fiesta, and I had another reason to hope very hard that we got there soon— because I did not want to find myself trapped in the car with an enraged bear. Reaching into my laptop bag and bracing myself as Suze took a turn way too fast, I checked to make sure that the Ithaca and the Colt were both fully loaded.

Gil's house was a tidy little gray cape that had all the features I'd come to expect from a *metsän kunigas* property—right on the edge of the woods, with a high fence, and a good-size property in exchange for a smaller house. Suze pulled the car over a few houses down, and we piled out and ran down. There was a small sedan parked in the driveway, and I reached over as we passed it and pressed a hand against the hood—still warm, so Carmen hadn't beaten us by much.

The plan had been hashed out in haste on the drive over. Glancing at Gil, whose face was now completely covered in a layer of dense black fur and whose hands were looking extremely pawlike, I hoped like hell that Suze, who was already using her fox tricks to keep any neighbors from noticing that I was openly carrying firearms, was also preventing them from catching a glimpse of him. Frankly, even under the painful pressures of the moment, I kind of wished that she could've prevented *me* from seeing that.

We crouched under the windows of the living room, and Suze held up three fingers, then counted them down silently. On one, I snagged her under the hips and popped her up long enough for her to take a quick look around the room, then eased her down again. Suze's fox tricks might've been more than enough to keep the neighbors from seeing something that they wouldn't normally expect to see, but as Suzume had explained to us both in the car, Carmen would be on alert and paranoid. To prevent any bad-luck moments of our ursine sociopath glancing at the window at the exactly wrong instant, it had to be Suze peeking in, using as much of her fox mojo as she could muster to keep any eyes on the inside distracted. As I dropped her down and she shook her head, I noticed a sheen of sweat on her face, even in the cold weather, and I knew that whatever she was working, she was *working* at it.

Gil led the way farther into the property. Luckily, unlike Dahlia, he'd settled just for fences on the sides of his property, but not fully ringing it on all sides, so we didn't have to worry about pulling ourselves over anything. Slipping around to the back of the house, we found a well-maintained porch and a large bay window that looked into the kitchen. This time there was no need to give Suze a boost—we could all see Dahlia. Still wearing the clothing from this morning, but now with a large bruise on her cheek and blood dripping out of her mouth, she was standing rigidly, talking to someone. I craned backward, easing slowly away from the covering angle, and the rest of the tableau spread out in front of me. Kevin was tied to a chair a few feet in front of Dahlia, looking pale and strained, and behind him stood Carmen. She was still smiling that sweet and innocent Swiss Miss smile, looking completely normal in a neat sweater and pair of slacks, her workplace name tag actually pinned on her chest. Meanwhile she was handling a gun with frightening comfort, keeping it trained on Dahlia. She was crouching down a little, then standing back up, and I realized that she was trying to figure out what angle she'd have to fire it from to make it look like Kevin had shot Dahlia. Whatever scenario she had in her head, she was committed to it.

I leaned over and tugged Gil back until he could see what I did. Suze stayed where she was, squeezing her eyes shut and screwing her face up in concentration, and I knew that she was making sure that if Carmen happened to glance out the window, her eyes would be drawn to the trees, or the fence, and not to me and Gil. With my hand on his back, I could feel a strange fluctuation in the formation of Gil's spine—from second to second, it went from straight to curved, and I wondered exactly how hard it was right now for him not to just shift and run into that room.

But he managed it, though the strain was showing on his face. Gil pointed to himself, then the porch. The porch doors were, unsurprisingly in this season, closed, but there were also drapes across them—apparently Carmen had grabbed Kevin before he'd had a chance to open them. This was lucky for us, since that would allow Gil to get as close as possible to an entrance without being spotted, though I knew that Suze would be throwing up some cover.

While Gil moved into position, I set the Ithaca down carefully on the grass and drew the Colt from my waist holster. I eased it out—Suze had her hands fisted in the ground, and she was actually panting with the effort of keeping all eyes away from me as I carefully aimed the gun at Carmen's head. I paused, hesitating. I did my due diligence down at the shooting range every week, but I'd never in my life shot through glass, or even expected to shoot through glass. I had no idea what this was going to do to my line of fire, and I was worried about the bullet ricocheting into either Kevin or Dahlia. Even worse, Carmen's finger was on the trigger of her gun. She had a silencer on her gun, but I didn't, and the sound of my shot would probably result in her firing automatically— which, given the direction she was holding it in, would go right into Dahlia. And if I missed Carmen completely, then everyone would be at risk.

I saw Kevin's mouth move, and whatever he'd said, Carmen definitely wasn't happy about it. That innocent smile dropped off her face with shocking speed, revealing something very cold and frighteningly familiar to me. Carmen would've enjoyed meeting my sister, I realized, because they probably had a lot in common. But Kevin's comment made Carmen look at him, and even though her gun hand never wavered, that meant taking her eyes off Dahlia. And the other woman had been waiting for this chance, and was moving in an instant.

I'd run out of time, and I couldn't hesitate any longer. I had to take the shot, and so I just aimed as high above Kevin as I could while still keeping my chances of hitting Carmen alive, and I squeezed off the shot. Then several things happened at once—the bay window shattered from my shot, the gun inside fired, and Gil went crashing through the patio door like Rambo. Suze was already on her feet and running onto the porch to follow Gil in. I rolled, grabbed the Ithaca in my free hand, and was right on her tail a moment later.

Inside was a mess. Gil had Carmen pinned to the floor. From the blood surrounding her, I figured my bullet had at least winged her, but she was fighting hard against her cousin and screeching curses like a banshee, so apparently I hadn't gotten her anywhere particularly vital. Kevin's chair, with him still tied to it, was knocked over, but when Suze leaned down to check on him, he immediately yelled, "I'm fine! But Dahlia's been shot!" I looked around, and there was Dahlia, lying on the floor next to the table. She must've shifted as she went for the gun, because she was a weird mish-mash of bear and woman. Her shape was still human, but she'd suddenly acquired at least seventy additional pounds of bulk and a full layer of black fur, causing her clothing to snap open at every seam. Her pants were tangled in loose drapes of fabric around her legs, no longer attached to anything, and her blouse remained fixed only at the seams resting on her shoulders—the remainder was, again, draping. The bones of her face were completely distorted, with her dark brown eyes staring at me from above the distinct beginnings of a bear's muzzle. Most disturbingly, there was a lot of blood at her midsection. I lunged forward immediately to try to put pressure on the wound, but found myself swatted away by a half hand–half paw that packed enough muscle to nearly send me sprawling.

"Don't worry about me." Dahlia's voice was lower, rougher, and having issues with forcing consonants through a mouth not designed for speaking. Her teeth were distinctly no longer human. "All I need is a dish towel, but Kevin might've hit his head when he went down."

"Don't you dare listen to Dahlia!" her brother-in-law yelled, looking completely outraged. "She just got shot! She's probably in shock! I just got tipped over!"

There was a low, rumbling sound from Dahlia, and then she shook herself and shifted completely—proving that Gil and Kevin's kitchen had definitely not been designed with a three-hundred-pound black bear in mind. She looked at me and gave a very serious growl, then jerked her head again toward Kevin.

"Suze, maybe you'd better get Kevin untied, and maybe slap some ice on his noggin," I said cautiously. "Gil? Care to weigh in on this situation?"

"I've got Carmen's gun, and it's a .38. Dahlia? Did you shift fast enough before it hit you?" There was a low, chatty sound from the bear. "Okay, yeah, she'll actually be okay. She shifted fast enough, and a bullet this size couldn't penetrate her fat layers. We'll have to tweezer it out, but she'll be okay." Gil nodded, though I noticed that he was using a lot of strength to keep Carmen in check. I crouched down and set the muzzle of my Colt right behind her ear, and let her hear me cock the gun. She was smart enough to stop struggling, but the expression in her eyes would probably show up in a few of my nightmares. No regret—just an incredible cold rage.

"Carmen?" I asked, keeping my voice level. "I think it's time for a bit of a chat."

"I should've been named *karhu*," she snarled. "I *deserved* to be named *karhu*. I was taking what should've been given to me."

"That's it?" Gil said, disbelieving. I wished I could've been as stunned as he was, but I'd seen too many people who weren't bothered by killing anyone who stood in their way. Carmen would've gotten along well with the Ad-hene. "You killed your own father, you killed Alison and Peter, who must've loved you, you were going to shoot Kevin and Dahlia, and let the vampires kill me for that—Carmen, *what the hell is wrong with you?*"

She turned her face very deliberately to look at her cousin, and disgust dripped from her voice. "What's wrong with me? What's wrong is that I didn't just put a bomb in the kitchen during Thanksgiving dinner and let you all burn. But fucking Peter had to be a literature student instead of an engineer."

Gil let loose a torrent of Finnish, and Carmen smiled, her flat blue eyes gleaming. "I accept," she replied.

"What the hell did you just do, Gil?" I asked, very suspicious of anything that would make Carmen smile like the Joker.

Gil got off Carmen slowly, letting her get up on her knees. I kept the gun trained on her, darting glances at him. "Gil?"

"Carmen was willing to kill to become *karhu*, as if we're back in the old days when the entire generation of a ruling family would rip itself to shreds until one of them was the sole survivor. Well, if that's what she wants, that's what she'll get. I've challenged her to a dominance battle."

"Oh, for fuck's sake," Suze snapped from where she was pressing a paper towel against a cut on Kevin's forehead. "Don't be a twit, Gil. Let Fort shoot the bitch and we'll call it a day."

There was a sudden movement, and the bear was giving Suze an extremely unfriendly look, those black lips pulling back to give her an excellent view of ursine dental hygiene. Apparently Dahlia was on board with her brother on this. The kitsune shook her head in disgust. "The two of you are nuts," she said flatly.

Gil's eyes never wavered from his cousin. "I held you when you were an hour old," he said to Carmen. "You are my baby cousin, and I love you. So whatever horrible thing went wrong inside your brain, or whatever you think that the rest of us did to you that justified this, I am sorry. And I'll let you have this chance of living and getting what you've apparently been willing to sacrifice your own family for, rather than just letting the vampire put you down like a rabid animal." He didn't look away, but he tilted his head just slightly at me. "Fort? I think I might need Scott permission for this one. Are you willing to sign off?"

That put all the attention of the room on me while I

weighed things. I knew even without looking that Suze was probably exerting all of her expressive power to get me to tell Gil not to be a moron, and shoot Carmen in the head. But that was the problem—I knew I would've been able to kill Carmen during the fight, and from the oozing cut on her left arm, I'd done my best to do so. But standing here, with all of us talking . . . that was different. That felt like an execution, and I didn't want to do that. But telling Gil no and calling up my sister to come down to execute Carmen wasn't any less a murder on my part.

And then there was the look on Gil's face—I still didn't like him, but I understood him all too well. Carmen was a monster, but even knowing that, he and Dahlia still loved her. She was their cousin, and that tie wasn't something you just shrugged away. It would've been easier for both of them to tell me to kill Carmen, just push it onto the Scotts and keep their own hands clean, but that wasn't what they were going to do.

"And if you win?" I asked. "How many more of the *metsän kunigas* die?" My hand tightened on the gun.

"When I'm *karhu*, I'll respect the will of the Scotts in all things," Carmen promised, those blue eyes glittering like the sunlight on frost. A sly expression slid onto her face. "Unlike Gil, after all, I've never questioned the right of the vampires to rule." A muscle twitched hard in her cousin's cheek.

I hesitated. I knew this wasn't how Chivalry or Prudence would do things—they would choose who they wanted to lead the *metsän kunigas* and force everyone in line. It would be so easy to just ignore what Dahlia and Gil wanted—but I couldn't help thinking of my conversations with Valentine and Lilah. Decisions were made by my mother and siblings, and then the other races were the ones who had to live with them, finding a way through the dictates that shaped their lives and community.

One person in this room would be *karhu*. Two weeks ago I hadn't even known any of them, but the ramifications of this decision would ripple out for decades. And I knew what it was like to have choices taken away from you, and to live with the burden of those outcomes. The names of my foster parents were written across my heart.

Carmen saw the answer on my face, and laughed, high and loud.

"Get in the backyard, Carmen," Gil said roughly. "We're settling this."

"Whoa!" a sudden protest emerged from Kevin. "Honey, wait a second, our fence is not that high!"

Beside him, Suze sighed heavily. "Don't worry. I can cover them up. This isn't something that anyone would be expecting to see, so it'll be easy to hide."

That was how we ended up in the backyard, watching Gil and Carmen disrobe with a complete disregard for the ambient temperature. The two were intent on each other, but something about the expression on Carmen's face made me nervous, even with the clear size disparity between the two of them. She looked like someone finally living out a lifelong dream, while Gil just looked grimly resolved.

Suze was to my left, working her fox tricks to make sure no one got an eyeful, while Kevin stood at my right. Dahlia had followed us all outside, apparently not bothered by the blood drying on her stomach, and now crouched next to her brother-in-law, her eyes fixed on Gil and Carmen as they stood silently, watching each other. There had been a brief break before the fight while Gil had pulled the bullet out of her belly wound with a set of tweezers.

I looked over at Kevin, and said hesitantly, "Is this kind of weird for you? You know, with . . ." We were currently standing in his backyard while his husband prepared for a fight to the death with his cousin, not even thirty minutes after Kevin had been held hostage. It seemed rather hard to find the right way to phrase that, so I settled with, ". . . well, kind of everything?"

Kevin shot me a short look. "Believe me, *everything* is weird when you marry a guy who can turn into a bear." Beside him, Dahlia gave a low, bear grumble of mild protest, but rested her head against Kevin's leg. He reached down and rubbed her round furry ears—both were clearly tense and extremely worried.

The fight began suddenly—one minute it was just the two of them looking at each other, and then Carmen and Gil were both changing, a process that forced me to glance down at the ground as their bodies warped and shifted, gaining bulk, muscle, and paws while their skulls pulled and changed. Suze's changes were always almost too fast for my eyes to process, but this was slower, more physical, and viscerally painful. Carmen was moving before her change was even complete, throwing herself straight at Gil, her jaws snapping and ripping at his throat. He smacked her away with his paws, but I saw blood on his fur when she finally pulled back. Then it was just a mass of ripping, snapping black fur as the two bears fought. Gil was larger and outweighed her, but Carmen was faster and seemed tireless, her jaws snapping and locking into any flesh she could get. Gil was taking her shots, using his larger bulk to keep knocking her back and away, but he wasn't able to land any solid shots or bites.

I felt Suze's hand on my arm, and she leaned close and whispered, "It's okay, Fort. This won't last much longer."

"That's what I'm afraid of." My hand wrapped around the handle of the Colt as Carmen ripped away a chunk of fur from Gil's shoulder.

"No, watch." Her voice was completely confident, and I forced myself to trust Suze and let go of the Colt. A moment later, Carmen again lunged out, but this time Gil moved, dropping his head, and his jaws wrapped fully around his cousin's neck. She thrashed, scrabbling wildly at him with her paws, but he rolled, bringing his weight down and onto her, and hung on, his jaws bearing down relentlessly. Carmen's eyes rolled, her rage still burning, and then her movements became weaker. Her mouth opened and closed in a snapping motion, but there was no expression of fear, until finally her whole body went limp. Gil continued holding on for another long minute, then let go slowly and stepped back. In two steps his fur began to recede, his long tan muzzle pulling inward, and the heavy bulk of the bear tightening and forming a recognizable human shape. Then the fur was gone, and a naked man knelt on the grass, the deep bites on his shoulders, arms, and chest still dripping blood. But it was the expression on his face that seemed the most painful as he looked down at his cousin's dead body in front of him.

Kevin was running before any of the rest of us moved, and he threw his arms around his husband. He planted a solid kiss on Gil, and, holding his husband tightly against his chest, began a spirited rendition of what sounded like a series of reasons why Gil was a complete idiot for not just letting me shoot Carmen. Gil meekly accepted both Kevin's berating and his help getting up, wrapping one long arm around his husband's shoulders, and the two began a very slow walk back to where the rest of us were waiting.

Dahlia shifted, and for the first time I had the experience of seeing her short, mom-cut black hair completely disheveled. She was also naked, but there was a lot of naked happening at the moment, and I decided that the polite thing would be just to ignore it. In human form, the bullet wound on her stomach looked smaller, and even though it was still seeping a little, I understood now why no one had seemed overly concerned before. When her brother approached, she gave him a deep, formal bow, and said, "My *karhu*."

Gil reached out with his free arm and yanked his sister into a hug, pressing his face into her neck and saying, "Forget that shit for a second. Are you okay?"

That Vulcan calm of hers finally broke, and for just a brief second I saw exactly how much she loved her younger brother, and I realized that while Gil might wear everything on his sleeve while Dahlia kept it all bottled up, the siblings were actually very similar. I remembered Dahlia's absolute rejection of the idea that Gil could've been the one framing her, and I couldn't help but feel envious of how strong their bond was.

"I'm fine," Dahlia was saying. "Are *you* okay?"

"Nothing that won't heal," he said. When they looked at each other, something deeper passed between them, and I wondered if this would be all they ever said to each other about Carmen's betrayal. "But are you really okay?" Gil pressed, a deep look of worry crossing over his face. "With me being *karhu*? Uncle Matias wanted you to have it."

Dahlia shook her head vigorously. "You won it in combat, Gil. And I have no desire to fight you to the death for it." A smile broke across Gil's face, and his sister gave him a small peck on the cheek. "After all, we know I'd kick your ass, so you can have it. Unless"—she looked back at me—"the vampires are going to raise a fuss."

"Are you sure you don't want it?" I asked, surprised. She'd seemed so natural in the role.

"I'm actually a little relieved," she replied. "I'm a businesswoman, not a politician."

"I'm not sure your brother is what I'd call diplomatic," Suze muttered. It had, after all, been a bit of a long morning with Gil.

A small smile tugged at Dahlia's mouth. "Maybe not," she acknowledged. "But he *is* political. And he wants the job, which I don't."

"And as my first official action as *karhu*," Gil said, his arms still draped over both his sister and Kevin, and looking like he needed the support, "I'm making you president of Kivela Mutual Insurance." He pressed a kiss to the top of her head. "I know you'll be so much better at it than I ever would've been."

I shook my head, accepting what was in front of me. "You're a pain in the ass, Gil, but maybe you are the right one for the job. Carmen thought that she was going to have Prudence come out and just kill the first most likely suspect—and that probably is what would've happened. So maybe you have a point about the *metsän kunigas* being able to investigate their own problems, not that I'm touching that one with a ten-foot pole today. So in my mother's name, I support your ascension to *karhu* ... ness. Whatever." I looked around. We needed bandages, extra clothing for the naked people, a cleaning crew for inside the house, and frankly I really could've used a drink. But first things first. "We need to do something about the body."

Gil didn't look over at it, and I realized that neither he nor Dahlia was acknowledging Carmen's remains at all. Maybe that was cultural, or maybe it was just how they were handling things. "Dahlia and I will pull it into the forest in another few minutes," he said. "If someone runs across her, no one will be worked up over the body of a bear."

I called my mother as Suze drove us back to my apartment a few hours later. There'd been a lot of things to clear—publicly absolving Dahlia of the murder accusation, the revelation that it had been Carmen's work all along, the pronouncement of Gil as the new *karhu*, the dispatching of a group of people to collect poor Alison's body.

"We found the real killer, and she's dead," I said to Madeline, feeling a mixture of exhaustion and a certain dull satisfaction. I regretted the death of Alison, and even the death of Peter, the apparent patsy, but I knew that I'd handled things a lot better than Prudence would've, and that I hadn't been the cause of any innocent person's death. "Everything is resolved with the *metsän kunigas*."

"Bravo, my dove," my mother said, sounding pleased. "Will you be joining us for dinner to tell us all the details?"

I glanced over to Suze, whose face was illuminated in the early-afternoon sunlight. She looked back at me, and the expression in her eyes made my heart pound. "Actually, I don't think so," I said to my mother, never glancing away from Suze. "I'll come down tomorrow. My car is wrecked, though, so I'll need a ride."

"Very well, dear. I'll send the car at five." We exchanged good-byes, and then I shut the phone off. It was Suzume's, my own still being completely destroyed and in need of replacement. But I wasn't thinking about that.

We walked into my apartment, not speaking. Dan was still at classes, so it was just the two of us, looking at each other from across the living room.

"You've decided," I said, not even bothering to phrase it as a question. The room suddenly seemed very warm, but I didn't move, not even to take off my jacket.

Suze gave me that slow, lazy smile that made all of my insides give a flip. "I think you've gotten all the warnings you need about who I am," she said, her voice rubbing me like velvet, and she began walking toward me.

A pang of worry slid through me, even as her hands began sliding up my arms, and her face was so very close to mine. "Suze, if this doesn't work—"

Her hands wrapped in my hair, and my head was very firmly yanked down to hers, and her mouth pressed against mine. My brain was spinning when she let me up and said, "Then we deal with it. But right now we're both on the same page, so . . ."

That was enough, and this time I kissed her, feeling a deluge of joy when she kissed me back eagerly, her tongue sliding into my mouth while her hands began busily working at my clothing. I wrapped my arms around her and lifted her up, her legs looping around my hips and her mouth never leaving mine. I walked us blind into my bedroom, kicking the door shut behind us. I eased us both down onto the bed, and then it was a flurry of clothing removal and skin, and as I pressed my mouth against the smooth line of her collarbone while I reached behind her back to unhook her bra, I decided that everything in my life was worth it just to end up in this moment.

Then Suze gave my shoulders a playful shove, and I dropped back against the bed. Her hands were unhooking my belt, then sliding the button free, and easing the zipper down. The sight of her there, her dark hair swinging forward, her long fingers easing the fabric away, was almost too much, and I forced my eyes up at the ceiling to distract myself and avoid possible embarrassment.

Directly above my bed, glued to the ceiling, was a pair of googly eyes, each one bigger around than my hand. They stared down at me, and I stared up at them, my jaw completely dropping. Suze's hands were still below my waist, tugging at the resistant denim, and I started laughing, a deep, belly laugh that filled my entire body. I tore my eyes away from the ceiling and looked down at Suze. I was still laughing uncontrollably, and I saw her smile, a pure, wide smile of unadulterated pleasure and foxy glee. My heart beat faster, and I reached up and pulled her down to kiss that smile, feeling the echoes of the laughter still rattling in my chest as I rolled us over and felt her skin against mine.

Chapter 9

I woke up slowly, with a general feeling of good-will toward everything and anything, but most particularly toward the black fox curled up on my pillow. I had a small crick in my neck from my head having been slowly nudged off that pillow while I was sleeping, but given the very pleasant state of the rest of my body, I considered it a fair trade. I reached over and ran a finger over the soft, downy fur behind Suze's ear. Her ear flicked under my hand, and then her eyes opened, all amber and vertical pupil.

"Good morning," I said, feeling bemused at this morning after.

In response, Suze got up and gave a bone-defying stretch, then rubbed her vulpine face affectionately against me in long, smooth strokes, her tail flipping lazily from side to side. After a few minutes of this, she stopped, stretched again, and then there was a very content and very naked woman lying beside me.

"Right back atcha," she said with another full-body stretch that had me blessing that complete absence of body-consciousness that all the shape-shifters seemed to possess. I rested my hand on her hip, feeling the smooth-ness and warmth of her skin.

"So, what changed your mind, Suze?" I hadn't asked last night, because we'd been thoroughly occupied, and

I'd decided that deep conversations could wait. Our one break had been when I'd pulled on some clothing and made us omelets for dinner.

She gave me that amused, foxy grin. "I've been window-shopping you awhile. I guess yesterday I decided it was time to try you on and wear you home."

I leaned over and kissed her, sliding my hand upward to press lightly against the curve of her shoulder blade. Everywhere my hand ran over, I felt lean, powerful muscle. Well—almost everywhere, I amended, as my hand slid forward and over her chest. "So, our relationship is like a pair of jeans to you. Sexy." She laughed against my mouth, and then rolled on top of me, and that was the last conversation that we had for a while.

We finally made it out of bed an hour later, for a very leisurely brunch. I cracked the remaining googly-eyed eggs and made French toast, while Suze eyed me with an expression of approval as I prepared food for her. Later, she took a shower, and I cruised the Internet's offerings of used cars, addressing the challenge of filling a certain Fiesta-shaped hole in my life.

Suze came up behind me, rubbing her hair dry with a towel. She'd gotten her pants and her shirt on, but hadn't bothered with socks, which I found both extremely adorable and rather impressive, given the limited effectiveness of the old-fashioned steam radiators in the building. She glanced at the screen.

"You know, Fort, your car got destroyed in a completely work-related incident. I say have your mom buy you an actual new car."

I tugged at the neck of her shirt until she'd leaned down close enough for me to press a kiss against her mouth, marveling internally even as I did it. "You knew what you were signing up for." I knew that it was probably a good idea to play things cool at the beginning of a new relationship, but I couldn't stop the big, shmoopy grin that I knew was spreading across my face. But since my brain was basically engaging in the hamster dance at the moment, maybe this was as cool as I was going to be able to manage.

Suze, meanwhile, was definitely occupied by the thought of my impending automotive purchase. "Just remember that I'm now dating the owner of this car." She peered closer at the screen, and then said flatly, "You're not buying someone's old Cadillac DeVille. Aren't you at least going to get some insurance money out of the Fiesta?"

I shook my head. "All I had on it was liability." It had been the cheapest plan I'd been able to find. I considered. "Though I do have some connections with Kivela Mutual Insurance, now. Maybe they'll give me a good deal on a new policy." Technically I'd saved Dahlia's life—that had to be worth a decent monthly rate.

"So how long will I be chauffeuring you? Remember that my no-eating-in-the-car rule is nonnegotiable."

I wrapped my arm around her waist. "Don't worry. I had some money saved up to fix the Fiesta, so I can get a car with it."

She eyed me suspiciously. "This is less than a thousand dollars, isn't it?"

"Considerably less," I admitted.

"You know, most people just get a car loan instead of buying whatever wreck they can get with their couch-cushion cash."

I regarded her seriously. "Most people should read Elizabeth Warren's books." I had read them in college, and her sections about controlling fixed expenses had made a serious impact on me. And given the jobs I typically ended up with, her lessons had been very useful.

Suze looked very unimpressed. "Hey, are you going to work today?"

I shrugged. "Hank e-mailed me to offer some afternoon stuff." Then I slid my hand a few inches lower and smiled at her. "But I don't have to."

She gave me the foxy smile that made my stomach tie in knots, and then a kiss that sent my brain pleasantly spinning. When she finally let me up for air, she grinned. "Nah, take the work. Maybe it'll help you get something other than"—leaning over, she snagged my mouse, clicked onto my other tab, shook her head, and sighed—"a Yugo."

"Are you sure?" I'd just had more sex in the last twelve hours than I'd had in the last six months, but I was more than willing to add some more, just to well and thoroughly declare the dry spell over.

"This is day three in these clothes, Fort. I want you to fully appreciate just how much I sacrificed to bang you last night."

I laughed. "At least that sacrifice was not in vain, right?"

Suze snickered, and then began kissing me again, which eventually led straight back into bed. When I finally walked her to the door forty-five minutes later, we were both in very nicely mellow moods.

Dan was sitting on the couch, ostensibly working on his flash cards, but as soon as the door had closed behind Suze, he stood up and gave me a slow clap. I pumped my fist and made a victory lap around the room.

"Congratulations, Fort," Dan said once we'd completed the celebration and were slacked out on the couch. "Maybe now she'll have something else to do rather than set up pranks."

I looked at him seriously. "Do you *really* think so?"

His face fell comically. "No, but I can dream, can't I?"

I was reminded of that conversation when I went to work. The dogs definitely didn't like whatever scent mark Suze had left on me, and I received something very different from the usual tail-wagging, tongue-lolling greeting. Pip, the long-haired dachshund, came straight at me with the intent to kill (or at least to maim my ankles), and it was only his elderly owner's solid obedience training that called him back. The rest of the dogs had more moderated reactions, but they made it extremely clear that they were walking with me under extreme duress, and that it was only for the sake of their suffering bladders that they were consenting to this. Even Codex and Fawkes, usually the most exercise-centric dogs, looked very unhappy about the situation, giving me grumbling growls whenever one accidentally came too close to me. When I delivered them back to their house, I reflected that this was the end of yet another job.

Not that I minded. I would very gladly trade sleeping with a kitsune for walking other people's dogs. And, after all, if there was one thing I had learned over my years of underemployment, it was that there was always another shitty job out there, just waiting for me.

My mother's Rolls-Royce pulled into the parking lot precisely at five. I had showered and changed into a clean pair of khakis and a sweater that passed the sniff-test with flying colors. The temperature had plummeted, and not only was my breath visible in the evening air, but there were mutterings on the weather channel about possible snow flurries. There was no accumulation predicted, but Dan volunteered to do our duty as New Englanders and join in the rush to divest the grocery store of all its stock of toilet paper, milk, and eggs. After all, there was an established record of predicted snow flurries suddenly turning into three feet of accumulation, and it was never a bad idea to be on the safe side.

I started toward the car, then stopped when I realized who was getting out of the driver side to hold the back door open for me. It was James, the white edge of his bandage just visible under a sliding fold in his scarf.

"I'm so sorry," I said, the words bursting out of me and sounding so terribly pathetic when weighed against my memory of my attack on him. "So very, very sorry."

His grandfatherly face looked at me with compassion that I knew I didn't deserve. "I know, Mr. Scott," he said.

"That's why I volunteered when your mother asked one of the staff to drive up and fetch you tonight."

He was shivering in the cold, and I allowed myself to be ushered into the backseat so that he could tuck himself back up front. With the doors closed, the car was actually better heated than my apartment, and I loosened the neck of my parka. "Why would you want to see me again?" I asked, looking at his eyes in the reflection of the rearview mirror, and wishing that I could see more of his face. "I bit you. I hurt you. I was trying to kill you."

There was a long silence as James merged the car into traffic and settled in for the drive. Then he met my eyes in the mirror, just once, and very quickly, and I saw wisdom and hard-earned knowledge there. "But you didn't *want* to kill me," he said, so quietly that I almost didn't hear him, even with the smooth purr of the Rolls's engine. "Maybe for a second there you would have killed me, when you didn't know who I was and all you saw was food, but you didn't want to. And I've lived among your family since I was fourteen and got a job raking the leaves in the autumn, and I know what you are." The word *vampire* hung in the air, unsaid even in this moment, so complete and engrained was James's loyalty to our secret. "I know how rare that is, that not wanting to kill."

I didn't have any response to that, and James didn't seem to expect one, since he reached out and turned on the radio, and the dulcet and measured strains of the NPR *All Things Considered* hosts filled the car as we continued down to Newport.

When James dropped me off on the mansion's doorstep and drove off, probably to tuck the Rolls safely away in the small carriage house nestled against the side of the property, I could feel the steady pulse of all of my family gathered together, and I followed it unerringly into the side parlor.

I stepped into the room, and all of my attention focused on my brother, who hopped off a small sofa and hurried to meet me. The lines of strain and unhappiness were gone from his face, and his weight was back where it usually was, giving him the tall, lean, yet muscled appearance of an A-list action star. All of the roiling, painful energy from the last time I'd seen him was gone, and for the first time I was truly conscious of how, when his hand touched my shoulder in affectionate greeting, my own control over that dark, cold part of myself became stronger, the effort of doing so becoming lighter and easier.

I knew even before the words came out of his mouth that Chivalry was in love again, and had found his newest spouse/victim. Whatever he said rolled over me unheard as he hooked a hand under my elbow and steered me to the sofa, where a tall woman with a riot of beautiful black curls and an almost palpable aura of vitality and health was already standing to meet me, a wide smile of greeting spreading across her face. She wanted me to like her, of course. They always wanted me to like them, since they loved my brother so very, very much.

I forced a mechanical smile across my face and returned her half hug of greeting cordially, if awkwardly. My mother, bundled into an armchair and swathed with brilliantly colored chenille throw blankets, was looking tired yet quietly amused at the interplay. Prudence was dressed to impress, in a floor-length gown of blood-red silk that should've clashed with her red hair yet didn't. Leaning dramatically against the fireplace mantel, she was watching Chivalry's new love with an expression of barely concealed irritation.

I stayed quiet while Chivalry fell over himself to introduce me to Simone Gastel, an expression of deep pleasure filling his face just from the act of saying her name. Her skin was a rich gleaming brown, and whereas Bhumika had been tiny, Simone was tall, her head nearly at level with my brother's. There was a strange pattern of dimpled scars across the tops of her cheekbones that I tried to examine without being obvious, but she immediately caught me and smiled.

"Everyone wonders, so don't feel bad," Simone said, completely unruffled. "When I climbed Makalu, my balaclava slipped and I didn't realize it for hours. I got just a little line of frostbite where the skin was exposed."

"Did it hurt?" I asked, knowing that I was asking the question that everyone always asked her, yet completely unable to restrain myself.

"Like the very devil," she said, a smile playing at her lovely full mouth at my predictability. But it wasn't a mean smile, just an amused one. "Taught me a good lesson, though, and respect for the Himalayas. Makalu was my first eight-thousand-meter peak."

"Simone is a mountain climber," Chivalry said, staring at her with completely unveiled rapture. "She's climbed to the summits of Makalu, Lhotse, Broad Peak—and that one that I'm still working on pronouncing."

"Cho Oyu," Simone said, smiling back at him, and so clearly, unreservedly, and tragically happy. I remembered meeting Bhumika in this very room, and seeing that same expression on her face. "I'm training for Annapurna right now," she continued, oblivious to the direction of my thoughts. "There's an expedition next May that I'm hoping to travel with that has an open spot on their visa."

"That sounds really incredible," I said, and meant it. A Himalayan mountain climber—no wonder she looked so incredibly fit and vital. "Do you get sponsorships or something?" A big part of me really wanted to find out that she worked at Best Buy or Walmart when she wasn't climbing. Like those Olympic athletes in sports like curling or rowing who had completely innocuous day jobs.

"Not yet, but maybe if Annapurna works out. I work as a winter guide on Mount Washington."

"Fort," Chivalry said as he rushed in, his enthusiasm

almost bubbling over, "did you know that the high parts of Mount Washington can have winds up to two hundred thirty-one miles per hour, and temperatures as low as fifty degrees below? Right over in New Hampshire!"

"Yes, Chivalry, you were very eloquent on the subject over dinner last night," Prudence said shortly. I blinked hard. The moment felt too similar to when I'd met Bhumika and Chivalry had extolled about the world of competitive rose breeding. The conversation swept past me—Simone was packing up her apartment in New Hampshire and moving down to the mansion. The wedding was already scheduled for the day before Thanksgiving.

"But, you know . . . You're sure about . . ." I couldn't stop myself from asking, interrupting the stream of discussion about dresses and colors and food. Chivalry always did love a wedding. And why not—he was so good at it.

Simone paused and looked at me, and her large eyes were completely serious. "Your brother told me everything," she assured me. "I was nearly caught in an avalanche on Broad Peak. If I hadn't stopped to hammer in an extra piton, I would've been swept off the mountain. Believe me—I understand what risks mean."

And looking at her, I realized with a sinking heart that everything that Bhumika had once told me was true. Chivalry had told Simone what she would sacrifice by being with him, and that the end was inevitable. She'd nodded and said that she wanted to be with him anyway, but she hadn't really accepted it. She hadn't believed in her heart that being with him meant that she would die, decades sooner than she would if she left him behind and never thought of him again. In some quiet place in her soul, she was sure that she would survive this, that she would do what every one of his wives before her had been unable to do. And how could she not? This was a woman who had conquered mountains, who trusted her body in the most dangerous places on Earth—how could she possibly believe that her body would fail her?

And Simone loved my brother. It was clear from every line in her body, and every expression that crossed her face. She loved him, and she would have him, and it would kill her.

Madeline's voice slipped into the conversation with a social finesse honed over centuries, subtly suggesting that Simone give us a moment to discuss business matters. Simone agreed readily, explaining that she still had a lot of calls to make to coordinate her move, and she'd go up to Chivalry's bedroom and get a few more of them done before dinner.

"I committed to guiding three groups up Washington next month," she explained to me, "and I'm trying to find a substitute guide. But if I can't find anyone I trust, I'll have to do them myself."

Chivalry cut in with a smile. "If you want to lead the expeditions, of course you should. I meant it when I said I supported your career. I'll just tuck myself down at a hotel and keep the hot cocoa ready for you."

I had to look away from the look the two of them exchanged. The moment the door had closed behind Simone, Prudence said sourly, "I guarantee, Fort, dinner will be nothing except tales of alpine adventure. Apparently above a certain altitude, climbers choose to pee in their old water bottles. I had not thought that physiologically possible for a woman, but Simone has assured me that every female climber she knows also does it. What a very pleasant addition to our table." The glare she gave Chivalry was cutting. Apparently her attempt to line up a "suitable" partner had failed dismally.

"Darling, you've made your opinion extremely clear," my mother said mildly. "Now, I'm very eager to hear about your brother's success with the *metsän kunigas*."

So I told them the highlights of the last few days. They listened with interest, with occasional compliments or critiques (my sister very notably responded to the discovery of the bloody knife with the question of why I didn't simply kill Ilona and Dahlia then and there)—until I got to the part about allowing Gil to become *karhu*. Then, very suddenly, the mood in the room changed, and both Prudence and Chivalry began excoriating me for poor management and worse decision making.

"It solved everything!" I protested, not surprised that Prudence was angry with me, but worried at the way that Chivalry was very vocally joining her side. Usually, even when I pissed him off, he avoided yelling at me until after Prudence was out of the room.

Now, however, his voice was cutting. "It solved *nothing*, brother, save your own desire to avoid your duty and execute Carmen. Instead you allowed, and not simply allowed, but *raised up*, a completely unsuitable leader."

"Your inexperience led to the problem," Prudence said, aggravation clear in her blue eyes, but her voice actually more moderated than Chivalry's. "Perhaps this is one of those teachable moments that our productivity consultants are always nattering on about at work. I'll go over tonight after dinner and kill Gil. Then the problem will be solved."

"You can't do that!" I yelled, and she simply gave me a long-suffering look, and raised one eyebrow, daring me to find a way that she couldn't.

It was my mother who stopped things, tutting softly from her blanket cocoon. "My darlings, no one will be killing Gil Kivela. At least, not tonight."

"Gil is the best leader for the *metsän kunigas*," I said quickly, trying to capitalize on the first part of my mother's comment while ignoring the more ominous second part. "His sister doesn't want the job, and he's really committed to trying to do what is best for the bears!"

"We're not talking about what's best for the bears, Fortitude." Chivalry's use of my full name, plus the glare he was sending my way, let me know just how pissed he was with me right now. "We're talking about what is best for our interests, which would've been to have a conservative leader like Dahlia."

"But we rule them, and that means we have a responsibility for their welfare!" I argued.

"No, little brother." Prudence's voice was icy. *"They serve us."*

Chivalry was pacing, clearly trying to calm himself down. "Gil will be a problem. He'll push for more self-rule, more rights—and what happens if we give those to him? Will we then give those things to the Neighbors, or the ghouls, or, heaven help us, the witches? And what concessions will Atsuko Hollis then push for, since I have no doubt that she will have a choice list waiting. Brother, I know that it is difficult for you to understand, but the wisest thing to do in that situation would've been to kill Gil and appoint Dahlia."

I sputtered. "Yeah, she would've been so eager to follow our orders after I *murdered her brother!*"

My mother's voice was quiet but hard. "She has children, Fortitude. Dahlia would've swallowed her brother's death to protect her children." She sighed loudly, a frumpy, elderly little puff of irritation. It would've been cute had it not been expressed over my reticence over murder and threats to children. "But now you have appointed Gil as leader in my name, and now is not the time to show a division by sending your sister to rectify the situation. So Gil remains *karhu*. But *you*, my son, will be dealing with him." She locked her flinty blue eyes on me. "And for his sake, I would strongly recommend that you keep him in line with whatever lovely friendship you seem to have formed. Because if you cannot control his demands, it is no difficult thing for Prudence to dispatch both siblings, and let little four-year-old Anni become *karhu*. Child rulers always make such convenient puppets." There was a low knock on the door behind me, and she smiled genially. "Ah, supper is ready. How timely."

Prudence leaned down and lifted our mother into her arms as if she had the weight and consistency of cotton candy. My brother, meanwhile, grabbed my arm with bruising force and kept me from following them.

"You're acting without considering consequences, Fortitude," he hissed at me. "That will catch up with you, probably very soon, and this time I will not step in to rescue you."

My head was filled with the knowledge of just how many dangerous plans and webs I'd gotten myself involved with. Not just Gil and his hopes for the *metsän kunigas*, but Valentine's movement for witch unionization, and Lilah and the Neighbors as they tried to restructure their world. The knowledge that it wouldn't just be Prudence who would argue against any support I gave them, which I'd expected, but Chivalry as well, was frightening. But at the same time, I could feel the deep wrongness in choosing only the path that served the vampires and ignored what the vassal species wanted for themselves.

I was angry at my brother, I realized as I turned to look at him. Maybe for reasons that weren't even fair, since I knew that he didn't look at things the way that I did, but I wanted to hurt him when I asked my question. "Did you feed Simone your blood?" His face became a cold mask of insulted outrage, but I kept pushing. "She loves you so much—is that actually real, or because you gave her a glass of your blood and told her that she loved you?"

"I'm not our sister," he said, and I'd never seen Chivalry look at me like that before. His voice was controlled and measured, but there was a deep, awful rage beneath it. He stared at me. "We will not speak of this again." Then, not looking to see if I would follow, my brother turned and left the room, leaving me with that terrible uncertainty.

Dinner was awkward. Mother sat at the head of the

table, and I watched her hand shake as she lifted her wineglass. Simone did indeed turn out to have a number of alpine stories. I purposely triggered the pee-bottle story by asking how people went to the bathroom at such high altitudes and cold temperatures, just to see Prudence grit her teeth. It was worth the expression on her face to have to sit through a lecture about the existence of products like GoGirl.

Prudence stalked away from the table as soon as the dessert dishes were cleared away, and at a signal from our mother, Chivalry collected Simone and made himself scarce as well.

She stared at me very seriously, and said, "Don't antagonize your sister, my son. Now is the time for all of you to bridge your differences." Looking in her eyes, I knew that this was the closest she would ever come to admitting to me that she was dying. Then she cleared her throat and fussed with her thick glasses, the ones that she liked to wear for effect. "Now, what fine plans do you have this evening?"

I looked at her across the table. She was a monster, a killer. And she was also my mother, and even though her love for me was a terrible thing, it was still love. She wouldn't be alive much longer, and I couldn't even imagine my world without her.

"I'm going to look at a used car over in Middletown," I said abruptly. "Would you like to come with me?"

She looked startled for a moment, and paused.

"I know it's only seven," I said, "But it is November. It's completely dark outside."

A slow smile spread across Madeline's face, one of rare, real delight, exposing those long dangerous fangs. "Yes, my darling," she said. "I believe I would like to go. Very much."

That was how I ended up driving my mother's Rolls-Royce, with my mother ensconced in the passenger seat and Prudence, Chivalry, and Simone clustered awkwardly in the back. Middletown was right next to Newport, and we followed Route 138 over.

"Really, Fortitude," Prudence said. "New cars are nice. They run, they smell good, they assist the economy. Don't you want to help out some job-creating business owner running a car dealership?"

Chivalry cut in. "If it's about the money, you know that I'd give you any sum to keep another of these wrecks from being inflicted on all of us."

"I'm buying my own car," I said firmly, for at least the fifth time. "A car I can afford."

"Then will you let me lend you the money?" Chivalry asked. He wasn't quite begging, but there was an edge of desperation in his voice. "I'll even do it at a ruinous interest rate if that makes you feel better."

My mother just smiled.

The owner of the car was waiting for me at his house, just as he had promised over the phone. He seemed extremely surprised at who exactly had come to look at it.

It was a first-generation Volkswagen Scirocco, the "S" version in Cosmos Silver Metallic, and it was older than I was. A three-door coupe with a five-speed manual transmission, it was remarkably light on rust.

"It was my winter beater," its owner explained. "But my wife finally insisted that we get a Volvo." He looked at me, impressed. "Most people haven't even bothered to come out and look at it because of its age."

"It's even uglier than the last one. How could you possibly have managed that without it being an express desire?" Prudence sounded almost wondering as she stared at the car. She leaned closer to peer in the window, then curled her lip. "There is *trash* in the backseat."

"Those are parts," I explained to her. "Replacement parts for the car. That's actually kind of a bonus because it will make maintaining the car easier." I hoped.

She stared at me for a long minute, then turned with incredible dignity and wordlessly returned to the car.

Chivalry just looked at me mournfully. "Really, Fort. A *German* car?" Two world wars had left my brother with strong feelings about certain European countries.

A truck pulled into the driveway behind us, and the lanky form of my mother's mechanic, Lou Gilliard, unfolded. Chivalry must've placed the call before we'd left the house. Lou gave a long-suffering sigh at the sight of what was in front of him, then popped the hood, pulled out a small flashlight, and began his examination. He started it, listened to the engine, then took a quick look at the undercarriage. Turning to me, he said flatly, "You really know how to pick them, don't you? Go ahead, and on your head be it. You'll be fixing it before the groundhog looks for its shadow."

"We appreciate you coming out," Chivalry said. The expression on his face clearly indicated that his final hopes that this car would not be purchased were ebbing away. Simone looked quietly amused by our strange little passion play, but she reached out and slid a comforting arm around Chivalry. I tried to suppress a shudder as I looked quickly away, my mind all too ready to supply the image of Jon gazing adoringly at Prudence in her kitchen.

"Always a pleasure, Mr. Scott." He nodded to the rest of my family. "Mrs. Scott. Ms. Scott." He looked at me and gave another long-suffering sigh. "Fortitude." Then headed straight back to his truck.

I pulled two hundred dollars from my pocket and handed it to the slightly stunned owner, receiving the title in exchange. My siblings looked at me stone-faced, but my mother laughed and shook her head. "Have a safe drive home, darling."

I kissed her lightly on one frail cheek, the skin so thin that it felt like waxed paper under my lips.

She reached one hand up to catch my chin, holding my face near her. I stared at her in the cold night. "My littlest baby," she said, so softly that I could barely hear her. "What a strange delight you are to us." Then she gave my jaw a small, affectionate pat of dismissal, and turned, reaching for my brother's strong arm and the support he would give her to the Rolls.

I got into my new car, feeling the ancient and cracked leather and every spot where it had been held together with duct tape, and drove away. The heat worked, in a certain petulant way. The radio was broken, but there was a *Born to Run* cassette in the ancient player, so I had music while I drove. I headed over the bridge, up to Providence, and didn't stop until I'd pulled into Suzume's driveway.

I honked the horn, and saw the face of a fox peep out from under her front curtains. A moment later, Suze came out the front door, pulling up the zipper to her parka. She was wearing sweatpants and a pair of slippers, but I wasn't entirely certain that there was a shirt on under that lime green parka. She took a long look at the Scirocco and shook her head slowly, then crossed over to the driver side window.

I rolled the window down with the hand-crank and smiled at her. Bruce Springsteen was singing about love, and everything seemed magical. "So is this a car you'd be willing to be seen in?" I asked her.

She leaned into the open window, resting her elbows on the door, and said, "Absolutely not." Then she leaned farther in and kissed me, her tongue sliding into my mouth and her scent filling my head. She pulled back and reached inside to open the door.

Climbing in, she straddled my lap, and her dark eyes gleamed under the flickering interior light. "But apparently I'm willing to make a few compromises, as long as you're the guy driving it."

ABOUT THE AUTHOR

M. L. Brennan lives in Connecticut with her husband and three cats. Holding a master's degree in fiction, she teaches basic composition to college students. Her house is more than a hundred years old, and is insulated mainly by overstuffed bookshelves. She is currently working on the fourth Fortitude Scott book.

ALSO AVAILABLE FROM

M.L. BRENNAN

GENERATION V

*Fortitude Scott's life is a mess. He has a terrible job,
a terrible roommate, and he's a vampire…sort of.*

Fort is, actually, still mostly human. When a new
vampire arrives in town and young girls start
going missing, he decides to help. But without
having matured into full vampirehood, Fort's
rescue mission might just kill him…

**"Engrossing and endearingly quirky, with a
creative and original vampire mythos, it's a treat
for any urban fantasy lover!"**
—*New York Times* bestselling author Karen Chance

Available wherever books are sold or at
penguin.com

facebook.com/acerocbooks

ALSO AVAILABLE FROM

M.L. BRENNAN

IRON NIGHT

Underachieving film theory graduate and vampire
Fortitude Scott may be waiting tables at a snooty
restaurant run by a tyrannical chef who hates
him, but the other parts of his life finally
seem to be stabilizing.

That is, until he finds his new roommate's dead
body. A cover-up swings into gear, but Fort is the
only person trying to figure out who (or what)
actually killed his friend. His hunt for a murderer
leads to a creature that scares even his sociopathic
family—and puts them all in deadly peril.

**"An entertaining and thoughtful urban
fantasy thriller."
—SF Signal**

Available wherever books are sold or at
penguin.com

facebook.com/acerocbooks

r0190